A DETECTIVE IN

A DINNER TO DIE FOR

JACK GATLAND

MEDIA

INSPIRATION • PRODUCTION • PUBLICATION

Published by Hooded Man Media.
Cover photo by Paul Thomas Gooney

Before LETTER FROM THE DEAD...
There was

LIQUIDATE
THE PROFITS

Learn the story of what *really* happened to DI Declan Walsh, while at Mile End!

An EXCLUSIVE PREQUEL, completely free to anyone who joins the Declan Walsh Reader's Club!

Join at www.subscribepage.com/jackgatland

Also by Jack Gatland

DI DECLAN WALSH BOOKS

LIQUIDATE THE PROFITS

(Short story - free when you join the Mailing List)

LETTER FROM THE DEAD

MURDER OF ANGELS

HUNTER HUNTED

WHISPER FOR THE REAPER

TO HUNT A MAGPIE

A RITUAL FOR THE DYING

KILLING THE MUSIC

A DINNER TO DIE FOR

BEHIND THE WIRE

(Coming February 2022)

DAMIAN LUCAS BOOKS

THE LIONHEART CURSE

(Coming January 2022)

ELLIE RECKLESS BOOKS

PAINT THE DEAD

(Coming March 2022)

As Tony Lee

DODGE & TWIST

For Mum, who inspired me to write.

For Tracy, who inspires me to write.

CONTENTS

PROLOGUE

MARSHALL HOWE HAD LOOKED FORWARD TO THIS FOR A WHILE.

He'd been the lead food and restaurant critic for *The Guardian* for a good three years now, and in the main it was a satisfying existence, and he definitely understood the advice he'd received from his predecessor when he arrived, saying he had to be *very careful of the power he gained from entering a five-star establishment*, knowing that his opinion, when written could make or even break them.

He *relished* that power. And he'd used it with abandon.

At least four restaurants he'd criticised had gone bust in that time, while two of the eateries he'd promoted, waxing lyrically over their menu choices and table strategies had found themselves awarded Michelin stars, perhaps the highest culinary award in the world.

Marshall Howe believed these awards were because of him.

Therefore, they were also *his* Michelin stars.

He'd known for a long time that he'd never have a star of his own; ever since he'd been beaten in a BBC cooking show twelve years earlier, he'd found his love for sweating in kitchens was long gone. He'd been a pastry chef for one of the big London hotels at the time and had worked with many of the names out there; Ramsey, Oliver, even Blumenthal and Waring were chefs he had on his extensive résumé, although if you asked them, they wouldn't remember the small, fat bespectacled man who sweated over a hot stove night after night while they took the credit.

Well, they knew his name now. Gordon Ramsey had even famously called him 'that little shit' when asked about a review Marshall had written on the *Savoy Grill*. Marshall didn't care about the insults. When a celebrity hated you, it meant they were aware of you.

And tonight, Marshall would ensure that Leroy Daniels didn't forget his name.

Entering through the glass doors of *Essence*, the London City restaurant owned by Daniels, Marshall took a deep breath, inhaling the aroma from the tables, the mixture of starters, mains and desserts that all mixed, creating a heady sensation, an *essence* even of extreme hunger. He'd heard rumours that Daniels deliberately piped various aromas into the doorway to prime the customers into being hungry, subconsciously suggesting to them the direction they should go when ordering, but he couldn't see any vents around. The smell was purely the restaurant.

The receptionist at the counter beamed widely at Marshall as he entered.

'Welcome to *Essence*,' she said, glancing at the book in front of her. 'Are you Mister Floyd?'

Marshall nodded. He'd used *Floyd* as his booking name, a nod to the television chef Keith Floyd. He never used the same name twice, ensuring that nobody would pick up his quirk, but he liked to use old, usually dead chefs as his *nom de plume* when attending a restaurant. In the last month alone he'd used Stein, Lawson and Cradock, the last a nod to Fanny Cradock, the television chef that had inspired him to want to cook as a child.

'I am,' he said. 'Table for two.'

He didn't expect a dinner partner to be joining him, but Marshall had noted over the years that when he booked a table for one, he garnered interest. Food critics always ate alone. Sometimes he did book a solo spot though, purely to gain the service and attention that he deserved, but on days like this, days where he wanted to slide in under the radar, he was happy to play the lie.

The receptionist nodded to the Maitre d', who walked over to Marshall. 'May I take your jacket?' the receptionist asked, but Marshall was already leaving, following the Maitre d' as she led him to his table. It was a warm June evening, and all he wore was a suit jacket, so he was happy to keep that on for the moment.

The table they led him to was beside the wall, set out for two and with easy access to both the kitchen and main entrance. Marshall smiled at this, nodding as he was asked whether this was okay for him. They placed him out of the way, but not *too* out of the way. When a restaurant knew, or rather guessed he was attending, they would go one of two directions. The first would be to place him front and centre, to almost shout out *look at us, we have a Guardian food critic here, we mean something,* but sometimes this would backfire, especially when he tore their service and menu apart.

The other times he'd find himself almost hidden from the other customers, to keep his opinions and cynicism away from the masses, in case he somehow infected them with his presence.

This was neither. This was a table that anyone would be given. And Marshall liked that. To the others in the room, it meant they didn't know who he was, or that he was here.

Which meant, as far as anyone watching was concerned, that Leroy didn't know he was here.

Marshall hid another smile at this.

People were going to get a show tonight, as they watched Leroy Daniels' glittering career collapse and die.

HELEN CAGE PEERED THROUGH THE DOOR OF THE KITCHEN AT the man sitting alone beside the wall, Darryl, the teenage pot-washer, standing beside her.

'He looks smaller than I expected,' he muttered before a hand pulled them both gently away from the entrance. The owner of the hand, a genial Indian man in his late-thirties, dark, shortcut hair matching his neatly trimmed beard, tugged gently at his chef whites as he grinned back at them.

'What he loses in height he gains in weight and sheer bastardness,' he said as Darryl, realising that he was in line of sight, disappeared as if by magic, heading for the dish-washing station. 'And if you keep staring at him, he'll work out we're onto him. Are you sure you should even be here?'

'What's the option?' Helen replied, a little too harshly. 'Stay at home and mourn? What happened was terrible, but I made my choice and he couldn't live with it.'

Realising she'd shared a little too much, Helen sighed audibly and, as the bearded man nodded and walked back into the midst of the kitchen, Helen, now alone, wandered back to the pastry station. As the Pastry Chef for *Essence*, she was in a position of control for the desserts, but she was new to the role, only recently moving up from cook a couple of months earlier. This was the first time a critic would judge her work.

Well, technically *Leroy's* work.

She glanced across the busy kitchen at Leroy Daniels, currently in an intense discussion with the bearded man beside the fish counter. Harnish Patel had been the *Essence* Sous-Chef since Helen had joined as a cook a couple of years earlier, and was easily the most competent chef in the kitchen. There was even talk that Harnish would replace Leroy for three months while Leroy started his new hotel-based restaurant in Croatia, but there were also rumours that the hotel he was partnering with had been a nightmare to deal with, backed up by Leroy's terrible mood since returning from Dubrovnik last week.

Leroy was a tall, muscular man, his blond beard standing out from his tanned face and bald, tanned head, his chunky black *Ray Ban* glass frames giving him the appearance of a mask across his eyes. You didn't want to be near Leroy Daniels when he was in a bad mood. And since he'd entered the kitchen an hour ago, Leroy had barely spoken to anyone, replying in grunts or waves of the hand.

Tara Wilkinson, the manager of *Essence,* walked over to Leroy; she was the same age as he was, early forties, and they'd known each other since catering school. In fact, it was Leroy who'd introduced Tara to her now husband, Harnish, a few years earlier, making the restaurant very much a family and friends affair.

Tara whispered into Leroy's ear, and he gave a whoop of triumph, his face finally breaking out into a wide grin. Helen knew Tara had just informed Leroy that Marshall Howe was in the building. They'd been waiting for over a week for this, ever since Howe had made a booking two weeks earlier under the name *Rhodes*, cancelling it the moment he learnt Leroy wouldn't be there. After that, all they'd done was wait until some random booking arrived for another dead chef, the well-known name game that Marshall Howe played.

As Leroy left his station, walking towards the door to the restaurant, Darryl strolled over to Helen once more.

'I don't get it,' he said. 'Why the hard-on for this guy?'

'Because he almost killed Chef's career,' Helen replied. 'On some Saturday morning TV cooking show about six years ago, he paid a stage hand to swap *tumeric* for *scotch bonnet* powder. Nearly killed the celebrity guest, made Chef look stupid. He's been waiting years to get his revenge.'

Darryl nodded, returning to his station. He'd most likely heard scuttle about the TV debacle, everyone had, but Helen also knew the rivalry went back to *Masterchef* a good decade back, when Leroy Daniels had beaten Marshall Howe in the final round.

But then Leroy had a lot of enemies. She knew that personally.

Shaking her head to get back into the moment, she looked at her station. There were dessert orders coming through, and her team were already at work. Pushing all thoughts of Chef Daniels and his rivalry with Marshall Howe out of her head, she started preparations.

―――――

MARSHALL GAVE A LOOK OF SURPRISE WHEN LEROY DANIELS emerged from the kitchen, walking over to his table and sitting down. The other guests in the restaurant were shocked too, as they started talking excitedly to each other, several pulling out phones and snapping candid shots of the two men. Marshall visibly groaned. Social media was about to have a field day as the diners shouted out to the world about the cosy chat Marshall was about to have with the owner of the restaurant he was critiquing.

'Howe,' Leroy said with a smile, his deep voice booming as he sat in the empty seat opposite. 'Hope you don't mind, but I'm guessing your dinner partner won't be joining.'

'Mister Daniels,' Marshall started, but Leroy raised a hand.

'*Chef* Daniels,' he interrupted. 'Please.'

'Chef Daniels,' Marshall replied, accepting the change with all the grace he could muster. It was Daniels' restaurant, after all. 'I usually critique anonymously.'

'I know,' Leroy smiled still, but it was colder now, less genuine. 'But we also know you're not here to critique. You're here to set up a hatchet job.'

'You call my professionalism into dispute?' Marshall leaned back. Leroy, in return, shrugged.

'Last time you were here, you likened my shrimp dumplings to fish-filled condoms, with a flavour that lingered like the swab bin in a sexual disease clinic. And you as good as said earlier today that you'd be gunning for me.'

'You heard?'

'I heard.'

Marshall nervously shifted in his seat.

'I say as I see,' he replied nervously.

'And of course before that, we have the scotch bonnet powder incident.'

Marshall smiled at this.

'You're not still pedalling that conspiracy theory, are you?'

he asked. 'I told you then, and I'll tell you now. I never swapped the powders. You made that mistake all on your own.'

Leroy bristled at the insinuation.

'I knew exactly what went into that curry,' he snapped. 'And the poor bloody actress didn't deserve what you did.'

'I did nothing,' Marshall shrugged. 'You're the one who made her splutter-vomit on BBC Saturday morning television.'

He looked around the restaurant.

'Hasn't hurt you though, has it?' he continued. 'I mean, this blank emptiness you've developed has what, two Michelin stars now?'

'Three,' Leroy leaned forward, lowering his voice. 'Three, and you know it.'

There was a murmuring. Marshall didn't need to look around; he knew the diners were excitedly commentating about the free performance they were getting. Changing the narrative, he picked up the menu now, waving it lazily at Leroy.

'This is a bit insipid and bland,' he stated as he read down it. 'Mushroom soup served with crème fraiche and truffle oil. Beef carpaccio with honey-mustard sauce. Baked lobster with black noodles, cherry tomatoes and broad beans.'

He gave a theatrical sigh.

'Been there, seen it,' he tossed the menu back to the table. 'Every other restaurant in Cornhill has this. I expected more from you. The *Committee* expects more.'

Leroy nodded at this, as if expecting the comment.

'I guessed you'd say that,' he replied. 'That's why you're not eating off the menu tonight.'

'I'm not?' Marshall was intrigued.

'No,' Leroy rose now. 'I'm giving you the *Chef's Special.* A onetime main course never created before today, and likely never to be created in the same way again. Two plates in total, one for you and one for me. Something I came up with while in Dubrovnik recently; a fire-baked potato filled with sea-urchin caviar with a whipped onion sauce, served on hot coals next to an ice-based clementine cut to look like sea urchin, served in a sea urchin shell and drizzled with Manuka honey, it represents fire and ice, from the show *Game of Thrones,* which was filmed there.'

'Sounds complicated,' Marshall sniffed, hiding the excitement he had inside. 'And we remember from *Masterchef* how complicated things always set you back.'

'We also remember how I beat you,' Leroy nodded as he moved to leave the table. 'Pick whatever starter you want, Marshall. The main is already decided.'

'Is this a prank?' Marshall asked. 'Is this revenge for the powder, which you still believe was me?'

'Oh no,' Leroy smiled, and for the first time, it looked genuine. 'I want to remind you why you lost to me. I want you to taste something so incredible that you can't help but write an excellent review, because if you don't, I'll know you had to lie.'

And with that, he bowed, nodded to some other customers and left the restaurant floor, returning to the kitchen.

Marshall picked up the menu again.

Things were getting interesting.

HE'D CHOSEN THE *SAINT JACQUES IN A GINGER AND CABBAGE sauce* for the starter, sliding the scallop meat into his mouth, savouring the tender, buttery texture as he chewed, the taste reminding him of a slightly almondy-flavoured lobster meat. And, when the main course appeared, it was exactly as Daniels had described it; a baked potato, still cooking on hot coals, placed into a wide wooden bowl. The ice to the side, currently holding up the honey-drizzled clementine, was already melting, creating a hissing noise as the water vaporised into steam on striking the hot coals. Visually, it was incredible, and Marshall almost didn't want to eat it.

Almost.

Taking a knife and fork to the baked potato, he placed a large piece of caviar and potato onto his fork, feeling it hit his tongue with an explosion of taste, the onion-whipped cream giving it a contrasting flavour, only added to when he placed a single piece of clementine into his mouth to join this.

'Not bad,' he mentioned to the Sommelier, currently hovering around the table, most likely ready to send back every comment Marshall made to his Chef. 'It's passable.'

It was more than passable. It was exquisite, inspired in design and possibly the best main course he'd eaten that year.

Damn Leroy Daniels.

He knew that Marshall would have to give a good review—

He coughed as he felt his throat tighten slightly, his lips now numb to the touch; he'd been eating so fast, he'd likely swallowed one of the pieces of coal, although he didn't feel any burning sensation, and the acidic taste of the stones, although pungent, hadn't been there when he took a mouthful—

Another cough, this time more of a splutter, as Marshall Howe clutched at his throat, dropping his knife and fork as he did so, finding his arms becoming leaden, gasping with wheezing breaths as he fought to grab air into his lungs, feeling his throat closing up.

Oh, you prick, he thought to himself as his eyes streamed with tears, blurring his vision of the restaurant patrons as they stared at him. *You trusted him. You believed he wouldn't fill the bloody thing with chilli powder.*

No, this was something else, something scarier, he realised as he scrabbled for water, unable to swallow it, the liquid falling back out of his mouth as he croaked for help. The Sommelier was now calling for help, with waiters running over, pulling him from the table, loosening his tie.

'He's going into anaphylactic shock!' one shouted. 'Grab the epi pen from the counter.'

Marshall was reddening now, unable to breathe but at the same time trying to speak, to say that *it couldn't be anaphylactic shock as he wasn't allergic to anything,* but before he could say it the receptionist ran over, slamming the needle of the epi pen into Marshall's thigh, causing him to yelp with pain as the epinephrine flooded into his system. His breaths were still shallow, unable to grab lungfuls as he felt the room spin away from him, fading into blackness as he collapsed to the floor, passing into unconsciousness, still unable to breathe...

———

THE KITCHEN HAD FALLEN INTO CHAOS THE MOMENT MARSHALL Howe collapsed to the floor, the other meals forgotten as everyone stood in horror, staring out of the kitchen door at the scene unfolding in the restaurant.

'Did he do this?' Harnish looked at Helen. 'I mean, *could* he have done this?'

'I don't know,' Helen's usually smiling face was turned into a picture of genuine shock as she called out. 'Has someone called an ambulance?'

'He couldn't have done this,' Harnish shook his head. 'I mean, he's a prick at the best of times, and he might have wanted to send a message, but this is—'

Helen looked around.

'Where is Chef, anyway?' she interrupted. 'I thought he'd be here.'

'He was eating in his office,' Harnish was already running for the door, Helen following. 'He never eats his own food in front of people, and he probably doesn't even know what's happening out there.'

Leroy Daniels' private office was at the back of the kitchen, the door closed. Banging on the door, Harnish opened it, already talking as he entered.

'Howe's had an allergic reaction to—' he started, but then stopped as Helen entered the room behind him, bringing her hand to her mouth to stifle a scream.

Leroy Daniels was at his desk, his half-eaten main course in front of him, a half-eaten main course that he now rested the left side of his dead forehead against, having fallen forward into it. His eyes were open and vacant, staring off into the distance, his skin mottled and blue, and his mouth was covered in both a mixture of vomit and blood, a trickle of which now led from his lips to the plate beneath him.

'We need another ambulance,' Helen said, turning to leave, but Harnish grabbed her, stopping her from leaving.

'It's too late for that,' he whispered. 'He needs the police instead.'

'The police?' Helen was confused. 'For an allergic reaction?'

'No,' Harnish looked back to the kitchen, where at the other end of it the crowd of cooks could still be seen watching the activities in the restaurant.

'Because I think he was poisoned. And if Marshall Howe dies, I think they were both killed by the same dish.'

1

A RETURN TO FORM

DECLAN LAY BACK ON THE BENCH IN THE CELL HE WAS currently in and stared morosely up at the pock-marked, paint-flaking ceiling.

This wasn't the first cell he'd been in, nor was it even the first cell he'd been in while being accused of something he hadn't done, but that didn't stop it being frustrating and incredibly annoying to once more be in such a predicament.

He'd not expected Detective Constable Ross and her officers when they'd arrived; he'd known something was amiss with Francine Pearce when he'd found her phone in an abandoned warehouse a week earlier, but he hadn't seen the complete picture as he passed the phone into forensics. He hadn't realised that Francine had recorded him threatening her, a threat made of fatherly protection for his daughter Jess, nor had he worked out how Francine's blood could have been found in his Audi.

Whoever was doing this, they were good. And they'd played him from the very start, knowing exactly which buttons to press to get him to do what they wanted.

That was possibly the only thing that worried Declan right now, that the person who was framing him was *better at this than Declan was.*

The door opened, and DC Ross appeared in the doorway, a file in her hand.

'Good night's sleep?' she asked. 'Sorry nobody was here to tuck you in, *sir.*'

Declan rose to a sitting position, stretching his arms as he did so. He was in trousers and shirt, his jacket and tie having been removed when he was brought to Bishopsgate. His shoes were slip-ons, so there were no laces to remove, although that was something that rarely happened outside of the movies.

'I'd like to call my Command Unit,' he said. 'I've been stuck in here all night without my phone, or any way of contacting the outside world.'

'You'll get your phone call soon enough,' Ross replied, using her free hand to pull back her long red hair as she looked down at the notes on the file in her other. 'We have some questions first. Your Police Representative will be here in a few minutes, so come with me, please.'

Rising, Declan followed DC Ross out of the cell and down the corridor. He knew Bishopsgate well; he'd interviewed people here during the Rupert Wilson case, this being one of the few police buildings in the City of London that had both interview rooms and cells within their walls.

'You worked out I didn't do this yet?' he asked conversationally as they entered the interview room; a dark, featureless room with one desk in the middle, four chairs in a two and two arrangement on either side of it, with a recording device on the edge, closest to the wall where detectives interviewing suspects could record the meetings. Ross ignored him, sitting in a chair as the escorting officer ushered Declan to sit facing her. Declan smiled at him, fighting back the urge to make a sarcastic comment. It wasn't his fault Declan was there. It was Declan's.

Because if Declan had been even half on his game right now, he would have realised what was going on from the very start.

'You want to begin?' Declan asked, leaning back on the chair. 'I mean, my Rep will be here soon enough, and I really want to get out and have a shower.'

'You think you'll get out?' Ross raised an eyebrow at this.

Declan leaned across the table, moving closer.

'I know I'll get out,' he said with utter conviction. 'Because I know I'm being framed. And if you had any sense, you'd already be looking into that rather than witch-hunting me.'

'Okay,' Ross replied, placing the folder on the table. 'Hypothetically. While we wait.'

Declan relaxed back, nodding for Ross to continue.

'You threatened Francine Pearce, a threat that was record-ed,' she started.

'She was deliberately goading me and had been spying on my daughter,' Declan shrugged the accusation off. 'She knew I'd get angry. I'd get confrontational. She banked on it.'

'You said you could make her disappear.'

'I wasn't going to.'

Now Ross shrugged.

'Seems like you might have,' she said. 'The blood in the car, and on the phone—'

'The phone was there when I arrived,' Declan shook his head. 'I don't know why it was covered in blood, nor do I care. She arranged the meeting, you can see that from the text.'

'And the car?' Ross spoke softly now, slowly. 'Explain how the blood was in the boot of your Audi?'

Declan didn't reply for a moment.

'I can't,' he said. 'Someone had to have placed it in there.'

'When?' Ross was warming to the questions, and Declan knew this was because she believed she was in the right. 'I mean, you had the tracker off, you were driving around unchecked—'

'I didn't turn my tracker off!' Declan snapped.

'But it was turned off, yes?' Ross persisted.

'Yes,' Declan reluctantly agreed. And it had been; Tom Marlowe had turned off the tracker when they'd driven to the black site to see Karl Schnitter. However, Tom had agreed that the tracker would only be off for twenty-four hours at most before *Section D* eventually fixed it, and even if it wasn't, Billy would have made sure it was working again.

'Why?' Ross asked.

'I can't tell you.'

'Can't, or won't?'

Declan looked up.

'Can't,' he replied again. 'It's above your pay grade.'

'Oh,' Ross nodded now, opening up and reading Declan's file. 'Is this to do with the shadowy Whitehall people you've been reported as dealing with? Charles Baker and his pet secret service?'

Declan couldn't help it; he smiled.

'Yeah, pretty much.'

'Must be so lovely to be special,' Ross replied, nonplussed. 'Also, must be so lovely to have an instant excuse for why you turned off your tracker when you needed to dispose of a body.'

'I didn't dispose of a body,' Declan snapped.

Now it was DC Ross' turn to smile.

'Oh, so you still have it?' she enquired innocently. 'Wonderful. That *will* save us time.'

Declan was about to continue with his argument when the door to the interview room opened and Doctor Rosanna Marcos stood there, a duffel bag over her shoulder. She was in her usual jeans and sweater, casual because her working clothes were mainly disposable PPE suits. But even in a comfy jumper and with her curled hair loose, she looked like the wrath of God made flesh.

'What the hell's going on here?' she demanded, sweeping into the interview room, an iPad in her hand. 'You'd better not have started without me.'

'You're my Federation Rep?' Declan was surprised at this, but Doctor Marcos ignored him, turning her ire onto DC Ross.

'This clown car of a case is over, and I'm taking DI Walsh out with me right now,' she said. Ross, leaning back in her chair to look up at Doctor Marcos, sighed.

'I've had this already with your superiors,' she started. 'We have enough evidence—'

'You have *nothing*,' Doctor Marcos almost slammed the iPad onto the table. 'Tell me your evidence. Or shall I tell you?'

DC Ross stared sullenly at Doctor Marcos.

'Please, make a fool of yourself,' she said.

'First off, you have this phone with blood on,' Doctor Marcos was walking around the interview room, ignoring the offered chair. 'A phone we already know was there when Declan arrived, because it was pinging off the local cell tower a good hour before Declan's did.'

'He might have turned his own one off so it didn't appear,'

Ross suggested, only to receive a barked laugh from Doctor Marcos.

'He was on an underground train!' she replied. 'Of course it didn't appear! And we have his contactless payments!'

'Anyone could have done them.'

'CCTV—'

'We're waiting for that.'

'Okay, fine, moving on then, we have the blood on the phone.,' Doctor Marcos sighed. 'To paraphrase you, anyone could have done that. There's no proof Declan caused this. In fact, there's no proof whatsoever that Declan Walsh even saw Francine Pearce there.'

'Actually, I agree,' Ross replied. 'I think he took her the previous night.'

She rose now to face Doctor Marcos.

'I think that directly after threatening her that evening, he walked back to Temple Inn, grabbed his car, knowing his tracking was off, drove to wherever Francine was, kidnapped or even killed her, placed her body in the boot of his car, drove somewhere dark and secluded, dumping the body before driving back to Hurley. There's a ton of places you can dump a body in Berkshire. Or maybe she's still in Hurley, in a basement somewhere? He grew up with a serial killer who's still out there, so maybe he had help?'

Declan didn't comment on this. As far as the world was concerned, Karl Schnitter had escaped. They didn't know he'd been taken away by Tom Marlowe in an unregistered van.

'And what about his partner?' Doctor Marcos politely enquired. 'She was in the car as well.'

'Well, there's a case to be made for her being a partner in

more than just the job,' Ross sneered. 'I heard they've been cohabiting for weeks now.'

'She's my housemate, nothing more,' Declan snapped.

'That aside, let's talk about the dumping of the body,' Doctor Marcos replied, and her voice was relaxed, almost goading. Declan felt that there was something about to be revealed, but he couldn't work out what it was.

'What about it?' Ross sat back down, tired of the confrontation.

'How do you know Francine was in the car?'

DC Ross stared at Doctor Marcos with genuine confusion.

'I thought you were the Divisional Surgeon for his team of misfit toys?' she shook her head. 'Let me spell it out nice and simple for you, Doc. Blood. Spatter. All over the inside of the Audi's boot space. What more do I—'

'Now let me spell it out for you,' Doctor Marcos tapped on the screen of the iPad, bringing it back to life. 'Because you obviously haven't read the *forensics report.*'

'What report?' Ross looked around the room now, as if expecting to see a file slid under the door. 'My forensics haven't come back to me yet—'

'Ah. Yes. I forget sometimes how good I am, and how people struggle to keep up,' Doctor Marcos grinned, and it was the cold, dead smile of a shark. 'The blood on the phone was definitely Francine Pearce's, and upon testing, was fresh —well, at least within a day or so. Which matches the time spent before DI Walsh could get it to forensics.'

She tapped the screen, where visible was a PDF document of a forensics report.

'Now, the blood in the car, though, that's a different matter,' she said. 'You see, there are two issues. The first, as you said, was that there was blood spatter all over the boot space. If I was to cut you up and dump you in my boot, and trust me, the thought *has* come to mind, the blood would pool, not spatter everywhere. And if it *did* spatter, your own body, by the simple act of being in the boot, would block a lot. The boot looked as if someone squirted the blood all over it. Does the job just as well, but isn't how an actual crime scene would look. And, if you read the report, one I'm sure your own forensics will come up with in time, you'll see that there's also a degradation to the blood, enough to mean this had to have been withdrawn from Francine Pearce's arm approximately fourteen days ago.'

'That can't be,' Ross shook her head. 'Francine Pearce—'

'Was in prison two weeks ago, yes,' Doctor Marcos nodded. 'Yes. And checking the records, a private doctor visited her around the same time. Which gives us a week for someone to break into the Audi's boot and squirt it about, if we're going by your timeline.'

She looked at Declan.

'Any time in the last two weeks where someone could do that?' she asked.

Declan nodded. A week earlier, he'd left his car keys with guards while visiting Karl Schnitter. It'd only been twenty minutes, but that was ample time to do what needed to be done.

'I can think of a location or two,' he said.

Doctor Marcos looked back at DC Ross.

'DI Walsh has blood from a week before Francine Pearce's disappearance, blood that logically cannot have been from her body being in his boot, so someone placed it there to frame him. Likewise arranging for him to meet Pearce in a location where only her bloodstained phone was to be found.

I've spoken to your superiors and they've agreed that until you find some genuine evidence which improves your case, maybe her body even, DI Walsh here is free to go.'

She nodded to Declan.

'Grab your shit. We're going now.'

Declan rose before DC Ross could argue this, but stopped, turning to the Detective Constable.

'This seems personal,' he whispered, leaning closer. 'Have we met in the past? Did I do something?'

'No,' Ross rose finally to meet him. 'It's just that everyone you meet gets destroyed, and everything you touch turns to shit. You're toxic, Walsh. I've read your file. From punching out priests to entrapping cyber-crime operatives, you live by your own rules, and you're the wrong kind of copper for the force.'

Declan nodded at this.

'Well, luckily, that's not for you to decide,' he said, following Doctor Marcos to the door. 'And until your superiors believe your conspiracy theories, stay out of my life.'

Walking down the corridor and towards the exit, Declan exhaled as Doctor Marcos passed the duffel bag to him.

'Here,' she said. 'It's your go bag.'

Declan nodded. A *go bag* was a holdall a lot of detectives kept in their police lockers; a change of underwear, shirt, sometimes a suit, all with a *dopp bag* wash kit that contained shampoo and deodorant. Sometimes you never knew when you'd get back home, and many was the time Declan worked through the night in the office, changing the following morning. Not to mention the times his suit was covered in blood.

Doctor Marcos nodded to a door on the right.

'Gent's washrooms,' she said. 'Get in there, fix yourself up. Grab a shower too, as you're hitting the ground running.'

'What's going on?' Declan asked, standing by the door. 'Why isn't Bullman or Monroe here instead?'

'It's been a busy night,' Doctor Marcos admitted. 'Bullman's in North London.'

She paused, as if deciding whether to explain more, before continuing.

'Karl Schnitter's transport was hijacked yesterday. Masked attackers broke him out. He's free, Declan.'

Declan leaned against the wall as the corridor started spinning.

'He's free?' he whispered. 'Is—'

'Jess and Liz are safe,' Doctor Marcos added. 'That's where Bullman is. But that's not all. Tom Marlowe was driving the transport.'

'Is he...' Declan left the question open, unable to answer it.

'Alive, but critical,' Doctor Marcos replied. 'Shot in the leg and the chest. Touch and go last night but he's stable right now.'

'Monroe?'

'Doesn't know,' Doctor Marcos shook her head. 'He's in Edinburgh. Long story, but we decided to keep this from him until he returns. De'Geer's gone up with him.'

Declan looked around the corridor now, as if expecting someone to appear, to tell him this was all a joke. Tom Marlowe was shot, Karl Schnitter was out there, and Francine Pearce—

'Francine and Karl must have worked together,' he said. 'Or at least known each other. The best time for them to frame me with the blood in my car was when I was at the black site. Which means that someone there had her blood, and they knew I was going to them.'

'We can work all that out later,' Doctor Marcos nodded towards the door again. 'You need to freshen up, wake yourself. With Bullman and Monroe off the reservation, you need to take the lead in our next case.'

'We have a case?' Declan was surprised at this.

Doctor Marcos nodded.

'We do,' she said. 'And we might even blag some breakfast in the process.'

MARTYR CHEF

FOLLOWING A FRESHENING UP AND A CHANGE OF CLOTHES, Declan and Doctor Marcos arrived at *Essence* around half an hour after they'd left a furious DC Ross in the Bishopsgate interview room, and fifteen minutes after Declan had shaken the cobwebs out of his brain with a cold shower.

During the journey, one that was mainly spent walking down side roads, southwards from Bishopsgate and towards Cornhill and the restaurant's main entrance, Declan spent the time getting himself up to speed with what had been happening, learning about Monroe's sudden discovery of family and the problems this entailed in Edinburgh, as well as the medical status of Tom Marlowe from a phone message sent by Bullman which said that despite being shot twice, Tom was luckier than the others on the detail, many of whom had been killed in the attack. Bullman had also sent a second message that gave Declan solace; Liz and Jess had been taken somewhere safe for the moment.

As he read this though, it had reminded Declan of a part of a conversation, words Karl had said when they met just over a week earlier, three comments that all stated the same thing.

'No matter what happens, Declan, I would never hurt your family.'

'Daughters are different. They are sacred, untouchable in this business.'

'I am always here for you, even when you do not know that you need me. And because of this, Jess does not need to fear me. No matter what.'

Declan believed Karl then, and even now he still believed him. Karl's problem, his issue wasn't with Jess.

It was with Declan.

Or was it? Had Karl decided in some crazy manner that their rivalry was over? That because the coin, the East German Mark that the *Red Reaper* had used to decide his victims' fates had landed face side up, Declan was now safe?

No matter what happened with Karl, Declan knew this was mainly to do with *Phoenix Industries*, the rebranded *Rattlestone* mercenaries who now worked for Trisha Hawkins; the only way they could have had Francine's blood was for them to have been working with her, and Trisha had been Francine's right-hand enforcer before things had fallen apart for *Pearce Associates*, and in turn *Rattlestone*.

Declan also knew that the blood could only have been placed into Declan's Audi in the twenty-four hours after Tom Marlowe had taken him to the black site, as that was the time the tracker was off. And, with Declan driving around North and West London that day, the only time they knew exactly where he would be, with the tracker off, would be when he spoke to Karl Schnitter. In fact, Karl demanding Declan visit him in the prison might have been the very catalyst for the frame up. Helping Francine attack Declan in return for his own freedom.

No, Karl wasn't built that way. And his comments had stated a far different decision that Karl had made. So what was the real story there?

The only way that Declan would get an answer was to find either Francine or Karl, and soon. Which was likely to be very difficult, especially with DCI Monroe missing in action and Tom Marlowe still in an ICU ward.

DC Davey was waiting for them as they walked up to the blue tent that covered the entranceway to *Essence*. She was as ever in her PPE suit, mask currently down, with the hoodie still over her frizzy red hair.

'PPE suits,' she said as Declan went to walk past her, Doctor Marcos already pulling out one of her own specially made ones.

'It's been hours,' Declan protested. 'Surely the bodies have been moved, and the scene examined? Can't I just stick with boots and gloves?'

'It's not for the scene, it's for you,' Doctor Marcos stated as she zipped up her own PPE suit. 'You've got two men; one dead, one in intensive care, both poisoned by something. Two other diners are also in hospital with similar symptoms. This might be an airborne contaminate, this could have even been targeted at the *restaurant* rather than the individuals. Think Salisbury, put your suit on and shut up.'

Declan nodded at this, taking the offered suit, opening the bag and pulling it out. Doctor Marcos' mention of Salisbury had sobered him. In 2018 Sergei and Yulia Skripal had been poisoned while in Salisbury, taken ill after dining at the *Zizzi* restaurant. While investigating, the police had found traces of the *Novichok* nerve agent on site, a Russian-made military grade weapon, a container of which, later found in a bin, had held enough of the nerve agent to potentially kill thousands of people.

Two police officers investigating the attack had also been poisoned by trace elements of the bio-weapon seeping through their forensic suits. While this current situation might be nothing like that, precaution was understandable.

Now fully covered, his mask and gloves on, Declan entered the tent and walked through the doors into the restaurant. The PPE-wearing DS Anjli Kapoor, seeing him enter, finished up her conversation with a forensics officer and walked over to him.

'I heard Marcos went full *Old Testament* on them. You good?' she asked.

Declan shrugged.

'I've had better days, but these poor bastards here have beaten me,' he said. 'What do we have?'

'Leroy Daniels,' Anjli looked around the crime scene. 'Celebrity chef, well, as much as chefs are celebrities these days. Won *Masterchef* a million years ago, turned that into a franchise of restaurants, does the Saturday morning cooking shows.'

'Not a fan?' Declan asked.

Anjli smiled.

'I find in my experience that the more expensive the meal, the smaller the meal,' she said. 'Look at Billy. The poor mite is literally wasting away.'

She led Declan to one of the tables placed beside a wall.

'Marshall Howe, one of the go-to food critics for *The Guardian*,' she said, pointing at it. 'Came in under a fake name, but they were ready for him, with a special, off-the-menu dish.'

'You make it sound like an ambush,' Declan examined the remains of the cutlery as he spoke.

'In a way, it was,' Anjli nodded towards the back door, where some forensics officers were walking through. 'Seems that Howe and Daniels had a rivalry that had spilled over a few times. They were on the same series of *Masterchef*, and Howe narrowly lost out to Daniels in the final. Checking some interviews he did around the time, he claimed Daniels had sabotaged his soufflé.'

'Ah, the war cry of the wronged. So what happened after that?'

'Daniels started working for a few Michelin restaurants, moving his way up the chain,' Anjli said. 'Started on the fish station and worked up to Sous-Chef.'

'And Howe?'

'Went the other way. Started reviewing restaurants. Bit of a prick, according to most people here. Actively enjoyed pissing people off. Got the attention of national press, started working for *The Guardian's* weekend supplement about seven years back, became lead food critic three years ago.'

'And they kept in touch?' Declan was surprised at this. Anjli, however, shook her head.

'Christ no,' she half laughed. 'Made a career of avoiding each other. Then a few years back they were both guests on a TV show where Daniels accidentally used scotch bonnet powder instead of turmeric, causing some actress from *Hollyoaks* to throw up live on TV. He claimed someone had sabotaged him, that Howe had paid someone to switch the bottles, but nothing was proven.'

'I'm starting to think the wrong person died here,' Declan mused. 'Sounds like Daniels might have had a reason to want Howe dead.'

Anjli nodded. 'They've been waiting for him to appear at *Essence* for a while now,' she continued. 'Apparently, he has this thing where he books a table under the name of a dead chef, thinks nobody gets it. The moment they saw *Keith Floyd*, they knew it was him. It didn't hurt that he also tried to book two weeks back and when he learnt Daniels was away, he cancelled the booking.'

'So Daniels knows Howe is turning up, and he makes him an off-the-menu main course,' Declan stretched as he glanced around the restaurant. 'Was it just Daniels and Howe?'

'That ate the meal, I believe so. Only two dishes were plated.'

'Does that mean two plates of food?'

Anjli grinned. 'It's how they told me it,' she said. 'I'm just the messenger.'

Declan considered this.

'If only two of them ate it, how do we have others sick?'

'That's why we're dressed as Smurfs,' Anjli tapped at her blue PPE suit. 'We don't yet know what caused the death.'

'Also, why would Daniels eat the same meal that he gave Howe if he intended to kill him?' Declan shook his head. 'Who else touched the food?'

Anjli pointed across the restaurant floor, towards the door to the street where, outside *Essence,* was a nervous looking Indian man in chef whites.

'The Sous-Chef, Harnish Patel helped, and the Pastry Chef, Helen Cage, added a drizzle of honey to the meal. Apart from that, nobody went near it outside of Chef Daniels.'

'I'll have a chat with him then,' Declan nodded to Anjli

before walking outside, pulling the mask and hood off as he did so.

'Mister Patel?' he asked. Harnish, jumping at the sound of his name, nodded.

'That's me,' he said before realising that this was a little redundant.

'Shouldn't you have gone to the hospital?' Declan asked. 'I thought—'

'I did, but I came back when I was given the all clear,' Harnish replied quickly. 'My wife is the manager, and I wanted to check in with her, make sure she was okay.'

'And is she?'

Harnish shrugged, and Declan could see the restrained anger on his face.

'I don't know,' he snapped. 'You won't let me inside to talk to her.'

'She's inside?' This surprised Declan.

Harnish nodded.

'Someone had to give the guided tour,' he looked back through the window. 'I'm waiting until she appears.'

'I understand you made the dish with Leroy Daniels,' Declan changed tack now. 'Was there anything different in the making?'

'Anything made from scratch is always different,' Harnish explained. 'Leroy was in Dubrovnik and came up with it. Said it was going to be the basis of a brand new signature dish, but needed a guinea pig before he went to press.'

'Howe?'

Harnish pursed his lips, as if debating whether or not to agree.

'He was going to give us a shit review anyway, he'd die before he said a good word about the restaurant—'

He stopped for a moment, realising what he'd said.

'I mean—'

'I get what you mean,' Declan smiled. 'So Leroy thought nothing ventured, nothing gained?'

Harnish looked around, as if looking to see if anyone else was listening.

'He didn't want to hurt Marshall,' he half whispered. 'Leroy wanted to impress him. He might have given the impression of a man who didn't give a damn what anyone thought, but he wanted to be liked by everyone. Even the people *he* didn't like. So the meal he made for Marshall would have been the best he could make, you see?'

'And that's why he made his own plate?'

'Yeah. Leroy wanted to ensure it was perfect. If his tasted exceptional, he'd be able to walk away from Marshall Howe's shit review with his head held high.'

'Did you try any of the meal?' Declan asked.

Harnish shook his head.

'I'm vegan,' he explained. 'Besides, it was Chef's meal to try, not mine.'

Declan nodded at this.

'Anything seem strange last night?' he asked. 'Aside from Howe's appearance?'

Harnish considered this.

'He was stressed, Chef that is,' he said. 'He's usually the first person in here, but last night he turned up an hour into service, already stressed out. Probably to do with the Dubrovnik trip; something happened there, but nobody mentions it. Even Tara wouldn't talk about it. She's been off all week too.'

'Tara is...'

'Tara Wilkinson, my wife. She's the manager here.'

'And she went to Croatia with Chef Daniels?'

'He might be the name and it's his dishes that people eat, but everything else, the look, the feel, even the attitude of the staff, that's all her,' Harnish explained with more than a hint of pride. 'But when they got back, he started talking about other opportunities. I got the impression he was considering pulling out of the deal.'

'And he was late to work?'

'Kind of,' Harnish was uncomfortable answering, as if worried he was betraying secrets. 'He was definitely in earlier today as he still does a lot of the setup in the kitchen, but when I arrived to take in the afternoon delivery, he'd gone out. Turned up an hour before Marshall did, he didn't say anything, so I assumed it wasn't important.'

'He usually do this?'

'Not really. But it's been a tough month, you know?'

Declan noted this down on the page. 'How so?'

'We, that is the industry, already had another chef die up in Scotland. A lot of us knew him.'

Declan jotted this down. He could get Billy to check on that. 'Anything else?'

Harnish was silent as he thought for a long moment.

'Actually, yeah,' he said. 'His knife was missing.'

'Knife?' Declan paused as he realised. 'He had his own, I'm guessing?'

'We all do,' Harnish looked disgusted at Declan, as if stunned he could even consider that the Chef would use someone else's blade. 'A good knife creates a skilled chef. Many of us have a set we've used since we started, or ones that we've learnt about from a mentor and then purchased when we were able. Me? I use a *Yoshihiro* layer hammered one as my go-to. Leroy, he preferred the *Miyabi* knives. The set he used was one of a kind, all ice-hardened with *Basur Birch* handles and Damascus blades. A couple of grands worth, easy.'

'So they could have been stolen, maybe during the chaos?'

Harnish shook his head.

'No point,' he replied. 'They're unique. The moment you try to sell them, you'd be found out. Everyone would know whose they were. Besides, I don't remember him using the knives last night. He borrowed an eight-inch one from Helen, and I remember thinking that was strange.'

'Helen?'

'Helen Cage, the Pastry Chef,' Harnish was scratching his head now. 'She helped with the honey.'

Declan noted the name in his notebook before sliding it back into the PPE suit.

'If you can wait around for some more questions, that'd be appreciated, and if I see your wife, I'll tell her you're out here,' he said to a grateful smile from the Sous-Chef. 'Is there anything else?'

'I think you should speak to Tara about the Gala,' Harnish replied a little nervously. 'I've been NDA'd.'

'Gala?'

'Sorry, I can't talk.'

'We're police.'

'This was Government, so I don't know if it trumps you.'

Nodding at this and deciding not to push the matter, Declan pulled his mask and hood on once more and walked back into the restaurant, only to find Doctor Marcos pulling hers off.

'No need to worry, Deckers,' she smiled, using her annoying, recently decided nickname for him. 'We just heard from the hospital. The other two patrons were allergic to nuts, didn't realise that they were in the dessert and had panic attacks when everything hit the fan here. Whatever killed Leroy didn't reach them.'

'So it's only in these two meals,' Declan looked back to the table where Marshall Howe had sat. 'Either Daniels wanted to kill Howe, one of his chefs wanted to and Daniels mistakenly ate the poison, we have someone trying to kill Daniels with Howe being collateral damage, or someone wanted them both dead.'

'That gives us a lot of alleyways to look down,' Anjli said as she walked across, overhearing. 'Lists of people who wanted both of them gone, and reasons for these hatreds.'

'I want to find out what else is in play here,' Declan looked around the restaurant. 'Who gains from seeing Daniels dead? What happens to that hotel deal, things like that? Harnish, the Sous-Chef, said that Tara Wilkinson is still here, and mentioned something about NDAs and Government Galas. Do we know where she is?'

'Her office, talking to PC Cooper,' Doctor Marcos replied, pointing to a side door on the other side of the restaurant, away from the kitchen. 'When she got back from the hospital with an all clear, we kept her in there in a PPE suit while we talked. She'll still be there.'

'Then I'll have a quick chat and see if she can give us anything before I leave here,' Declan said as he pulled off his PPE suit, finally happy to be rid of it. 'DS Kapoor? Go back to Temple Inn and get DC Fitzwarren on this. I want anything he can find on these people. I want suspects with motives by the time I get back.'

'You sound just like Monroe,' Anjli grinned as she turned

and left. Doctor Marcos was still waiting beside Declan, though, and so he turned to look at her.

'What?' he asked.

'You haven't told me what I'm supposed to do,' she smiled. 'You're lead, after all.'

'Oh, right,' Declan flushed. 'It's been a long day already. Find out what the hell killed Daniels and why it hasn't yet killed Howe. And then work out how it got into the food.'

With Doctor Marcos already off to the main entrance, most likely back to her forensics lab and the body of Leroy Daniels, Declan started for the door to the offices.

This looked like a poisoning gone wrong, that Daniels had perhaps tried to prank Howe and it'd spiralled out of control. Anaphylactic shock meant allergies, so what had it been that both victims were allergic to?

Declan hoped this was a straightforward answer, because the alternative was murder.

3

NEW MANAGEMENT

TARA WILKINSON WAS STRANGELY COMPOSED WHEN DECLAN walked into the back office, PC Cooper sitting with her, both still in PPE suits, although the hoods were off and the zips were open. It was little more than a broom cupboard in size, and Declan was surprised to see how small the room was.

'Guv,' Cooper said as she rose, backing away to give Declan the chair. 'Mrs Wilkinson has been giving me the details of the evening.'

Declan took this moment to observe the *Essence* Manager, sitting calmly in the office chair facing him. She was in her forties, short, pixie-cut black hair over large, silver earrings as she watched Declan in return. Even in the chair, Declan could see she was tall, maybe even six feet in height, with the slim, lithe frame of a ballerina. Under the PPE suit, she wore a black suit jacket and skirt over a pale blouse, and apart from her earrings, she wore no other jewellery.

'Sorry to keep you here longer than you wanted,' Declan said, sitting in the chair facing Tara. 'As you can understand—'

'My husband was sent to hospital, possibly poisoned and I've been stuck in this room since I returned while people try to work out if I can walk into the kitchen without dying,' Tara snapped. 'I don't understand much of what's happened in the last twelve hours.'

'Your husband's fine,' Declan forced a smile. 'He's outside, waiting to see you.'

At this news, Tara's posture relaxed into a shrug, and she cried.

'I thought—' she started as Declan pulled a tissue from a box on her desk and passed it over to her.

'So far, nobody else has taken ill,' he explained. 'The two diners were allergic to nuts. Only Leroy Daniels and Marshall Howe seemed to have been targeted.'

'It was just that Harnish helped with the meal,' Tara replied.

Declan nodded.

'Well, it looks like he didn't try any of it,' he said calmly. 'So, in a minute I'll let you go to him, and get yourselves home. Before that though, I do need to ask some questions.'

Tara nodded, the relief flowing from her in waves. Declan pulled out his notepad and pen, a carbon-tipped tactical one he'd used since his days in the Military Police.

'Can you think of anyone who might have wanted to see Leroy Daniels dead?' he asked.

'I thought these were quick questions?' Tara almost laughed. 'He's a chef. A bloody good one. Was. That is, he *was* one. When you're that good, you piss people off. Lots of them.'

'Enough to kill?'

Tara's eyes widened.

'You think that's what this was?' she whispered. 'Murder?'

'It's a line of enquiry.'

'It can't be,' Tara shook her head. 'Only Leroy, Harnish and Helen touched the food.'

'What about the ingredients?' Declan pushed. 'Could they have been tampered with before he made the meal?'

Tara didn't answer, frowning as she mentally went through a checklist, nodding to herself as she checked off each line.

'It's possible,' she said. 'But it's such a small list of people involved. And it was only dependent on Howe returning. More likely that Leroy did it himself.'

'You think Leroy deliberately tried to murder Marshall Howe?'

'We'll never know,' Tara shrugged. 'But Leroy was a passionate man, you know? He wasn't shy of a fight, and God knows he had enough of them, even though he wanted everyone to like him. Papers, however, loved him. He always gave them a scoop.'

'Do you think he hated Marshall Howe enough to kill him?'

'I would have said no, but now I'm not sure,' Tara replied, and there was a slight hint of caution in her voice, as if she was making sure she gave nothing away. 'I know they seemed to be okay, and for the last few years there's been issues with people that Howe has paraded in front of him—'

'Paraded?'

'Marshall Howe was a bitch at the best of times and a snake at the worst,' Tara shifted in her chair. 'He'd find any new chef that could push Leroy's button and he'd make sure he shouted their praises loud enough for Leroy to hear.'

'Any in particular?'

'Jean-Michel Blanc,' Tara nodded. 'Although that ended while we were in Dubrovnik.'

'How?'

Tara stared at Declan as if he was mad.

'Because he was killed in a robbery,' she said. 'Someone stabbed him while he was in his restaurant kitchen.'

'Now I understand what your husband was talking about outside,' Declan wrote it down. 'How was Leroy with his staff?'

'Good,' Tara replied. 'I mean, a lot of them stayed with him for years. Old hands make good work.'

'You met him in catering school, right?' Declan changed the subject, hoping to put Tara off balance slightly. She nodded.

'Yeah, but even then you could see he was going to be massive. I was never more than a cook. He was a chef.'

'There's a difference?'

'A cook does what they're told. They stick to the recipe. A chef creates the recipe, even if it means tearing up the established one.' Tara chuckled. 'I was—I am a bloody good cook, detective. Even my husband, the Sous-Chef, says so. But I couldn't plan a dish. Create a meal. All that arty food stuff I never got the hang of. So, when we graduated I moved more into the admin side, working in kitchens and building up a more managerial aspect of the role. And then, when Leroy created the idea for *Essence*, the first one, he called me in to help manage it. That's where I met Harnish, as he'd come with Leroy when they left *The Ivy*.'

'You said first *Essence*?' Declan looked around the office. 'This wasn't—'

'God no, this is the third, at least,' Tara laughed. 'We had a small place off Smithfield Market to start with, then there was a bloody awful slop-house in Mayfair, which still exists as *Little Essence*, and then there's this, which we moved into about three years back. It's a franchise.'

'So the Croatian hotel—'

'Would have been another *Essence*,' Tara sighed. 'We're looking to open restaurants in Paris, Berlin and Dubrovnik right now. The last of those is part of a five-star hotel.'

'Which you and Chef Daniels went to a couple of weeks ago?'

'For six days, Monday to Saturday, yes,' Tara tapped on her keyboard and the screen lit up, showing an image of Leroy Daniels, in full chef whites and on a beach, blue sky behind him, shaking hands with an elderly man in a suit. 'Beautiful, brand new hotel, private beach, all the stuff the higher echelons of holidaymakers want. This wasn't an all-inclusive *Thomson Holidays* location, detective. This was *money*. We did some press stuff to announce it, then Leroy spent three days working in the kitchen and on a menu for the place, and we had a public tester meal on the last day.'

'Quick turnaround,' Declan wrote this down. 'So when does that open?'

'It won't,' Tara replied sadly. 'Apart from the obvious, we fell out with the hotel. They'd expected more client-facing events with Leroy over the week we were there, while he felt they wanted a performing seal. It didn't help that he was working on two menus at the same time.'

'Two?'

Tara smiled.

'He could multi-task, detective, even when he didn't want to. It meant the hotel pulled him from pillar to post on a daily basis. But they didn't feel loved enough, and after we came home last week, we haven't heard from them since.'

'You mention home,' Declan looked up from the note-book. 'Did Chef Daniels have a wife? Family?'

'No, this was his family,' Tara waved a hand around the room. 'Not this exactly, but the restaurant. I mean, he had affairs and flings, all that. He'd broken up with Helen about a year back, and I think he was hoping they'd get back together.'

'Helen Cage, the Pastry Chef?' Declan frowned.

Tara laughed at this.

'Pastry Chef is a bit much for her talent, but yeah.'

'You don't think she should have had the role?'

Tara shook her head.

'We had a perfectly fine Pastry Chef before Leroy made his changes,' she said. 'Usually I'd be the one discussing this with him, but this time he was adamant. He wanted her exclusive to *Essence*.'

'Because of their relationship?'

'No, because of her bloody *honey*.'

Declan leaned back in the chair.

'You're going to have to explain that one to me,' he said. 'Is *honey* a sexual—'

'Manuka honey,' Tara replied. 'Super expensive, super healthy. It's what all the rich bio-hackers and health gurus eat now. It protects the body against damage caused by bacteria. Some also boost production of cells that repair tissue damaged by infection and have anti-inflammatory actions that help ease pain and inflammation. But you can only get it from certain places, usually New Zealand. Helen's family owns one of the few UK-based hives, and because of that Leroy wanted exclusivity to the brand, because it carried on with his 'British food' remit.'

'So they gave Helen the job on the condition that she also brought the honey?'

'In a roundabout way, yeah,' Tara was a little more cautious in her reply. 'I think there were other things, but it wasn't my place to ask.'

'You're the manager here,' Declan pursed his lips. 'Surely this is exactly the sort of thing that's your place to ask?'

'You'd think,' Tara stated, crossing her arms. 'But the name over the door isn't mine.'

Declan couldn't help wondering whose name would be over the door now that Leroy Daniels was dead, but he decided it wasn't the time to ask that question.

'Thank you for your time,' he said, rising to his feet. 'I'm sure you have a lot to get on with right now, with your husband outside and everything.'

'That's it?' Tara seemed quite surprised. 'Will you need me again?'

'Probably,' Declan was puzzled by Tara's response. Usually people were content to be released, not surprised it was actually happening. 'We're waiting for toxicology reports. After that, we'll probably have a whole new round of questions to ask, mainly based on what we find. What will you do now?'

Tara looked around the office, as if realising how small it actually was.

'I can't say.'

'Is this because you don't know, or because of an NDA?' Declan asked. 'Your husband mentioned there was something about a Gala, but I should mention this to you?'

'There was a meal,' Tara nodded. 'Leroy was supposed to be arranging it. Only booked last week, a big event. It's the other menu he was working on. Would have given us one of those crests to put on the wall and everything. I suppose I ought to see whether that'll still happen now he's gone.'

Declan went to reply, to ask whether Harnish Patel would now move into the Chef role, but something about the way she spoke stopped him.

'Crest? You mean a Royal event?'

Tara nodded.

'Prime Minister stepping down, big Gala Dinner at the Houses of Parliament, we got the call during Dubrovnik that they wanted Leroy to do the menu.'

'But if he's dead, how can he continue?' Declan asked. 'I mean, you say it like it could still happen.'

'Leroy did the menu,' Tara pointed at a sheet of notepaper on her desk. 'Finished it yesterday. With that as the blueprint, we can still make the dinner he planned. You can still read a book by an author after he died.'

Declan nodded, finally understanding this, but also understanding that with Leroy gone, this was an opportunity for Tara and Harnish to appear from behind the curtain.

'One last thing,' Declan said, walking to the door of the office. 'Your husband said that Chef Daniels wasn't using his usual knives last night, and that he had to borrow one from Helen Cage.'

'That's not uncommon,' Tara dismissed the comment.

'That's not what I got from your husband,' Declan retorted. 'I got the impression that chefs and knives are very personal.'

'Well, they are,' Tara continued, and it felt very much like a back track. 'But at the same time, a knife is just a knife, you know? If Leroy left his knife somewhere, he'd always be able to borrow someone else's. It's not like a sword master and a blade that's individually balanced and all that. It's just a tool. A hammer for a carpenter.'

'So he did this a lot?'

Tara paused, considering the question. Eventually, she shook her head.

'Actually, now I come to think about it, I can't think of a time when he didn't have his knife set with him, in its little leather case. Maybe he left it somewhere?'

Declan threw out a hunch.

'Has he been seen with the knives since he returned from Dubrovnik?'

Tara shrugged.

'I don't do kitchens,' she smiled. 'I'll ask Harnish though and come back to you.'

'I was told that Chef Daniels left the restaurant last night,' Declan added. 'Do you know where he went?'

Tara shook her head.

'I'm not his PA,' she replied. 'But I know he was gone for a couple of hours, left around four, if that helps. Probably to do with the Gala.'

'Which you as manager should have learnt about?'

'As I said, detective, Leroy was a force of nature. Chains of command and all that meant nothing to him. I learnt when I learnt.'

Declan nodded a thank you and with PC Cooper beside him, left the office, returning into the restaurant.

'Did anything strike you as odd when you talked to her before I arrived?' he asked. Cooper shook her head.

'To be honest, she just went through the schedule of events, Guv,' she replied. 'I got the impression she wasn't doing a lot though, like the position she had was honorary?'

'What do you mean?' Declan stopped, watching the officer as she considered her words.

'My cousin's a restaurant manager in Windsor,' Cooper said. 'Granted, it's not as swish as London, but she spends her days training staff, doing all the Human Resources stuff, literally an agony aunt for the whole place, and then in the evening she's involved in taking bookings, meeting clients, working with the Chef and his team in the kitchen, she's everywhere, right?'

'And that's not the case here?'

Cooper shook her head.

'I was taking statements when I got here,' she pulled out her own notebook, checking the notes as she spoke. 'Many of the kitchen crew hadn't really seen her around for weeks. She spends all her time in the office, only speaks to Chef Daniels one on one, and never ever spoke to her husband when they were working. Seemed to be a bit of a coldness between them. And, more importantly, when she was in Dubrovnik for five days, her replacement, the usual Maitre d' did more in that time than she had in a month, and they all felt that finally someone was listening to their issues.'

'So she's not as good as she thinks she is,' Declan mused. 'Or, she's got the job because Leroy Daniels wanted people he could trust around him.'

'There's something else,' PC Cooper said, lowering her voice. 'I only recognised the name because my cousin mentioned him. Jean-Michel Blanc? He used to call himself Johnny Mitchell, real Jamie Oliver wannabe. When I heard he'd been murdered a couple of weeks back, I checked him up before you arrived.'

'And?' Declan didn't like the direction this conversation was going.

'I called my cousin, asked for the skinny on him,' Cooper continued. 'Restaurant managers all know each other, and she was able to put a quick call around. Johnny Mitchell cut his teeth under Leroy Daniels, before he changed his name and focused on Anglo-French fusion cuisine.'

'Interesting.' Declan opened his notebook, writing this down. 'Harnish said the restaurant knew him, so perhaps he even worked here. Anything else?'

'Yes, Guv,' Cooper straightened a little as she gave the report. 'Mitchell had a Richmond restaurant, but three months ago he upped sticks and opened a new restaurant in Scotland. That's where he was robbed and killed.'

'So? Many people change locations,' Declan replied.

Cooper nodded.

'Yeah, but not all of them break up out of a six-month relationship with Helen Cage right before doing so.'

'The Pastry Chef?' Declan whistled. 'She's very popular right now. How do you know this?'

'Waiting around with the manager, Guv,' Cooper smiled. 'She mutters to herself.'

'We'll need to have a chat with her as soon as we can,' Declan nodded. 'That woman seems to have her fingers in a lot of different pies.'

Declan looked around the restaurant; the forensics teams were finishing up now, and Declan knew that it'd only be a matter of hours before the place was left alone again.

'Do you think it was murder, sir?' Cooper asked. 'I heard the SOCO say it was allergic reactions.'

'We're still waiting to see on that,' Declan replied. 'But it seems strange that a chef who's spent years working with foods dies of an allergic reaction the same day he cooks a meal for his most hated rival. Especially as he's had no reaction in the past.'

'Maybe something in Dubrovnik sparked one off?' Cooper suggested.

'That is something we need to decide,' Declan nodded. There was a lot going on, and Declan had no clue where they needed to start.

'Damn you, Monroe,' he muttered, half under his breath. 'Why did you pick this week to bugger off on whatever crusade you're on now?'

4

GRASSED MARKETS

'I HATE THIS BLOODY PLACE,' DCI ALEXANDER MONROE griped, waving a hand around the Grassmarket with one hand as he sat outside *The Last Drop* pub, cradling his pint glass, currently filled with orange juice and lemonade with the other. 'It feels so fake. Like Scottish Disney.'

PC Morten De'Geer followed the hand, casting his gaze around the Grassmarket. A historic marketplace, it was primarily located in the heart of the city's Old Town, and comprised a continually changing collection of pubs and restaurants situated around the large open square on the southern side of Edinburgh Castle, all of which offered seating areas outside and on the cobbled pavements of the square itself.

Calling it a square though was a bit of a stretch of the imagination; in reality it was a long rectangle that ran from west to east, with a pedestrianised cobbled walkway along the north side, a middle area interspersed with trees and pub seating and then a road on the south side that ran from the castle in the west, towards Cowgate in the east. Along the north face were pubs and restaurants, all filled to capacity on this warm June day, while along the south wall were hotels and vintage clothing shops, equally busy.

'The Grassmarket is one of the oldest parts of Edinburgh and it was originally used as a marketplace for horses and cattle before falling into ruin in the 19th-century,' De'Geer read from his phone. 'Nowadays it's a very popular visitor destination that offers an exciting assortment of places to eat and drink as well as a hub to explore nearby tourist attractions like Greyfriars Kirk and Edinburgh Castle.'

He looked up.

'Doesn't sound like Disney to me.'

Irritated, Monroe pointed at a small group of tourists who stood around West-Bow Bell, a drinking fountain at the far east of the Grassmarket. They were watching their tour guide intently, a man in a long black robe, a yellow and red scarf and with a pair of black spectacles on as he waved what looked like a wand around.

'There,' Monroe muttered. 'Bloody *Harry Potter* tours everywhere. He's telling them that Victoria Street was an inspiration for Diagon Alley, when there's no proof of it anywhere. All that Edinburgh really has is that JK Rowling once lived here. Probably still does, who knows.'

'That's no different from where we work,' De'Geer frowned. 'Come on, Guv, half the time we walk out of the office we bump into some tour group talking about how Temple Church is the one from *The Da Vinci Code,* or how Shakespeare had his inspiration for *Richard the Third* outside Middle Temple Hall. And pretty much every old pub in North Kent and Essex claims Charles Dickens wrote his books there.'

Monroe sniffed.

'Suppose so, laddie,' he muttered. 'I'm just angry that my favourite pie shop closed. I loved their haggis ones.'

He leaned back in his chair, looking up at the sky.

'I suppose I can't really complain,' he said. 'I mean, I only come up here when the Festival's on. I'm as much a tourist as the rest of them.'

Changing the subject, he looked back at De'Geer.

'I appreciate you coming,' he said. 'I'm guessing your lassie wasn't happy.'

'Lassie?' De'Geer looked uncertain where this conversation was going.

'DC Davey,' Monroe continued. 'You're a thing, aren't you?'

'Ah,' De'Geer flushed at this. 'No.'

'Really?' Monroe sat up now. 'I was sure you were together.'

'We had a date, but it didn't work out.'

'You choice or her choice?'

'Bit of a mutual choice,' De'Geer replied, but his expression gave away the fact that it wasn't that way at all. 'We thought it was a good idea not to date someone we worked closely with. Always leads to heartbreak.'

He stopped, paling.

'I mean, usually,' he backtracked. 'I'm sure you and Doctor Marcos—'

'Are older,' Monroe smiled. 'We've done all the bullshit you're yet to go through. We understand each other better.'

'And how did she take this?' De'Geer asked. 'That you needed to come here?'

'Well, she ordered you to come along with me, so I reckon she either doesn't trust me to stay alive, or she doesn't trust me to tie my shoelaces.'

Monroe stopped talking as a squat, muscled man in his late sixties, no taller than five feet in height, walked over to their table. His white hair was trimmed down to an almost shaved cut, and his stubble was flecked with red, matching his cheeks and nose. In fact, if it wasn't for the tweed suit, one that would have made Billy Fitzwarren jealous, De'Geer would have classed the man to be some kind of promoter, pushing another guided tour of the city.

'Ali,' the white-haired man said as he held out a hand to Monroe. 'Been a while, laddie.'

De'Geer stifled a snort, and the man looked over to him.

'Problem?'

'No, sorry,' De'Geer regained his composure. 'It's just that I hear the Guv call people 'laddie' or 'lassie' so much, it's just strange hearing someone do it to him.'

The man smiled at this, looking back at Monroe as he sat in one of the empty chairs around the table.

'When I met this man, he was a wee nipper, only four-teen,' he said.

'I was sixteen.'

'You were still wee.'

Monroe nodded, looking at De'Geer. 'This is Willie Moss,' he explained. 'Retired Police Sergeant from Glasgow. When he was a beat copper, he was the one that suggested I change my life, made me the man I am now, for good or bad.'

Willie held out his hand, and De'Geer shook it warmly.

'PC Morten De'Geer, Sarge,' he said. 'It's an honour.'

'Ach, he's a polite one,' Willie grinned. 'Could have done with a few his size back in the day too.'

He rummaged through his inside jacket pocket and pulled out a wad of folded A4 paper, opening it up and flat-tening it out on the table.

'I see you're as tech savvy as ever,' Monroe mocked. Willie raised an eyebrow as he looked up.

'Can you hack this with all your fancy London tech?' he enquired politely. 'No? So shut yer wee trap.'

Monroe grinned as Willie pulled out a pair of reading glasses, placing them on as he read down the sheet.

'Claire Doyle has been making a bit of a name for herself, it seems,' he said, looking back up. 'Moved across to Edinburgh last year at sixteen, and she's been hanging out with a bad crowd.'

'How bad?' Monroe asked. 'Drugs? Worse?'

'Activists,' Willie replied, spitting the word out. 'Lots of climate change arguments, all that sort of thing.'

'Wait,' Monroe shook his head. 'She's hanging out with climate change protestors, and this was enough to put a bounty on her head?'

'Sort of,' Willie turned the page. 'She's been involved with a group buggering around in Leith, north of here. Hassling a councillor named McCavity, and stopping a developer tear down some manky ol' buildings, concreting over some marshland, that sort of thing.'

'Let me guess,' Monroe looked at De'Geer briefly before replying. 'The developer is Lennie Wright?'

Willie didn't answer, but his expression gave Monroe everything he needed.

'He's legit now, Ali,' he said. 'He's got friends in the council. McCavity and him? Thick as thieves.'

'Legit? Not what I've heard, Willie,' Monroe retorted. 'I heard he's cleaning house in Glasgow, proving he should be top dog again, and that's spilling out over here.'

He leaned closer.

'Does he know that Claire's a Monroe?' he wondered carefully. 'I mean, I'm guessing she's not using the surname.'

Willie shrugged.

'I don't really know, but from what I heard, Kenny's kids, if they even exist, have never been a concern to the Wrights. And as I said, Lennie's legit. I don't know who's been feeding you information, but they're a drama queen and taking things to the next level when there's no level to go to.'

'It's Derek Sutton,' Monroe leaned back. 'You want to tell him he's a drama queen? To his face and all that?'

'I'm no' scared of Sutton,' Willie shot back. 'He's nothing but a thug. He doesn't see how the world changed while he rotted in Belmarsh. This apparent grandniece of yours has rubbed a lot of folk the wrong way, but she's a bee sting, nothing more. Lennie knows he'd gain more trouble going for her than by setting solicitors on them. You and your attack dog here have come all this way for nothing, and I'd suggest, as your friend for almost forty years, that you call it a day, turn around and go back to London before the Wrights think this is some kind of incursion on their territory.'

'Glasgow's their territory,' Monroe whispered, his voice cold and lacking any emotion. 'This here isn't anything to do with them. And if my grandniece is touched—'

'Christ, Ali!' Willie snapped. 'You didn't even know you *had* a grandniece until this week! She must have known about you, though! Her and her mum? They most likely knew about you all their lives and they never once came to find you. Maybe you should think about that before you get on your white horse and pull your magic sodding sword out of your arse!'

Monroe sat silent for a moment.

'You're right,' he eventually replied. 'They don't know me. I was an idiot to come.'

He let out a deep breath, staring up at the buildings that surrounded Grassmarket.

'Thanks Willie,' he nodded. 'Stay for a drink?'

'I can't,' Willie rose, placing the paperwork away. 'I've a council thing to do before I catch the train back to Shettleston. You take care now, okay? And keep me in the loop on how you're doing down there with these City folks.' He aimed the last line at De'Geer who bristled as the short man walked off quickly towards Cowgate.

'So I'm guessing we're not really going home just yet?' De'Geer asked as Monroe rose, finishing his drink.

'No, son we are not,' Monroe motioned for De'Geer to finish his drink. 'I think we need to stretch our legs a bit first.'

Finishing his coke, De'Geer rushed after Monroe, already following Willie as he walked out of Grassmarket.

———

THEY DIDN'T HAVE TO WALK FAR; AS SOON AS THEY HIT Candlemaker's Row, De'Geer saw Willie Moss duck right through an arched gate, entering Greyfriar's Kirkyard via the stairway on the other side.

Smiling, Monroe followed him.

'Looks like it's your lucky day, laddie,' he said. 'We get to see a wee doggie and have a bit of a *Harry Potter* tour at the same time.'

Greyfriar's Kirkyard was enclosed within four walls of old, tall Edinburgh buildings, with Greyfriar's Church, or *Kirk* itself, to the far end of the entrance that De'Geer and Monroe had entered through. There were several paths through the graveyard, and along the walls were old graves and mausoleums, many of which had been moved over the years to provide access along the tarmac'd paths that wound their way through the small amount of trees remaining.

In the middle of the Kirkyard was Willie Moss, standing nervously beside a gravestone and speaking to two men; the first was obviously a bodyguard, or muscle-for-hire; no older than late twenties, he wore full tracksuit and trainers, but was easily six feet in height. Beside him was a man in his late sixties, bald apart from a short white cut around the sides, matching the soft white beard that he wore over a plaid shirt and long, black jacket. It was warm for June, and the shirt and jacket looked overly warm for the climate, but the man didn't seem to be bothered.

Moving closer, Monroe waved for De'Geer to be silent. There wasn't that much they could hide behind, as in this area the gravestones and markers were smaller than the ones to the side, and eventually, realising they couldn't get close enough to overhear the conversation Monroe straightened up, adjusted his coat, made his way back to the path and started towards the men who only now noted the two new arrivals.

'Well, as I live and breathe, Willie,' Monroe said with a smile. 'Fancy seeing you here! There I was, taking young Morten here to see Greyfriar's Bobby, but who should I find, but you!'

He turned to the older of the two strangers, now glaring at Monroe with undisguised hatred.

'Standing with Lennie Wright,' he finished. 'Hello Lennie, how are things going?'

'You're interrupting a private conversation,' Lennie replied. 'I'd appreciate it—'

'That's the joy of *this*,' Monroe interrupted with a smile, pulling out his warrant card. 'Means I can interrupt any conversation, public or private.'

He pointed at his ID.

'See? *Detective Chief Inspector Monroe*. That means I can walk up to old friends like you and ask why you're chatting in the middle of a graveyard, acting all suspicious-like?'

'ID says City Police,' Lennie pursed his lips. 'London. Not Edinburgh. You're out of your comfort zone.'

'As are you,' Monroe moved closer, nodding to tracksuit and trainers, who'd moved to intercept. 'Down, boy. Or my man there will arrest you for assaulting a police officer.'

As if emphasising this, De'Geer straightened. He had almost a foot in height on the man, and with his blond Viking beard, he looked a dangerous man to cross. Tracksuit and trainers, at a nod from Lennie, backed down.

` We seem to have started off on the wrong foot,' Monroe continued to Lennie. 'I'm here on a family matter, and I'm trying to stop a repeat of what happened forty-odd years ago.'

'Forty-odd years ago, you killed my brothers,' the words were flat and cold as Lennie looked at Monroe.

'Derek Sutton killed your brothers.'

'Aye, and you'd been with him as you hunted them down.'

Monroe shook his head, nodding at Willie.

'I'd been a copper for a year by then,' he said. 'Ask Willie. He was the one that proposed me.'

'You may have worn the uniform, but you were as corrupt as all the others,' Lennie sniffed. 'I heard the stories.'

Monroe's posture tightened, as if realising that De'Geer could hear all of this.

'I didn't want them dead,' he replied. 'I wanted them in prison for what they did.'

'What they did?' Lennie almost laughed. 'They got rid of a *grass.*'

'Now that's unfair,' Willie said, almost apologetically for interrupting. 'Kenneth was an informer for us, but not on you.'

'But you killed him anyway,' Monroe finished.

There was a long moment in the Kirkyard, almost as if everything had frozen in place. Even the tourists by the church had stopped talking, although this was mostly by chance, as nobody outside the five men on the grass in the middle of the Kirkyard were involved in the discussion.

'I killed nobody,' Lennie smiled, showing a row of yellow, tar-stained teeth. 'You'd have to speak to my brothers about that. If you hang around, I can grab you a ouija board.'

'This was all long ago,' Monroe continued. 'It doesn't need to start up again. I've left you alone.'

'Then why are you here?' Lennie shrugged. 'Tell me you're not here because of that little bitch, the one that's got herself in my way?'

'She's family,' Monroe almost pleaded. 'You don't need to put a hit on her. Let me speak to her.'

Lennie thought for a moment.

'Family?'

'Kenny's granddaughter.'

Lennie Wright went to speak, but shook his head, as if silently telling himself not to continue.

'Walk with me,' he eventually said, turning and walking away from the others. Motioning for De'Geer to stay, Monroe followed.

'Speak to her,' Lennie said matter-of-factly. 'If she agrees to no longer be a problem, I'll step back. No harm done. But if you don't, or if you think that it's a great idea to join her? I'll make damn sure you both regret it.'

'Threatening an officer of the law?' Monroe smiled.

'Not at all,' Lennie stopped, looking at Monroe. 'I never threaten. I make promises.'

He leaned in.

'I won't say it's been nice to see you, Ali, because it hasn't,' he hissed. 'I know what you did, even if your blond pretty-boy copper there doesn't. And if you even consider trying to play the blue card on me? I'll ensure that everyone knows the truth of *Detective Chief Inspector* Alexander Monroe.'

He punctuated every word of Monroe's title with a tap on Monroe's chest.

'But I will give you something,' he added, finally smiling. 'Something you've probably never known, and something neither Willie over there nor Sutton ever told you. When my brothers killed your brother? They weren't looking for him.'

He tapped Monroe one last time.

'They were looking for *you*.'

Monroe felt a tightness in his chest as Lennie watched him silently.

'I was a nobody back then,' he argued. 'A teenager.'

'You can lie to yourself all you want, Ali,' Lennie shrugged, turning to walk back to the others. 'But we know the truth, you and I. About your love for *fire*.'

Monroe's hand grabbed Lennie's wrist, turning the elderly gangster back to face the angry DCI.

'If we're giving out truths, here's one for you,' Monroe hissed. 'If you hurt my family, whether or not I'm aware of them, if you touch even one hair on my grandniece's head? I'll *end* you.'

Lennie nodded silently before wrenching his arm from

Monroe and walking back to his bruiser. Monroe, meanwhile, stood shaking beside a gravestone.

For forty years he'd wondered if it had been his own actions that had damned his brother.

Now, Alexander Monroe knew they had.

And now, Alexander Monroe needed to *repent*.

5

BACK IN THE SADDLE

BILLY WAS WAITING FOR DECLAN WHEN HE ARRIVED, A CUP OF coffee in his hand, his waistcoat a blue tartan today.

'Thought you might need this,' he said, passing it over as Declan walked to his desk. 'You know, to get the synapses going and all that.'

'Thanks,' Declan sipped at the coffee and sighed with delight. It was from the swanky machine in the canteen and made even the local coffee shop's best flat white taste weak in comparison. 'Where are we on things?'

'Case, or... other things?' Billy enquired tactfully. Declan smiled at this.

'Your choice.'

'Well, we can go into the case when the others arrive, so let's talk about the other stuff.'

'Please,' Declan took his jacket off, hanging it on his chair. 'All I know is that Tom was shot, that's it.'

'Karl had a photo that he wanted sent to his daughter,' Billy explained. 'While looking at it, I realised it had data hidden inside. A latitude and longitude and a message saying *Avenge Me*.'

'Yes, you passed it on to Trix,' Declan sipped at his coffee. You've told us this.'

'Yeah, but I didn't mention this was purely to get Trix and *Section D* to move Karl, which they did yesterday.'

'Because they thought the location was compromised,' Declan shook his head. 'Christ, it wasn't a command to get him out, it was a dog whistle to get *Section D* to bring him out to them.'

Billy nodded. 'There was a team of five,' he said. 'Two vans caught the transport in a choke point a mile from the location. Assault weapons, well trained, took out three guards with extreme prejudice, injuring Tom.'

'How many guards were there in total?'

'Four, including Tom,' Billy lowered his voice. 'Declan, he should have been killed as well, but he was in the driver's seat. The chassis of the van took the brunt of the bullets, and the two hits they got were, shall we say, bloody? They probably didn't think he'd make it and grabbed Karl out of the back before leaving.'

'Tom's still in ICU?'

'Yeah, but he's out of surgery, so that's a plus,' Billy admitted. 'He's probably finished in active service though.'

Declan groaned at this. He'd seen enough wounds in the army that killed careers, and he hadn't even considered something like that could happen here. *James Bond with a Zimmer frame* had never really occurred to him.

'Trix is with him,' Billy carried on. 'Bullman is making sure Liz and Jess are somewhere safe for the moment.'

'I think Karl won't be after them,' Declan replied, placing the cup onto the desk. 'I get this feeling he's done with me.'

'I'd rather we kept them safe, just in case?' Billy had the tone of a man who knew the person he was talking to thought they were making sense, but was instead being a bloody idiot.

'Yeah, of course,' Declan accepted. 'Anything on Pearce?'

'Nope, nothing since around a week back,' Billy replied. 'We're still checking in on it. I know we'll get a hit somewhere. It's just a matter of time.'

His tone changed, less professional now.

'It sucks what they tried to do,' he said. 'Why go to all that hassle to screw you over?'

'Apart from revenge?' Declan shrugged. 'Makes sense, really. Francine Pearce already had one personality change, when she went from being Frankie Wilson, assistant to Sarah Hinksman into Francine Pearce, Personal Assistant in *Devington Industries* twenty years ago.'

'You think she's doing it again?'

'I think she has nothing left,' Declan continued. 'She had *Pearce Associates,* but that burned when we solved the Victoria Davies murder and arrested her. She still had links to *Rattlestone*, but that died off when we arrested Malcolm Gladwell, proving the connection with the company, and closing it down. Now there's *Phoenix Industries,* but I didn't see Pearce's name on the list of directors.'

'That doesn't mean she's not on there,' Billy had already moved over to the monitor screen and was typing on his keyboard. 'If she's changing identities, she could already be on there in another guise.'

'Double check all female board members and major shareholders,' Declan nodded. 'You could have something there. And she's got the money to change identity. Alter the hair, change clothes, pay someone an inordinate amount to create a new persona, complete with passports and ID cards—'

'She's still in the system though,' Billy looked back from his monitor station. 'You can't fix that.'

'She was blackmailing the heir apparent to the Tory Party,' Declan almost laughed. 'Who else did she have in her pocket? All it takes is a Whitehall slip of the fingers and that entire file disappears. And, if Francine Pearce is disappearing, to be replaced by *name to be announced later,* why not kill two birds with one stone and land the missing person case on the one copper who's been making her life hell?'

'You make a compelling argument,' Billy leaned against his desk. 'Francine is never seen again, and you're unable to be charged with murder or kidnapping, but it'll hang over your head forever.'

'They didn't want me arrested,' Declan spat the words out. 'They wanted my reputation. To be an outcast, shunned by the police. Well, more shunned than I have been for a while. With, of course, the serial killer that has a grudge against me out in the wild.'

'So how do we stop this?'

'Find Francine Pearce,' Declan sighed. 'It's the only way we can get it out from under us. Once she's no longer missing, then she's no longer on our radar. We can move on.'

Anjli walked in through the doors now, noting Declan and Billy talking.

'Am I missing anything?' she asked as she dumped her messenger bag onto her own desk. Something about how she did this stopped Declan from continuing.

'I thought you'd be here earlier,' he said. 'I chatted to Tara before returning.'

'Yeah, but you came straight from the nick in Bishopsgate,' Anjli protested. 'I had to go find where I'd parked my car, and then drive back.'

'Bloody hell, you're just like a married couple,' Billy laughed, but stopped when Declan spun around to face him.

'Is that what people think?' he asked.

'How do you mean?'

'Do people think we're a couple?' Declan glanced back at Anjli. 'DC Ross was under the impression we were.'

'DC Ross also thinks you can kill a government whistle-blower, hide her body and return as if nothing's out of the ordinary,' Anjli scoffed. 'DC Ross is an idiot.'

'She thinks I could do this because you helped me,' Declan added. Anjli thought about this.

'Well, I am the more competent of all of us here, so yeah, I can see why she'd think it could work if I was—'

She stopped.

'Wait, she thought I was involved?'

'Well, you are the more competent of all of us,' Declan smiled.

Anjli went to reply to this but cursed as her phone beeped.

'The case?'

'Bloody Eden Storm,' Anjli tossed the phone onto her desk. 'Guy won't take a hint. Keeps trying to take me out for dinner. In Rome.'

Declan laughed at this; Eden Storm was a tech billionaire who'd recently taken a shine to Anjli, mainly because she kept telling him to sod off.

'Maybe you should just go on one date to shut him up?' Billy suggested. 'I mean Christ, woman, he's fit and rich and he flies his own helicopter.'

'What you're saying is you want to date him,' Anjli side-eyed Billy, who instead of taking issue with this actively beamed with delight.

'In a bloody heartbeat,' he said. 'Could you at least ask if he swings both ways? I could be the Anjli he wanted.'

'This is wrong on so many levels,' Declan walked back to his desk, pulling his own phone out of his pocket. Dialling a number, he held it to his ear. After a few rings, it was answered.

'*Declan,*' the voice of Liz Walsh, his ex-wife, sounded stressed and tired. '*Are you okay?*'

'I should ask you that,' Declan walked away from the others, entering the empty glass-walled briefing room as he continued. 'Are you and Jess doing alright?'

'*We've had better days,*' Liz was making light of it, but Declan could hear the anger in her voice; anger at having her routine altered '*Your boss has us in a posh hotel for the night though, so Jess is watching all the pay movies while I'm working my way through the room service menu.*'

'I'm sorry, Liz,' Declan added. 'You shouldn't—'

'*I shouldn't what?*' Liz was still strangely calm down the line, and Declan knew she was barely holding in her anger. '*I shouldn't have to uproot my life because some mad serial killer my ex-husband couldn't put down like a rabid dog is now back out in the world and gunning for my daughter?*'

'That's unfair, Liz, and you know it.'

'*What I know, Declan, is that your childhood bloody mechanic's daughter tried to kill Jess while she was staying with you,*' Liz wasn't even trying to hide the anger now. '*Now I gave you the benefit of the doubt, and you told me he was gone, but now he's not?*'

'I genuinely think you don't need to fear Karl coming

after you,' Declan shook his head, realising after he did this there was no way Liz would have seen it. 'He said as much to me when we met—'

'*So you've been meeting him?*' Liz was almost shouting now, and as much as Declan was regretting making the call, he knew she needed to vent. '*What, like Agent Starling and Hannibal sodding Lecter? Do you do lunch? What else aren't you telling me?*'

'When I get more information, I'll keep you in the loop,' Declan replied stiffly, disconnecting the call before Liz could shout at him again. He got it, he really did; Liz had never married him for the job, and the job had split them apart in the end.

But it had been the hours, the long shifts and the slow cases that did that to them. Here in the *Last Chance Saloon,* the cases were far more frantic. In a way, Declan was silently glad that they were divorced. If she'd wanted to leave him before, she'd want to kill him now.

Who was he kidding? She did want to kill him now.

'Trouble in paradise?' Anjli asked across the office. Emerging from the briefing room, Declan shrugged.

'I get why she's angry,' he said. 'But at the same time, I'm getting the same problems. It's not like I've just dumped them all on her. It's not my fault that having Jess together meant she couldn't just make a clean break from me.'

'Maybe she's pissed about something else, and you're just a good foil?' Billy suggested. 'Wasn't there a guy on the scene?'

'Rob, yeah, but they broke up a few weeks back,' Declan walked back to his desk, checking his watch. 'Maybe I should call him, see why they did.'

'Will it help?' Anjli asked.

'Probably not,' Declan sighed. 'What should I do?'

'Find Karl Schnitter and stick him in the bloody ground,' Anjli muttered, and Declan could hear the passion and anger in her voice. But then again, everything about this was personal to every member of the team. Even Bullman, who wasn't part of the *Last Chance Saloon* back then, had turned up and helped Monroe in Berlin.

'Don't worry, that's my plan,' Declan replied as he turned to his phone again, sending Monroe a text.

About to hold a briefing. Any notes?

A moment later, a reply came through from Monroe.

Don't pander to them. Be a boss. You're lead and everyone, no matter their rank, works for you.

Except Rosanna. Do whatever she says.

Declan laughed at this, typing.

Are you ok?

Far from it. Say hi to everyone.

Declan wanted to mention Tom, but he understood why he couldn't. Tom had been like a nephew to Monroe and his then-wife Emilia, and if Monroe learnt that he'd been off gallivanting around Scotland while Tom was in hospital, Declan didn't know how that'd affect the gruff Scottish DCI.

Remembering something, he typed another message, sending it.

Hey, you're in Edinburgh right? Could you check into something for me?

I'm not on bloody holiday.

I know. And you just told me I'm lead. The boss. And if you're not on holiday, you're working for me.

There was a long pause, and as he waited for a reply, Declan saw Doctor Marcos and DC Davey enter the office, ready for the briefing. He could almost feel Monroe stewing as he read the message. So, with a smile, Declan added to it.

If you are, then Edinburgh becomes police business and you can claim the travel, like Berlin…

After another long moment, there was a beep, and Monroe's last message appeared.

Bloody pedant. Send me what you need.

Declan almost laughed.

'So, are we doing this or what?' Doctor Marcos asked. 'Because I'm in a rush to keep playing with a dead body.'

She glanced at the phone.

'Messaging Jess?'

'Monroe,' Declan admitted. 'Asking him if he had any advice for me in the briefing. He said to listen to whatever you say.'

'You see!' Doctor Marcos grinned, punching his arm as she walked past. 'Now you're catching on to who the *real* power in this office is.'

Nodding to the others to follow them in, Declan entered the briefing room.

6

GOSSIP BRIEFS

'OKAY, SETTLE DOWN,' DECLAN SAID, TRYING TO MAKE HIS voice as gruff as Monroe's usually was during these briefings. 'Anything and everything. Let's all get on the same page.'

The briefing room was half-empty; with Bullman still away at the hospital, and with Monroe and De'Geer up in Edinburgh all that were there was Billy, as ever connecting his laptop to the computer screen, Anjli, reading from her notepad and both DC Davey and Doctor Marcos, sitting in their usual spots at the back and deep in discussion.

'Right then,' Declan tapped on the plasma screen behind him, hoping that Billy had already front-loaded the crime photos. Luckily for Declan, Billy had, as an image of Leroy Daniels appeared on the screen, a press photo of Marshall Howe appearing beside him. 'Leroy Daniels, Head Chef at *Essence*, found dead last night, affected by the same food that almost killed Marshall Howe, food critic for *The Guardian*, leaving him currently in a coma. Doctor Marcos?'

Doctor Marcos shifted in her seat as she gathered up her notes.

'We've found something curious here,' she said, nodding to Billy who, with a few keystrokes, changed the image of Leroy Daniels to that of a fish.

'A fish,' Anjli was unimpressed.

'A *puffer*fish,' Doctor Marcos rose now. 'Normally of the genus *Takifugu, Lagocephalus* or *Sphoeroides* species, or a porcupinefish of the genus *Diodon*, to be precise. Does anyone know what they have in common?'

'They're used in the *Fugu* dish,' Billy chimed in.

'Well, of course you knew that,' Anjli grinned. 'It's probably what you ate when you weren't eating pheasant.'

'Unlikely, DS Kapoor, because even DC Fitzwarren isn't stupid enough to dice with death on a daily meal basis,' Doctor Marcos replied, looking back at Billy. 'You're not, are you?'

'That and it's pretty much illegal in the EU,' Billy added, almost wistfully.

'Okay, so what does a Fugu dish have to do with this?' Declan asked.

'Fugu contains lethal amounts of the poison *tetrodotoxin* in its inner organs, especially the liver, the ovaries, eyes, and skin,' Doctor Marcos explained. 'Anyone who prepares this dish has to take three years of rigorous training before they're allowed by Japanese law to remove toxic parts of the fish, to avoid contaminating the meat.'

'And what does the poison, this tetra-whatever do?' Anjli asked.

'The poison's a sodium channel blocker that paralyzes the muscles while the victim stays fully conscious,' DC Davey said from the back of the briefing room. 'The poisoned victim cannot breathe and eventually dies from asphyxiation.'

Doctor Marcos nodded to Billy, and Leroy Daniels' toxicity report appeared on the screen.

'As you can see here, Chef Daniels had a fatal amount of tetrodotoxin in his body the night he died,' she said. 'Marshall Howe had a far smaller amount in his system, which is why he didn't die instantly, and why they've been able to keep him alive, if critical.'

'So someone poisoned the food?' Declan asked. However, Doctor Marcos shook her head.

'No,' she replied. 'There's no sign of it in the dish they ate. Also, tetrodotoxin poisoning can have either *rapid onset,* somewhere between ten minutes or half an hour, or the more common *delayed onset,* which is generally within three to six hours. Death may occur as early as twenty minutes, or as late as a full day later after exposure, but it usually occurs within six hours.'

'So not as quick as it did last night,' Declan mused.

'Wait,' Anjli shook her head. 'So Leroy Daniels and Marshall Howe could have been poisoned around three hours *before* the meal?'

'That's the most likely option,' Doctor Marcos nodded. 'We're working out now how it could have been passed. There's talk on whether it's more harmful through skin contact or airborne contaminates, but the most common and dangerous form is ingestion.'

'It also means that Marshall and Leroy may have met before the meal,' Billy added. 'Maybe even had a spot of tea somewhere. The manager said Leroy was away from *Essence* between four and six last night.'

'Good thinking,' Declan nodded. 'I want both men's movements for the—' he looked at Doctor Marcos for confirmation.

'I'd say three hours,' she replied.

'—for the three hours before that meal. See if they met, or they were at the same place, whatever we can find out,' Declan paused. 'Is there a cure for this?'

Doctor Marcos shook her head.

'Not that I know of,' she replied. 'Most people who survive Fugu poisoning do so because their bodies could purge the toxin, of which there was a minuscule amount.'

Declan now looked at Anjli.

'Okay, so apart from fatal poisons being thrown around, what else?'

Anjli read from her notebook.

'Marshall Howe and Leroy Daniels hated each other, and for seemingly good reasons. They each blamed the other for derailing their careers. But according to witnesses, not enough to actively try to kill each other.'

'Where does *each other* come from?' Billy asked. 'You think Howe could have done this?'

'If they met before the meal, it becomes a possibility,' Anjli stated. 'And Marshall Howe was quick to anger apparently, as was Leroy.'

'What do we know about Howe?'

'Been a foodie for years now, started as a critic a few years after *Masterchef*, known for having his favourites. Most recently, he's been shouting the virtues of Jean-Michel Blanc.'

'Who's dead, from what we've heard,' Declan added. 'What do we know about *him*?'

'Well, that gets a little confusing,' Billy smiled as he pulled up old news clippings onto the screen. 'Jean-Michel Blanc is actually Johnny Mitchell, who trained under Leroy Daniels for five years.'

An image of a good-looking young man with dark, wavy hair appeared on the screen.

'Okay,' Declan looked at the image. 'So what, he's Leroy's protégé?'

'Was,' Billy replied, turning to face Declan. 'He was the winner of another series of *Masterchef*, six years back, one where Leroy was one of the guest-chef tasters. Obviously he impressed Leroy, because he offered him a job the moment the series ended. Started on the fish station, worked his way up over the years.'

'So what happened? Why the split?' Declan asked. 'I mean, according to Harnish Patel and Tara Wilkinson, the place is a family where barely anyone leaves.'

'The problem, it seems, *was* Harnish,' Billy read from his own hastily written notes, quitting as he tried to make out his own handwriting. 'Only way Johnny could rise higher was to become Sous-Chef, and that meant *dead man's shoes*. Harnish had to leave for Johnny to rise, and with Tara as manager, that wasn't happening soon.'

'So Johnny left?'

'Not immediately,' Billy explained. 'While he was working for Leroy, he played about on social media. Created this character of Jean-Michel Blanc.'

'French for Johnny Mitchell White?'

'Probably because of the chef whites, or maybe he was a closet racist, we'll never know,' Doctor Marcos muttered.

'So Johnny does these *TikToks*, some *YouTube* videos, getting over on social media. Think of him as a Joe Wicks for cooking, way more personable than the current crop of TV chefs, and his market was growing massively. So much so that he was invited onto the same Saturday cooking show as Leroy, as his alter ego, *while* working for him as Johnny.'

'Which didn't go down too well, I'm guessing?'

'Leroy no-showed, probably didn't want to be overshadowed by one of his own employees and Johnny, as Jean-Michel and probably furious about this, made a joke on TV, one connected to the whole scotch bonnet incident. That night there was a massive fight in the kitchen between the two of them and after it got physical, Johnny walked out,' Billy read from the screen. 'A month later, he's got financiers backing a new Anglo-French fusion restaurant in Richmond. Uses social media to really attack Leroy around this point, and it's not for the clicks. The others in the kitchen, who knew them both, said it felt personal.'

'And how does Helen Cage fit into this?' Anjli was writing everything down as she spoke.

'Helen's family make honey,' Declan interrupted. 'Tara Wilkinson mentioned it. Said they were one of the only UK-based hives of Manuka honey, and Leroy wanted exclusivity, because it carried on with his 'British food' remit while giving diners some kind of sexy Instagram-friendly honey.'

'So Helen was working on the pastry counter as nothing more than a line cook,' Billy carried on reading his notes, currently on his laptop monitor. 'Had been for about a year. But when Johnny left, Helen went with him. And so did the honey.'

'They were together?'

Anjli spoke up now.

'One of the waiters I spoke to said that while she was at *Essence*, Helen had been with Leroy, but they split badly. She left with Johnny for a while though, after dating for a few months, but then came back.'

Billy looked up from his notebook, tapping on the screen.

An image of Johnny Mitchell, as Jean-Michel Blanc, standing outside a restaurant, appeared on the screen.

'They were apparently together for a good six months before it fell apart. A month after Helen returns to *Essence*, Johnny shuts up the Richmond restaurant completely and moves everything to Edinburgh. This was spring this year. And then a couple of weeks ago, a month after their big opening, someone breaks into the restaurant after hours, not realising that Johnny's still there. There's a scuffle, and Johnny is fatally stabbed before the killer leaves with the takings.'

'Would there be takings?' Anjli asked. 'Don't they take mostly card payments?'

'I'm just going on what Edinburgh police are saying,' Billy nodded. 'But yeah, there won't be as much there as there would have been, say, ten or twenty years ago.'

'What do we know about the killing?' Declan looked to Anjli. 'Am I the only one that thinks this is too coincidental? That Johnny and Leroy both die within weeks of each other?'

'Currently nothing, but that might change,' she said. 'We have an asset up there though that can sort that for us.'

'Funny enough, I've already requested that DCI Monroe and PC De'Geer check into this while they're in Edinburgh,' Declan said as he paced back and forth. 'So we have a chef murdered in a restaurant who dated another chef's ex-girlfriend, who then also dies in a poisoning accident that might have been when he was meeting with his sworn enemy, someone who championed the first chef...'

Declan scratched at his chin.

'Could Howe have done this as revenge for Johnny's death? And if so, why would he think Leroy had anything else to do with it? This was at the time Leroy was in Dubrovnik, so we'll have to come back to that later. Next.'

'The manager and the Sous-Chef,' Anjli rose now. 'Tara has known Leroy Daniels since catering school, but only started working with him when she met and started dating Harnish Patel. Since then they've become quite a culinary power couple.'

'Enough to carry on after Daniels dies?'

'If anything, his death would free them,' Billy nodded from his chair. 'Leroy was a bit of a prick, according to the internet. Gordon Ramsey level shouting, but without the charm. Regardless of what the staff said, looking at it from the outside, *Essence* was far from the family they reckoned. Although, there might be a little more closeness than people realise.'

'What do you mean?' Declan frowned. Billy grinned widely.

'Okay, so this is gossip and possibly untrue, but I checked into the hotel this morning and gathered a thimble of tea from the head chambermaid when I phoned for information on their stay.'

Declan looked confused at this until Anjli tapped him on the shoulder.

'It's not actual tea,' she said. 'Tea is gossip.'

'I knew that,' Declan lied. 'What did they say?'

'Well, when Tara and Leroy arrived, they were given a suite, the hotel's version of the Presidential one,' Billy pulled up images from the hotel website. 'Two rooms, a dining area, a TV and sofa and an office space. The idea was that Leroy could relax here when he wasn't doing press events or hanging out in the kitchen, while Tara would be close by if needed. They were there six days, so five nights, flying in Monday and leaving Saturday morning.'

'Okay, so where's this going?' Declan asked. 'Currently I'm—'

'Let the man spill the tea,' Doctor Marcos muttered, leaning forward, her eyes sparkling. 'Chambermaids are the people who make the beds. What did they find?'

'It's more what they didn't,' Billy replied. 'You see, they came in every day and made the beds in the suite, and also did a turn down service in the evenings. Most of the time they were chased away by Leroy from doing the latter because he was working on menus in the suite and they'd distract him, but in the mornings they could clean the rooms. On the first and second nights, both beds, both *king size double beds*, were used. But, on the third and fourth nights, Leroy's bed was untouched, while Tara's kingsize bed was *well used,* to quote them. And then, on the last night, both beds used again. The maid I spoke to hinted it was as if for two nights, Tara and Leroy shared the bed.'

'Dubrovnik's a romantic city,' DC Davey muttered. 'I went there a couple of years back. Maybe the closeness, the location, it moved them to...'

'Or, this is something that's been going on for a while,' Declan nodded. 'Billy, keep on with this. If Leroy and Tara were having an affair, I want to know. And if not, I want to know *whose* bed he was in for those two nights.'

He straightened, looking around the room.

'I'll have a chat with *The Guardian*, see if they can shine any light on Marshall Howes's last movements. DS Kapoor, have a chat with our Pastry Chef, see what she says. With Monroe and De'Geer in Edinburgh, we should gain some more info about Johnny's death soon, and Doctor Marcos,

DC Davey, keep on with the body, see what you can find, if anything more. If we hear anything more about Howe coming out of the coma, we'll see if we can chat to him too.'

Everyone nodded, noting their jobs down, but before anyone rose, Declan continued.

'So while we're here, and while we don't have anyone else around, I'd like to discuss the other issues we have,' he said. 'Bullman will be back soon with an update on Tom Marlowe, but at the moment we're in the dark about what happened with Karl Schnitter. What we do know is that he's out there somewhere and he'll remember that all of us in this room assisted, in Hurley, in placing him in a dark hole. So be careful.'

'What about Francine Pearce?' Anjli asked.

Declan looked over at Billy now.

'She's in hiding, and we don't know why,' he said. 'We think this could be a way for her to change her identity while causing me harm, and Billy's been looking, seeing if he can pick anything up on CCTV.'

'Nothing yet,' Billy replied, 'but I've also got Trix looking, too. In fact, everyone in *Section D* have taken this very personally. They know Schnitter couldn't have escaped without help, and the people who did this seem to have also tried to frame Declan for Pearce's disappearance, so it's safe to say they're connected.'

'Anything on the copper who's hunting Declan?' Anjli added. 'She seemed to be a little too eager to see him go down.'

'I found something, and I think it explains a lot,' Billy pulled up DC Ross's file onto the screen. 'I had to go back to her training class to find it, but it was what she said to the Guv here that did it.'

'You're toxic, Walsh. I've read your file. From punching out priests to entrapping cyber-crime operatives, you live by your own rules, and you're the wrong kind of copper for the force.'

It was Doctor Marcos who spoke, shrugging as everyone looked at her.

'What? I have a photographic memory. You all know that.'

'It was the cyber-crime bit that did it,' Billy pulled up another file onto the screen. This time, another woman's image appeared.

'DC Sonya Hart,' Anjli hissed. 'Mile End cyber-crime officer. Or, that is, she was until you had her and DCI Ford arrested.'

'Ross and Hart were classmates back in Hendon,' Billy explained. 'Really close, too, from what I heard.'

'So it *is* personal for Ross,' Declan nodded, staring at the screen. 'She won't stop. Good to know.'

'Jess and Liz?' Anjli asked.

'The Guv's putting them into protective custody for the moment,' Declan replied. 'With luck it won't be for long, because I think Liz is in a race with everyone else to see who'll kill me first.'

There was an awkward, silent moment in the briefing room, curtailed as Declan clapped his hands together.

'Right then,' he said. 'Let's go catch a killer.'

But, as the team filed out past him, Declan stared up at the image of DC Sonya Hart.

He knew many in the force were split on how they felt about Declan, and a lot of that was from this one moment. Even before the terrorism charges had been laid at his feet, Declan had moments where officers had called him a grass for turning in Ford and Hart.

One had even spoken out at his father's funeral.

And DC Ross was likely to be smack bang in the middle of that group.

Shaking his head to clear it, Declan took a deep breath and walked back to his desk.

They needed to sort *this* investigation out before they worried about any others.

7

STRAWBERRY FIELDS

Sᴇᴀɴ Aꜱʜʙʏ, ᴛʜᴇ ꜰᴇᴀᴛᴜʀᴇꜱ ᴇᴅɪᴛᴏʀ ꜰᴏʀ *Tʜᴇ Gᴜᴀʀᴅɪᴀɴ,* ʙɪᴛ into a Cornish pasty as he looked across his desk at Declan.

'I was sorry about her,' he said between half-filled mouth-fuls, the insides of the pasty repeatedly visible in the inside of his mouth as he spoke. 'She was a hell of a woman.'

Sean was talking about Kendis Taylor, onetime investigative reporter for the paper before her murder several months ago; Sean and Declan had become acquainted in the aftermath of her death, although Declan was loath to give Sean the full details of the situation, in particular how he'd started an affair with her the night before she died, an affair that nearly had him thrown in a black site as a terrorist handler, and eventually punched out beside her grave by her angry, widowed husband.

'That she was,' Declan toasted Sean with the mug of coffee in his hand. It might only be instant, but at least it was caffeinated, and despite the one he'd had at the Unit, Declan was feeling the tiredness seep back in after his night in a cell.

'So then, Howe,' Sean had finished the pasty now, crumpling up the paper bag it had arrived in and tossing it into the bin like a basketball. 'What do you need?'

'An idea about the man,' Declan pulled his notebook out. 'Getting a feel who might have wanted him dead.'

'It wasn't Daniels?' Sean seemed surprised at this. 'We were going with the headline tomorrow that it's Daniels. They really hated each other, and it was in his restaurant, over his meal.'

'I'd hold on that,' Declan tapped his nose with a finger. 'But that's all I can give you.'

'Interesting,' Sean jotted this down on his notepad. 'Well, if it wasn't Daniels, it could have been a ton of other people. Every other day he pissed off a restauranteur or a chef.'

'Because of his reviews?'

'Partly,' Sean nodded. 'Also, because he liked to do these little hit pieces that really nailed home how much he hated some of them. He would come up with incredible metaphors and note them down. Then, when reviewing, he'd rummage around in that folder for some really juicy lines, something to punch that meal in the face.'

'Sounds like he had a bit of a chip on his shoulder.'

'No,' Sean shook his head, but it was mockingly. 'People with chips on their shoulders can still be argued with. Howe had a sodding chip shop on his.'

'How so?' Declan had guessed this would be the answer, but he wanted Sean to explain a little more.

'Don't get me wrong, Howe was an amazing writer, and he could literally make you taste the meal on the page when he wanted, or else we'd have kicked him out years ago,' Sean laughed. 'But no matter how brilliant he could be on his best days, the worst driver is a backseat driver, and the worst chef is a failed one. Marshall Howe was convinced he was better than every chef he reviewed. It became a bit of a running joke, that the only places he raved about were either people he didn't class as a threat, or where he thought the review would piss off someone else.'

'How was he on Johnny Mitchell?'

'You mean *Jean-Michel TikTok?* He loved the guy. First off, this was another person who hated Leroy Daniels, so he had something in common with him, and secondly, he had a massive following. More people watched his TikTok's in a day than read Howe's reviews in total. Marshall wasn't stupid. He knew Johnny, or his alter-ego was going to be the next big thing and he hitched his wagon to that horse a long time back.'

'And after Johnny was murdered?'

'The robbery? Howe was distraught. For about two days. I think it helped that Mitchell had been cold to him the last few times they met, perhaps realising Howe may be good in the short term, but he didn't give much in the longer frame of things. I think the last thing they worked on together was the meal.'

'Meal?' Declan waved a hand. 'Care to give me a bit more than just 'meal' there?'

'Some Westminster thing,' Sean shrugged, gulping down some coffee before continuing. 'Gala dinner. He claimed it was NDA'd up to the hilt, but it didn't stop him telling everyone about it at any chance he had. Howe was brought in on the organising committee, because of his knowledge and all that. He'd pitched Jean-Michel as the perfect option.'

Declan looked back through his notes, finding a quote from Tara Wilkinson earlier that day.

Prime Minister stepping down, big Gala Dinner at the Houses

*of Parliament, we got the call during Dubrovnik that they wanted
Leroy to do the menu.*

'This wasn't the Prime Minister thing, was it?' he asked
cautiously. 'Because he's stepping down?'

'You know of it then?' Sean was surprised, but this soon
faded. 'Of course you do. You're probably invited. Your mate
Charles Baker sort you a ticket?'

Declan smiled, refusing to reply, while trying to work out
the timings in his head. They had hired Johnny Mitchell to
create the menu for the event but, after his death, someone
had immediately passed this on to Leroy Daniels, who was in
Dubrovnik but returning home soon.

Both the murder and the request had happened within days.

'Who would have made the decision?' Declan asked. 'You
know, who decided finally who would have taken over after
Mitchell died?'

'Why, do you know who's doing the meal?' Sean leaned
forwards now, all ears. 'It's been a bloody nightmare working
that out.'

'That's because the replacement died last night,' Declan
threw Sean a bone; after all, he'd likely find out, anyway.

'Bloody hellfire!' Sean exploded as he slammed back into
his chair. 'What are the odds of that happening?'

'Exactly,' Declan placed his notebook back into his coat
and rose. 'Thanks for the chat, Sean.'

He went to leave, but stopped.

'Oh, one last thing. Do you know what Howe would have
been doing yesterday afternoon, before his poisoning?'

Sean tapped on his laptop.

'All our calendars are synced, so hold on,' he said, checking. 'Yesterday Howe was in the office, it was a deadline day

so he'd have been filing copy before three, and then he had a dentist appointment.'

'Does it say where?' Declan leaned over, looking.

DENTIST - FIRST FLOOR, 9, STOREY'S GATE

'Thanks, Sean, again,' Declan said, offering his hand.

'Thank you,' Sean replied, taking it and shaking it warmly. 'I can start looking into the setup now I know Leroy would have had to keep the menu.'

'How do you mean?'

'Well, the dinner's tomorrow,' Sean explained. 'Even with the chef change a couple of weeks ago, it's too late to alter anything. We're talking State Dinner here. The food will have been picked, the supplies already ordered. Leroy Daniels would have had to use what he had available to create his own twist on Mitchell's designs, and that would have really hacked him off, especially with a committee signing off on it.'

He burped, most likely the pasty fighting back.

'Anyway, let me know if we can use anything from your investigation, because although menus for dinners are a bit *Daily Mail*, we do have a juicy murder attached here,' he winked. 'And I know you passed a couple of things to Kendis back in the day.'

'That was one time, and I was still in love with her,' Declan shook his head as he walked to the door. 'Stay safe.'

'If it gets me a story, you can be in love with me,' Sean offered, wiping the fallen pieces of Cornish pasty off his jumper.

Declan laughed.

'I'll think about it,' he said as he left.

———

Helen Cage lived in a very cosy but expensive looking house just around the corner from Strawberry Hill train station. It was an affluent area, if only from the cars that Anjli saw parked on the street as she pulled up in her police issued *Hyundai* vehicle. *Bentleys, BMWs, Mercedes Benz* and *Land Rovers* were surrounding her, none of which were older than three years, judging from the number plates. They weren't all like that though, and as Anjli walked towards the house in question, she saw more average vehicles parked up in driveways, worrying that she felt more relaxed when *average* things were around.

She was spending too much time with Declan, she supposed as she knocked on the door, surprised that the thought made her smile. After a moment, it opened and a young woman faced her across the threshold.

'Helen Cage?' Anjli held up her warrant card. 'DS Anjli Kapoor. I'm here about—'

'I know what you're here about,' Helen nodded, opening the door wider for Anjli to enter. 'It's all I've been thinking about since I got home. Come in.'

Entering the house, Anjli followed Helen into a side living room. Sitting on the sofa, with Helen facing her in a matching armchair across the coffee table, Anjli pulled out her notebook, placing her iPhone onto the table with the recording app on.

'You mind?' she asked, continuing at a nod from Helen.

'So is this because I put the honey on the poisoned meal?' she shifted in the chair nervously.

'It's a little more, but we can start with that,' Anjli forced a smile. 'You used your honey?'

'*Hill's Honey*,' Helen nodded back. 'It's the only Manuka created in the UK. Well, there's a couple more but we're the closest to London and we have the best reviews.'

'And *Hill's Honey* is...'

'Made outside,' Helen angled her head to show the back garden. 'We have an incredibly large back garden outside, and a large apiary located there. We're on a hill which helps with moisture.'

'Is that why—'

'Oh, no,' Helen smiled. 'We named it *Hill's Honey* because of Strawberry Hill.'

'And it's exclusive to *Essence*?'

Helen shook her head.

'It was, sort of, but not anymore,' she said. 'Basically, the honey was exclusive, sure, but to Leroy, not the restaurant.'

'And now he's passed, the agreement is void?'

'Pretty much.'

'I'm sorry to ask this,' Anjli leaned forwards on the sofa. 'But it might be connected to the case. I heard about the death of Chef Daniels. I believe you were dating?'

'A long time ago,' Helen's reply was terse and quick. 'The relationship we had when I returned was purely business.'

'Still, Someone who was—'

'Look, let's cut to the chase,' Helen interrupted, reddening as she did so, as if this was foreign behaviour for her. 'Leroy was abusive. He was a bully. And more importantly, he would groom you and squeeze you like a lemon until there was nothing left.'

'And he was like this with you?'

'Not at the start,' Helen relaxed into her chair, although her expression was still wary. 'I dealt with him in relation to the honey, back at the start. He was charming and good look-ing. I was young, just out of university.'

'Not catering college?'

'Oh no,' Helen smiled at this. 'I never did that. I have a Biology Degree from the Uni of Bristol. I did a postgrad course in Newcastle, but by then I was burned out. I'd worked with pastries all my life; you find yourself working with a lot of desserts when your family creates honey, and Leroy offered me a gap year, or a *see what you want to do* year in his kitchen as part of the deal.'

'So becoming the *Essence* Pastry Chef wasn't your goal?'

'Far from it.'

'Tell me about Johnny Mitchell,' Anjli sat back now, changing subject. 'It could help the case.'

Helen nodded at this.

'I'd kinda dated Leroy by then,' she said, 'but eventually I realised the truth.'

'Which was?'

'Leroy didn't see me as a partner, but more as stress release,' Helen explained. 'At the start he took me on dates, grand dinners, the food was amazing, the sex brilliant. And when he brought me into the kitchen, I thought it was because he wanted to see more of me.'

'And it wasn't?'

Helen's face darkened.

'Yes and no,' she said. 'He wanted me close by so that when he wanted sex, I was right there. He didn't have to travel, you know?'

'Must have been hard to realise that.'

'I didn't,' Helen admitted. 'Johnny did. He was working as Fish Chef around then, we were very close. He pointed this out to me one night when we were both drunk, I think it was after some awards we catered, and it was like all the pieces slotted together.'

'And so then you broke up with Leroy and started seeing Johnny Mitchell?'

'It wasn't quite that easy, but yeah,' Helen shrugged. 'I wasn't technically seeing Leroy then, and Johnny and me, we'd been kinda dating for a month or two, but obviously losing his *all you can eat sex buffet* pissed him off. There was a confrontation between him and Johnny, partly because of Johnny doing his *TikTok* things and making fun of Leroy on TV, and partly because of me, and Johnny knocked him spark out.'

'He hit him?'

Helen grinned.

'He beat the living shit out of that prick,' she said, and Anjli noted the gleam in her eye.

She hated Leroy Daniels.

'And then you left?'

'I went with Johnny when he started his new restaurant,' Helen got up, walking to the cabinet and pouring herself a drink into a tumbler, something that resembled a vodka. 'And it was great at the start. But, after a few months, I realised that, in his own way, Johnny Mitchell was as self-absorbed as Leroy Daniels.'

'How so?'

'He wanted to beat Leroy at every opportunity. He was posting social media jokes, but they weren't funny, recreating the splutter-vomit TV incident, all targeting Leroy. Sure, he had anger issues with him, but it was childish. And I realised that I didn't want to be with a man that only had eyes for a chef that treated him like shit, basically Stockholm Syndrome at its finest.'

"So you broke up?'

'I said we needed a few weeks apart to consider things,' Helen sat back down, swirling the clear liquid in her tumbler as she stared down at it. 'I moved back here, which was only a ten-minute drive from the restaurant, but he fired me the next day, telling my parents he was going to source his honey from Cornwall now. And then a month later he upped sticks and disappears to Edinburgh, taking anyone else who wanted to go with him, and giving generous severance packages to those who didn't.'

She took a long draught from the tumbler.

'He didn't even ask me to consider joining him, and I sure as hell didn't get what the others got for not moving.'

'And so you returned to Leroy Daniels.'

'No,' Helen vigorously shook her head. 'Not at first. But then the Pastry Chef left, and Harnish and the others were in a bind, and I knew the dishes, and he offered me the exclusivity deal at five times the price he paid last time. My mum needed the money. I agreed.'

'How did you feel when you heard about the Edinburgh stabbing?' Anjli asked carefully.

'How the hell do you think I felt?' Helen snapped angrily. 'I was bereft! I loved Johnny, no matter how it ended! He was too young to die.'

She looked into her glass, and Anjli could see the tears running down her cheeks.

'He was too young to die,' she whispered.

'I'm sorry,' Anjli said softly. 'Are you okay to go on?'

'Yes,' Helen wiped her eyes. 'Leroy and last night, yeah?'

Anjli nodded. 'Did anything seem off last night?'

Helen considered this.

'There's been a tension since they got back from Croatia,'

she admitted. 'Something happened between Tara and Leroy while they were over there. Don't know what, didn't care. Chances were he probably tried to shag her, and she kicked him in the nuts.'

'She wouldn't sleep with him?'

Helen stared off for a moment, thinking about the question.

'She'd probably do it if this meant she'd keep her job,' she said, following quickly with 'no, actually she would if it meant *Harnish* kept his job.'

'Harnish was likely to be fired?' Anjli paused from writing this down.

'Harnish is better than anyone in that place,' Helen nodded. 'But he'll never leave. They're tied to Leroy. *Till death do us part* and all that.'

She paled.

'I mean, you know, they were loyal.'

'I get what you meant,' Anjli looked back at Helen. 'Did you know why he was late to the restaurant last night?'

'He had a dentist appointment, well at least that's what I was told,' Helen shrugged again.

'And where were you around five in the evening?'

'In the kitchen,' Helen's reply was quick and precise. 'I started around two in the afternoon.'

'Do you usually start that early?'

'Depends on who's in,' Helen finished the tumbler, placing it on the coffee table. 'We knew Howe was in last night, we'd recognised the name and the Maitre d', who took the booking knew the voice. We needed to make sure we were on point, so we all came in early.'

'All?'

'Well, all of us in the kitchen,' Helen looked at Anjli now.

'Tara got in about ten minutes before Chef did, in the end. We assumed she'd been trying to salvage whatever screwed up in Dubrovnik.'

Anjli turned off the phone app, placing it and the notebook back into her jacket.

'Can you think of anyone who wanted to kill Leroy Daniels?' she asked.

'Get your notebook out,' Helen half laughed. 'There's a whole load of people.'

'And who wanted to kill Johnny Mitchell?' Anjli rose now as she spoke.

'Only one comes to mind, but he was dead serious when he said it,' Helen replied as she rose to meet the detective.

'And his name?'

'Leroy Daniels.'

8

SCOTTISH KISS

Monroe hadn't been happy to receive his orders from Declan, even if his student was being the master in Monroe's absence, but he understood why he'd been asked. It made sense for Declan to use every resource he had on the case, and after De'Geer and Monroe had been brought up to speed, it was decided that they should have a chat with the Edinburgh police to see what additional information could be picked up. It irritated him he couldn't continue on his own mission, but he wasn't completely sure what that was now in actuality; whether it was to stop Lennie Wright, or to reunite, or rather unite for the first time with his grandniece.

And besides, PC De'Geer was like a bloody puppy when he realised that with Doctor Marcos and DC Davey still in London, he'd be allowed to go over the forensics by himself.

Johnny Mitchell's restaurant, *Monet* was situated off the Lawnmarket, as you headed towards the castle, and the closest *Police Scotland* Unit was actually the regional one, on the junction of St Leonard's Street and St Leonard's Lane, about a mile southeast, a brisk fifteen-minute walk from Greyfriar's Kirkyard.

Monroe had been silent during the walk; it was a glorious day and De'Geer was happy to be out in the sun, but Monroe was mulling over the recent conversation with Wright in the Kirkyard. The revelation that his brothers had been looking for *him* the night they killed his brother was preposterous, but at the same time incredibly chilling. At the time of the murder, Monroe had fallen in with the wrong company, and he'd been working as a lookout for several of the dealers.

And one night he'd distracted the police with terrible repercussions.

Monroe shook the memory aside. He didn't want to remember. It'd been over forty years earlier, and he'd been offering to help with any problems that the Hutchinsons had, trying to live up to the larger-than-life image that his brother Kenny had with the firm.

It was an arson attack that painted the target on his back. The problem was that while Lennie seemed to know more about this, Monroe didn't.

Maybe Derek Sutton could shed some light, he thought to himself. *Yes, he'd meet with him later that day, before Sutton returned to Glasgow.*

Once in the Police Unit Monroe had shown his warrant card, De'Geer doing the same and, after the regulatory time was spent being mocked for being a Scot who turned to the dark side (the dark side being London), they were passed through to meet with a DCI Hendrick, who was the lead on the murder enquiry.

Hendrick was a tall, well-built man with medium length brown hair in a centre parting, and a khaki tweed waistcoat over his shirt and tie, currently loose. He smiled, leaning over his desk to shake Monroe's hand as he offered them the two chairs placed on the other side.

'Good of you to come up,' he said, sitting back down. 'Although I didn't know they'd send you all the way from London for this.'

'They didn't,' Monroe replied. 'We were in the area, anyway.'

'You were?' Hendrick raised an eyebrow. 'We weren't informed.'

'Personal business.'

'That you brought a police officer with you as backup for?'

Monroe smiled.

'He's here to make sure I don't make it *too* personal.'

Hendrick laughed at this, leaning back in his chair.

'Well, we can get back to that in a minute,' he said. 'First, let's talk about your English chef. Why's it so important? On paper, it's nothing more than a robbery gone wrong. An investigation, sure, but not one that warrants... well, you.'

Monroe pulled out his notebook as he spoke.

'We've got another chef dead in London,' he explained. 'Had issues with *your* dead body when they were both alive. We're just making sure there's no connection.'

'Actually, I'd bloody hope there *was* because, to be frank, it might help me,' Hendrick replied. 'We're up the creek with no paddles, to be sure of that.'

'Really?' Monroe looked up from the notepad. 'No leads at all?'

'Apart from the supernatural,' Hendrick laughed, but cut himself off. 'Your man Mitchell, he moved into the new restaurant a couple months back. Big hoo hah, too. A Michelin Star in his first year down south and he was up for a second, so they said. Popular location, great reviews, and then a couple of Wednesdays back, he sends his staff home as usual at the end of the shift, and is alone in the office. Someone comes in, tries to rob the place.'

'Tries?' De'Geer asked.

'We don't think they expected Mitchell to be there,' Hendrick continued. 'Snuck in through some roof entry, came down and was surprised by Mitchell, sometime before midnight.'

'Why then?'

'That's when we have time of death,' Hendrick waved a file. 'All in the forensics report.'

'Do you mind?' De'Geer took the folder from Hendrick, leaning back into the chair as he started reading it.

'Are all PCs forensic experts in London?' Hendrick asked, half-annoyed yet half-impressed. Monroe, in turn, made a non-committal shrug.

'Well, they're not all *experts*,' he smiled. 'So you know how they got in?'

'Och, there's a dozen ways,' Hendrick waved a hand. 'The whole place is seventeenth century. There're tunnels underneath that often lead into communal cellars and then there's four floors above the shops and cafes along there, all with roof access. Batman would have a field day running around up there.'

Monroe was going to argue this, but remembered Declan had once escaped custody in Temple Inn by running along the rooftops of the buildings.

'We think they clambered up from further down, or got up onto a roof around the back, near the Mound, bollocksed around up there a while, found a way in and then snuck down, possibly completely random and opportunistic,'

Hendrik continued. 'Once they were there and saw what they had, they most likely wanted the safe's contents, but didn't expect to find themselves in a fight.'

'You think there was a confrontation?' Monroe asked. 'They didn't just kill Mitchell and take the money?'

'No sir,' De'Geer looked up from the notes. 'The blade that killed Jonathan Mitchell matched that of an eight-inch knife, likely from the kitchen.'

'Anyway,' Hendrick, annoyed at being interrupted, shifted in his undersized chair. 'After the attacker, or attackers killed Chef Mitchell, they emptied the safe and left.'

'How did they empty the safe?' Monroe interrupted again, following with a hasty 'Sorry.'

'We think they either forced Mitchell to open it, perhaps with the knife, or he'd already opened it when they found him,' Hendrick said. 'We don't know what was in it, but we assume anything expensive would have been in there.'

'And nobody saw them leave?'

'There was nobody in the building,' Hendrick shook his head. 'Poor bloody cleaner found him dead in the office around seven in the morning.'

'We'd like to talk to the cleaner.'

'That can be arranged, but just don't get her talking about the bloody ghost.'

'Ghost, sir?' De'Geer looked up.

'Yeah, reckons she heard sounds, like walking about and doors opening in the basement when she arrived seven hours after the murder, assumed that Mitchell was down there until she found him in the office. Problem is, these buildings are all old as hell and creak constantly, so she probably did hear it, but not in the way she thought.'

Hendrick sighed.

'But when you see a dead body, I guess your mind just goes off on one.'

Monroe nodded as he stared down at his notes. At least he understood now what Hendrick had meant earlier when he made the *supernatural* joke.

'And the basement?'

Hendrick shook his head.

'No secret doors, nothing.'

'And he had no enemies? Nobody he'd angered while he was here?'

'Not to my knowledge,' Hendrick shook his head. 'Barely any of the team he had in Surrey came with him when he moved his restaurant. Most of the hires were local, none of whom have priors or any history. From what we saw, there was nobody in that kitchen or in the main restaurant that wanted him dead.'

'Anyone outside the immediate team?'

Hendrick scratched at his nose.

'Well, we have little about his personal life while here, but we had a couple of the newer team mention a woman who visited him when he first moved up.'

'Any name?'

Hendrick shook his head.

'No, but she was from his life in London,' he replied. 'She turned up, stormed into his office and slammed the door behind them. Team got the impression she was an ex-girl-friend or spurned lover, because although the argument was muffled, they heard her shouting that *she needed him*, that *she risked everything for him*, but then it ended and she left.'

'And when was this?'

'About a month back, shortly before he launched.'

Monroe wrote this down. Billy had messaged that

Mitchell had split with Helen Cage before moving to Edinburgh, and there was a chance she'd followed him, albeit briefly.

'Thank you,' Monroe said, putting away his notebook as De'Geer passed back the forensics notes. 'If we can grab some phone numbers, mainly the staff and the cleaner, we'll be on our way.'

'Do you really think it was murder?' Hendrick asked. 'I mean, that they faked the robbery to lead us away from the actual crime?'

'Honestly, I think it was both,' Monroe rose from his chair. 'I think they intended to kill him, and they also wanted whatever was in the safe. What I have to do now is work out how this connects to my own case—'

'You can sit back down,' Hendrick's tone was forceful, and even though Monroe was technically the same rank, he complied. He was in Hendrick's office, on his patch, and in reality, Hendrick had home field advantage.

'I said we'd discuss why you're here,' he said. 'Why I've got two City of London coppers wandering around my town with no remit, apart from a murder a couple of weeks back.'

'It's personal,' Monroe replied curtly.

'Aye, you mentioned that, and I don't give a shite,' Hendrick leaned forward now, and the jovial officer was gone. 'I'm worried that you're up to something that's going to get people hurt, and I'm not having that.'

'DCI Monroe is looking for his estranged grandniece,' De'Geer replied, much to the chagrin of Monroe, who glared at him in betrayal. 'He's going to find out anyway, Guv. We might as well tell him.'

Monroe sighed at this.

'I come from Glasgow,' he said. 'Moved to London

decades ago, after my brother died. However, I found out that he had a kid, unknown to me, and that kid also had a kid, who's now seventeen and in Edinburgh.'

'So what, this is a family reunion?' Hendrick scoffed. 'Forgive me for not buying that, but nobody looking to connect with a teenage bloody woman brings a hulk of a man like your fellow there with him!'

'She's in trouble,' Monroe continued. 'She's an activist, something to do with climate change. She's been causing a stink in Leith, and she's pissed off a nasty bastard named Lennie Wright.'

At the name, Hendrick's demeanour totally changed.

'Walk away,' he said. 'You want nothing to do with the Wrights.'

'I know,' Monroe replied. 'They're the ones that killed my brother forty years back. And now it looks like the last of them wants to remove my grandniece too.'

'He won't do that,' Hendrick shook his head. 'He's too visible these days. Bit of a public figure on the various committees, if you get what I mean. Always meeting with councillors, in particular a corrupt wee shite named McCavity, and making buddies in Holyrood.'

Monroe understood what Hendrick was saying; Holyrood was the home of the Scottish Parliament, in the same way Westminster was the home of the Houses of Parliament.

'So what, he's untouchable?' De'Geer asked, and Monroe could see it surprised him that Hendrick would roll over so easily.

'At the moment, aye,' Hendrick tapped on his laptop, turning the screen to show Monroe a scrolling list of files. 'But we're gathering what we can on him, and eventually we'll get him.'

'And if it's too late?' Monroe snapped. 'If he kills Claire before he's taken down?'

Hendrick sat back, watching Monroe carefully.

'Claire's the grandniece?'

'Aye.'

'So, what's your plan?'

'I don't have one yet,' Monroe admitted. 'But it's sure as hell not going to involve sitting around. I thought I'd visit Leith, see if I could find—'

'Claire,' Hendrick interrupted, tapping on the keyboard. 'Do you have a surname?'

'Doyle,' Monroe replied.

'Mother's name Sherie Doyle by chance?'

'That's her grandmother,' Monroe leaned closer now. 'How do you—'

'It's not only the mob that she's got a problem with,' Hendrick smiled. 'We've picked her up a couple of times.'

He turned the laptop to face Monroe and for the first time he saw the face of his grandniece, taken against a wall, her expression showing annoyance and anger, but also triumph, as if she was irritated she had been arrested, but proud of the fact. She was slim faced, with dark red hair to her shoulders, a fringe across her forehead. Monroe was almost amused to see she didn't have any of Kenny in her looks.

Then again, that was probably a blessing.

'In fact, she's in custody right now,' Hendrick looked back up at Monroe. 'She's enjoying the facilities in our Queen Charlotte Street cells.'

Monroe half-stood up.

'She's in danger,' he stated, looking at De'Geer. 'We need to—'

'*You need to calm bloody well down,*' Hendrick closed the

laptop, slamming the lid as he spoke. 'She's in a cell, alone, and nobody's looking for her there. Come on, I'll drive you both up and we can check for ourselves.'

Monroe slumped a little as he stood, the weariness of the last few days finally catching up with him.

'While Lennie Wright's out there, she's not safe,' he protested.

'Then let's nail the wee bastard together,' Hendrick smiled.

CLAIRE DOYLE'S HEADACHE HADN'T GONE AWAY, EVEN WITH THE painkillers she'd taken. She'd timed it right, to be honest; she'd taken them just as the police cars arrived and the uniforms pulled them out of the road.

Some of the more diehard activists super-glued their hands to the tarmac, or handcuffed themselves to chains, but Claire wasn't about to screw up the skin on her fingers for this. She wanted to help stop the planners, but there was a limit as to how far she'd go. And now she simply waited to be released; it had been a peaceful protest, and she'd made sure not to strike an officer as they bundled them all into vans and brought them to the station. In fact, she'd been thrown a little when, on hearing her name, the desk sergeant had ordered her into a cell.

Something was wrong, she just knew it.

There was a rattling in the lock of the cell door, and it swung open, revealing two burly female officers.

Nervously, Claire rose.

'Am I being released?' she asked. The first of the two women, a peroxide blonde, barked a quick laugh.

'No, love, you're being moved,' she said. 'Got interest in you elsewhere.'

The way the officer said this sent shivers down Claire's spine, and she backed against the wall.

'I haven't spoken to my solicitor,' she said. 'I'm supposed to speak to my solicitor.'

'Feck your solicitor,' the other woman, with short peppered hair, moved into the cell, pulling out a yellow plastic police-issue taser. 'You're coming with us now, and if you make a noise, I'll shoot you in the feckin' face. Got it?'

Nervously, Claire nodded.

This wasn't good.

And suddenly, all the bravado she had for helping the protests was gone, blasted away by the sight of two brutal looking women who were going to take her away from the safety of this cell, no matter what she did to stop them.

9

GALA MENUS

IT DIDN'T TAKE DECLAN LONG TO TRAVEL DOWN FROM *THE Guardian's* London offices; they were just north of King's Cross, and only a thirty-minute Circle Line trip on the London Underground to Westminster. From there he walked past the Houses of Parliament, or more accurately the *Palace of Westminster*, crossing Parliament Square, making his way across Little Sanctuary and heading past the *Queen Elizabeth II Centre*, turning left opposite the imposing white-bricked *Westminster Central Hall*, where he had a slight moment of déjà vu, remembering how he'd attend the monthly comic marts held there as a teen.

To the right of him was Storey's Gate, the street where Marshall Howe's alleged dentist had been. Apart from the fact Leroy also claimed to have visited the dentist at the same time, Declan had felt warning bells when he saw the address, as it seemed a little off the trail for a *Guardian* food critic. There were plenty of capable dentists around the King's Cross basin, and to travel all this way for a dentist within prime Westminster real estate—

He stopped and chuckled as he reached number 9, Storey's Gate. He'd been right.

A dentist here would be a miracle.

The Westminster Arms was a narrow pub with a black-painted frontage, the name of the pub written in gold letters above. And above those was a plaque, inserted between two windows, stating that the *Red Lion Restaurant* had been rebuilt there in 1913. Declan knew that nowadays the upstairs area was known as the *Queen Anne Dining Rooms*, and that in the basement there was a wine bar, as this was where his father met up with Anthony Farringdon when he worked across the road as head of security for Westminster and Whitehall a few years back, and he'd read about that in his father's notes.

There sure as hell wasn't a dentist here, but instead it was often filled with journalists and MPs as it was also one of the few bars around Westminster to have a *Division Bell,* a signal that a vote was occurring in Parliament, and that any members of the House of Commons or of the House of Lords that were currently drinking in the bar had eight minutes to get to their chosen division lobby to vote for or against whatever resolution was in discussion.

And of course, the journalists would be there, listening intently to any conversation within earshot, so it made sense that Marshall, working with journalists, would have learnt about this place—although why he felt the need to disguise it was a mystery.

Entering the pub, Declan walked over to the bar. It was late afternoon, and quiet for the time, but this was also because MPs would be in session right now. The drinking often happened later, usually with raucous dinners upstairs.

Were Marshall Howe and Leroy Daniels at one of these dinners?

Along the left of the bar were four-person booths in dark wood, while the bar itself ran along the right, an extensive variety of rather expensive spirits on display. There was a young man, slim with his hair shaved serving at the counter, nodding at Declan as he looked over.

'With you in a minute,' he said, pouring an ale for an elderly man in a business suit. With nowhere to urgently be, and glad for the moment to simply relax, Declan leaned against the bar, looking up at the television in the top left of the room. It was on *BBC Parliament,* the sound off, subtitles on, and currently showed a familiar face on the screen.

Declan looked away. He wasn't in the mood to watch Charles Baker gurning for the camera. The last time he'd even seen the man, he felt like he was being used as some kind of celebrity endorsement, and that annoyed him as much now as it did then.

The shaven-headed barman walked over, wiping his hands on a tea towel.

'What can I get you?' he asked. In reply, Declan reached into his inside jacket pocket, pulling out his warrant card, showing it to the barman.

'Information,' he said, realising how clichéd that sounded the moment he spoke it. 'Do you have CCTV here?'

'Outside and over there in the corner,' the barman pointed. 'Is there a problem?'

'Not for you, don't worry,' Declan forced a smile. 'Investigating a murder and I think the victim was in here yesterday afternoon. Any chance of seeing the footage?'

'Do you have a warrant?' the barman asked carefully.

Surprised at the out-of-the-blue question, Declan leaned closer.

'Do I *need* one?' he replied softly.

The barman, backing away, slightly shrugged.

'I dunno,' he said. 'It's just we have a lot of important people here, having a simple drink, you know? Many of them are hiding from their Whips, all the usual things—'

Declan mentally shook his head at the term *hiding from their Whips*, reminding himself that the barman didn't mean actual whips; this wasn't a BDSM club, or anything remotely like that, as far as he could tell. In the Government sphere, the 'Whips' were MPs or perhaps Members of the *House of Lords* appointed by each party, officially created to help organise their party's contribution to parliamentary business, but in reality their role was that of enforcer, of bulldog, making sure the maximum number of their party members voted the way their party wanted.

If you didn't want to vote the same as your party, however, perhaps for ethical reasons, and you couldn't be seen as voting against them, then abstaining from the vote by missing it entirely was your only option. It made sense that the barman would be worried about either party's Whips learning that an unavoidably delayed MP was in fact hiding in the back room bar of *The Westminster Arms*.

'I get you,' Declan relaxed a little, holding a hand up. 'I'm just trying to confirm if two people met, that's all.'

'Well, unless they stood over there, you wouldn't know,' the barman pointed to a corner of the bar. 'Only place the CCTV hits, because—'

'Because people don't want to be seen.'

'Exactly,' the barman was relaxing also now. 'I suppose it won't hurt, you looking. Anyone in particular?'

'This man,' Declan held up his phone, a photo of Marshall Howe on it. Glancing at it, the barman nodded in recognition.

'Him? Yeah, he's been here a lot. Part of the committee.'

'Committee?'

'Yeah, some dinner thing this week,' the barman was more chatty now he knew what the problem was. 'He's one of the judges who picked the menu. They meet upstairs.'

'You don't have cameras upstairs, do you?'

'Not working right now,' the barman was apologetic. 'But there's four of them who turn up for these things. First is an old guy, the Minister on the TV there—' he pointed at Charles Baker, and Declan almost smiled, envisioning the incredibly vain Charles Baker learning that he was categorised as *old* '—the man on your phone, and usually two women I've never seen before. Sometimes there's others, but that's the usual crew that turns up.'

'Would you recognise them if you saw them?' Declan asked.

The barman nodded.

'You mean on the CCTV?' he asked. 'Yeah, I reckon so. They're in here enough. Let me get someone downstairs to take over the bar here and I'll show you myself.'

As the barman wandered over to the end of the bar, speaking quickly to another member of the bar staff, a young woman who seemed annoyed that she was being hassled on her break, the barman motioned for Declan to follow him as he walked through the door at the side of the bar itself. Making an apologetic smile for the now glowering woman, Declan followed.

In the back office, the CCTV monitor was small and compact, as was the room itself, half filled with boxes of crisps, reminding Declan that apart from a rather overdone tuna bake in the Bishopsgate cell the previous night, he hadn't actually eaten anything, and now it was past lunchtime. Unknowing of Declan's internal hunger strife, the barman, now known as Paul, scrunched in next to Declan as they went through the previous day's footage.

'I wasn't in yesterday, had the day off,' he said, as if apologising for daring to be away from his post. 'There wasn't a booking for them, so it had to have been a walk-in. They had a few of them, often when they were auditioning.'

'Auditioning?'

'You know, doing the whole *Dragon's Den* thing with chefs. Had a fair few of them in here a few months back. That woman from *Bake Off,* too.' He was loading the footage for the afternoon as he spoke. 'Do you know the time?'

'Let's say between three and six,' Declan suggested, watching the side-by-side images as they sped through the day.

'This is just before three,' Paul slowed the speed down. 'You can tell by the timestamp in the corner.'

Declan withheld the urge to reply, explaining how he had already used his razor-sharp detective skills to work out that the clock in the corner was the timestamp, and instead leaned closer to the screen, watching intently.

'There,' he said as a familiar man with lustrous white hair walked into the pub. 'That's Charles Baker.'

On the other screen, they could see Charles pass through the bar, making his way to the back.

'Heading for the dining room upstairs,' Paul nodded, allowing the footage to carry on. Over the next five minutes,

Paul indicated two other people, both women he believed to be part of the committee, as they arrived. However, when pushed, he didn't know their names, and Declan didn't either, as he didn't recognise either of them. He knew the next one though, as Marshall Howe entered the bar. He seemed nervous, possibly sweating, as he walked through to the back. Declan asked to watch the footage again, confirming to himself that Howe was concerned about something before allowing Paul to speed up the feed until they stopped again twelve minutes later.

Walking into the pub, a briefcase in his hand, was Leroy Daniels.

He wasn't in chef whites, and he had a baseball cap over his bald head, but it was obviously Leroy. And, watching the inside feed Declan saw Leroy stop in the bar, confused as he looked around the tables. He spoke to a member of bar staff and then, directed by them, continued to the back.

Probably asked where the committee was, Declan assumed. *Which means he's never been here before, or met with them here. This has to be the meeting with the committee.*

The timestamp read three fifty-six; he was probably there for a four pm meeting.

'And there's no other footage in the pub?' Declan tried not to let his frustrations be heard in his tone, but he knew he wasn't doing a very good job of it.

'Sorry, no,' Paul was speeding up the video feed again now, and Declan watched the drinkers in the bar blink in and out of existence as people entered and left at incredible speed. Eventually, though, Paul slowed the footage down again, and after a few more moments, Declan watched Leroy Daniels leave the pub, briefcase still in hand. The timestamp showed that only thirty-two minutes had passed since he arrived, and then, one by one, as the footage continued on Declan saw the others leave, Charles talking passionately to the two women as he did so. Declan wondered if this was flirting, Baker putting on his usual charm, or something connected to the dinner—and then felt bad for instantly assuming Baker's smarm in this situation.

Marshall was the last to leave, a few minutes after the others, munching on what looked to be a sandwich, while wiping his forehead with his other hand as he did so.

Declan leaned back.

'That looks like a sandwich. Was there food up there?'

'They usually ate picky food during the meeting, yes,' Paul picked up a book and ran a finger down it.

'Picky food?'

'You know, food you can pick at,' Paul tapped a line of text in the book. 'Plate of sandwiches. Enough for six people.'

'And were they made here?'

Paul looked offended that Declan would think otherwise.

'It's just sandwiches, mate,' he said tersely.

Declan nodded, considering this.

'I wasn't saying anything against your food, but I am following what looks to be a fatal poisoning, so if they ate here and the poison started *ingesting* around now, well, you can see where I'm going with this.'

Paul's face paled as Declan looked back at the screen, ignoring him as he worked through this once more. If Marshall Howe and Leroy Daniels *were* poisoned before the restaurant, it had to have been here, three hours before the fatal dinner. But if the plate of sandwiches had been poisoned, then why weren't the others at the meal showing symptoms? Baker had been on the television when Declan arrived, so he obviously wasn't sick, and this wasn't a poison you could keep off with some *lemsip* and good thoughts.

No, something else was going on.

'Can I get this footage on USB?' he asked. 'And the name of the person who prepared your sandwiches yesterday?'

'I'm not sure,' Paul looked concerned. 'I mean, of course I can give you the name, but the footage might be a problem. Looking is one thing, but there are politicians in that bar. They might not take kindly to it.'

Declan pulled out his phone. He'd expected this, considering Paul's reluctance earlier.

'I'll just take photos of the screen then,' he said with a smile. 'Just so I can show the timings.'

'Yeah, that'd be okay,' Paul nodded nervously, the uncertainty obvious on his face. 'I reckon that wouldn't cause any problems.'

'Is all this on the cloud?' Declan was taking a photo of the screen now, currently showing Leroy Daniels walking out with the briefcase in his hand.

'Yeah, but only for forty-eight hours,' Paul was already rising from the chair as Declan kept moving the footage to the point he needed and snapping another shot.

'That's all we need,' Declan rose too, shaking Paul's hand as he placed his phone away. 'You've done me a massive favour today.'

Walking out of *The Westminster Arms,* Declan glanced up at the camera that looked down at him with a smile. Beside the PC on the back office desk, there'd been a post-it note with what looked like a cloud file password on it. Declan had *accidentally* taken a photo while snapping the screen images, which was completely unintentional in every legal sense of the word. It wasn't his fault they'd put it there, after all.

And if it was the password to their cloud server, and with a good cyber operative, Declan reckoned he could get a copy of that footage directly from the source. But, until then, he needed to work out who the other people in the footage were and what really happened in that room.

Luckily, thanks to *BBC Parliament,* he knew exactly where one of them was, and he was sure he'd be able to chat to him that afternoon.

And, with a spring in his step, Declan headed towards the *Palace of Westminster.*

10

OLD GRUDGES

Bullman hadn't joined the force to be a babysitter, but even though she currently felt useless, she also knew that by simply organising security for Liz and Jessica Walsh, she was actively helping one of her own.

She felt useless though because she felt, deep in her heart she should have seen this coming; ever since she'd been involved with the *Last Chance Saloon,* she'd found herself tied into the conspiracies and secrets that surrounded the officers. Apart from her first case with them, working with Monroe and Doctor Marcos in Birmingham, before she even took the role in the Unit she'd attended Temple Inn as Declan's Federation Rep when he was accused of terrorism charges, a role that had ended with her learning of his escape from the building.

She'd assisted Anjli Kapoor in hunting down Will Harrison and Malcolm Gladwell, most likely burning any Westminster credit she'd ever gained over her career and had travelled to Berlin with Monroe to hunt down the truth about Karl Müller, although at the time they hadn't realised that the

Red Reaper was the friendly car mechanic that Declan had spent most of his life knowing. She'd even arrived with De'Geer, eager to save Jess from Ilse Müller's clutches, only to find that Billy and Anjli had already beaten her to it.

And that Jess had defeated Ilse by herself.

It was because of this that Bullman had wanted to ensure Liz and Jess were safe personally. One day, she hoped Jessica Walsh might be happy to take a role in her team; Bullman suspected that she'd be twice the detective her father was, and he wasn't too bad himself.

When he wasn't getting arrested, that was.

As Jess and Liz lived near to Declan's old Command Unit in Tottenham North, Bullman had drawn the police protection from there; they had a decade of history with Declan, and they also had a decade with Liz and Jess. In fact, DCI Farrow, Declan's old boss, caught up with her as she was leaving the Unit to check in on his onetime DI.

'He's a pain in the bloody arse, but he's a good copper,' he explained, wiping his wire- rimmed glasses with a microfibre cloth before putting them on. 'I only dealt with him for a couple of years, but he was a superstar in the making, if only he calmed himself down.'

'Yeah, he still does that,' Bullman was fascinated by the wispy tufts of hair that stuck out of the sides of Farrow's cheeks, giving him the nickname 'The Owl' around town, and had to really focus on Farrow himself to not let her attention drift.

'I worry about him being with Monroe, though,' Farrow sighed. 'I mean, he's a good copper but there's a ton of baggage.'

'Glasgow?'

'And the rest,' Farrow shrugged. 'Not my place to say,

Ma'am, and he's your boy, but you should be wary he doesn't catch you in his flames. You know, when he crashes and burns, eventually.'

Bullman resisted mocking the idea of Monroe being her boy and instead leaned in.

'Why would he crash and burn?'

'You always do when you fly too close to the sun,' Farrow shrugged again. Bullman noted he seemed to do a lot of shrugging and wiping of his glasses.

'Are you okay?' she asked. 'You seem on edge.'

DCI Farrow looked uncomfortable for an endless moment.

'So, I'm a Catholic,' he said.

'And that's a problem?' Bullman wasn't sure where this was going.

'No, no, not at all,' Farrow stammered. 'But you see, so's Liz Walsh.'

Bullman nodded. She'd heard a story from Anjli, that after Declan had punched a Catholic priest on live TV during an arrest, the Catholic Church had pretty much threatened to excommunicate his ex-wife.

'I've been smoothing things over,' Farrow explained. 'Making sure they're happy for her to return to the book club, all that. They know Father Corden was guilty as sin of dog trafficking, and they agreed with what happened, but the way it was done—'

'From what I heard, Father Corden told DI Walsh that Jess was going to hell for this harassment and DI Walsh took offence.'

'Exactly,' Farrow nodded. 'And they get that. And they allowed Liz to take the sacraments again.'

'Farrow, why are you telling me this?' Bullman was tired,

and now she was confused.

'Because I'm seeing Liz Walsh,' DCI Farrow blurted out. 'And I'm watching her go into protective custody because of a case Declan couldn't solve and as much as I feel for him, I want to punch the bloody idiot.'

He stopped, paling.

'Shit. Sorry, Ma'am.'

'Let me tell you something,' Bullman walked Farrow away from the building. 'The official statement is that Karl Schnitter has reappeared and the Walshes might be in trouble, but that's not the case. Declan caught him, fair and square. And then the Americans offered Karl a *get out of jail free card*, so in the end we made a shadowy Government organisation take him. One that, a couple of days ago, was infiltrated and betrayed, releasing Karl back into the wild.'

Farrow was silent, staring at Bullman, as if waiting for her to shout 'April fool!' as she continued.

'Now, the reason we're worried about Jess and Liz isn't because they're related to Declan, no no. It's because Jess managed to single-handedly take down Karl's murderous daughter, and people are worried there might be a reprisal.'

'Christ.'

'Yeah,' Bullman grinned. 'I'm guessing you haven't reached that stage of the relationship with Jess, where she tells you stuff like that?'

'Stuff like that?' Farrow shook his head. 'There's more?'

'What can I say,' Bullman shrugged now, half-mockingly. 'You North Tottenham guys are a little too pedestrian for us. We like the bigger game in our Unit.'

Farrow stared at Bullman for a moment, his mouth opening and shutting.

'I only wanted to know if I could visit Liz while the police were there,' he said. 'And, if they were reporting to you, whether I should speak to Declan first, so he doesn't hear from uniforms that their boss is hanging out with his ex-wife.'

Bullman groaned.

'Just tell him,' she replied. 'If it's serious, if you feel strongly about her, don't keep it a secret. They never work. Oh, and don't mention that I told you about Karl. You know, to anyone. Or I'll make a call and they'll put you in the same anonymous cell.'

It was meant as a joke, but Bullman watched Farrow pale even more at what he perceived was a veiled threat.

'I'll call Declan about it when this is all over,' he said. 'I mean, he's not guilty of hiding the body, right?' His expression was needy, as if really wanting Bullman to agree with him.

'Sure,' Bullman glanced at her watch. 'Not this time, at least. Call him when it's done, and in the meantime, do your best for his family.'

And, this said, she shook Farrow's hand and walked over to the waiting squad car to take her back to Temple Inn.

The *Last Chance Saloon* might be a nightmare band of misfit toys at the best of times, but by Christ, at least they had a fire inside them.

Although, Bullman thought as she raised an eyebrow, watching Farrow walk back into his building, *if Liz Walsh wants a piece of that, perhaps there's some fire there after all.*

CLAIRE HADN'T EXPECTED TO BE TAKEN OUT TO THE CAR PARK when they removed her from the cell; she'd hoped to be passed through processing at least, perhaps somehow pick up her personal possessions, her phone if possible, but the two burly women didn't seem to have received the same memo as everyone else did, and had hustled her out of the back of the building before anyone even noticed that Claire Doyle, inhabitant of cell five wasn't there anymore.

She should have taken the waving of the taser as a clue, but the peroxide-blonde officer had slapped her partner, telling her to *put it away and stop being a tit,* so Claire had assumed they were just trying to get a rise out of her.

It had worked.

The building itself had once been the Leith Town Hall, and as such was a four-storey Victorian cornerstone, complete with a doric order porch on the ground floor, tall sash windows on the first floor and smaller, square sash windows on the second floor. Although the front of the building, when seen from the main road was a picture-postcard delight of architecture, the back of the building however was a mish-mash of old and new, a narrow entrance road leading from the back of the police station into a U-shaped car park that served as parking for both the concrete and brick English School to the right, and the painfully modern styled new-build apartments that lined the other two sides.

There were a couple of squad cars and a van already parked there, and Claire assumed one of these was going to be her transport for the day, but the burly coppers weren't interested in those; instead they aimed for a nondescript Ford Mondeo, parked at the side of the station, bundling Claire into the back seat without an explanation.

'Are you sure about this?' she asked as she righted herself, glancing at the officer who'd pushed her in. 'I think we need to be in something a little more official.'

'This is as official as you get,' the officer replied grimly, slamming the door hard. As Claire now sat, scared in the back, her bravado now completely dissipated, the two officers clambered into the driver and passenger seats.

'Now put your seatbelt on,' the blonde one said. 'We don't want you getting hurt.'

From the laughter the two women gave to this, it must have been a hilarious joke, but Claire no longer found the humour in it. This wasn't the usual sort of prisoner transfer, it was an *extraction* and she didn't know how she could get out.

Before the Mondeo could move, however, a black Mercedes A-Class pulled into the entranceway, blocking their exit. The driver, a man in a tweed suit with brown hair waved a hand apologetically as he shifted the car into reverse, pulling to the side as the peppered-hair police officer sitting in front of Claire leaned out of the passenger window and shouted at them irritably to *get out of the bloody way*, but Claire saw that the man in the passenger seat, an elderly man with white hair and a beard, placed a hand on the driver's arm, stopping the car. Then, with the Mercedes still blocking the way, the white-haired man and a hulking blond police officer exited the vehicle, watching the Mondeo carefully for a moment before walking determinedly towards the car.

'Is that Claire Doyle in there?' the elderly man asked softly, holding up a warrant card.

'Nothing to do with you, so get out of the way,' the peroxide blonde officer snapped, her hand on the clutch, as if she was considering running him down and ramming the Mercedes.

'That's no way to speak to a Detective Chief Inspector,' the uniform with him, a massive Viking, moved to the back door. 'Open it. Now.'

Claire slid to the door, realising this was possibly the only chance she had of escape but the peppered-hair officer slid out of the car, opened the back door on the other side and pulled Claire out in a few quick motions, holding her as a shield, the yellow, police-issue hand taser, shaped like a gun, held to the side of Claire's head.

'Back off,' she said. 'Or we give the wee girl a lobotomy.'

'Well, lassie,' the elderly man smiled. 'If we didn't think you weren't police before, we wouldn't now. Tasers don't give lobotomies. They're too low a dosage. Anyone who's been given a taser to use would know this, as it's taught on day one.'

By now other officers, hearing the shouting or possibly because of the man in the car phoning them, emerged out of the building, and the peppered-hair officer, realising the futility of their situation dropped the taser, stepping away from Claire.

'I demand my solicitor,' she said defiantly as the local police now ran in, taking the two women and quickly cuffing them. Claire, realising she was safe from harm, finally allowed herself to lean against the Mondeo, still handcuffed as the white-bearded, elderly man walked over to her.

'You're lucky we turned up when we did,' he said. 'Another couple of minutes and you'd be gone. You know where they were taking you?'

Claire shook her head numbly.

'Och, no worry. They'll tell us eventually. Probably work for Lennie Wright.' The elderly man smiled at the flinch Claire gave when she heard the name. 'Aye, he doesn't seem to be a fan of yours either, lassie.'

'Were you telling the truth?' Claire asked. 'When you said about the taser not lobotomising me?'

'Sort of,' he smiled. 'They reckon you might get seizures or abnormal brain activity. But no lobotomy. Perhaps.'

'Christ, you bluffed them.'

'They looked like the type of women who'd bluff easily,' the elderly man smiled again, and although Claire knew it was a smile meant to calm her, she couldn't help but give in to it, relaxing at the sight of it.

Not wanting to consider the taser any more, Claire changed the subject.

'How did you know I was in the car?'

'I recognised you from your mugshot,' the elderly man explained as he uncuffed her.

'Mugshot?' Claire looked at the DCI now with suspicion. 'Why were you looking at my bloody mugshot? Just who the hell are you?'

'I'm Detective Chief Inspector Alexander Monroe, of the City of London Police,' the elderly man said, straightening as he did so. 'And I'm your great-uncle.'

There was a long moment of silence as Claire took this in, punctuated with the noise of two fake officers being dragged into the station, this time by force.

But after around twenty seconds, Claire finally replied to this revelation.

'You *what?*'

11

BACK IN BUSINESS

A<small>NJLI HAD JUST PULLED UP AT</small> T<small>EMPLE</small> I<small>NN WHEN</small> D<small>ECLAN SENT</small> a message to her.

> Did we find a briefcase at Essence?

She'd replied in the negative and a moment later, she'd had a response.

> Go check. Important.

An image had been sent with this, a CCTV photo taken of a monitor screen, and Anjli could make out the blurred form of Leroy Daniels holding a briefcase outside a pub.

Declan obviously found where Leroy had been going during his missing time.

It hadn't taken long to return to *Essence*, and Anjli soon found one of the kitchen staff, a young man who looked no older than fourteen opening the door and allowing her entry, once he saw her warrant card.

'I thought you'd be closed today,' Anjli said as she entered the restaurant.

'We are,' Tara Wilkinson said as she entered the restaurant from a door at the back. 'But we still need to clean up after your people made such a hash of the place.'

'Yeah, sorry about that,' Anjli fought to keep her anger in check. 'Solving a murder and all that is a real bind, you know?'

'Have you?' Tara stopped as she reached Anjli. 'Solved the murder?'

'Well, we're getting closer,' Anjli replied. 'Anywhere we can speak quietly? I have some questions.'

'I thought we went through that this morning?' Tara started towards the door at the back already, expecting Anjli to follow. 'With the other guy?'

'The other guy is *Detective Inspector Walsh*,' Anjli bristled as they walked into the manager's office. It wasn't the one that Leroy Daniels had died in; he had his own special one in the back of the kitchen.

'Sure,' Tara looked back, and she smiled, as if trying to make friends rather than score points. 'Sorry. My guys get pissed when they're not called *chef*, so I apologise.'

'The questions we have are new ones, as we've had some developments,' Anjli explained, sitting in an offered chair as Tara sat back at her desk. 'We now know that both Chef Daniels and Mister Howe were poisoned by tetrodotoxin.'

'We don't prepare Fugu here,' Tara was quick to answer. 'The EU—'

'We also don't think they were poisoned here,' Anjli continued, and Tara stopped, a surprised expression on her face.

'They weren't?'

'No, we think it was at *The Westminster Arms*, around four in the afternoon yesterday,' Anjli read from one of the texts that Declan had sent. 'We have CCTV footage of both men attending a meeting upstairs there, one where sandwiches were served that might have contained the poison.'

'Christ,' Tara leaned back in the seat as she weighed this up. 'Poor buggers.'

'Did you know that Chef Daniels would be meeting with Mister Howe?'

'It was a possibility, sure,' Tara nodded. 'He was on the committee.'

'This is a committee for the big Gala Dinner at the Houses of Parliament?'

Tara nodded.

'You told DI Walsh that you didn't know where Chef Daniels was yesterday, only that he left around four.'

'I didn't know he had a meeting, no,' Tara admitted, and her face was tight as she spoke. Anjli realised she was hiding anger here, anger at being kept out of the loop, perhaps. 'I didn't even know he'd left until someone told me. We've all been given NDAs, so we couldn't have told you anyway without a court order or something, that's what the guy from the Civil Service said, anyway.'

'Guy from the Civil Service?'

'When we signed up to do the dinner, they said we couldn't say anything. Even half the cooks don't know what it really was. Because of people finding out and all that.'

'You couldn't talk to the police?'

'No offence, but the police aren't exactly known for keeping secrets these days.'

Deciding to press on, Anjli checked her notes.

'Going back to Chef Daniels, Helen Cage said she'd been told he had a dentist appointment.'

'Helen Cage is a busybody who sticks her nose into everything,' Tara snapped.

Anjli nodded at this.

'You mentioned to my colleague that she wasn't very good at her job.'

'That's not what I said,' Tara replied. 'I said we had a perfectly fine pastry chef before Leroy made his changes, but these were his decisions and that it wasn't my place to ask.'

'So she *was* good at her job?'

'She was a good pastry chef for a provincial restaurant,' Tara sniffed. 'We, however, are a three-star Michelin eatery.'

'Are? Surely if Chef Daniels is dead, you mean *were?*'

'Yes, sorry, it's still new.'

'You hinted Leroy hired her for her honey?'

'It's not even that good, from what I've been told,' Tara laughed. 'But they're the only people making it at a price we can afford, so there's that 'British pride' we always hear of.'

She laughed.

'Make a shit car in the UK and they'll laud it up to the heavens because it's British made.'

'Leroy was very much into British pride?'

'You mean was he a *nationalist?*' Tara narrowed her eyes. 'Maybe. But he never treated Harnish any different to the others. In that he treated them *all* like shit.'

'Sounds like you're not a fan.'

'I loved him. And I hated him. Leroy had that effect on a lot of us.'

'Hated enough to kill?'

Tara stared at Anjli.

'How very *dare* you,' she snapped. 'I owe everything to him.'

'When did Mister Howe make the booking?' Anjli changed subject.

'About an hour before he arrived.'

'So after he met with Chef Daniels?' Anjli noted this down. 'Something must have spurred him on.'

'Probably had an argument with him, decided to get a kick in,' Tara shrugged. 'Who knows what that odious little prick thought?'

'Not a fan?'

Tara snorted.

'He's a cancer to restaurants,' she said tersely. 'He bigs up the ones he likes, the ones that suck up to him, even pay him, and shoots down anyone who dares speak against him.'

Anjli nodded at this.

'We have a witness who claims that everyone came in early yesterday because they had to be on their game for Mister Howe,' she said. 'It gave the impression that Marshall Howe had booked earlier than that.'

'Your source is wrong,' Tara stuck to her guns, folding her arms. 'Maybe she got confused after Howe tried the booking before.'

'Maybe,' Anjli smiled, noting that Tara, by using *she*, had already decided who the source was. 'Chef Daniels was seen with a briefcase, but our forensics didn't see it in his office. Would you know where it is?'

'Leroy never used a briefcase,' Tara frowned. 'Maybe he had it for the meeting? Ideas inside it or something? I don't know. Sorry.'

'Well, if you find it, please let us know,' Anjli turned the page in her notebook. 'When did you find out about the Gala Dinner?'

'That's two questions. When did we find out, and when did we find out we were doing it.'

'So answer both, please.'

'We found out there was a dinner, but didn't know the scale of it about six months back when Leroy pitched. But Howe wanted bloody Johnny, so we missed out.'

'And when you found out you were doing it?'

'When we were in Dubrovnik, so about a couple of weeks back,' Tara replied carefully. 'It's tomorrow night, so it's been full on, nose to the grindstone and all that.'

'A couple of weeks back... would that have been the Thursday?' Anjli asked, looking to watch Tara as she continued. 'The day after Johnny Mitchell was murdered in Edinburgh?'

Tara simply nodded.

'It's no secret he beat Leroy for the gig, but it was close,' she stated. 'When Johnny died, they needed someone who could take the meal over and hit the ground running. As I said, it took all of Leroy's time while in Dubrovnik.'

'But you came back on the Saturday, and there was a big meal he presided over on the Friday night before you left,' Anjli checked her notes. 'Chef Daniels was only working on this for a day at best?'

'I don't know. I never took the call.'

'But you're the manager.'

'Leroy is his own manager,' Tara was getting exasperated now. 'I manage all this. I manage his expectations.'

She stopped.

'*Managed.* I managed them.'

There was a long pause, held deliberately by Anjli as she turned her notebook page backwards, checking earlier notes.

'How were you and Chef Daniels before he died?'

'Fine.'

'We have reports he was a bit of a prick, sorry for the term, but it's what we were told. Was he like that with you?'

'No.'

'How was he with you?'

'Professional. Why?'

Anjli pressed the issue.

'We understand that for two nights in Dubrovnik, Chef Daniels didn't sleep in his own bed,' she said as she stared directly at Tara. 'Do you know what bed he slept in?'

Tara went to speak, to deny, but then stopped. She opened her mouth, shook her head, and then slumped in the chair.

'Was he in *your* bed, Mrs Wilkinson?' Anjli continued.

'That's a personal matter,' Tara snapped back. 'It's not relevant to this investigation.'

'Let me be hypothetical for a moment,' Anjli closed the notebook, holding her hands together. 'A chef finds his wife is sleeping with another chef. That chef then dies. Would you say the first chef had a motive to kill? Would you say that Harnish Patel had a motive to murder Leroy Daniels?'

Tara shook her head.

'Harnish doesn't know,' she whispered, and Anjli could almost see the gears in her mind whirring as she tried to work out how to get out of this. 'It was a fling, a memory, nothing more. We'd been drinking, it was late, and it was a fantasy.'

'Had this happened before?'

'Back in catering school,' Tara admitted. 'Look, Harnish

and I, we've had issues. It's tough living in a shadow, and Harnish wanted to move on.'

'You didn't.'

'I knew that whatever we did, Leroy wouldn't let us go,' Tara half-smiled. 'He needed us. We gave it a while. And then Johnny got the Gala deal and Harnish was furious.'

'Why?'

'Because Harnish had been Sous-Chef when Johnny ran fish,' Tara shrugged. 'Harnish was higher, but Johnny was living the life we should have had. It was tough for him.'

'You were in Dubrovnik the night that Johnny Mitchell died, but where was your husband?'

'He was here,' Tara waved a hand. 'He was holding the bloody place together with the Maitre d', and was here until at least midnight. And he's not magic, detective. He can't be in two places at the same time.'

Anjli nodded. Forensics had dated the time of death for Johnny Mitchell at around midnight.

'What did you mean, it was a fantasy?'

Tara rose, pacing around her small office.

'When we were in catering school, there was a trip to Croatia. Not Dubrovnik, but close enough. We'd just got together, and we joked it would be our honeymoon spot one day. But we didn't last; nothing lasts long in Leroy's world and after we graduated, we lost touch. But returning there, to the beaches, the streets... it brought it all back. And we allowed it to.'

'For two days.'

'Yes.'

'Was the affair still happening when you returned?'

'No, after a couple of nights we realised it was a bloody stupid idea and we stopped.'

'Just like that.'

'We weren't love-sick teenagers. We knew what we were doing, and we decided to stop.'

Anjli wrote this down. 'Did you tell your husband?'

'No, and he doesn't need to know,' Tara shook her head. 'He has enough on his plate now, with the Gala.'

'Have they confirmed you'll be taking over?'

'The bloody thing's tomorrow night,' Tara gave a laugh, but it felt like one that was bordering on the edge of hysteria than of humour. 'They don't have time to find anyone else. We have Leroy's menu plan and we have the food and supplies that were ordered by Johnny when he was running it all, so Harnish is working out a revised menu that covers both Leroy's and Johnny's ideas and merges them together, in a kind of tribute.'

'Why not just do Leroy's menu?' Anjli asked. 'You just said it was done.'

Tara waved her hand around.

'See this?' she asked, and Anjli guessed she was talking about the building more than the office they now stood in. 'I pay the bills, cover the rent, pay the wages, make sure the licenses are up to date, all of that. My husband cooks the food, keeps the kitchen running smoothly and confirms every plated meal that leaves the kitchen is worthy of the Michelin stars this place has. But the only thing people give a toss about is Leroy Daniels, as it's his name on the door.'

'I'm sure that—'

'You ever go to the cinema?' Tara interrupted. 'Go see a Ryan Reynolds or a Tom Cruise movie? Maybe you're more a Timothée Chalamet woman? You go because of the name on the poster. Daniel Craig is *James Bond*. Tom Cruise is *Ethan Hunt*. Gail Gadot is *Wonder Woman*. You might care who directed it, but you don't care who wrote it, who edited it, who was the colour grader, all of that.'

She sighed.

'These people all work in the background, but all of them made the film you're watching. Now consider a kitchen. Harnish oversaw every piece of food that came out of *Essence*, but people only gave a damn about Leroy, because he *created* the dish they're eating. Now, Harnish gets to create a menu that is eaten by the Prime Minister! That's eaten by royalty! Why the hell would he just stick with Leroy's, when he achieves notoriety with his?'

Anjli stared at Tara as, now finished, she sat back down in her office chair.

'You know to some, that could be a motive for murder,' she said.

'Then bloody arrest me,' Tara sighed, 'because I'm too tired for this shit. Come back on Saturday and I'll go quietly. But until this Gala Dinner is finished, I really don't need you people critiquing my every poor decision.'

Anjli nodded, rising from the chair and walking to the office door.

'If the Gala does well, are you hoping to keep this restaurant?' she asked as she opened it.

'That's just tempting fate,' Tara smiled. 'I'm not replying to that.'

And, her questions answered, Anjli left the office, closing the door behind it.

But she didn't leave; instead, Anjli wandered over to the kitchen, opening the door and facing the young man, working at the sink station.

'You a cook?' Anjli asked.

The young man jumped, having been singing to himself and facing away from the door.

'I'm the pot washer,' he said. 'Darryl.'

'You don't look old enough to be working,' Anjli smiled. 'Shouldn't you be in school?'

'I'm seventeen,' Darryl protested. 'Been here a year now.'

'Washing pots? That has to be a hard job.'

Darryl brightened at this.

'It's only temporary, until there's a place on the crew for me,' he said. 'And with Chef gone, that might be soon.'

'How do you work that out?' Anjli leaned casually against a counter, trying her best to sound conversational, allowing Darryl to talk.

'Well, everyone moves up,' Darryl explained. 'Chef Patel will take lead, Chef Hudson will move from vegetables to Sous-Chef, and so on.'

'Dead man's shoes.'

'If that's what it takes,' Darryl smiled. 'Almost moved up a couple of months back, but that got stopped by Chef Patel.'

'How come?' Anjli asked lazily, avoiding eye contact.

'He hired a new Pastry Chef to replace Linda, so we all didn't move up.'

'Chef Patel hired Helen Cage?' Anjli looked back at Darryl. 'Not Tara or Chef Daniels?'

Darryl now stared at Anjli like a deer in headlights.

'I might have got that wrong,' he said hurriedly, turning back to the sink. 'Sorry, but I have to work.'

Anjli left Darryl to his pot washing, leaving the restaurant before Tara realised she'd hung around. Harnish Patel hiring Helen Cage hadn't been mentioned before, and Tara had made a point of stating that Leroy had hired her. Which meant one of two things. First, that Harnish hadn't told his wife that he'd been the one to hire Helen, which made Anjli wonder why he'd done it in the first place. Was it to ensure that Leroy Daniels didn't have to ask, or was it done to either placate or distract him? And second, if Tara did know that her husband had hired her, why lie about it?

Either way, one thing was becoming clear.

Helen Cage was a lot more important here than she was letting on.

12

MEMBERS TERRACE

IT WAS A MATTER OF MINUTES FOR DECLAN TO CROSS Parliament Square once more, aiming for the Houses of Parliament as he did so, turning to the right and entering through St Stephen's Gate, showing his warrant card to the police on duty to allow entrance. Then, after heading through the metal detectors and x-ray machines all visitors had to go through, he exited out into New Palace Yard, and the entrance to Westminster Great Hall.

The last time he'd been here, he'd arrived with police, there to arrest Malcolm Gladwell. Before that, he'd been hidden away in a corner of the Members Terrace, during his first meeting with Charles Baker, then still organised and controlled by Francine Pearce and Will Harrison between them.

Declan chuckled to himself as he walked across the hall, away from the main doors and towards a large stone staircase leading up to a giant stained-glass window. He remembered Anjli mocking him when they had first arrived, days into his tenure at the *Last Chance Saloon*. The expert on all things

Parliament, she'd pointed out the small brass plaque on the floor where King Charles the First stood as he was sentenced to death, before leading Declan with glee over to another spot where William Wallace was sentenced to death and then an unmarked area by the staircase where Guy Fawkes was sentenced to death.

Basically, Anjli Kapoor knew where a lot of people had been sentenced to death.

Declan half-wished she was here with him now as he showed his ID to the security guard beneath the stained-glass window, turning down the corridor to his left. He'd called ahead, allowing Charles Baker's new aide, Jennifer *something hyphen something* to make sure he didn't hang around the Central Lobby for too long. Declan was known in the Houses now, and the BBC reporters still hung out in the octagonal hallway, looking for scoops between Parliamentary Sessions. And, as he entered, Declan saw a young woman, barely in her twenties, slim in a bright green dress, her long blonde hair pulled into a ponytail, squinting at him as he approached.

'I'm he,' Declan intoned ominously as he showed his badge. Hurriedly, Jennifer grabbed him by the arm and rushed him into the lobby, past the reporters and through the north walkway, towards the Terrace Cafeteria.

The terrace was outside, at the back of the Houses of Parliament, and looked out across the Thames. The first time they'd ever arrived here, Declan and Anjli met Charles Baker at the furthest possible table from the entrance, almost as if he didn't want people knowing he was talking to the police. However, the last time Declan had met Charles, it had been in the main courtyard of Portcullis House and, as the then hero of the hour, Charles had made damn sure everyone knew he was talking to *Declan Walsh, super cop.*

Today, however, Charles Baker was sitting at the same table he'd met Declan and Anjli at, all those months earlier, a frown upon his face.

When even Charles Baker didn't want to associate with you, it was time to admit you might be in trouble.

'Declan,' Charles forced a smile, but it was a sickly one. 'Meet my aide, Jennifer Farnham-Ewing.'

That's what the surname was, Declan smiled as he nodded to the blonde aide, who glared at him like a poisonous snake.

'I only have a few moments,' Charles carried on. 'I—'

'Don't want people to see me with you,' Declan finished the sentence. 'Don't worry. I get it. Any chance of a sandwich, though? I'm famished.'

'It's nothing personal, God knows I owe you, but Christ, Declan, *you kidnapped Francine Pearce?*'

'I didn't,' Declan snapped. 'She's faking her disappearance to throw me under the bus. You know her better than others.'

'Yes, I suppose I do, unfortunately,' Charles stared at the table before locking eyes with Declan. 'But the fact of the matter is that I'm about to be in a pretty vicious Leadership Campaign for Prime Minister, and the last thing I want is to be seen with the man who might have killed an MP's *sister*.'

'First, she's not dead. Second, good luck,' Declan leaned closer. 'But I'm here on business.'

'Daniels,' Charles looked up at Jennifer, who passed Declan a folder. 'In this file is everything we discussed in relation to the Gala. I shouldn't be giving it to you without—'

'An NDA? I know,' Declan smiled. 'Happy to sign one, but then there's a paper trail showing we chatted.'

Charles grimaced at this. 'This is the short list, how

Jonathan Mitchell beat Leroy Daniels, the offer we made to Daniels after Mitchell died, the lot.'

'Who was on the committee with you?' Declan asked. 'Apart from Howe?'

'Baroness Jones,' Charles replied. 'She's involved in a lot of these things. That's also why Howe was there, she absolutely loves his writing, constantly fights to have him involved. Poor woman needs to read better newspapers. Also Heather Gosine, a nobody MP from the other side. You know, to show the State Dinner isn't partisan, even though it's a farewell party for a Tory and all that.'

'Why are you on it?'

'Because I'm the heir apparent,' Charles had a slight hint of a smug expression on his face as he spoke. 'The Prime Minister wanted me beside him on the top table. Staking his claim, so to speak.'

'Yesterday, you met with Leroy Daniels upstairs in a pub. Why?'

'Church and State,' Charles tapped his nose. 'It's involving royalty, the Commons and the House of Lords, so it can't be discussed in rooms related to any of them. And the *Westminster Arms* does a solid party platter.'

He looked to the Thames.

'Should've bloody well used them instead,' he mused aloud. 'They do an awesome sausage roll too.'

'On that subject, any chance of a sandwich?'

'Get Declan a sandwich?' Charles asked Jennifer. 'To go.'

As Jennifer walked over to speak to a waiter, Declan leaned closer to Charles.

'And Howe and Daniels, were they cordial?'

'You think they poisoned each other?'

'I think they were both poisoned, yes,' Declan nodded. 'And I think it was at your meeting.'

'God,' Charles paled. 'Could I have—'

'If you had, you'd be dead by now,' Declan leaned back, relaxing. 'Although when you become king, maybe you need a good taster. Someone expendable.'

'I'll be sure to have you requisitioned,' Charles replied, and for the first time, the smile on his face seemed genuine. 'Look, Leroy Daniels came in, showed us his menu ideas, and then buggered off. That was it. They weren't even very different, because they couldn't be. No time to ask everyone if they wanted to change their choices and all that. We needed to get it done because the dinner's tomorrow night.'

'Did he eat anything?'

'We all did,' Charles shook his head. 'There was an argument though, now you mention it. Howe made Daniels a plate of sandwiches, making a big show of deciding which ones he should have, the stumpy little knob. In return, Daniels did the same back. Jonesy ended up shouting at them both to stop acting like bloody kids. They sat down and shut up.'

'Nobody else touched their food?'

Charles shrugged.

'What am I, their keeper?' he exclaimed. 'It was sandwiches, Declan. Bloody finger food. And we all ate from the same tray.'

Declan considered this. If that was true, then the sandwiches couldn't have been doctored.

'What did you drink?'

'Wine, I think Daniels had a coke.' Charles nodded. 'Yes, a bottle.'

'Howe?'

'Wanted wine, but you don't get those on a Civil Service budget, and nobody was paying out of their own pocket. We shared a bottle of sparkling water.'

Declan looked back at the folder on the table.

'Can I borrow this?' he asked.

'Declan, if you bugger off out of here and keep out of my way until I become Prime Minister, you can bloody keep it,' Charles rose now, nodding at Declan. 'Jennifer will escort you out once your sandwich arrives. I'm sorry we couldn't meet under warmer circumstances.'

He stopped at this, leaning over, close to Declan.

'She loved Wales, you know,' he whispered. 'St Davids. Big family connection in happier times.'

And, this cryptic message given, Charles Baker walked out of the Members Terrace.

'What did he say?' Jennifer asked, annoyance visible on her face as she passed over a paper bag filled with what was likely to be a hastily made sandwich, and Declan realised that Charles Baker had deliberately made it so she couldn't hear him speak.

Was Baker being controlled by Pearce again?

'How long have you been Charles' aide again?' he growled as he rose from the table.

'Three months,' Jennifer replied.

'When you make six, I'll tell you,' Declan said. In reply, Jennifer placed a hand on Declan's chest.

'My boss has a busy few months ahead,' she breathed. 'The most important job in the country. And the last thing he needs is anything that can stop that.'

'Such as being seen with me?' Declan asked.

Jennifer smiled.

'You get it,' she replied, stepping back, allowing Declan to

leave. 'So, until he's Prime Minister, and until you fix whatever toxic PR problem you currently have, I'm instructing
front gate to revoke any credentials you have to get in here.
No more free sandwiches from Westminster, Detective
Sergeant.'

'It's Detective *Inspector*,' Declan wasn't smiling.

Jessica shrugged at this, almost apologetically.

'For the moment,' she said as, folder and sandwich in
hand, Declan walked past her, out of the Members Terrace,
and out of the Houses of Parliament.

He tossed away the food when he found a bin, though.
After the discussion with Charles about their food, he'd
suddenly gone off sandwiches.

THE FOLDER STAYED UNOPENED ALL THE WAY BACK TO THE
Temple Inn Unit, where Declan found Billy working at his
monitor, Detective Superintendent Bullman behind him.

'Ma'am,' Declan straightened. 'I didn't know you were
back.'

'About an hour ago,' Bullman was tired, and Declan
guessed this was because she'd not only been trying to get
information on Tom Marlowe's status, but also protecting
Jess and Lizzie, after Karl Schnitter's escape.

'Are—' Declan started, but Bullman stopped him, already
expecting the question.

'They're home, and back to normal,' she said. 'We have
two cars watching them, and DCI Farrow's taken a personal
interest in helping, and if there's any hint of an issue, I have a
whole unit ready to move.'

'Thanks,' Declan didn't believe Karl would target them,

but he appreciated this. If anything, it'd calm Lizzie's fears, although he'd only just got her to relax over letting him see Jess after the events of Hurley; now he expected to have to start all over again. He was worried about Farrow being around, though; if he recalled correctly, Liz had never really warmed to the man.

'Billy's been catching me up on the Croatian gossip rags,' Bullman, noting that Declan was distracted, added. Declan glanced over to Billy, who pulled up a couple of fuzzy images of dark nightclubs. In them, the recognisable figure of Leroy Daniels could be seen.

'Apparently, he didn't just stay at the hotel,' Billy explained. 'He went into Dubrovnik on one evening, was snapped at a bar in the old town and then later in the night at a nightclub near Lapad Beach.'

Declan leaned closer; to the side of Leroy, here wearing a baseball cap over his trademark glasses, a long-sleeved sweater over his torso and currently holding up his right hand to stop the photographer, Declan could see Tara Wilkinson, holding a drink up to obscure her face, probably hoping her husband wouldn't see it.

'Seems to be a lot of trouble to stop the photo,' he said. 'Especially as everyone knows they're there, having made a massive hoo-hah over it when they arrived.'

'There's something wrong with the image,' Billy said, frowning as he stared at it. 'It's not right.'

'How so?' to Declan, it looked like every other hastily snapped nightclub photo he'd seen in the press; over exposed because of the flash, and stark in contrast to the surroundings. Billy shrugged.

'I don't know,' he admitted. 'But I'll work it out.'

Closing the image for the minute, he pulled up another sheet onto the screen.

'This is something else I found,' he said as Declan looked at a bank statement. 'It might mean nothing, but it could be important.'

'Whose statement is it?'

Billy looked back at Declan.

'These are the accounts of *Hill's Honey*,' he explained. 'They've been in a lot of financial trouble. Seems that growing specialised honey is expensive, especially when it goes wrong.'

'Go on,' Bullman said. 'How do you mean, wrong?'

'During winter at the start of last year there was a terrible cold snap in the UK, and that decimated *Hill's Honey's* incredibly limited supply of Manuka bushes,' Billy explained. 'These are the bushes that the honeybees get the pollen to create the honey from. It effectively halted their cottage industry.'

'Couldn't they carry on with other bushes?'

'They could, but they'd make nothing,' Billy replied. 'A hundred grams of honey goes for about a fiver if it's good quality. Manuka honey sells for five times that.'

'So they needed more bushes,' Bullman commented. 'Why not get them?'

'Because you have to ask New Zealand for them,' Billy spun in his chair to face Bullman and Declan. 'And New Zealand has been stating for years that the cuttings from their Manuka bushes were taken illegally and should be returned. However, the alternative position has been that the British took the European Honeybee to New Zealand in the first place, and without them...'

'No honey.' Declan nodded at this. 'Stalemate. So what happened?'

'Helen's parents begged for help from the Government, and the foreign office basically told them to piss off,' Billy was pulling up news reports from the time. 'They were pushing for a UK and NZ trade agreement at the time and knew this might cause issues.'

'Could they lean on the other honeys?'

'That's the problem,' Billy replied. 'The Cage's stopped diversifying a year earlier, throwing all their eggs into the Manuka basket as it was the most rewarding, but with no new bushes making expensive honey, and with their others making low-cost honey instead, they couldn't repay their loans. There was a chance they'd lose everything and Helen Cage's father suffered a massive heart attack, dying at the end of last year.'

'Christ,' Declan muttered.

'Now his life insurance payout gave them enough funds to keep the business continuing, but the bills kept coming.'

'And it was around here that Leroy Daniels offered an exclusivity agreement,' Bullman was walking back to her office. 'But looking at the sales figures, it was way below the current rate. She was beholden to him for more than just her own career. He was holding her mother's dying business hostage.'

'Sounds like a marvellous chap,' Declan muttered. 'Why are we trying to find his killer again?'

'Got something else for you,' Billy turned back to the screens now. 'You said Daniels was with a briefcase when he met with the committee yesterday? It looks to be a habit he passed to his protegé.'

On the screen was an interview from a style magazine,

taken around the time that Johnny Mitchell had opened *Monet* in Richmond. In fact, he was standing in front of the restaurant, holding up a similar briefcase to the one that Leroy Daniels had held.

'In the interview, he explains he uses the briefcase to hold his ideas in, to remind him that the restaurant is a business and not a plaything,' Billy grimaced. 'The whole interview is a puff piece and guess who wrote it?'

'Marshall Howe,' Declan had already noted the name on the byline.

'I called De'Geer, he checked with the DCI involved in the case in Edinburgh, and he confirmed that nobody saw this briefcase at Johnny's murder scene.'

'And nobody seems to know where Leroy's one went after he died, too,' Declan mused. 'The same case perhaps?'

'I'd need a better CCTV image to know for sure,' Billy smiled. 'Photos show imperfections better than—'

He stopped.

'Oh damn, I know what I saw now,' he whispered, pulling up the image of Leroy Daniels in the club. 'Yeah, I need to check on this.'

'What is it?' Declan asked, leaning in, as if trying to work out what Billy was thinking by staring at the same image.

'There was an interview,' Billy pulled up a video of Leroy Daniels at the opening press conference. 'He said to the press he was being careful shaking hands with the mayor, as he'd burned his palm that morning and he didn't want a strong squeeze.'

'Maybe he was making a joke?'

'Yeah, but look,' Billy zoomed in on the video; on the fleshy part of Leroy Daniels' right hand, under his pinkie finger was a fresh blue plaster, about the size of a fifty pence piece. 'He's burned. You can see it.'

He now pulled up the image in the nightclub.

'Look,' he pointed at the hand that Leroy was holding up to block the photo. 'The burn's not there.'

'Could it have gone down?' Declan asked. 'It's what, a couple of days later here?'

Billy slumped back in his chair.

'Maybe,' he conceded. 'I'll check the body, see if the burn's still there.'

'You will?' Declan grinned. 'You sure of that?'

'I'll get DC Davey to check for me when she gets back,' Billy smiled sheepishly. 'They still don't let me look at the dead bodies.'

'Probably for the best,' Declan walked back to his desk. 'I'm calling it a night, I'll go through these at home. If you hear anything, let me know?

Billy waved back from his station, already pulling up alternate photos from the night and Declan shook his head at this. Billy would likely sleep at the Unit again, or at least be leaving after midnight.

Grabbing his messenger bag, Declan threw the files in and, before he was pulled into anything else, left the Command Unit for his car and home.

If he was lucky, he might even get there in time to have dinner at a normal time.

13

FAMILIES AND FRIENDS

AFTER THE TWO FAKE POLICE OFFICERS HAD BEEN ARRESTED, Monroe had petitioned for Claire to be placed under his own protection, arguing that if she wasn't safe in a police cell, then where would she find solace outside of actual family. Hendrick, already fuming over the almost-extraction, agreed on the condition that Monroe didn't leave Edinburgh. Which was fine for Monroe, as he had no intention of leaving until he sorted out the problems he had with Lennie Wright.

The other problem he had, however, was with Claire Doyle.

'So your mother never talked about me?' he asked.

'Mother, grandmother, nobody,' Claire sipped at the coffee that Monroe had bought her, while sitting outside a coffee shop on Lawnmarket. 'No offence, but it doesn't look like you were that important.'

'Did you know your grandfather's name?' Monroe pressed.

Claire shrugged.

'I'd heard he was possibly some enforcer for the Hutchinsons, nothing more,' she replied warily. 'I didn't know he had a cop for a brother, or that I'd get into some kind of family dispute, though.'

'That's the problem,' Monroe watched Claire as he spoke. 'I don't think you've walked into any dispute. There's not been one for forty years.'

He leaned closer.

'I think you *are* the dispute,' he said. 'Something you've done that put you on Lennie's radar. And you can't tell me it's by random chance that Lennie's hunting you right now.'

'There's no chance about it,' Claire looked around, as if to see if they were being watched. 'We had something on him and he wanted it back.'

'Two things,' Monroe replied to this. 'Who's the *we* in that comment, and why is it *had?*'

'Because the guy who had it is dead,' Claire's eyes clouded as she replied, tears starting to form at the corners of her eyes. 'But Lennie doesn't know that. And when he does, he'll start bulldozing houses again and concreting over foundations.'

'So it's being held as ransom, this mythical information?' Monroe shook his head. 'You're bluffing with a pair of threes and when he finds out, he's going to kill you.'

'I think we've already reached that point,' Claire replied glumly. 'You turning up saved my bacon.'

'So tell me what it is you had on him,' Monroe offered. 'Maybe we can work together on it?'

'No offence, DCI Monroe—'

'Call me Alex.'

'No offence, *DCI Monroe*, but I haven't had much luck in the past with coppers.'

Monroe nodded, leaning back.

'Aye, I see that,' he said. 'So let's pretend for a moment that I'm helping because of a misguided belief that you're family?' he punctuated the question with a wink, hoping it'd relax the teenage girl in front of him. 'Where's your mother, anyway?'

'She's dead,' Claire spoke matter-of-factly; *too* matter-of-factly for Monroe.

'How?'

'Cancer,' Claire replied.

'Grandparents?'

'Dead.'

Monroe observed Claire.

'How?' he repeated.

'Cancer.'

Monroe decided not to reply to this; Claire had either had shit bad luck, or she'd realised that saying *cancer* was the way to stop conversations. He assumed it was the latter, and decided it'd be best to try again when they knew each other better. If they ever did, that was.

There was a long silence as Monroe waited for Claire to break. He wasn't sure if she would, although watching Declan and Jess over the last few months gave him hope that eventually Claire would give in and tell him.

He was right.

'So we're protesting because of some really hinky shit around here,' Claire explained. 'Some people in Leith started feeling sick, like *really* sick. People checked into it, started saying it was *cobalt poisoning*.'

'Is that bad?' Monroe had never heard of it before.

'Heart failure, blindness, deafness, what do you think?' Claire's sarcastic response left little to the imagination. 'It wasn't good. The problem was, it shouldn't have been happening full stop. There should have been no cobalt around to cause this.'

'I'm guessing there was?' Monroe nodded.

'Lithium-ion batteries,' Claire explained. 'They're in electric cars, phones, aircraft engines, laptops and tablets, they're everywhere. In small quantities, it's okay. But when dumped together, they can seep into the ground, poison water supplies—and worse.'

'So this is a battery landfill issue?'

Claire seemed genuinely surprised that Monroe had worked it out.

'You've heard of it?'

'The basic idea's been around for decades,' Monroe nodded. 'Toxic chemicals being dumped in a particular location were a favourite for years. People pay a lot for that. And it's better if you don't care if it hurts people. I'm guessing this is just the more twenty-first century model of the scam.'

'Aye,' Claire sipped at her coffee. 'And Lennie Wright's the one with the landfill, dumping it in the foundations of his new buildings, down in the docklands.'

'So we prove he's doing it,' Monroe slammed his fist on the table, surprising a nearby couple sipping at their chai tea lattes. 'We get him put away.'

'A mob boss, put away for illegal dumping?'

'They arrested Capone for tax fraud.'

Claire shook her head.

'We had footage of a construction site where the toxicity was off the scale,' she said. 'But we lost it when—'

She looked away, her voice becoming quieter.

'When Bazza fell off a bridge and broke his neck.'

'Fell or pushed?'

'Oh, he fell, bloody fool,' Claire replied. 'He was trying to get some extra footage so climbed up on a rail bridge over the A1 and slipped.'

'And the footage wasn't on the cloud?'

'It was, but we don't know the passcode. And by the time we went back to gain more, the building work had begun,' she shook her head. 'I'll get him another way.'

Monroe smiled.

'*We'll* get him,' he said. 'We have a laddie who can crack anything you want. I'm sure we can get—'

'*We* have someone who can do that too,' Claire snapped, and once more, Monroe realised he hadn't broken through to her as much as he'd hoped. 'We don't need police help. You didn't help us before and it sure as hell won't help now.'

'But we're—'

'Please,' Claire held up a hand. 'Please don't say we're family. I don't know you, and to be honest, I've got too much on my plate for *Hallmark Channel* reunions. It's not even Christmas, for Christ's sake.'

She rose from the chair, but Monroe went to stop her.

'You're not safe without—'

'Without your protection?' Yeah, that's convenient,' Claire snapped. 'Look, my *family* are activists, and they're back in Leith. I didn't want to come here, I don't need you holding my hand, DCI Monroe. Thank you for what you did for me earlier, but whatever family issues you had with your brother a million years ago, I don't need them hitting me right now.'

Monroe went to reply, but instead he nodded, pulling out a business card.

'I'm not leaving until I sort out Lennie,' he said. 'You can be involved or you can go your own way. But here, take my number. You never know if you'll need it.'

Claire looked for a moment as if she wasn't going to, but

eventually she took the card, sliding it into her pocket.

'No promises,' she said. 'But if you do find anything, you can contact me through Marcy, who owns the Vegan cafe on Newhaven Harbour.'

And before Monroe could say anything else, Claire slipped from his grip and left.

Monroe fought every instinct inside him not to rise and stop her, but he knew that deep down, she was right. He was a stranger to her. All he could do for her was remove the imminent threat to her life; that of Lennie bloody Wright.

Who, if he was dumping batteries, would be nicked very soon.

He looked up as De'Geer walked up to the table.

'I found the cleaner, Guv,' he said. 'She's going to meet us at *Monet*, but not until they close at nine.'

'They're still open?' Monroe was surprised.

'More a café than a restaurant, but yes, sir,' De'Geer nodded. 'They close at nine though because, well, nobody really wants to be there at midnight, in case...'

Monroe *hmph*'d an answer to this. With the murderer still out there, he understood the staff could be worried. But the chances of more than one attack at the same restaurant were just as high as a nine pm attack at a now rebranded café.

'Well, you can get me another drink, if we're hanging around here for another couple of hours,' he smiled. De'Geer went to speak, but then, as if realising something, looked around.

'Where's the girl?'

'Decided she doesn't need us,' Monroe replied, a little too morosely. 'Her choice, I can't force her. Just have to look out for her until she allows me in.'

De'Geer nodded at this.

'She'll be okay, sir,' he said reassuringly, but Monroe knew he was just stating what he believed his boss wanted to hear.

He was correct.

'Right then,' Monroe rose, finishing his drink. 'Go get me a refill. And later on we'll go talk to a cleaner about ghosts.'

TARA WILKINSON HADN'T MEANT TO STAY LATE, BUT WITH Leroy's death the previous day and the Gala Dinner tomorrow, she wasn't going to be heading home any time soon. Besides, Harnish was supposed to be here by now to check over the final touches to the menu, and he was getting later by the minute.

The Gala Dinner wasn't that much of a problem, to be honest. Leroy had created the best menu plan that he could under the circumstances before he died, based on an original that had been more than adequate, and this meant the diners had been able to carry on with their original choices, whether they were meat, vegetarian, gluten-free, vegan, now with slight additions and alterations that Leroy had provided.

Tara laughed to herself.

Yeah, that Leroy provided. All on his own. Without any help. Prick.

The problem that Harnish and Tara had now was how to take the items that were on the menu, items that Leroy had allegedly created the recipes for, and tweak them enough to state they were no longer just *Leroy Daniels* dishes. Now they also had to be *Harnish Patel* dishes, showcasing the new and upcoming chef on one of the biggest stages out there.

The main courses were easy; a change to the plating style,

a removal of a couple of the flavour-crutches that Leroy always fell back on, some little spice touches that added more of Harnish's heritage. The desserts however were a little more specific, and the only thing they could think to add in any way was that damned Manuka honey that Helen Cage brought to the table, which Johnny had already set in his first menu and had ordered the bloody stock for, before he died.

Helen bloody Cage.

Harnish and Tara had already argued enough about that damned woman. Tara was convinced Helen Cage was a curse made flesh, who destroyed anyone she shagged. Johnny Mitchell was destined for great things until she got her claws into him, and then he fell apart, with some weird quarter-life crisis move to Jockland. And Leroy had been like a lovesick puppy, agreeing for her to return to work for him even if it meant she never screwed him again.

And now they were both dead, and Helen Cage was sitting pretty. Well, not anymore. It was Leroy who wanted her, and the exclusivity of her bloody honey. And now he was dead, after the Gala they could dump her at the side and get some better product. As it was, her family was pretty much finished in the honey business, the debts were too high, she'd shagged her way through anyone that could help, and Harnish—

Tara looked at a photo on her desk; their wedding photo, taken four years back. They looked happier there. They *were* happier there. Things had been tough over the last year, and the things they'd both had to do to ensure their success were, by agreement, never to be spoken of, but at the same time Tara knew that the affair, even if you put aside the whole ethics of *sleeping with a co-worker*, was the one thing that could destroy everything.

We'll talk about it after the dinner, she agreed quietly with herself. *Nobody needs to know. We can build from this, move away from the old ways.*

Tara only hoped that Harnish was on the same page. After all, the fallout from the affair might end up forcing Harnish to leave.

Tara didn't think she could cope with that.

Looking at her watch, she tutted. Harnish still hadn't arrived. And now she was getting hungry, trapped in a restaurant where every piece of food could potentially kill her.

Actually, that was an overstatement. The police had explained the poisoning hadn't happened here; the food was fine. But, they still didn't know what else they'd need for the Gala Dinner, as the ordered stock had only been what Johnny had wanted, and the one thing Tara didn't want to do was find that a late-night snack meant they'd run out of something important.

But she needed something sugary. The last thing she'd had was hours earlier. Maybe a quick look wouldn't kill her.

Leaving her office, Tara walked through the unlit main restaurant, past the unused chairs and tables of *Essence* as she headed towards the kitchen area. A car drove past the windows and Tara stopped, momentarily caught in the evening headlights as they passed, but then the moment was over, and Tara checked the front door. It was still locked, although Harnish would most likely come through the back entrance into the kitchen, anyway.

Walking into the kitchen, Tara squinted at the brightness; the kitchen lights had been left on by Darryl when he left, and the movement from dark to light made her blink, holding up her hand to shield her eyes.

Was someone in with her?

'Hello?' Tara whispered, looking around. 'Harnish?'

After a moment of silence, Tara found she couldn't help herself.

'Leroy?'

Again, nothing. And, after a moment, Tara laughed.

'Oh, you bloody idiot,' she muttered to herself, walking over to the freezer. Maybe there was some gelato or sorbet she could steal, something sweet to stop the sugar crash that she was having. Or maybe she'd just slice up a loaf and have some toast? Thinking about it, apart from a nibble or two, she hadn't eaten for almost twelve hours, and she'd been up for most of the night, too.

Hearing her stomach rumbling, she considered ordering out for a pizza, realising the lunacy of such a scenario, and imagining the press if they found out. *Michelin restaurant orders Dominos*. No, everything she needed was here. And she was still good enough a chef to make it. Although, there was an easier option here.

Tara pulled out her phone, typing on it.

Are you coming to the restaurant

A moment later, a reply appeared.

On my way now.

Good do me a favour pick me up a milkshake and an apple pie from McD

That's not a healthy dinner

Screw healthy I'll detox after tomorrow x

Will do then

Tara noted the lack of an x at the end of Harnish's farewell, but as long as he brought her food, he'd be forgiven.

She stopped, feeling a little faint, the room spinning as her phone tumbled from her fingers and fell to the floor. She definitely needed something sugary and fast, as her balance was off, and her lips were tingly, numb—

Tara Wilkinson's legs gave out as she fell to her knees in the doorway to the kitchen. She didn't know what was going on; she'd fasted for way longer than this before and never needed to rest, but then with the stress of the last twenty-four hours...

A memory of the night before, of seeing the Maitre d' eating a *Twix* came to mind. It had been before the incident yesterday, she might not have finished it and it might still be behind the desk. Slowly, Tara pulled herself to the counter, trying to put aside the fears that now came up. *Was this a stroke? Christ, was she paralysed or something?*

She was halfway across the floor when her arms gave out, and Tara's cheek slammed to the carpet as she stared blankly at the restaurant windows, struggling to breathe, feeling her airways close but unable to take a breath.

She didn't care about the affair now. She wanted Harnish here; she wanted to tell him she still loved him, and that she regretted what was done to Johnny—

But as her glazed, lifeless eyes stared out into the street and her final breath wheezed out, Tara Wilkinson would never speak another word again.

14

DATE NIGHT

It had taken Declan another hour to get home, but even at just after eight in the evening, it felt early for him; usually he'd end up coming home right before it was time to sleep, and often Anjli would do the same. On the rare occasions they didn't, they still spent the hours discussing the case while in the background, ignored, the television would play episodes of *Repair Shop* or similar. Declan never really paid attention to it, mainly as he focused on whatever was currently on his radar.

And right now, a file was in his sights; a file marked *EYES ONLY*, one that gave the impression of secrets far more important than a dinner in a fancy room in Parliament.

With nothing in the fridge, and with no appetite for delivery pizza, Declan grabbed his jacket and made his way into Hurley itself, leaving a message for Anjli that he was going to grab something at *The Olde Bell* before they stopped serving food. Although not usually a 'pub grub' man, he'd gained an affection for the menu while using the pub and hotel as a base during the *Red Reaper* case a few months back.

A case that didn't want to die.

As it was, Declan had barely placed his order and sat down at a table with a pint of Guinness before Anjli wandered in, nodding at him as she walked to the bar to order her own food and drink.

'I heard you have an exciting folder,' she smiled, tapping it with her finger as she finally sat down facing him. 'Is that it? Is it filled with secrets?'

'Dunno,' Declan sipped his Guinness. 'Haven't opened it yet.'

'Why not?' Anjli frowned. 'Not like you to get cold feet on something like this.'

Declan leaned back, staring at the ceiling for a moment.

'I'm finding it hard to concentrate right now,' he replied. 'Bullman says Jess is okay, and that Liz and Jess have police outside, but until we find Karl, I just—'

'You think he'll go after them?' Anjli sipped at her gin and lemonade.

Declan shook his head.

'Weirdly, no,' he said. 'I really don't. But I think he's planning something, and with Francine Pearce playing games...'

'Billy's already on that,' Anjli soothed. 'And if anyone can do it, it's him. He's checking holiday homes from Haverfordwest West to St Nons right now, based on what Baker said to you.'

'Anything from *Essence*?' Declan changed the subject. 'Maybe Leroy's missing knife?'

Anjli shook her head.

'No briefcase or kitchen utensils, but I got some interesting tales.'

'Like?'

'Well, Tara admitted she slept with Leroy while in

Dubrovnik, which explains why he hadn't slept in his bed. Also, she was quite clear on the fact that her husband Harnish did all the work there, and that Leroy was known for taking the credit. I also talked to the pot washer, a guy named Darryl, and he said that it was Harnish that hired Helen, not Leroy.'

'Not what I expected,' Declan raised an eyebrow. 'Tara gave me the impression she blamed Leroy for it. Any reason he'd keep that from his wife?'

'Apart from the fact she was sleeping with the boss?' Anjli shrugged. 'I think it's enough to ask more questions about Cage. I got the impression that it was a bit of a sympathy hire.'

'Billy said the same thing,' Declan said as he took a mouthful of his Guinness. 'Although he thought it was more a case of Leroy finding out that Helen's family was under financial duress and using this to force her to work for him.'

'Harsh,' Anjli replied. 'Billy dropped me the basics in an email. I can't imagine how she felt.'

Declan didn't respond to this; of everyone he knew, Anjli was the one that would most likely understand Helen's predicament. She'd been held to ransom by Johnny Lucas after her mother had needed cancer treatment. It was long passed, her mother was cancer-free and Anjli no longer owed the gangster, but the debt had been there, and she'd had to make the choice as to whether or not she informed her team-mates about it.

That she had done so pretty much saved her career.

Unaware of Declan's thoughts, Anjli reached across to the file, opening it.

'Come on then, let's see what shady shit goes on in the

world of Governmental party planning,' she said as she pulled out the first sheet. 'I mean, how bad can it be?'

'No wine at the committees, for one thing,' Declan said as he joined her.

BILLY STRETCHED HIS ARMS, YAWNING AS HE RECLINED THE gamer chair he'd requisitioned for his default monitor station. He hadn't intended to stay late, but there wasn't much to do when he got home, and fewer people there than here in the Command Unit at this time of night. In fact, it'd been one of the other people in the Unit he'd just been to see downstairs in the morgue. He hadn't looked in person, and DC Davey had mocked him for that, but she'd checked the hand of the body of Leroy Daniels and confirmed that yes, *when he died, there was still the slightest scarring of Dubrovnik's burn.*

A burn that couldn't be seen in the nightclub photo.

Billy had then spent the next hour checking through image searches, guaranteeing this wasn't some kind of cache error, that perhaps the image used was from a different event, as sometimes these things happened. It could have been from the first night they arrived, maybe even hours before he burned his hand on the morning of his first meeting with the mayor, but Billy doubted it. If they flew in knowing there was a big event the following day, surely they'd make certain they were ready for it.

No, this was after the event.

Billy had played with the raw data of the image in *Photoshop*; perhaps the camera flash had bleached the hand closest to it, and therefore wiped out the scar? Perhaps the shadows of the club changed the light values?

All of these came up negative.

Leroy Daniels didn't have a scar, although the body downstairs did. Which meant that unless there was some other way Billy hadn't considered, the man holding up the hand in the photo who was dressed like Leroy Daniels *wasn't* Leroy Daniels. And if this was the case, that a lookalike had been involved to fool the press, then Tara Wilkinson had to have known this, purely because she was in the shot beside him.

Now that Billy knew there was an imposter in the midst, he looked more closely at the other photos, comparing them to this; the face was similar, but the eyes were narrower. Of course, this could have been because of the flash, so he needed more proof. This Leroy was a little shorter, compared to Tara, but then the shoes couldn't be seen, and she might have worn higher heels here. The beard was a little lighter, again, possibly because of the flash bleaching out the colour...

There was a logo, faint in the background and matching it to another image on a Dubrovnik party site, Billy now knew which nightclub it was. And, after a quick call to the club, where he spoke to a fluent English speaker, Billy learnt this photo was taken on the Wednesday night, two days after Leroy and Tara had arrived on the Monday, and the first night they apparently slept together.

But which Leroy did Tara sleep with?

Billy leaned back in shocked revelation; *Tara didn't sleep with Leroy because this wasn't Leroy.* And this fake Leroy was seen with Tara because the *real* one was elsewhere.

Flicking through the press shots, photos taken during the week, Billy noted that on the two days that Leroy reportedly shared the bed with Tara, he kept away from the photos, with only distant shots of the kitchen available. Yet on the last day he was all smiles, close up and personal.

The imposter could have been used for the long shots, Billy surmised. *The kitchen staff didn't know Leroy that well, and more importantly, they were all strangers. And if Tara was vouching for him, then he had to be Leroy.*

In none of the photos was Leroy doing anything remotely chef-like. No preparation, no cooking. He was standing, watching, not even ordering them to do anything.

Because he wouldn't know what to say. And possibly didn't even speak English well.

Leroy Daniels hadn't been at the restaurant in the hotel for two days. He hadn't even been in the hotel, no matter what Tara Wilkinson claimed.

So where was Leroy Daniels?

'I TELL YOU ONE THING,' ANJLI FINISHED A CHIP AS SHE READ the folder to her left. 'I can see why Helen Cage broke up with Johnny Mitchell. If you think your parents had been royally screwed over by the Government to the point where dad dies, you wouldn't be over the moon about doing a fancy dinner for them either.'

Declan snorted. 'You think that was enough to stop her from taking the job?' he asked between his own mouthfuls of dinner. 'From what was said today, she didn't really have an opportunity to find other work, and they needed the money to keep the lights on.'

Anjli wiped her mouth with a napkin.

'Yeah, but the timing seems really dodgy here,' she said. 'Look. Johnny gets the gig to create the Gala Dinner, which was not known then to be the PM's last public appearance before the Leadership contest, about six months ago. That's when Leroy loses out to him, too. Within a month, Johnny and Helen split up, and a month later, he's off to Edinburgh to open his new restaurant.'

'Maybe there were other reasons,' Declan argued. 'Maybe Johnny was having other people looking over his shoulder while he was down south, and he realised that going north would eliminate that.'

'You think Leroy Daniels?'

'Maybe, or perhaps it was Marshall Howe,' Declan pulled a page of notes out of the folder. 'He's all over this. Pushing for his favourites to get the roles, arguing against the people he didn't like...'

'Maybe Marshall had something on Johnny?'

'Or it was the other way around.'

Declan shook his head.

'No, I don't think so. I reckon Marshall just liked Johnny because it pissed off Daniels.'

'Why Edinburgh?' Anjli asked. 'He could have gone to Liverpool, Birmingham, anywhere in the country. Why up sticks to Scotland?'

Declan typed a message on his phone.

'I'll check this with Billy,' he replied. 'Maybe he just wanted distance though.'

'Interesting thing though,' Anjli read the minutes of a meeting held a couple of months earlier. 'Even though he lost out, Leroy still kept badgering them, trying to get onto the ticket. Says here he actually offered to be Johnny's Sous-Chef if it meant he could be involved.'

'He actually said that?'

Anjli *hmm*ed to herself as she read.

'Scratch that, it wasn't Leroy,' she carried on reading. 'It was Tara that made the offer.'

'I bet that didn't go down well.'

Anjli stopped eating for a moment as she picked up another sheet of paper.

'Wait, hold on,' she said as she read down it. 'When Johnny Mitchell died, Leroy wasn't a shoo-in. In fact, Marshall Howe was petitioning for someone else to run the gala.'

'Who?'

'Harnish Patel,' Anjli looked up at Declan. 'With Helen Cage doing desserts.'

'Howe knew Patel and Cage?' Declan considered this. 'Makes sense. Howe wants anyone connected to Daniels, but not Daniels himself to be involved here. That's harsh.'

'And yet he allowed him to take over,' Anjli tapped at a line in the minutes of the final meeting. 'That said, even at the very end he argued Leroy wasn't right for the role, even if he was keeping to the menu ideas.'

'How do you mean?' With Anjli's permission, Declan took the piece of paper, scanning down it. 'Christ, the menu is almost exact here. Did Leroy have advanced knowledge of what Johnny was planning?

'Perhaps,' Anjli finished her plate, wiping her mouth. 'After all, by then Helen was working for him, and we know she was there when Johnny was working it out.'

'That would be a better reason to hire her back than *I want to try our relationship again*,' Declan mused. 'Actually having information that vital, that useful...'

'Only if Johnny couldn't continue,' Anjli pointed out. 'Which leads us again to whether Johnny Mitchell was killed deliberately.'

'By who, though?' Declan leaned back in his chair. 'Tara and Leroy were in Dubrovnik, Helen and Harnish were in the restaurant until around the same time that Johnny was killed in Edinburgh. They could have paid someone, I suppose, but from what I hear in the witness statements about the man, Leroy seemed the type who would want to see things done personally.'

Dave the barman, walking over to clear the food away, smiled as he saw the folder on the table.

'You know, one of these days you'll have to actually have a date without the paperwork,' he said, picking up Declan's plate.

Anjli, looking horrified, shook her head.

'It's not a date,' she protested. 'It's—'

'It's whatever you say it is,' Dave tapped his nose before taking her plate, adding it to the other. Before he walked off, he looked back at Declan.

'You still hunting Karl Schnitter?' he asked softly. Declan, shaken by the change in direction, nodded. Usually he would have agreed to this without a second thought, purely as the cover story had been that Karl Schnitter had escaped, rather than been taken away by a dodgy covert Government black-ops unit, but as Karl had escaped from that, technically he *was* still hunting him.

'You know Flossie? Runs the sweet counter in the shop on the high street?' Dave asked. Declan nodded. Calling it a sweet counter was as amusing as calling the line of three shops a high street, but he knew what Dave meant.

'What about her?'

'She reckons she saw him this morning, outside his garage,' Dave leaned closer. 'Utterly convinced, she is. Says he even gave her a wave as he walked off.'

Declan glanced at Anjli, also listening intently.

'Thanks, Dave, we'll look into it,' he said as he gathered his papers together, closing the file and, after finishing their drinks and with Anjli behind him, he walked out of the pub, scanning the street as he did so.

'You don't think he's that stupid, do you?' Anjli asked. 'To return here?'

'Actually, I think he's exactly that stupid,' Declan nodded. 'He was looking to escape when we caught him, remember? Maybe he had a *go bag* ready, one we never found? Makes sense he'd come back to grab it.'

'You look tense,' Anjli watched Declan carefully. 'You need to watch that. Gossip in a small town isn't the be all of intel gathering.'

'Yeah,' Declan nodded. 'I used to go to a gym when I was in Tottenham. They had a thing called a *Boxmaster*. Whole load of pads you could just go to town on, like a heavy bag but more focused. I haven't found anything like that here yet.'

'You need to find an easier stress relief,' Anjli laughed as they started north.

'Oh yeah? I haven't seen you de-stressing lately,' Declan mocked. 'Physician, heal thyself and all that.'

'I have my ways,' Anjli replied coyly.

'Oh yes?' Declan asked.

'I take long, luxurious baths,' Anjli smiled. 'In fact, I'll be doing that when we get in, so expect nothing from me, as I won't even be considering work.'

Declan went to reply to this, but stopped as he realised that the thought of Anjli Kapoor in a bath had made him blush. Looking away from his partner, he stopped in the high street, looking south, towards St Mary's Church.

'Go have your bath,' he mumbled. 'I need a little space.'

'You okay?'

'Yeah, just need to walk off the Guinness and have a think,' Declan forced his best smile. 'And besides, I don't want to walk in on you when you're all—' he waved a hand up and down his body, as if this explained what he meant.

'I'll have you know, I've had men line up to see— ' Anjli did the same motions, pointing at her body, mocking Declan, before paling. 'Although that's not quite what I meant.'

'Go have the bath,' Declan was already walking south. Anjli, sighing, started off north, confused by why the thought of Declan seeing her nude was now the main focus in her mind.

Declan walked purposely towards the entrance to St Mary's Churchyard, entering the darkness on the other side and stopping, listening to the surrounding emptiness.

'You can come out now,' he whispered. 'I know you're here.'

There was a rustle of movement and a man walked out of the hedge to the side of Declan. He was in his sixties, his white hair cut short, as if with a razor, his beard now removed. He wore garage overalls and a donkey jacket, and he smiled widely as he faced the detective.

'Hello, Declan,' Karl Schnitter said. 'Been a while.'

———

15

FACE OFFS

'GIVE ME ONE REASON WHY I SHOULDN'T ARREST YOU RIGHT now,' Declan hadn't realised that he'd done it, but his extendable baton, always secured in his jacket sleeve had now slid down into his hand, ready to be flicked open at the slightest command.

'You do not want to arrest me,' Karl smiled. 'You had that opportunity once before, and you let me rot in an unknown room instead.'

'For what you did, you deserved it.'

'Maybe, maybe not,' Karl shrugged. 'We will never know.'

'Why are you here,' Declan flicked his wrist, and the baton extended. 'You here to finish your deranged game?'

Karl glanced at the weapon in Declan's hand.

'You won the game,' he replied calmly. 'The *Red Reaper* will appear no more.'

'You still need to pay,' Declan stated. And, for the first time, anger appeared in Karl's eyes.

'You think I have not paid?' he snapped. 'I lost my life! My home! My family! For decades I belonged here, and now I cannot return!'

'Perhaps you should have thought of that when you killed teenagers and old women,' Declan's anger was also rising. 'Or when you threatened my child.'

At this, Karl's expression softened.

'I would never hurt Jess!' he exclaimed. 'I have known of her all of her life.'

Declan stared at the insane serial killer in front of him and realised that there was the slightest possibility that Karl Schnitter might be telling the truth.

'You killed my parents,' he snapped back. Why the hell wouldn't I think you'd *not* stop there?'

'I killed your mother and father, that is true,' Karl bowed his head. 'Your father was a good man, but he was going to stop me. I tried to work a way out of saving him, but Ilse... she changed the way I felt. I allowed her to lead on that one and I regret it.'

'And mum?'

'Christine was sick,' Karl replied. 'She was looking at months of great pain before a terrible death. When she realised who I was, *what* I was? She begged for me to—'

'*Don't say that!*' Declan raised the baton, using every ounce of willpower to hold back from striking the German to the ground, to keep striking him. 'She wouldn't—'

'You were not there,' Karl half-whispered now. 'She was in terrible agony. Patrick would not do anything, the doctors would not—'

'*They wanted to save her!*'

'*There was no saving her, Declan!*' Now it was Karl who shouted. 'I loved your mother like a sister! She befriended me before anyone else did, and at the end she saw me for what I really was, an angel of mercy that could end her torment!'

A tear ran down his cheek.

'She was pure of heart and clean of soul,' he finished. 'Helping her on was the biggest failure of my life.'

Declan went to reply to this, but found he had no words. Karl genuinely believed that he'd done Declan's mother a great service here.

'So why are you here now?' he asked. 'To kill me? To finish the job, if you're not after Jess?'

Karl shook his head.

'You beat me,' he explained. 'I have no argument with you. And, now I have done one last thing, I will hand myself in.'

'And I'm supposed to believe that?'

Karl didn't speak for a moment, and the silence in the churchyard was deafening.

'I offered myself up to your superiors before,' he said calmly. 'You were the one that threw me into a black hole of anonymity.'

'You don't think you deserved that?'

'I deserved my trial,' Karl snapped. 'I deserved my chance to explain.'

'But now you're free so you can go explain to everyone,' Declan closed the baton. 'Because I'm done with you.'

'Maybe I'll tell them how a Detective Inspector had me kidnapped by Government operatives and thrown into a nameless gulag.'

'Go wild,' Declan shrugged. 'But if you're in the mood for telling people things, tell me instead how you got out? I guessed you had guards working for you, but how?'

'They were not working for me,' Karl replied, and Declan nodded.

'Francine Pearce,' he said. 'I'm guessing she pulled the strings because they planted her blood in my car when I saw you. So do you work for her now?'

'I was happy,' Karl replied. 'I had been beaten. And I understood my place. But then something happened.'

Declan felt a chill slide down his spine at these words.

'Go on.'

Karl stretched his arms as he continued.

'I learnt quickly that the guards in this unknown place? They once worked for other agencies. Names like *Rattlestone* and *Pearce Associates*.'

Declan nodded at this. He'd guessed as much.

'Anyway, they did not talk to me, they did not know much about me. And Tom, the man who kidnapped me, he would interrogate me. One day, he brought a friend. A woman.'

Declan felt the same chill again. *That's how Francine had worked it out. She'd heard about Trix.*

'It seems that one of the guards recognised this girl, that she had worked for the same company.'

'She worked for *Pearce Associates*.'

Karl nodded.

'She was Francine Pearce's mole in your unit,' he said. 'And with this information, it was easy to guess what happened. A woman who had been revealed as a spy against Declan Walsh, who had been instrumental in helping him escape terrorism charges created by *Rattlestone* is now meeting with an unknown man who was brought in from Hurley, Declan's home town. Obviously, I was a person Francine wanted to speak to.'

'And did you?'

Karl smiled at this.

'Of course we spoke,' he said. 'Through the guards. She wanted you dead and needed my help in finding the way to do so. I, however, did not want you dead. And so I suggested a joint operation.'

'You call me in, she places blood in my car, you pass a message that gives us a belief that you're about to be sprung and you're moved.'

'Yes, although I had specified no deaths,' Karl shook his head. 'That was not part of the agreement.'

'They're deaths that have been added to your tally,' Declan snapped. 'And a good man is still in hospital, fighting for his life.'

'You should be angry at me, I get that,' Karl was insufferably calm. 'But your true anger should be aimed at Francine Pearce and her friend, Trisha Hawkins.'

Declan was surprised at the latter's name being mentioned.

'I'm hunting them both,' he growled. 'And when I find Pearce, I'll make damn sure she's targeted.'

'She is in St Davids, in Pembrokeshire,' Karl stared around the graveyard as he spoke. 'She is staying at her sister's old house. When I die, promise me you'll bury me here?'

'You know this how?' Declan asked, reeling a little at this. Karl's words were almost identical to Charles Baker's earlier that day.

'Because I came from there this morning,' Karl replied, and his tone was dark now. 'I needed to make things right. As you said, many good men died in my escape. Men who were not supposed to die. Innocents.'

'And you care about innocents now?'

'I always did,' Karl shrugged. 'It was always justice. And now one more will face it.'

Declan didn't like the sound of this.

'You spoke with Pearce?'

'I said I needed to make things right,' Karl replied calmly. 'I did not say that involved conversation.'

'You need to come with me,' Declan said, moving closer. 'You need to face the crimes you've created.'

Karl nodded and pulled his hand out of his overalls. A small snub-nosed pistol was in his hand.

'I will not be doing that, I'm afraid, Declan,' he said. 'This was a courtesy. You will never see me again, but I will do what you have asked.'

'I want you to *face justice!*' Declan snarled.

'And I will,' Karl replied. 'For you have taken everything I love; my family, my home, my life, from me. I have nowhere to go, except one last destination. I will leave you to deal with Miss Hawkins.'

He stood to attention, nodding slightly and Declan wondered if there was a chance here to make a jump for the gun, but before he could start, Karl slipped through the gate, back into the street. Declan turned, following him out—

But Karl was gone.

From where the gate was, there were at least four different directions he could have taken, all down hidden country paths. He could have run to the Thames path, crossed the bridge, even doubled back to the old crypts. Declan had no idea where he was heading, or even how he'd be able to follow.

Swearing to himself, Declan started north, back towards his house. He was annoyed, but at the same time there was an element of satisfaction here. That Karl wasn't gunning for Jess or Liz meant Declan could finally relax.

Declan pulled out his phone, dialling Temple Inn. Unsurprisingly, it was Billy that answered.

'Do me a favour,' he said down the phone. 'Anjli mentioned you're already looking at holiday homes, so have a look for any properties in St Davids that were owned, or still are owned by Sara Hinksman. If you find one, send police immediately.'

With Billy already typing as he disconnected, Declan leaned back, stretching his spine as he considered this. Sarah Pearce had become Hinksman by marriage, and Francine had begun her career as her sister's assistant before Sarah's untimely death twenty years ago, a death that sent Frankie Pearce, as she was then into a spiral that created the woman Declan constantly faced.

If Francine Pearce was hiding in St Davids, it was well past time for them to have a chat—if she was even still alive, after Karl's visit.

As Monroe and De'Geer arrived at the doors of *Monet*, a short, muscular man with a full beard and shaved head stood nervously waiting for them.

'DCI Hendrick said to meet you here,' he said, holding out a hand. 'I'm Rich Ashby. I was the lead SOCO.'

Monroe nodded. He didn't expect Ashby to have a rank; normally SOCOs, or *Scene of Crime Officers* weren't usually police officers, but were employed by the relevant police forces. Doctor Marcos was just that, a doctor, even though she often believed she outranked everyone in the office.

'DCI Monroe, and this is PC De'Geer,' Monroe shook Ashby's hand. 'Can you show us what happened?'

'I can, but it's up to you to talk to the cleaner,' Ashby opened the restaurant door, allowing the other two through. 'She's bloody mad, utterly convinced there were ghosts bouncing around at seven in the morning.'

'De'Geer, if you would?' Monroe smiled at the PC. 'You're so much better with people than I am.'

As De'Geer, directed to a scared-looking woman in a cleaner's tunic that stood to the side of one of the large windows, walked off, Monroe nodded at Ashby.

'So what do you think?' he asked. 'Robbery? Murder?'

'A bit of both, I'd say,' Ashby scratched at his beard. 'I mean, obviously it's both, but I get the feeling that it's mainly one, with the other being a bit of opportunism.'

'Aye, but which one was the planned one?' Monroe muttered as he looked around the restaurant. 'So, has much been moved since?'

'Surprisingly no,' Ashby led Monroe through to a back room, nodding to some waiting staff. 'The staff haven't been using Mitchell's office yet, I think they were waiting for the police to completely finish the investigation before deciding what to do with it. They have the place pre-paid for another three months, rent wise, so it makes sense for them to do something here, especially with the Edinburgh Festival in just over a month.'

Opening the door, Ashby led Monroe inside a larger than expected back office. Against the back wall was a metal safe, around three feet in height, and with a combination lock. The door had been swung open, and it was currently empty.

On the shelf was a leather wrapped collection of kitchen knives, and on the desk against the side wall was a selection of menu printouts, with a large, framed map of Edinburgh above it, the words *Plan of Edinburgh and its Environs, a survey by John Knox, 1825* on the right hand side.

'Doesn't look like that anymore,' Monroe commented, pointing at it. Ashby moved closer, having a better look.

'Aye, it's got the Nor Loch on it for a start. That's now the park by Princes Street, as well as the train lines to Waverley Station. Which isn't built here yet.'

'Wonder why he has it on the wall?' Monroe asked. 'And one that's damaged?'

'Damaged?' Ashby looked at Monroe, confused.

'Aye, all the sharpie marks drawn on it,' Monroe indicated the various lines and squiggles over the Old Town.

Ashby laughed.

'Nah, they're nay squiggles,' he replied. 'That's the tunnels.'

Monroe looked again.

'I thought the Edinburgh Vaults were under South Bridge, over there?'

'Well yeah, but that's just one of the many tunnels we have under Edinburgh,' Ashby said with the slightest hint of pride. 'When the New Town was built in the mid eighteen hundreds, they covered over tons of places. Sometimes entire streets. This line here, it runs underneath this very street, heads all the way east to New Street, passing under Flesh-market Close.'

He smiled.

'That's my favourite Ian Rankin book, that is.'

Monroe nodded absently, remembering something Hendrick had said earlier.

'The whole place is seventeenth century. There're tunnels underneath that often lead into communal cellars.'

'Could they have come from the basement?' he asked. 'Especially as the cleaner heard noises from down there?'

'The basement's filled with boxes of stock, and the cleaner's mad,' Ashby shook his head. 'We think the killer came in along the roof, made their way down the stairs, exited onto the kitchen roof through a back door, came in through a skylight and entered here while Mitchell was counting the takings. There was a scuffle, and Mitchell was killed.'

'How do you know the skylight?'

'Because there was glass all over the floor,' Ashby was tiring of the conversation now. 'Bit of a give-away, sir.'

'Weapon?'

'Eight-inch blade, with the depth and width matching a similar sized kitchen knife,' Ashby opened up the leather wrap, unravelling it and pointing to a vicious-looking blade. 'That one there. Well, not that one, but the same.'

Monroe took the blade out, looking at it.

'And nobody's found one like this?'

'Not around here,' Ashby walked Monroe out into the kitchen now, pointing at a small skylight in the ceiling. 'That's the window whoever did this broke to get in.'

There was a good eight feet of space between the ceiling and the skylight. Monroe stared up as he spoke.

'Was there anything here?' he asked. 'Table, chairs perhaps?'

Ashby shook his head.

'This is pretty much as seen.'

'Then how did they get out?' Monroe looked around. 'Hendrick said the outside CCTV didn't pick up anyone, so they didn't exit out the main door. They had to get back through that, but even without their spoils, that's a hell of a jump.'

'Maybe they had a rope?' Ashby suggested. 'Apart from a locked back door and a front entrance, that's pretty much all they could do.'

'And what did they take?' Monroe was shaking his head in disbelief.

'Takings, some papers, oh, a couple of frying pans—'

'Frying pans?' Monroe was surprised at this, but Ashby, unrelenting, continued.

'They're worth a hundred each. Probably thought they could get some money for them.'

Monroe looked back at the office.

'He has a wrap of knives in there and an antique print,' he muttered. 'Good set of chef knives are probably worth a bit, likewise the map. They could have taken those and made five times the pans amount, and the pans would have been bulky.'

He tutted to himself.

'This doesn't feel right, laddie.'

Undaunted by the criticism, Ashby took Monroe through the restaurant, showing him the places where the killer was believed to have moved around while Mitchell was in the office, confirming that the time of death was around midnight. Monroe believed Ashby knew his thing and so he accepted the information, but felt the scene had been fabricated.

That someone had entered, killed Mitchell and then created a story for the police to follow, including the removal of mildly expensive pans. Alone, and in the restaurant, they could have taken hours setting the pieces of the puzzle to lead the police down the wrong route. In fact, the only witness who hadn't been guided was the poor bloody cleaner who thought she saw ghosts.

'So the cleaner thinks it was a ghost,' De'Geer explained as he walked outside with Monroe at the end of the tour, nodding farewell to Ashby, who was probably eager to be rid of the suspicious, cynical DCI and his assistant. 'Says she came in at half six and started to clean—'

'Why so early?'

'Special needs kid,' De'Geer read from the notes. 'She works the hours her husband doesn't, so there's always someone around. Anyway, she's here just before seven and she's in the kitchen, doing the floors when she hears a door close somewhere, but she knows all the doors are shut because she closes them as she's done. She's all alone, so she holds the mop like a weapon and goes to see.'

'And what does she see?'

'Nothing spooky,' De'Geer admitted. 'However, she claims the door to the storeroom in the cellar and the office door, earlier closed, are now both half open. That's when she sees the body.'

'Maybe she cleaned the storeroom and forgot to close the door?' Monroe frowned. 'Makes more sense than a bloody spirit.'

'True, but she seemed quite insistent that she didn't,' De'Geer explained. 'I had a look down there at her insistence, and there's a locked trap door, leading to God knows where.'

'Maybe one of these communal cellars,' Monroe mused. 'Who has the keys?'

'No idea,' De'Geer replied. 'That is, she had no idea. As far as she was concerned, it's not been open for years. Even when she cleaned the café that was here before *Monet*.'

'So Mitchell is murdered around midnight, and the killers wait around for seven hours before leaving?' Monroe shook his head, stopping as he watched a black SUV drive towards them. 'That can't be right. Maybe a tramp was hiding out there? Realised he had to get out before he was found—'

He stopped as the SUV pulled up beside them and two burly men emerged from the back doors, walking towards Monroe and De'Geer.

'Mister Wright would like a word,' the closest man, the same tracksuit and trainers bodyguard they'd met in Greyfriar's Kirkyard said, with as much menace as he could.

'Threatening a police officer?' Monroe smiled. 'You sure that's the way you want to go, laddie?'

'No threats, just a request,' tracksuit and trainers replied, emphasising the word *request*. 'Mister Wright would like to speak with you before you return to London.'

'And who says we're returning to London any time soon?' De'Geer asked politely. Tracksuit and trainers didn't seem to have an answer to that and, after a few seconds of awkward silence, Monroe patted him on the arm.

'We'll just get in the back, shall we?' he asked, nodding to De'Geer to join him. 'Keep up the good work.'

And with the two officers now in the back, and with the second burly man sitting with them, tracksuit and trainers climbed into the front passenger seat as the black SUV drove off into the Edinburgh night.

16

FOLLOWING THE RECIPE

'MA'AM, CAN I HAVE A WORD?' BILLY LOOKED NERVOUSLY AT Bullman through the door to her office. 'I think I might have something, but it's pretty detailed, and I'm just filling in puzzle pieces like a mad conspiracy theorist.'

'Currently, mad conspiracy theorist is a good thing,' Bullman nodded. 'Here or at your station?'

With a nod, Billy led Bullman back to the computer monitors, sitting at the keyboard as Bullman walked up beside him. Across the banks of screens she could see images of Leroy Daniels, pictures of planes, scans of flight manifests and close ups of what looked to be blue plasters.

'Wow,' she muttered. 'You weren't kidding when you meant—' she stopped herself. 'Go on, tell me what you have.'

'First off, I don't think Leroy Daniels is who he says he is here,' Billy said, pointing at the photo of Leroy in the Dubrovnik club. 'But I'm getting ahead of myself. I need—'

'DC Fitzwarren,' Bullman spoke calmly, but with authority. 'Take a breath, clear your mind and start at the beginning.'

'Yes, Ma'am,' Billy reddened. 'Sorry.'

He turned back to the screen where, front and centre, was the image of Daniels taken in the nightclub.

'Okay, so everybody in the world knows that Leroy Daniels was in Dubrovnik at the time of Johnny Mitchell's death, thanks to the extensive media coverage the hotel pushed for,' he started. 'But looking at this, I don't know if he was.'

'What do you mean?'

'Well, they arrive on Monday morning, right? Big arrival on a private jet, lots of press in Dubrovnik Airport snapping them. They didn't meet anybody, instead they take a waiting car and go straight to the hotel, where they look at the restaurant, probably meet with the management staff and discuss what's needed, as well as planning out the week's events.'

'Okay, so apart from adding to the carbon footprint, I see nothing wrong so far.'

'Because at this point, there isn't anything wrong,' Billy smiled. 'So now we're later that day, and Chef Daniels is in the kitchen, seeing how everything's set up before the big press event that afternoon. He's visible, and he's close up and personal with the cooks, even working on the hobs. And that's where the problem happens.'

'Problem?'

'He burns himself,' Billy brought up a photo of the press photo of Daniels and the Mayor of Dubrovnik, standing on a beach together. 'Monday evening they have a reception with the mayor and a ton of other dignitaries, where Leroy states he can't shake hands with his right hand because he burned it.'

He pointed at the scene, zooming in on Leroy Daniels' obviously blue-plastered hand.

'You can see there's a small blue burn plaster on his wrist now, and the following day, Tuesday, he's seen at a couple of smaller events, both with the same plaster; there's one with a distributor, there's one on another beach with someone dressed like a character from *Game of Thrones*—and then, after around four o'clock, there's nothing.'

'Maybe he was sick of cameras?'

'That's what I thought,' Billy nodded, returning to the screens. 'But now, looking into this, it seems he finished early on the Tuesday, went to his room with Tara telling everyone he was working on the menus... but here's the thing. The menus are already finished.'

Bullman raised an eyebrow. 'You're sure?'

'They did them before they arrived,' Billy continued. 'There's an interview he has with one of the press on the Monday where he even talks about this. But now it's Wednesday, and suddenly Leroy Daniels doesn't want to speak to people. He doesn't want to be around people. There's a few candid photos taken of him at the back of rooms, or watching in the kitchen's corner as the cooks practise on the menu, but it's like he's phoning it in.'

'Tuesday night was the first night Tara and Leroy slept in the same bed,' Bullman mused. 'Maybe he was tired out.'

'We'll come to that in a minute, Ma'am,' Billy had one of the Wednesday photos on the screen, and zoomed into the image, enhancing the fuzzy, distant shot of Chef Daniels in his chef whites, watching the proceedings. 'See here? There's no plaster on his wrist now.'

'He could be wearing skin coloured plasters?'

'He wouldn't do that if he was in the kitchen,' Billy argued, looking back around to his superior. 'Most chefs wear blue plasters in the kitchen when they cut themselves, because that way they see if it falls into the food.'

'That's put me off a later dinner,' Bullman muttered. 'Thanks for that.'

Ignoring the barbed reply, already engrossed in the clues he'd found, Billy brought up more images, taken over the week, concentrating on the now familiar image of Leroy in a Dubrovnik nightclub, his hand held up.

'During the day, he keeps away from people, and he's a bit distant according to reports. Also, and more importantly, he refuses to meet with management. No photos taken apart from this one in a nightclub on Lapad Beach. And here you can see he holds his hand up to stop a photographer taking a shot. The same one he burned.'

'Which isn't burned.'

'Exactly. Tara's in the background, and you can see from body language she's uncomfortable as well, but the photographer told the paper he sold this to, that someone at the hotel contacted him, in English, to give him the scoop of where they'd be.'

'So Tara calls him in, but plays the part in the picture. I can see that working.'

'I've checked everything on this photo and there is no way it's been doctored,' Billy was serious now as he spoke. 'It's not been bleached out, it's not been affected by quality issues... this is the raw image, and I can tell you with my hand on my heart that this is *not* Leroy Daniels.'

'What do you mean?' If Bullman had been prepared for that answer, she made a good act of not revealing herself. 'Who is it if it isn't?'

'I don't know,' Billy shook his head. 'I've compared his height on images to other people, and I've checked other pictures of him. Leroy has a small mole under his left eye which this man doesn't seem to have, although the image could've wiped it out or bleached it, but he's not as tall, he's got a slimmer face—'

'Christ, if he isn't there, he could be anywhere.' Bullman was pacing now.

'If you look at him, he's an easy person to impersonate,' Billy watched Bullman from the chair. 'Someone with a beard, of around the same height who shaved his head, wears a bandana, put a pair of thick black glasses on... think about it. Nobody in the kitchen knows who he is, and if Tara's with him and speaking for him, then they're going to listen to what he says. From what I can find out, he didn't really talk to the kitchen staff; this was a problem that came up with management.'

'So what do you think happened?' Bullman stopped pacing and faced Billy. 'I'm guessing you have a theory?'

'Yes, Ma'am, and this is where conspiracy part slides in.'

'Only now?' Bullman sighed audibly. 'God give me strength.'

'Okay, well, it seems to me that from Tuesday afternoon until Thursday morning Leroy Daniels literally phones in his work, doesn't really stretch himself, make an effort, all that sort of thing. Then, around Thursday afternoon, he's back, front and centre again. He's talking to people, there's a large dinner on the Thursday night which he happily attends and he shows the new menus that he's created.'

'Complete one-eighty.'

'Exactly. But by then the hotel isn't talking to him, they're unhappy with Daniels, saying they thought they'd get more press out of the week he had with them and then he spends all of Friday in his room before a final dinner in the evening and then flying home on Saturday morning. My contact at the hotel claims on the Thursday and Friday he slept in his own bed again, with only Tuesday and Wednesday nights the times he didn't.'

'Well, Tara Wilkinson stated for the record that they'd slept together, maybe they realised it was a bad idea?'

'That's one option,' Billy smiled. 'But what if he wasn't in the bed, because he wasn't in the hotel room? They probably didn't consider the cleaning staff telling anyone, so Tara makes up the affair story on the fly when questioned by Anjli. I mean DS Kapoor.'

'To do that though, she's risking her own marriage,' Bullman whistled. 'Which means she had a major part in this.'

'Oh, I think Tara and Leroy were completely in this together. All of this? It's a perfect alibi for anything that happens during that week.'

'Are you talking about Johnny Mitchell's death?'

'Possibly,' Billy admitted. 'And here's the conspiracy. I realised that with him in Croatia and Johnny in Scotland, Leroy murdering Johnny could be a bit of an issue, unless he *wasn't* in Croatia.'

'Go on.'

Billy shrugged. 'It's a working hypothesis. And currently it goes like this. Leroy Daniels came into Croatia by private jet Monday, and that jet was in and out of the airport twice before picking them up on the Saturday. He could've got back onto it late Tuesday afternoon or early Tuesday evening, flown into England that night, get to Edinburgh by Wednesday afternoon where he breaks into *Monet*, finds a hiding spot to hang around until the shift ends, and then kills Johnny Mitchell when they're alone.'

'He then returns to Dubrovnik first thing Thursday morning with nobody knowing,' Bullman exclaimed. 'That's a hell of an accusation, Detective Constable. You'll definitely need to have something more than guesswork to support this.'

Billy tapped on his keyboard, and a new photo appeared on the screen. It was a cargo plane, dressed in the same livery as the private jet seen in the arrival and departure photos.

'This is *Apex Transport*,' Billy explained. 'Run by Dan Lane, they provide a lot of refrigerated and non-refrigerated transportation services for restaurants around the world. You need something fast? *Apex* does it.'

Some further typing and a man, in his forties, bearded and with a greying hipster haircut, appeared on the screen.

'This is Dan Lane,' Billy carried on typing as other scans of flight manifests appeared. 'He's worked with *Essence* since the beginning on hard-to-import items, and has some kind of agreement with Leroy for personal transportation.'

'Partners?'

Billy brought up some corporate documents onto the screen.

'I think it's more that he has a gambling problem, and from what I can work out owes Leroy Daniels about fifty grand after a failed investment that happened about three years ago. Money he's not been able to pay, as his horses haven't come in.'

'So Daniels uses him as a high-class *Uber* until the debt is paid,' Bullman shook her head. 'Classy.'

'I've dug into the flight manifests from the airport that week, and I've learnt that on Tuesday evening the *Apex* jet returned to the UK, arriving at a private landing strip, Eshott

Airfield in Northumberland for required maintenance, before returning Thursday morning to Dubrovnik.'

'So technically someone could have hitched a ride on the plane,' Bullman was nodding now as she worked this through in her head. 'Eshott. How far is that from Edinburgh?'

'Only a two-hour drive, Ma'am,' Billy showed a map on the screen. ' Leroy Daniels could've climbed onto that flight, flown to Northumberland and stayed the night before making his way to Edinburgh, finding a place to hide, waiting until midnight and then killing Johnny Mitchell. This done, he gets in a car, drives back to the jet and he's back in Dubrovnik at seven in the morning, sneaks back into the hotel and suddenly happy and waving as he's seen by the cameras.'

He tapped the monitor screen to emphasise his point.

'Nobody is the wiser, and then on the Thursday morning he gets a call from the Government, stating that Johnny Mitchell is dead, and they need a replacement for the Gala Dinner.'

'And it's easy curating a new menu when you've just been in the office where the previous menu could be seen,' Bullman was coming around to this now. 'Would also explain the open safe, as anything secret about the Gala would have been in there. Maybe even this briefcase they both seem to have had.'

'Surely he'd have dumped the case though?' Billy considered.

'Maybe not,' Bullman stroked her chin as she thought. 'He's all about ego and trophies. Maybe he wanted Howe to see the briefcase, send a message of some kind?'

Billy shuddered.

'That's cold, Ma'am.'

'Well, death is a dish best served and all that,' Bullman smiled. 'What else?'

'Well, this is the clincher for me, but I've heard that Tara Wilkinson tried to get Johnny to agree to let Leroy be involved with the dinner, but he turned him down,' Billy continued. 'Leroy isn't known for his calm demeanour, and it makes sense that he'd want to do this himself rather than by proxy. It also explains why Leroy's knife is missing, as it's the same size as the one that killed Mitchell, and is probably somewhere in the ocean over international waters.'

Bullman stared off into the distance, and Billy could see she was working things through in her head, putting the pieces together.

'We need to get Tara Wilkinson in as soon as possible,' she said. 'I want to know for certain that this was an imposter in these photos before I speak to her. Because if Leroy did go to Edinburgh and kill Johnny Mitchell, she had to be involved with it.'

'And Harnish Patel?'

'I'm not sure,' Bullman shook her head. 'Everything after Leroy's death fits the angle of someone helping him, but Mitchell's death doesn't. The Gala Dinner going to Leroy doesn't help unless...'

'Unless they already knew that Leroy Daniels was going to die as well.'

Bullman stormed to her office.

'*Get me Tara Wilkinson!*' she cried out. 'And call Monroe and find out what he's learnt in Edinburgh! We're supposed to be investigating the poisoning of Leroy Daniels, not his protegé! I want this solved and off my table before we move onto the *actual* problems!'

Billy smiled as he moved to his phone. Bullman was right; their cases often fell into an over-confusing mess around now, and this added murder, even if created before the actual murder, raised up new and intriguing options.

First, Johnny Mitchell was in a relationship with Helen Cage, who was now part of Leroy's kitchen, but hired by Harnish Patel. How would she react if she heard that her new boss had killed her old boyfriend? Second, how did Marshall Howe fit into this? Declan had the paperwork there, so that was likely to be found tomorrow, but it didn't stop Billy wondering.

More importantly, how was the Gala Dinner the following day going to work, when two of the chefs involved were already dead?

'It's me,' he said into a phone. 'Get a couple of uniforms out to *Essence* in Cornhill, see if Tara Wilkinson's there. If not, try her at home.'

PC COOPER WAS ABOUT TO FINISH UP FOR THE EVENING WHEN the call came in. And, being the closest to the restaurant as they drove back to Temple Inn from Shoreditch, Cooper and the driver of the squad car, Sergeant Dalton knocked on the door of *Essence*, to at least have a brief look before sending someone else to the home, wherever that was.

The restaurant looked closed, and the lights were off in the main dining area, only a sliver of light from the kitchen visible as Cooper hammered on the glass door to the restaurant, peering through the shadowed and tempered glass to see if there was any movement.

'Tara Wilkinson!' she shouted. 'City police! Open up!'

There was something on the floor, near the Maitre d's station, and Cooper pulled out a torch, shining it through the glass, trying to angle the light, half reflecting off the glass and back into her face, onto the figure that seemed to be asleep on the carpet.

The torchlight fell upon the open, dead eyes of Tara Wilkinson.

'Oh, crap,' Cooper said as she reached with her other hand to her radio. 'Command, we have a problem. Ambulance needed to *Essence*, on Cornhill—'

She stopped as she noticed another figure stood beside her. Harnish Patel, a *McDonald's* paper carry bag in his hand, stared at her.

'Why does an ambulance need to come here?' he asked, confused.

'Mister Patel, do you have a key that can open this?' Cooper showed the door. Harnish dropped the bag to the floor, rummaging in his pocket.

'I think so, but Tara has keys,' he replied. 'Bang on the door and she'll...'

As if realising everything now, his mouth dropped open for a moment.

'No, no, no,' he repeated as he pulled at the door now, fumbling with the keys. 'You're wrong. She's okay.'

Unlocking and pulling the door open, he ran into the restaurant, seeing the prone figure on the floor. Stumbling to the body, he turned it over, his wife's dead eyes staring up at the ceiling, dried bile running down her cheek.

'No no no,' he repeated, half in shock.

'Chef Patel, you need to step away from the body,' Cooper said in her most authoritarian voice, pulling at his shoulder to gain his attention.

'My wife—'

'Is dead, sir, and we don't know what did it,' Cooper continued. 'Please sir, let us do our job.'

As Harnish stepped back numbly, Cooper clicked on the radio again.

'We've got a major problem here,' she said, in as calm a voice as she could muster. 'Tara Wilkinson is dead, and I think she's been poisoned.'

17

GLASWEGIAN STANDOFF

'YOU KNOW, AS MEETING INVITES GO, THIS IS A REALLY SHITE one,' Monroe smiled darkly as he exited the SUV, glancing around the dock they currently had parked on. They were in what looked to be an abandoned industrial site to the north of Edinburgh, and judging from the water to the side, it was likely one of the Leith properties that Lennie Wright owned in the area. Monroe had decided during the drive that appearing arrogant and insulting from the start would be the best plan here, mainly because he was now convinced Wright intended to kill both him and De'Geer tonight, and most likely dump the weighted-down bodies in the harbour. Therefore, he had nothing to lose here.

At least if he started strong, he'd die strong.

It wasn't the best option; staying alive was always the preferable choice, and more importantly, he didn't want De'Geer caught up in this. The lad was still green, still fresh, uncorrupted. There was actually a future for him, and Monroe cursed himself for bringing De'Geer along.

Lennie Wright waited in the doorway to an old ware-

house building, the soot-stained bricks around him a testa-
ment to the time these buildings had stood here, facing the
North Sea as the water made its way slowly towards the Forth
Bridge, eventually becoming the River Forth as it travelled
west past Stirling and ending at Loch Ard, to the west of
Scotland.

Monroe had always wanted to follow the river to the
source, spending a week strolling along its banks as the river
wound its way through Scotland. He'd never managed it,
though, and now it looked like he wouldn't be adding this to
a list any time soon.

'You don't seem to be gone,' Lennie muttered. 'I said you
had one conversation to change the bitch's mind before you
pissed off, and my people tell me you did that, and now she's
back with the activists, already planning their next protest.'

'You said you'd leave her alone until I spoke to her, but
when I found her, your people were trying to remove her
from the police cells,' Monroe snapped back. 'You reneged on
your promise.'

'I never said those two women were mine.'

'And I never said they were women,' Monroe folded his
arms. 'In fact, it hasn't been released out there yet. So either
your sources are shit hot, or you sent them.'

Lennie grinned at Monroe. It was the grin of a piranha,
seeing his next meal, and Monroe didn't like it.

'When are you going home?' he asked. 'I hear she doesn't
want to connect with long-lost family, and that pretty much
means you can bugger off back to London, right?'

'Working a case,' Monroe shook his head sadly. 'Murder
in Lawnmarket. Might have to stay around for a while.'

He moved closer.

'You know, really sniff around.'

'Oh? And what will your detective nose sniff out?'

'Let's start with cobalt poisoning.'

It was as if someone had fired a gun; at the mention of the word *cobalt*, the four bruisers that stood around Monroe and De'Geer all pulled out guns, now aimed at the two officers.

'Now that's interesting,' Monroe looked around. 'You know how many years you get for that?'

'You have nothing,' Lennie smiled still, but now it was plastered on. 'Nothing but lies and conspiracy theories from vegan activists. They should eat some steak. Might clear their brains.'

'I have a video on a broken camera that had a cloud account linked to it,' Monroe smiled back, as humorous as Lennie's was. 'And I have a computer expert that'll crack it in a day or so. I reckon I've got time to see how you're updating the *gangster burying his rivals* trope.'

'You should be careful, or we could start with you,' Lennie grinned. 'All this, over a child who isn't even connected.'

'Connected?' Monroe frowned. 'Connected to what?'

'*To you!*' Lennie exclaimed. 'Claire Doyle isn't your grand-niece! Amy Doyle wasn't your brother's daughter! Did you even check for a DNA test before you leapt onto the train like feckin' *Zorro?*'

Monroe shook his head.

'You're just playing games now,' he muttered.

'Come on,' Lennie waved his hands around the bay as he spoke. 'You've never heard of these additions to the family until now? How so? You're a copper! You'd have heard of this years ago! Even Willie Moss tried to warn you about this!'

Monroe could feel the open space spinning around him now. *This was a lie. He was being pushed off balance.*

'Who's kid was she then?' he whispered.

'Derek Sutton's,' Lennie replied with a hint of gloating. 'Had Amy right before he was nicked. Spent his whole life in Belmarsh, away from them until you got him out a few months back.'

He chuckled.

'All that shite he did, and he was set up by kids in the end. Who would have thought it.'

Monroe stared at De'Geer, who watched back almost pityingly, as the Glaswegian DCI played every conversation back in his head. He'd never checked the DNA as he hadn't any. Derek had spun a story, and he'd believed him instantly. He'd *wanted* to believe him, to believe that somewhere, a little piece of Kenny still lived. And in Edinburgh, Willie Moss never stated that Claire was his grandniece, and even Hendrick had skirted the issue. Claire herself had given him the truth.

'I'd heard he was possibly some enforcer for the Hutchinsons, nothing more.'

Derek Sutton had also been an enforcer.

Derek Sutton, who couldn't face Lennie one-on-one, as he'd killed the other Wright brothers.

Derek Sutton who needed a copper on his side for this one.

'*Bampot*,' Monroe muttered.

'You're realising now, eh?' Lennie nodded. 'That you were played like a prize prick? And you claiming to be a bright DCI as well. Shame on you.'

'Kin of mine or no', I'll still make sure you don't get away with what you're doing,' Monroe hissed. 'Your illegal dumping ends now. Clean it up.'

'Or what?' Lennie was laughing now. 'You'll set your grandniece on me?'

He nodded to the surrounding bruisers, and almost as if choreographed, they took a step closer, raising their guns.

'You've nothing here,' Lennie snapped. '*You're* nothing. And now you've threatened me, I'm rethinking my suggestion that you leave.'

'What, two dead London coppers on your patch aren't going to cause you issues?' Monroe was mock surprised.

'Who said they were gonna find you?' Lennie replied calmly. 'I'm gonna dump you with the batteries. You can bleed out with them and nobody's finding you until I sort things with my pet councillor and the next building gets built here.'

'That McCavity?'

'He's one of them,' Lennie nodded. 'And by then, we're all long gone. They'll be using bloody *Time Team* to find you.'

'If you really wanted to do that, you'd have done something earlier,' Monroe moved in close to Lennie, almost standing nose-to-nose.

'Oh aye? And what's that?'

There was an audible hiss of shock from the bruisers as Monroe pulled a *Glock* 17 out of his jacket, jamming the muzzle under Lennie Wright's now quivering chin.

'You'd have had your guys search us first,' Monroe said. 'Tell them to drop the guns, or I'll blow you to Hell and back.'

'Bullshit,' Lennie shook his head. 'You never had the *stones* to do this before.'

'My life wasn't on the line before,' Monroe hissed, pushing the gun deeper into Lennie's chin.

'Sir,' De'Geer said softly. 'You can't do this.'

'You heard him, lad, he wants to kill us,' Monroe snarled, his eyes never leaving Lennie's. 'We need to end this now.'

De'Geer softly took his hand and placed it on the gun as he stared at Monroe.

'You can't do this,' he repeated. 'You're a decorated detective, close to retirement, with a career behind you. If this gets out, you'll lose everything.'

He took the gun from Monroe as the elder police officer wavered. But before Lennie could speak, De'Geer had the gun back aimed at him, now between the eyes.

'I should do it,' De'Geer said simply, to the stunned Monroe. 'I'm new, I can weather something like this. People with agendas aren't after me. I can claim it was self defence.'

'You can't kill me,' Lennie hissed. 'You're young, too innocent. It does something to you.'

'My ancestors were Vikings,' De'Geer turned back to Lennie. 'We landed near here and pillaged our way to England. You think I'm scared of offing a broken down gangster like you? Get your pasty Celtic nobodies to back the hell down and drop their weapons before I turn you into a *stain on that wall.*'

'Drop the guns, lads,' Lennie whispered, staring with fear in his eyes at the furious De'Geer. Monroe walked around, picking them up off the ground as they did so.

'I think you should leave,' he said to Lennie once they were all gathered. 'We'll make our own way home, so sod off and don't come back.'

'You'll regret this,' his eyes still locked on De'Geer, Lennie backed over to an SUV, entering it as his now unarmed bruisers did the same. 'Being a copper won't help you this time.'

'I don't know,' Monroe grinned. 'Being a copper put me in contact with this Viking here, and we can both agree that he's helped a lot tonight. Tell McCavity we'll be having a wee chat with him tomorrow afternoon once we gain a warrant.'

As the SUVs sped off in a trail of gravel and dirt, Monroe let out the pent up breath he'd been holding.

'Jesus lad, you almost killed me when you took the gun,' he said. 'When did you know?'

'The moment I saw it,' De'Geer passed the *Glock 17* back over to his boss. 'It's the one Doctor Marcos stole from SCO 19, isn't it? She said she still wanted to make comparisons between ammunition and simunition markings in barrels.'

'Aye, that's the one,' Monroe took the gun back, placing it back into his jacket. Rosanna Marcos had 'acquired' the gun during an SCO 19 training session a few months back and, after using it to scare away Macca Byrne and his men when they attempted to attack Monroe in a Birmingham church, she'd kept it as a keepsake in her nightstand, where Monroe had himself borrowed it before heading to Edinburgh. 'What would you have done if they called your bluff?'

'The same as you,' De'Geer smiled. 'I would have shot him in the face and run like hell while he tried to wipe the paint from his eyes. Apparently it's really bad to do that, something about Ant and Dec?'

'Aye, in *Byker Grove,* PJ is shot—' Monroe started, but De'Geer shook his head.

'Sir, there's no point telling me about this,' he said. 'I looked it up, and it happened before I was born.'

'Well, now I feel bloody ancient,' Monroe patted De'Geer on the shoulder. 'But the evening isn't over yet. If we run, we can grab something to eat before the pubs shut. We need something to calm the adrenaline we're currently feeling.'

'And then?' De'Geer didn't want to comment on what he'd heard. That DCI Monroe had been on a wild goose chase, in relation to his believed grandniece. 'I'm guessing none of what you recorded can be used?'

Monroe pulled out his phone, having been quietly recording on the app since they were taken. Turning it off, he stared at the screen for a moment.

'It's good, and it'll get Lennie some shite, but I want the others,' he said. 'This McCavity, it's a name I keep hearing. If Lennie's gone, he'll just work with someone else.'

'So what next?'

'Next we get Derek Sutton to come visit us,' Monroe was already walking towards the main road. 'And we get some bloody answers.'

Monroe didn't mention that he wanted more than just family answers from Derek Sutton, though. He wanted truth about a house fire forty years ago, and why it warranted his death right after.

THE AMERICAN EMBASSY HAD BEEN HOUSED IN GROSVENOR Square in Central London since 1785, when John Adams became the first ambassador to the Court of St. James's, but after security concerns a few years back, it'd moved to a brand new, state-of-the-art complex on the South Bank, near Vauxhall Bridge, created specifically for the thousands of people who walked through its doors every day. Designed as a transparent crystalline cube set atop a monumental colonnade, the Embassy was twelve floors of office space held within a wall of laminated glazing and an outer envelope of transparent film, shaped to minimise solar glare. Even the interior garden you walked through to get to the entrance was specially created, inspired by different regions of the United

States, including the Canyonlands, the Gulf Coast, the Potomac River Valley and the Mid-Atlantic. Costing a billion dollars, all funded from sales of other US Embassy houses, it was indeed a magnificent structure.

Karl Schnitter understood it completely. This was a building with a *purpose*. This was a structure designed to help cool down in the summer and retain heat in the winter. It was a building that apparently created a physical representation of America's core democratic values of *transparency, openness,* and *equality*, although that was something he couldn't see too much of when looking up at it.

There were a few tourists still around; even though it was almost ten in the evening, the June sun had only recently set, and the streetlights bathed the building in a strange, ethereal glow. It was a great beast, and it wanted to sleep, but there was one more thing left to do before Karl could allow this.

With a determined stride, he started towards the main entrance, following what looked like a water feature on his right-hand side. At the glass doorway, a US Marine in his dress uniform stepped into view.

'Can I help you, sir?' he asked warily.

'Yes,' Karl smiled. 'I would like to speak to someone.'

'Office hours are over,' the Marine intoned. 'Come back tomorrow.'

'I would love to, but I made a promise, and by then I might have been found by another agency,' Karl replied cheerfully. 'Please let someone know that Karl Müller is here? I might be under the name Karl Schnitter.'

'As I said sir—'

'I know what you said,' Karl walked closer now. 'And I told you I would like to speak to someone. Let me be more specific here. I wish to speak to one of the many office workers and state officials here that actually have a head-quarters in Langley, Virginia, yes?'

Karl watched the Marine, noting the understanding now in the guard's eyes. By mentioning *Langley, Virginia,* Karl had asked to speak to whoever worked for the *CIA* in the building.

'That's right,' he said now, smiling. 'I am Karl Müller, and I would like to give myself up to you for multiple crimes and murders carried out over many decades.'

At this, the guard pulled up his assault rifle, training it on Karl.

'Now get me a handler, so I can finish this up and go to bed,' Karl continued, unfazed. 'It has been a very long day, and I would like my sleep.'

HAVERFORDWEST POLICE RARELY FOUND MUCH ACTION ON A weeknight. If anything, it was mainly nightclub or bar fights, the occasional misunderstanding, that sort of thing. And as for the city of St Davids? Well, Sergeant Owen remembered a month around ten years back where the greatest crime, written up in the local paper was that of a ladder being stolen.

A bloody *ladder*.

St Davids wasn't really a city; it was a town, little more than a village in fact. But, as Saint David himself had been born in a small hut only a mile or so away in St Nons, the church had become a cathedral, and in that moment a city had been created, because of the rule that a Cathedral can only be in a city, or something like that. Owen knew little about this sort of thing, even though he was devout Church of Wales. All he knew was St Davids was the smallest 'city' in the whole of the United Kingdom; a city with a roaring tourist trade, thanks to the upsurge in coastal activities and surfing.

Owen didn't surf. He'd always wanted to, but he'd blown his knee playing rugby, and you needed to be able to pop up onto the board, while the best he could usually manage was a slow crawl.

He was in a squad car, driving down Goat Street, heading out of the central—well, the *only* part of the city, and if he had to be brutally honest, he didn't really know what he was doing. All he knew was the front desk had a call from London, asking if officers could check a particular address, see if some woman was there and, if so, bring her in. It sounded like a waste of time, but one thing they had in Haverfordwest was time. And besides, it meant if she wasn't there, he could end his shift with a quick beer at *The Farmers Arms*.

The address in question was a property on Bryn Road, apparently a holiday cottage that'd been empty for close to a year now. However, as he pulled up outside the cream-painted stone building, he could see a light on. Walking to the door, he put his helmet on, mainly for appearance's sake, rapping three times before stepping back.

After a moment, the door opened and a woman, with slicked back wet hair over a towelling robe, stared out at him.

'What?' she asked, irritated.

Sergeant Owen looked at the image on his phone before looking back up at the woman in the doorway. The hair was cut differently, but that could be because it was wet. The woman was as close a match as she could be.

'Miss Pearce?' he said as professionally as he could muster. The woman, hearing the name, seemed to slump a little.

'Yes,' Francine Pearce admitted reluctantly, wiping a hand through her wet hair. 'What's going on?'

'I think you need to come with me,' Owen said. 'Once you get dressed, that is.'

And with this, the now no-longer-dead Francine Pearce swore silently to herself and walked away from the door, leaving Sergeant Owen alone as he waited.

18

HANDS-FREE INVESTIGATION

DECLAN HAD RECEIVED THE CALL FROM BULLMAN JUST AFTER midnight; not only had Karl Schnitter been taken in by the US authorities, but also a local bobby had spoken to a very much alive Francine Pearce, who was now sitting in a cell, held until questioning in the morning.

And, besides that and connected to the *actual* case, Tara Wilkinson had been found dead.

Basically, it'd been a busy night.

Declan offered to return to the office there and then, but Bullman had told him to get some rest but come in bright and early; with the Gala Dinner the following night, it was likely to be a very long day, and tired officers might cause issues when wrapping things up, especially at an event involving royalty.

Declan hadn't even considered he'd be seeing royalty, and this one thought kept him tossing and turning for much of the night. He made one call to Trix, as he'd promised, to let her know about both Karl and Francine, although Karl turning himself in to the Americans was no surprise to either of them. They both knew Karl had friends in the US agencies, ones who thought he would be a valuable asset; it was the reason Section D had taken him away in a van before the CIA arrived.

By now, the CIA had probably given him a new identity and a nice new house.

Of course, Trix already knew, and Declan disconnected wondering whether she'd intended to inform him before he called her, or whether she'd leave him in the dark.

Eventually, after struggling to sleep for most of the night, he ended up in the living room in his dressing gown, going through the paperwork that Charles Baker had given him. And, when Anjli had finally wandered down in a dressing gown at seven, looking like she'd had the best night of sleep ever to Declan's annoyance, they both showered and dressed, individually of course. After making some truly excellent and well-needed coffee from the machine, they drove back to Temple Inn in their separate cars, for by then Doctor Marcos had already emailed to go straight in, as there was nothing worth looking at in the restaurant.

While on the M4, Declan made use of his time alone.

First, he phoned DC Ross.

'*Phoning to confess?*' she said as an introduction, obviously recognising his number.

'I told you I didn't kill her,' he said. 'I'm really not the enemy here. Francine Pearce was found last night in St Davids, and is currently sitting in a cell in Haverfordwest.'

There was a silence down the line.

'*I don't have anything on this.*'

'No but you will,' Declan smiled. 'Consider this like the forensic report we had first. You're just a little behind in the details. Go ahead, call them. I'm sure they'd love to chat to you. Probably Francine, too. And if you need anything when you go after her—'

'*Hold on, go after who?*' Ross sounded confused through the car speakers.

'Tricia Hawkins,' he said calmly, as if he'd expected her to have already considered this. 'Come on, we both know she set up the phone, covered in blood. Francine might claim she's clueless, but you got played by someone. And if it's not Pearce pulling the strings, then it's Hawkins.'

He waited a moment to let that sink in.

'Personally, if I'd been made to look a fool, I'd be going after the culprit pretty quickly, and definitely before the press get hold of this, as they will.'

'*Are you telling me what to do, DI Walsh?*'

'No,' Declan sighed. 'And just for the record, I didn't tell DC Hart what to do, either. She chose to work with DCI Ford to steal millions in crypto coins. That wasn't me, and I'd appreciate you not blaming me for her greed.'

And with that parting shot, Declan had disconnected the call, immediately dialling the second number on his list for the morning.

'*Hawkins,*' the voice said down the line, a woman's tired voice. '*Who's this and how do you have this number?*'

'Hey, Trish,' Declan replied lazily. 'Declan Walsh here. You know, the guy you tried to set up and failed.'

'*I don't see a failure,*' Trisha's voice became more measured. '*And I'd like you to tell me where my friend is. I know you took her.*'

This was not the answer he expected, and it took a moment before he realised why she'd said such a thing.

Keep playing the game in case I'm recording you. Clever, Declan thought to himself.

'Don't worry,' he said. 'You're not on speaker, I'm on hands free and alone. Just wanted to give you the good news.'

'*What news?*'

'We found your friend,' Declan said, realising that he couldn't keep the smile from his lips. 'Could you imagine it? All that hassle hunting for her, and she was in her sister's old cottage all along.'

Again, he gave it a moment to sink in. He knew Trisha wouldn't have heard yet, because they had given Haverfordwest police strict instructions to bring Francine in for questioning, but then leave her in the cell, contacting nobody until further notice. And, at seven in the morning, there was little chance of anyone calling in yet. Trisha was on the back foot here, and he intended to make the most of it.

'Fun fact,' he continued. 'You spent a ton of summer breaks in that cottage, so I'm completely stunned that you didn't remember the place when giving your statement to the police.'

'*Must have slipped my mind,*' Trisha's voice was tight. She was angry. Declan grinned. *This was nothing. Time to really turn the screw.*

'I mean, you probably know *all* the hiding places.'

'*What's that supposed to mean?*'

'I mean, Trisha, that half an hour after the police took Francine to a police station fifteen miles away, and let her rot in a cell for the night while waiting for permission to talk to her, a team of very clever people, controlled remotely by someone with a real axe to grind and a personal knowledge of Pearce broke into the cottage and went through every room with a fine-tooth comb.'

There was a long silence on the other side.

'You'd be stunned at what they found,' Declan continued.

'Especially the fake IDs and passports. You know, the ones for when you pretend you're dead to screw over a detective and need to start a new life somewhere warm.'

'You're lying. You found nothing.'

The voice was icy, but trembling a little.

Trisha was scared.

'Interesting response, Declan mused aloud. 'Not actually denying that these things even existed. Well, must dash, you're about to have a very angry Detective Constable and her team hunt you down.'

'Why?'

Declan raised his voice so that the car's microphone caught every word.

'Because when you frame someone, you can be vague. There's plausible deniability which covers the cracks in a story. But when the victim is found alive and well, people start to question those cracks. Things like blood covered phones appearing out of nowhere, or random blood spatters in a police boot become more than evidence, they become *investigations*. Have fun with all that.'

And, his point made for a second time, he disconnected before Trisha Hawkins could reply.

Then, taking a deep breath, he dialled his third number. He'd wanted to do this the night before, but the thought of calling Liz and accepting another barrage of anger felt easier now he'd arranged the other ducks in a row.

'Dad?' Jess spoke through the speakers. *'You okay?'*

'Get your mum, put it on speaker,' Declan requested, waiting until Jess came back, telling him she'd done what he asked. 'Liz, Jess, it's over. Karl Schnitter gave himself up last night. He won't be coming for anyone ever again.'

There was what sounded like a held back sob down the line, and Liz spoke.

'I don't know what you did to sort this, but thank you,' she said. *'Thank you from both of us.'*

'I've asked the police to stay on guard, though,' Declan grinned. 'Jess is sixteen after all, and this gives us a great excuse to decide on who she dates—' he stopped, laughing as Jess started shouting through the speaker at him, saying how *he was mean and cruel* and *this was so unfair.*

'Hey, sorry about DCI Farrow.'

'What do you mean?' There was a strange tone in Liz's voice, something that immediately made Declan suspicious.

'I know you're not a fan, and he made a point of being involved,' Declan replied.

'Oh, yes,' Liz laughed nervously. *'That's fine. He's a good man.'*

Declan wanted to push, to see what was truly going on here, but, knowing that they were both safe, Declan made his farewells, promised to call Jess later and disconnected the phone for a third time.

He had one more phone call to make.

Dialling a number, he pressed *connect* and sat back in the driver's seat, waiting for an answer. The phone connected, but nobody spoke.

'I know you're there,' he said.

'Have you spoken to her yet?' The voice of Trix spoke now through the speakers. Declan nodded, realised that was pointless, and then replied.

'Yup, I reckon she's calling the troops right now.'

The plan had been simple when he called Trix the previous night; gain access to the cottage once Francine was out, and place tiny cameras all over the place before spooking Trisha and Francine to see what happened. There was no way they'd find hiding places in the cottage on their own without taking the entire place apart over days, weeks, even, mainly because there were so many small nooks and crannies that could be used. Movies lied in this respect; when people go through a house, it takes hours. It was always far easier to watch them do it for you.

'The moment I see Francine opening up anything, we've got them,' Trix replied. *'Chances are she'll open it, check it's okay, decide you're screwing around and then look to move things later on. Which gives us a chance to have a peek when we kick the doors in under anti-terrorism charges.'*

'You think they'll agree to it?'

'You saw what the Star Chamber did when they thought you and Kendis were threats,' Trix chuckled down the line. *'There's enough hatred of Francine and Rattlestone still in Westminster to enable that she'll get the VIP treatment. And, once we find the hidden holes, we'll work out what her plan was.'*

'Keep me in the loop,' Declan said before disconnecting. He almost felt sorry for Francine; she'd engineered the escape of Karl Schnitter to get at Declan, and in the process had taken down *Section D* agents. She might have felt that this wasn't a problem, but all she had done was body-blow Emilia Wintergreen, head of *Section D* and Monroe's ex-wife.

And when you'd pissed off the head of a covert and off-the-books agency, you were right royally screwed.

By now Declan was driving through London, winding his way through the traffic with the ease of a man who knew the journey like the back of his hand. He'd come in along the Embankment, dropping south off the A4 in Earls Court, and now drove past the Houses of Parliament, noting the early morning barricades being placed around the main gates. If the Queen, or one of the higher-up *Premier League* royals, was attending the dinner tonight, there'd be a ton of security. He'd have to remember this when driving back that night, maybe head south around Blackfriar's instead.

Something about this was itching at the back of his brain, and he knew there was an unspoken line here, something he hadn't considered. *What was it? Why was the security at Parliament so important to him?*

Declan tried to think back to the paperwork he'd been reading earlier that morning. Leroy had wanted to be better, more successful than Johnny Mitchell, that was always going to be known; Leroy was definitely the sort of man who'd take offence at an underling doing better than him, especially if this ended with the underling gaining one of those hard-to-get *By Appointment To* crests for their headed notepaper.

But was it enough to kill?

Declan had read Billy's conspiracy email, explaining how he believed Leroy Daniels had snuck back to Edinburgh and it fit the narrative, but at the same time, why risk it? Why not hire someone to do it? Or arrange for something bad to happen at a later time?

To go to all this length, with secret plane rides and doubles and all that, it felt more like something that had a far bigger payoff for the risk. Something that Tara Wilkinson and possibly even Harnish Patel wanted to be involved in, or at least were happy enough to be helping so they wouldn't call the authorities.

That itch was still there as Declan turned left onto the Embankment, passing Portcullis House. The last time he was here, he'd been welcomed as a friend by Charles Baker, a far cry from the concerned man in a corner of an outside terrace the previous day, but Declan was an unknown quantity at that point, DC Ross still claimed back then that Francine Pearce was dead, hidden somewhere, most likely under Declan's patio. Security would have been tight, and nobody would have—

Security.

The word flared up in his mind like a beacon. The itch he had was connected to security. What was the reason?

Declan almost crashed his Audi as he realised what it meant, the shock causing him to slam his brakes on suddenly. Waving an apology to the cab behind him, he started driving again, working through his hypothesis in his head.

Leroy didn't want to be the Chef for the Gala. *No,* he wanted it, his ego needed the validation. But it wasn't why he *needed* to be the Chef.

If he was the Chef, it meant he'd be at the Gala. Otherwise, he'd be on the outside looking in. To be the Chef meant he would have been at the Houses of Parliament, serving Cabinet MPs and royalty. The itch was there and Declan was so close to scratching it as he glanced at the folder beside him.

'I can see why Helen Cage broke up with Johnny Mitchell. If you think your parents had been royally screwed over by the Government to the point where dad dies, you wouldn't be over the moon about doing a fancy dinner for them either.'

Anjli's words from the previous night echoed through his mind. Maybe this wasn't about Leroy? Maybe this was about Helen, and a revenge mission?

Declan tapped the keys on his phone again; he was almost at the Command Unit, but he had an itch and it needed to be scratched now.

'Guv?' Billy's voice answered.

'Are you in the office?'

'I never left,' Billy replied. 'Crashed in the cot upstairs for a couple of hours.'

'Do you have a list of who's attending the Gala tonight?'

There was the sound of Billy tapping on the keyboard.

'Yup, who are we looking for?'

'The Foreign Secretary.'

A pause.

'Yup, she's there. Why?'

'I'm almost in. I'll come back to you when I arrive,' Declan disconnected the call, his mind racing. Marshall Howe had been pushing for Harnish and Helen to take over the Gala, an event where the woman who Helen believed had made the decision that effectively killed her father would be at.

But Leroy couldn't have known this. *Was Leroy using Helen too?* Tara hadn't seemed to have wanted it.

But Tara was also now dead.

And the itch in the back of Declan's mind was screaming to be scratched now.

19

DUNGEON CRAWLING

DE'GEER STRETCHED AS HE STOOD OUTSIDE *MONET*; THE DAY was still early, but he'd already spent an hour in the waiting area of Edinburgh City Chambers, sitting amongst eager couples looking to plan their weddings as, in full uniform, he arranged a meeting for noon the same day.

From there it had been a walk back to *Monet*, and what he believed to be a quick examination before returning to Monroe, most likely screaming at Derek Sutton in a café somewhere. De'Geer had no intention of being around for that, and so he smiled as, entering the restaurant-turned café, he nodded to the members of staff at the counter. He was hoping they remembered him from the previous evening; for once he was glad for the fact that, with his height and stature, he was hard to forget.

'I had a couple of questions, and I wanted to check something,' he said to a mid-thirties woman who identified herself as *Sandra with an S,* although De'Geer didn't really know how else to spell it. And, with Sandra beside him, they walked down into *Monet's* cellar and storeroom.

'Did you ever see this open?' he asked, kneeling beside the trap door in the floor, pulling at it. The wooden exit was solid and locked, and Sandra shook her head as she stared down at him.

'Nah, bloody thing gives me the creeps,' she said. 'John had an idea to turn whatever's underneath into some kind of speakeasy cafe, or a cabaret venue for the Fringe. There's a couple like this on South Bridge. Police had a look the morning they found the body, but it don't go anywhere and they were more interested in the skylight.'

De'Geer noted the use of *John*; yet another identity change for Johnny Mitchell.

'He worked here as a teenager, I hear?'

'Maybe, I dunno,' Sandra shrugged. 'I know he worked somewhere around here. But we didn't have that much time for chat. The launch was pretty full-on.'

De'Geer tugged at the door again. 'Do you have a key?'

'Yeah, hold on,' Sandra walked to the wall beside the door, pulling a bunch of keys from a hook beside it. 'It'll be one of these.'

De'Geer started to test the keys in the lock.

'Did you ever see John bring anyone down here?' he asked.

'All the bloody time,' Sandra half-chuckled. 'Well proud of it, he was. Never went in though, just opened the door and talked about the history. He has a map in his office with the tunnels on it. All found when he was a teenager.'

'Johnny Mitchell made the marks on the map?'

'Well yeah, there's not gonna be an official one now, is there?'

De'Geer nodded, trying another key. Teenage Johnny

Mitchell seemed quite the adventurer. He must have found this door while working here, and started exploring.

There was a click, and the key turned.

'Oh, and he brought the woman, Tara whats-her-face,' Sandra remembered. 'Again, I think he was just showing off.'

De'Geer pulled open the trap door, shining his torch into the hole. A steep staircase led down into the darkness. Taking a deep breath, he looked back at Sandra.

'Keep this open, yeah?' he asked.

'You're not going down there, are you?' Sandra was horrified. 'People have got lost down there. Died down there.'

'So keep the door open,' De'Geer smiled as he started down the stairs. 'I won't be long.'

The vault under the trap door wasn't as big as De'Geer had expected, and reminded him of the ones they'd seen under Greenwich. It was pitch black, musty smelling and, as De'Geer's torch scanned the walls, he could see years of graffiti on them. There was nothing around, and De'Geer understood why the police would have given this up as a lost cause.

The torch stopped, however, as he saw a small, torn piece of plastic and paper on the floor.

Walking over, De'Geer crouched beside it, being careful not to touch, in case it was relevant. It was small, easily missed, but unmistakable once De'Geer recognised it, looking around to see if the other parts of it was around. It wasn't; the killer had taken their rubbish with them, but forgotten this torn-off scrap.

It was the bottom half from the front packaging of a sandwich, the kind you saw in service stations or 'food to go' areas in shops; triangles of cardboard that held, within, a single, usually white bread sandwich. It had been torn away when the package was opened, and probably fell to the flor, missed as the killer ate. However, it was the worst part to leave, because in the bottom corner was a *best before* date; now showing the day after Johnny Mitchell's murder. With the short time frame for consuming that sandwich companies gave on these, it had to be around the time of the death when this was eaten.

Which meant it was likely that the killer was down here, and was waiting.

De'Geer pulled out a plastic forensics bag and carefully placed the piece within. There was a chance for fingerprints, and even if it wasn't connected, De'Geer had to assume so until proven wrong.

The scrap of paper now secured, De'Geer stepped back, scanning around. There was a dark mark on the wall a few yards down, as if a leak had trickled down it. From the smell though, De'Geer knew this was urine.

Someone sat down here, ate a meal and took a piss in the corner, the day that Johnny Mitchell died.

This couldn't be a coincidence. This had to be the way the killer got in. De'Geer couldn't see any signs of a second meal, so assumed it had to be one person. But which person?

De'Geer's torch shone on the east wall, revealing a doorway, leading into more communal cellars from the Seventeenth Century, and De'Geer knew he couldn't return just yet. The killer had to come in from somewhere, he just had to find where. And, rising up, he started eastwards, Lawnmarket itself somewhere above him as he made his way through the pitch black cellars.

The problem was, they weren't straight; there were small bends, turns, even junctions, and within five minutes, De'Geer realised with a small amount of nervousness that he was lost. He thought he could retrace his steps, but the certainty was gone. And now, in a tunnel that veered sharply to the right, heading southwards, his torch was starting to flicker.

'Don't you bloody dare,' he muttered as he shone it around desperately, looking for another exit. There had to be one.

And there was, to the east, a small wooden staircase that headed to a square door in the roof; another trapdoor, leading to God knows where. As the torch flickered again, De'Geer ran to it, scrambling up the stairs as, to his horror the torch spluttered and died.

Now in pitch blackness, De'Geer hammered on the wooden door above him.

'Hey!' he shouted. 'Hey there! Police! Open up! Can anyone hear me!'

There were no sounds above him, and De'Geer cursed his own stupidity as he kept hammering on the wood. 'Come on! Open up!'

With a realisation he pulled out his phone; there was no signal, but it did give him a little light as he kept banging—

And then he was blinded by light as the door opened and a young woman in a black shirt and jeans stared down at him.

'Jesus, there was someone!' she shouted to the side before turning back to De'Geer. 'What the bloody hell are you doing down there?'

De'Geer climbed gratefully out of the vault, shaking himself.

'Working a case,' he said. 'Torch went. Where am I?'

'Pumproom of the Halfway House on Fleshmarket Close,' the woman replied. 'Where were you wanting to be?'

'I'm following the path south, looking for a way out,' De'Geer explained.

'Then you're bloody lucky I heard you, because there ain't no way out down there,' she said. 'We do ghost tours during the Festival. All that's south is a metal door.'

At De'Geer's confused expression, she smiled.

'Loads of small streets got covered over down here when they built up,' she explained. 'Because of the height between streets, you can have a cellar look out over another building's garden. That's Edinburgh for you. But the streets weren't filled in. And you used to be able to go from here into the South Street Bridge Vaults.'

'Used to be able?'

'Yeah,' the woman pointed to one of the walls, and De'Geer assumed she was pointing south. 'Tron Kirk was built over several small closes including Marlin's Close, which you can see inside it. And when they built Hunters Square, some of the buildings used the alleys in the foundations. One of those is now an Ibis Hotel on Blair Street, and the door is a blocked off exit in an access tunnel.'

'So the metal door at the end stops at the Ibis?'

'Yeah,' the woman laughed. 'Hell of an anticlimax, eh?'

'Actually, it helps me a lot,' De'Geer was already walking to the bar's main door. 'Which way—'

'South down Fleshmarket, cross Cockburn, carry on to the High Street and then down between the Starbucks and the Kirk,' the woman smiled. 'You need anything more, come ask. I'm Alice. Anything.'

Resisting the urge to flirt back, De'Geer followed the directions and, after a few minutes of walking found himself outside the Ibis Hotel. He looked around Blair Street; there weren't any CCTV cameras that he could see on the hotel walls, and so he entered, asking to speak to the manager, his uniform the only calling card he needed.

After a couple of minutes the duty manager, a middle-aged, short man with red hair appeared and, after listening to De'Geer's request, took him into the bowels of the building.

'We don't use this floor anymore,' he said as they walked into what could only be described as a sub-sub-basement corridor. 'Nobody comes down here at all, really. It's mainly used to store chairs and tables for when we don't have weddings on.'

He was right; the old corridor was filled on either side with piles of stacked chairs and flattened, round tables. However, halfway down, the duty manager stopped, pointing at a pile of chairs stacked up on the left.

'There's a door behind all this,' he explained. 'No idea what it's for or why, but that's the one you want. I don't think I've ever seen it opened, and I've been here ten years.'

Declan examined the floor.

'Well someone's been near it,' he said, pointing at scuff marks. 'These chairs have been moved.'

With the duty manager's help, De'Geer pulled the stack of chairs out, creating a gap behind them. And, once he slid through into it, De'Geer saw that this was the exact stack needed to move to get to the door's padlock.

'It's been jimmied,' he said, carefully removing it with a pen, showing the duty manager. The padlock was open, but had been made to look as if it was closed. Now pulling on latex gloves and placing the lock in his hand, De'Geer tried closing it, only to see that it sprung open. 'Probably took a screwdriver to it. But behind all this, nobody would know. Are there cameras down here?'

The duty manager shook his head as De'Geer opened the metal door, staring into the blackness beyond.

'I don't suppose you have a torch, do you?' he asked.

* * *

They walked for about five minutes northwards, through the dank passage that led from the metal door, the duty manager following De'Geer reluctantly, as if taking personal responsibility for this open door on hotel premises.

Eventually De'Geer stopped, nodding as he shone the torch, provided by the duty manager, around.

'That staircase is the one I went up earlier,' he said, pointing at the corner of the cavern. 'Which means if I came from the left, the Ibis does connect all the way to Monet.'

'Wait, you mean the restaurant the chef was killed in?' The duty manager paled now in the torchlight, and De'Geer realised he was finally realising the full extent of the Ibis Hotel's role in this.

'Exactly,' he replied. 'Someone could have entered the tunnels through your hotel, and made their way to Lawnmarket.'

He turned to walk back, the nervous duty manager following.

'Do you have CCTV in your hotel?' he asked.

'Of course,' the duty manager looked affronted at the question.

'How long do you keep it?'

'Fourteen days.'

De'Geer cursed. Johnny Mitchell's murder had occurred before that, so CCTV wasn't an option anymore. Maybe the padlock had some fingerprints on it, or perhaps the fast food bag had DNA somewhere, but all De'Geer currently had was a potential escape route. As yet, there was no proof.

'You might want to try The Tron though,' the duty manager, now eager to help added. 'The pub across the street. They put new cameras up last month that look over the parking spaces, they might keep footage longer?'

De'Geer nodded thanks at this, although he reckoned it'd be a fool's errand. The problem with cases like this was the video evidence; with cameras now recording in high definition, nobody kept footage that wasn't relevant anymore, clearing memory for the next batch.

Still, nothing ventured and all that.

They'd almost made it to the doorway when De'Geer's torch caught a flash of white fabric to the side, low down, against the tunnel wall. Motioning for the duty manager to stop, he knelt down beside the item, shining the torch on it.

A tea towel, likely taken from *Monet* and wrapped around something slim had fallen onto the floor. Using a pen to unwrap it, De'Geer stared down, taking a breath as he realised what he was looking at.

An eight-inch chef's knife, discarded on the floor.

Pulling out his phone, De'Geer cursed again. There was still no signal down here.

'I need you to do me a favour,' he said to the duty manager. 'Go up to your office, or reception, the closest place a phone is, and call the police. In particular, DCI Hendrick. You got that?'

The duty manager nodded dumbly.

'What do I tell him?'

'Tell him that PC De'Geer needs him to send a forensic unit and a Scene of Crime Officer here immediately,' De'Geer replied. 'Right here. Not outside, but to the metal door and this knife.'

'What is it?' The duty manager stepped closer to see, but De'Geer held up a hand to stop him.

'If I'm right,' he whispered, 'I think this is the knife that killed Johnny Mitchell. And if it is, then the killer definitely entered and escaped from your hotel.'

He rose, stepping back.

'I'd start talking to your staff,' he said. 'If you don't have CCTV, we're going to be relying on a lot of witness statements. Anyone who remembers anything around that time would be incredibly helpful.'

'We get hundreds of people walk through the hotel each day,' the duty manager protested weakly. 'We can't remember them all.'

'Then you'd better hope we find another way to catch the killer you let wander around your hotel,' De'Geer. 'Go on! Call the police now!'

The duty manager ran off as De'Geer stared down at the knife. He didn't know much about blades, but he knew this didn't match the ones in Johnny Mitchell's collection, still in his office. It looked expensive, too. De'Geer wanted to leave, to phone Monroe and ask for advice, but he knew he had to secure the scene until Hendrick arrived.

Looking at his watch, he sighed. Just over two hours until the meeting he'd arranged at noon.

This was going to be tight. But on a plus note, at least the murder enquiry was advancing.

Just not in the way he'd expected.

20

DEADLINE DAY

'Right then, we need to go over this fast because I think we're further behind than we thought,' Declan said as he entered the briefing room.

'Wow, don't sugarcoat anything,' Anjli grinned. 'Channel your inner Monroe.'

Declan fought the urge to smile back; after all, he was indeed trying to mimic Monroe in his absence. In the briefing room were Anjli and Billy, both in their usual spots, DC Davey sitting where Declan usually sat and Doctor Marcos and Bullman standing near the door, as if guarding it.

'First off, parish notices,' Bullman said from the doorway. 'Tom Marlowe has been taken off the critical list and is now stable.'

There was a murmur of gratefulness at this, as Tom was a valued outside asset of the team, if only because he annoyed Monroe every time he arrived.

'Second, Francine Pearce has been found alive and well,' Bullman continued, nodding at Billy, 'thanks to the tireless actions of our resident hackmaster. And apparently a certain

DC Ross is so ticked off she's been made a fool of, she's already requested access to Trisha Hawkins phone records.'

'Sounds like she's got a new target,' Anjli nodded. 'Good.'

'Finally, Karl Schnitter, aka Karl Müller, has been taken into custody by the US Embassy, and we're waiting to hear what their plans are for him. If it's anything like last time, he'll likely disappear into the system, never to be heard from again, and I'm happy with that.'

'I spoke with him before he did this,' Declan added, noting the surprised faces that now watched him, and the cold emotionless expression of a likely furious Bullman as he spoke. 'He was the one that confirmed Charles Baker's message that Pearce was at Sarah Hinksman's holiday cottage. He'd apparently been there earlier that day to put things right.'

'Do you know what he meant by that?'

Declan shook his head.

'Probably nothing good, but we'll get back to that later,' he looked at Doctor Marcos. 'What do you have from the body?'

'A severe case of déjà vu,' Doctor Marcos admitted. 'On examination, Tara Wilkinson had a fatal amount of tetrodotoxin in her system, the same poison that killed Leroy Daniels and placed Marshall Howe into a coma.'

'She was fine when I saw her earlier,' Anjli mused. 'Maybe she took it after?'

'Time of death was around eight last night,' Doctor Marcos continued. 'Going on what happened with the other two attacks, I believe she ingested the poison around five, maybe six at the latest.'

'After I was there,' Anjli noted this down.

'Who was there when you left?' Declan asked.

Anjli considered this.

'Just the pot cleaner, Darryl Carr,' she replied. 'He was cleaning up, I got the impression he was leaving as soon as he was done. We checked in later and he'd gone to a family event almost directly after speaking with me.'

'Could Tara have eaten something else?'

'Possible,' Doctor Marcos nodded. 'We won't know until we've performed a full autopsy, but I don't think she ate a full meal or anything. When Harnish Patel arrived, he had a fast food bag for her. She'd apparently texted him asking for a milkshake and an apple pie.'

'Maybe she just wanted something sweet,' Declan mused. 'What did forensics find on the scene?'

'Nothing,' Doctor Marcos looked at DC Davey to answer this, and Davey stood up.

'Place was spotless,' she explained. 'Patel was still there when we arrived, and he explained the restaurant had been closed, so only two or three people had been in since we visited the previous day.'

'Darryl was really going to town when I arrived,' Anjli nodded. 'So it makes sense that things were clean.'

'Or he was cleaning a murder instrument,' Bullman muttered.

'Literally the only out-of-place item in the whole restaurant was a teaspoon in the sink,' Davey read from her notes. 'Probably used in a cup of tea or coffee.'

'If it was, it was after I left,' Anjli added. 'As I said, that place was spotless.'

'Have we checked the spoon?' Declan asked. 'I mean, we still don't know how the poison was passed to Leroy Daniels and Marshall Howe, so if a cup of tea did it...'

'It's with the lab, they're looking now,' Davey nodded.

'Might take a while though, as they're pretty backed up.'

'Pressure them to go as fast as they can, and check if anyone found any honey there,' Declan added.

'That's pretty specific,' Bullman commented. 'Care to share with the class?'

'I think we need to find Helen Cage and have a chat with her, Ma'am,' Declan turned to look at his superior. 'The paperwork we have from the Gala Dinner committee shows that Michelle Rose, the current Conservative Foreign Secretary is one of the high table guests of honour at the dinner tonight, and she's the same MP who personally turned down Helen's father's request for more Manuka bush cuttings. Because he wasn't able to do this, the business almost went under and he eventually died of a heart attack, brought on by stress resulting from this.'

'You're thinking Helen Cage might have set this up so that she could poison the Foreign Secretary?' Doctor Marcos frowned. 'That's a hell of a long way round to get to her target, especially as the poison is tasteless. She could have probably found a way to doctor food elsewhere.'

'If the targeted victim is *only* Michelle Rose, then yes,' Declan nodded. 'But Helen blamed the Government, plural. If you want to take out an entire Cabinet, then this is the perfect way to do this.'

'Christ, you're not talking murder, you're talking *terrorism*,' Doctor Marcos was already tapping onto her phone, sending a message across to the main lab. 'But that's a slippery slope to slide down, as you know personally.'

'I'm aware,' Declan agreed. 'So let's go through what we have already. Johnny Mitchell was killed in his restaurant in Edinburgh, and currently the lead suspect is Leroy Daniels.'

'Who's dead,' Anjli noted.

'And can't defend himself,' Declan looked over at her. 'But, from what Billy found out, there's every chance Leroy was able to come over from Dubrovnik on a private charter plane, kill Johnny Mitchell, dump the weapon and then return, hoping that nobody would be the wiser.'

'And it would have worked if he hadn't burned his hand,' Billy was already working on his laptop as he spoke. 'we definitely have a lookalike there for a couple of days, and it gives Leroy Daniels enough time to do what's needed to be done and leave.'

'Agreed,' Declan looked back to the group. 'But here's the thing. With Leroy dead, we don't know why he did it. Was it to kill a rival to gain the Gala Dinner job? Was it something more? We need to find out. Because if it's the former, then we have a solid suspect that works through the whole thing.'

'Helen Cage.'

'Who was Johnny's girlfriend but left when he announced he was taking on the Gala. Which, considering her recent bereavement at the time, was probably a major trigger. Who then worked for Leroy, as he went off-script in his war with his former student.'

'But Harnish hired her, not Leroy,' Anjli added. 'Although Tara, the manager of the restaurant didn't seem to know this, and from the sounds of things wouldn't have hired her if she had a choice.'

'Tara who also allegedly arrived in Edinburgh, begging with Johnny to allow Leroy to join in,' Declan replied. 'There's definitely something odd going on there, and with her now dead, we can't ask her about it, or ask her how much she knew about Leroy's plans to kill Johnny Mitchell.'

'Hold on, she went to Edinburgh?' Billy was flipping through his notes now. 'How do we know this?'

'It's in the committee notes,' Anjli raised up the folder that Charles Baker had given them. 'Apparently Tara turned up in Edinburgh, trying to convince Johnny to allow Leroy to be involved.'

'Hold on,' Billy was reading through emails now. 'I'm sure this matches something Monroe found from DCI Hendrick—'

He stopped at a line.

'Hendrick said the kitchen staff gave statements where a woman from London came to visit Johnny.'

'Tara. It has to be.'

'It was, as she even told them her name in a *do you know who I am* kind of way, but Hendrick said that witnesses claimed she said in a closed room *she needed him*, that *she risked everything for him*, before leaving.'

Declan looked at the room.

'Who did Tara need and how did she risk everything? Was it her husband, her boss, or even Johnny himself? We need to find that out.'

'If Tara was in on it, it makes sense that Harnish was too,' Billy mused. 'But I can't believe that Helen Cage would be so happy to be involved in some kind of revenge fantasy that killed her ex-boyfriend.'

'Maybe she wasn't?' Declan replied, leaning against the plasma screen, which burst into activity at the touch, posting up image after image until Declan jumped away, embarrassed.

'Sorry,' he said sheepishly as Billy closed the screen, rebooting it. 'But I mean what I said. Maybe she wasn't happy, or even wasn't involved? After all, if we go on the belief that Leroy killed Johnny, then a few days later someone kills him, we open up other options. Retaliation, perhaps?'

'But Helen wasn't at the pub meal, and it had to be someone there,' Doctor Marcos replied. 'Goddammit, I hate it when things get complicated.'

'I don't think it is,' Declan shook his head. 'I think we're missing something, and because we are, we're not seeing the straight line.'

'Something else,' Billy tapped on the screen, and an image of a teenage Johnny Mitchell appeared. 'I found out why he went to Edinburgh. It seems that he grew up near there and as a teenager worked weekends in a café on Lawnmarket. Can you guess the address?'

'You're kidding,' Anjli shook her head.

'Nope, apparently he'd always loved working there and, when the old owner sold up, he put in a cash offer immediately, selling up to move there.'

'So his move wasn't to do with Helen then?' Bullman asked. In reply, Billy shrugged.

'Might have been a catalyst, Ma'am,' he replied. 'But he was going there regardless.'

'De'Geer mentioned in an email that there's a ton of tunnels under Old Town,' Davey suggested. 'Maybe one was used by Leroy Daniels to get in?'

'Worth a look,' Declan nodded. 'Billy, email De'Geer and get him to go potholing.'

'Got something else, Guv,' Billy was reading an email on his screen. 'Apparently Marshall Howe has finally woken up and is talking. Well, croaking, really.'

'Right then,' Declan nodded. 'We need to have a chat with him. Anjli? Go speak to Howe, see if he knows how the textra-whatsitcalled—'

'*Tetrodotoxin,*' Doctor Marcos quietly corrected.

'Yes, that,' Declan nodded at her with a smile. 'We need to

find out if he had any idea how the poison went into his system. Billy? Find me Helen Cage. We need to speak to her right now. Doctor Marcos? Find out how Tara ingested the poison. What else?'

'We should speak to Harnish,' Anjli suggested. 'Although that could be tough right now. And confirm that Darryl washed all the spoons?'

'Right then, you know your roles, let's get to it,' Declan nodded, half to himself. 'And see if Monroe can speak to any of the staff at *Monet*, maybe anyone who worked in Richmond. I want to know if Tara and Johnny were a thing after all, and whether he ever talked about his time working there to her.'

DEREK SUTTON SAT IN THE CAFÉ AND, FOR THE FIRST TIME IN all the years that Monroe had known him, he looked embarrassed.

'I didn't know what to do,' he said. 'I needed to get someone to look after her, put the screws on Lennie.'

'And you couldn't do this yourself?' Monroe asked, sipping from a mug of builder's tea. They were in a greasy spoon trucker stop south of Edinburgh; a place where nobody would think twice about two men, one in a suit, one in a T-shirt having a chat. Among the other residents of the café this particular morning included truck drivers, travelling salesmen, door knocker crews preparing for the day and engineers about to start their rounds.

The only person who wasn't there was De'Geer, mainly because he had packed nothing that wasn't police uniform orientated, so Monroe had sent him back to Hendrick, to see if anything else could be learnt about Johnny Mitchell's last days on Earth, as well as investigating the tunnels that Monroe had seen marked on the map in Mitchell's office. There probably wasn't anything, but Monroe decided having one of the drawn lines go through *Monet* was something they should look into, in case it helped in any way.

Billy had sent a message explaining there was a strong chance that Johnny Mitchell had been having an affair with Tara Wilkinson, and judging from the way the conversation went, Monroe was actually glad he was hundreds of miles away right now, even if he felt sorry for Declan having to shoulder it all.

'I don't do that sort of thing any more, Ali,' Sutton dug into his breakfast, a greasy Scottish fry-up that included piles of haggis and black pudding. Just watching it made Monroe's arteries harden, and his mouth water a little. 'I've got too much to live for out here.'

'Like what?'

'Like not being back inside,' Sutton looked up. 'Seriously. I won't go back.'

'How did you find out?' Monroe asked. 'That she was yours?'

'One of the Twins told me,' Sutton explained, namedropping Johnny and Jackie Lucas, the gangland 'twins' of East London for the last thirty or so years, who Sutton worked for before being arrested and imprisoned. The worst kept secret in the London underworld was that it was Johnny, however, that ruled everything with Jackie as his 'Mister Hyde' multiple personality, one that came out now and then to scare the living hell out of everyone with violence and death. Suffice to say, people knew there weren't any real twins, but still agreed there were.

You never wanted 'Jackie' to come looking for you.

'They could have told me,' Monroe mused. 'That you were a lying bastard.'

'Och, Ali, you've always known I was a lying bastard,' Sutton grinned. 'Your problem was that you always wanted to believe me.'

He placed the cutlery down for the moment.

'Lennie's doing bad things,' he said. 'I get that Claire needs to get out of there and fast, but Christ, man, she's actually doing something worthwhile, fighting for something important. I think she might be the first Sutton to do that.'

'That's because she's a Doyle,' Monroe muttered. 'It was a shitty thing you did, Derek. I dropped everything to come here.'

'I know, and I'm sorry,' Sutton replied, and Monroe didn't for one second think he was. 'But I knew the moment I poked my nose in, I'd be recognised as the guy who whacked his brothers.'

'You shouldn't say things like that in front of a DCI.'

'I didn't say I *did* it, I said they'd recognise me as the guy they believed did it.'

Monroe almost laughed.

'Look,' he continued. 'I know you thought you were doing a good thing, but you used me. And you made me think I had family. Now, I want to sort Lennie out, but if you want to help Claire, you need to help me, yeah?'

'All I know is violence and pain,' Sutton looked at the plate as he mopped up the baked beans sauce with some toast. 'You think you'll need that?'

'Actually, I very much think we will,' Monroe grinned. 'I think it's time for Lennie Wright to remember exactly why his brothers feared Derek Sutton and the Monroe brothers.'

He stopped, the smile fading.

'On that note,' he whispered. 'Lennie spoke to me in the Kirkyard yesterday, said that the hit that took out Kenny was meant for me. Know anything about that?'

Sutton carried on eating.

'Dammit, Derek, did I do something without realising?'

Derek Sutton placed his cutlery down and looked at Monroe.

'Brigid Wright,' he said. 'Lennie's sister.'

'I know of her but I never met her.'

'Sneaky little bitch, real curtain twitcher. Liked to spy on people and grass them up to her brothers. Had a habit of climbing up onto decrepit buildings and watching with binoculars.'

The words *decrepit buildings* made Monroe's blood turn cold.

'The fire,' he whispered. 'The old warehouse. Was she on it?'

'Nobody knows, as the Wrights didn't want anything said,' Sutton replied. 'A body was found though.'

'Christ!' Monroe leaned back. 'How am I only hearing about this now?'

'Because two days later, they killed Kenny and all hell broke loose,' Sutton replied. 'By the time it came out that Brigid had been there, you were off to London. And there was no proof that *you'd* actually lit the fire.'

'You know I did.'

'I told them I didn't,' Sutton shrugged. 'And with Kenny gone, they decided it was an eye for an eye, kin for kin.'

'Kenny died because of me,' Monroe felt faint. 'I didn't even check the building. What if others had been there?'

'Then I don't think you'd have got into the police, pal,'

Sutton smiled. 'Look, Brigid snuck in and would have grassed us up. She got caught in the fire and she died. It wasn't your fault.'

'That might be how you sleep at night, but I'm not made like that,' Monroe growled. There was a commotion outside, and Monroe looked up to see De'Geer, in his uniform, striding to the door.

'Christ, the bairn can't even blend into the surroundings,' he muttered as he rose, waving De'Geer back out of the café as he followed him outside. 'I thought you were seeing Hendrick and booking our meeting?'

'I did,' De'Geer was excited. 'Booked us for around noon, straight in and out. But I had a thought about the *ghost*, and how he came and went.'

Monroe went to reply, but then stopped, realising it was far easier to just let De'Geer explain.

'Go on.'

'So the map was right, and the trapdoor in the storeroom does go down into an old cellar,' De'Geer explained. 'I had someone find me the spare key and checked.'

'Surely the police would have done that,' Monroe replied. De'Geer nodded.

'The woman in *Monet* said they did, but half-heatedly,' he explained. 'They were convinced it was a robbery gone wrong and focused on the skylight.'

'So, what did you find then?'

De'Geer looked around, as if scared someone was about to scoop his news. 'There's a torn piece of service station sandwich wrapping down there, and someone had a piss against the wall.'

'So it's being used by teenagers or the homeless?' Monroe shrugged. 'That's been happening for years now.'

'The date on the torn wrapping matches the days around Mitchell's murder, so this wasn't years ago, Guv. I think someone spent hours down there, waiting for midnight, having a snack, attending their call of nature...' De'Geer left the moment hanging.

'Christ,' Monroe muttered. 'Of course. That's how Leroy got in. But what about the broken skylight?'

'Probably a red herring, created by the killer,' De'Geer, now in full forensics mode explained. 'Problem with a broken window Guv, is the glass goes the direction of the force. So you break a normal window from the inside, glass falls on the outside. But the skylight was above, and if you broke it from outside or inside—'

'The glass would be taken by gravity and fall back in,' Monroe nodded. 'Good work.'

'I haven't even started,' De'Geer puffed out his chest as he continued. 'I took a torch and had a look around. The cellars lead east and turn south where I found a pub on Fleshmarket Close.'

'Another trapdoor to a cellar?'

De'Geer nodded. 'They explained that under Lawnmarket were a ton of paved over streets and tunnels from when they rebuilt the city, ones which went all the way to the Edinburgh Vaults, but stopped at a metal door connected to the Ibis Hotel. I went down into the sub-basement with the duty manager, and someone definitely entered through there, as the lock was broken and I found this.'

Reaching into hs jacket, De'Geer pulled his phone out, showing a photo of an eight-inch knife, resting on a tea towel, itself on the dusty ground of a cellar.

'Christ,' Monroe muttered. 'Is that—'

'An eight-inch chef's knife,' De'Geer was so proud of this,

he looked like he'd explode. It was beside a wall, probably fell out of a bag when the killer ran from the scene of the crime, and the tea towel muffled the sound.'

Monroe shook his head with admiration.

'Jesus, laddie,' he said. 'You solved the murder while I had breakfast.'

De'Geer smiled. 'And I have more, Guv. So, the killer escaped into an access tunnel under the *Ibis Hotel* on Blair Street.'

Monroe nodded. 'Did you get CCTV?'

'Not from the hotel, as they only keep the footage for two weeks,' De'Geer admitted. 'However, there's parking on the street, and a camera on the pub opposite, who keep footage for a month.'

'Okay, so what did we see on their CCTV?' Monroe asked. 'You're gaining a flair for the bloody dramatic from Declan.'

'It's a twenty-four-hour camera, and the Thursday after Johnny Mitchell died, you can see a car parking up on Blair Street at six-fifteen in the morning, leaving shortly after seven-thirty.'

'And this is important how?' Monroe rubbed at his eyes.

'I didn't Get a clear view of the driver, as they were covered up and had a hoodie on, but the car was a *2020 Audi Q5*,' De'Geer replied. 'Registration was held in the name of Harnish Patel, address in London.'

'Chef Patel was here at six in the morning?'

'Looks like it, sir,' De'Geer grinned as he finished. 'I believe the ghost that the cleaner 'heard' was actually Harnish Patel, leaving the restaurant through the cellar, seven hours after Johnny Mitchell was killed.'

21

BEDSIDE MANNERISMS

ANJLI KNEW *THE ROYAL LONDON HOSPITAL* IN WHITECHAPEL well; it was the hospital where Monroe had been brought after being beaten within an inch of his life by DI Frost a few months earlier.

Marshall Howe was likely to be in the same ACCU as Monroe had been in; the *Adult Critical Care Unit* was a ward at the back of the modern looking red-brick and glass building she walked into, waving her warrant card at anyone who looked official within the reception area, a wide expanse of glass and marble that, with its high glass ceiling, felt more like an airport terminal or exhibition hall than a hospital. And, now having informed the reception of her arrival, she headed to the elevators that would take her to the fourth floor of the South Tower on *Lift Core 5*.

The elevator doors opened out onto a shared waiting area, and Anjli turned through a door to the right that led into a bridge corridor, finding herself now in a familiar corridor with two options; one was to Ward 4E on the right, and on the opposite side, around a corner to the left was

Ward 4F. A nurse walked past, so Anjli waved her warrant card, stopping him.

'Marshall Howe?' she asked.

'Ward 4F,' the nurse replied, pointing off to the left.

Nodding thanks, Anjli entered the ACCU, the same one in fact that Monroe had been in, walking past the four bays with four beds in each, where privacy was nothing more than a screen around the bed, and six side rooms for single patients, heading towards the rooms to the sides where one room, a single patient room had the door open, with Marshall Howe, clearly visible inside, being tended to by another nurse.

'Marshall Howe?' Anjli said as she entered, waving the ID to both Howe and the nurse. 'I'm DS Kapoor. I was told you're well enough to talk?'

'I am,' croaked Howe as he reached to the side and picked up a plastic bottle of water, the size and style of a plastic sports bottle and sipped at it, groaning.

'God, my throat hurts,' he complained croakily.

'You're lucky it's just that,' Anjli responded and Howe nodded.

'They told me that Leroy died,' he said. 'Was it—'

'The poison? Yes,' Anjli nodded, but Howe, annoyed at being interrupted shook his head.

'No, no, was it slow?' he eventually managed.

'I don't know,' Anjli replied carefully, glancing at the nurse. 'Although reports state that death from tetrodotoxin isn't exactly speedy, if you know what I mean.'

'Shame,' Howe shook his head sadly. 'He was a prick, but he didn't deserve to go out like that. He wasn't supposed to die.'

The last part of the sentence set off warning bells in Anjli's head as she watched the ailing man in the bed.

'Wasn't supposed to die?' she asked as she pulled out her notebook. 'Would you like to explain?'

'The patient has just woken from a coma,' the nurse said, as if trying to minimise anything that Howe had said. Anjli, however, turned and glared at her, and the nurse wisely shut up.

Howe, looking up at the ceiling, tears forming at the corners of his eyes, didn't.

'It was supposed to be a small amount,' he said. 'Enough to screw him over for a few days.'

He waved at his bed.

'Like this.'

'You knew he was being poisoned?' Anjli exclaimed. 'Or are you assuming?'

'I knew,' Howe replied sadly. 'I know because I did it.'

'Are you admitting to the murder of Leroy Daniels?' Anjli was reeling here, not expecting this revelation. However, Howe shook his head.

'I—well, it's not like that,' he said. 'I wasn't trying to kill him. Just wanted to teach him a lesson, get him out of the way.'

'You didn't want him running the Gala Dinner.'

'No,' Howe nodded gently, the effort obvious on his face. 'He didn't deserve it after what he did.'

'And what did he do?' Anjli moved closer, softening her voice, turning on her voice recording app. Howe simply shrugged.

'He killed Johnny. My Johnny.'

'And you know this how?'

'Because Leroy told me,' Howe said. 'Well, he told everyone, and then *they* told me. He was drunk, it was Christmas, and he said that if Johnny urinated on his chips one more time, he'd kill him. Stab in the chest with a kitchen knife, looking at him in the eyes as he did so.'

'And you, or rather *they,* believed he was serious?'

'Leroy Daniels was a bastard, but he always carried out what he promised,' Howe whispered. 'And he promised to kill Johnny for taking the Gala gig from him. And then a couple of weeks ago, Johnny was stabbed. In the chest. With a knife.'

'While Leroy was in Dubrovnik.'

'Yeah, convenient,' Howe started to chuckle but stopped, groaning as he reached for the water again. 'He killed Johnny and the others on the committee handed him the Gala like a reward. I didn't think that was right.'

'You wanted Harnish Patel.'

Howe shifted in the bed, facing Anjli.

'I made no secret of that,' he said. 'Harnish and Johnny between them made *Essence* what it was, and Leroy took the credit. It's why Johnny eventually left. But even then Leroy couldn't let it lie. He chased Johnny out of London. Chased him out of England. He tried to take back anything that Johnny had, which he believed was his—'

'Helen Cage?'

'Yes, that for a start,' Howe nodded. 'Only when Johnny was back home in Scotland did the harassment stop. And even then Leroy was still furious that Johnny got the Gala gig. He killed him for nothing, too.'

'How so?'

'The menu was set, and Johnny bought the food months back,' Howe's voice was becoming a croaky whisper. 'We hired Leroy to be a pair of safe hands. He wasn't supposed to change the menu. We'd given the menu to the *Queen,* for

God's sake. You don't tell the Queen there's been a change. Arrogant sod turned up and demanded a reprint of the menu, saying he had a whole load of new ideas. We pointed out—'

Howe stopped, a coughing fit overcoming him.

After a moment, though, he was ready to continue.

'Sorry,' he wheezed as he sipped on more water. 'We pointed out it was impossible and he stormed out. But we knew before he even turned up that he was going to be a nightmare. That's why I did it.'

'Poisoned him.'

Howe nodded.

'He killed Johnny,' he wheezed. 'Bastard needed to pay.'

'You could have called the police.'

'I intended to,' Howe nodded. 'I wanted him to suffer first, though. If he was brought in after the Gala Dinner, he'd still have done the Gala Dinner. And if it'd been before, there was a chance he'd have got out of it. Better to strike.'

'And what was Johnny to you?'

'A friend, nothing more,' Howe replied. 'Critics don't get many. Johnny understood me. I tried to help his career.'

'Did you recommend him for the meal?'

Howe nodded again.

'I've done a few meals for Parliament now,' he said. 'God knows why they use me. Probably because Baroness Jones has a crush. But I'm the 'food expert' that they know, and I'm cheaper than the guy from *The Times* so my word has sway. They still had to *beauty contest* it, but Johnny won. Probably because he was cuter.'

'Leroy wasn't happy?'

'My dear, Leroy wouldn't have been happy even if he'd won,' Howe shook his head sadly. 'Prick never knew a good thing when he had it. He'd fold a flush because it wasn't a royal.'

'So how did you manage it?' Anjli asked. 'The poisoning?'

'In his sandwiches when I picked them for him,' Howe admitted. 'I had a small bottle, a phial of tetrodotoxin on me, and I popped a couple of drops onto Leroy's sandwiches when I chose them for him. Not much, just a little, exactly what she told me.'

'She?' Anjli looked up at this. 'Who's she?'

'Just an expert I asked about the drug,' Howe was floundering a little. 'I wanted a second opinion, as I knew about Fugu fish, but when it was concentrated, I knew it was different.'

'You haven't given a name,' Anjli replied coldly. 'I'd like it.'

'And you can whistle for it,' Howe snapped, his voice croaking with the words. 'She was a tool, as much as anything else. I needed someone who understood about toxins, and nothing more.'

'Where did you source the tetrodotoxin from?' Anjli asked, noting down Howe's previous statement. 'I heard it was banned in the EU.'

'Yeah, well, we're not in the EU anymore, are we?' Howe croaked as he sipped once more at his bottle. 'There's a lot of ways to get hold of it.'

'So your plan was to poison Leroy, but only enough to put him out of action before calling the police on him,' Anjli was writing as she spoke. 'So how did you come to fall ill?'

'Bloody Leroy,' Howe laid back on the bed, tiring. 'I picked his food, so he had to make a show of picking mine. At some point he must have put one of his picked sandwiches on my plate, there was a lot of choice but few of each. I was lucky really. If he'd swapped two, I might have died.'

Anjli nodded as she noted this down.

'And what did you do with the tetrodotoxin afterwards?'

'I disposed of it,' Howe replied with the certainty of a man who believed this to be true.

'Where?'

'It's in my waste bin, at home,' Howe replied. 'Wrapped it up in a shit ton of bubble wrap and then stuck it in an old pencil case before taping that up too.'

'Are you really sure about that?' Anjli watched Howe closely as he sat back up now, watching her suspiciously.

'Why the hell wouldn't I be?' he asked.

'Because Tara Wilkinson died of tetrodotoxin poisoning yesterday, as well,' Anjli turned the page back in her notebook as she read from it. 'Died in *Essence* around eight last night. Believed to have been poisoned between five and six pm.'

'Well, it wasn't me, because I was here,' it was a weak attempt at a joke, and Anjli saw it was a defence action.

Howe was shaken by this news.

'You see, Mister Howe, this is my problem,' Anjli leaned closer now, pressing on with the questions, pushing to see whether Marshall Howe would crack a little more. 'Johnny Mitchell dying wasn't even on our radar until Leroy died. He would have gotten away with it. Well, until someone else put the pieces together. Someone killing Leroy, it sounds like a revenge killing for the original murder, so someone who liked Johnny, who was angry that he was dead, could have been convinced to do this. But then we have Tara, who we also believe to have been involved in the murder, if only in a small manner, now also dead. You've said you had help from a 'she'. Would this have been Helen Cage?'

Howe coughed now, but after a moment Anjli realised it

was laughter, spluttering out like an illness onto the sheets as Howe chuckled.

'She was Harnish's little helper, nothing more.'

'And how did she help him?' Anjli pressed on. However, Howe seemed to have suddenly realised what was going on, as if the coughing fit had cleared his head.

'I think I need my solicitor,' he said. 'I think I've said too much. It's these drugs. I hallucinate, I'm delirious.'

'So what, you *didn't* poison Leroy Daniels now?'

Howe kept quiet for a moment, as if considering his options.

'Solicitor.'

Anjli sighed.

'Well, it doesn't matter,' she said. 'Whatever killed Tara was in the restaurant, and when we find it, we'll work out how it was doctored. Who knows, maybe we'll even find the little phial of thrown away tetrodotoxin you used to kill Leroy.'

'I didn't use anything to kill him,' it was almost a petulant whine. 'It wasn't my fault that he wasn't strong enough to fight the toxins.'

'Didn't you even consider that someone else could have eaten one of your doctored sandwiches?' Anjli closed up the notebook now, picking up the phone from beside the bed, where it'd also been recording. 'You could have poisoned Charles Baker, Baroness Jones, Heather Gosine, anyone else in that pub in the process! You could have killed tons of people, all because you *wanted to stop Leroy from going to the sodding ball!*'

'It wasn't supposed to be lethal,' Howe complained weakly, his voice only a hoarse whisper now. 'I don't understand how it was! I did exactly as I was told!'

'*Who* told you!?' Anjli half shouted now. 'Whoever she is, she didn't help you! She gave you the wrong amounts, and you almost died!'

Howe stopped complaining. In fact, his entire body language changed, relaxing. It was as if he'd finally come to a silent decision.

'It was Tara,' he said. 'Tara Wilkinson.'

'The manager of *Essence* gave you advice on *tetrodotoxin?*' Anjli shook her head. 'Come on.'

'It's true,' Howe folded his arms weakly as he looked at Anjli, glancing at her while still laying on the bed, rather than turning his head. 'She worked in Japan as a manager. learnt about Fugu. Check her history.'

'And why did she want Leroy out of action?'

'Because then she could get her husband in,' Howe said. 'With Johnny and Leroy both out of the picture, Harnish could ride in like the saviour.'

'When did she speak to you about this?'

'The week after they got back from Dubrovnik.'

Anjli watched Howe for a good, long moment.

'I think you're lying,' she said, unsure whether or not he was. 'I think you know we can't check Tara's alibi because she's dead. And that means you don't have to tell us the real person who helped you. Did Tara get you the tetrodotoxin too?'

Howe nodded, and Anjli turned the phone recorder off. This was a pointless interview now, as Howe had straightened himself enough to know that pinning everything onto a dead person kept enough plausible deniability in his story.

'Before I go, one last thing,' she said irritably. 'Helen Cage. Why did you want her in the Gala Dinner?'

'I didn't,' Howe sighed.

'We have notes in the committee report saying your choice instead of Leroy was Harnish and Helen.'

'I didn't say I wanted her,' Howe snapped, his voice a whisper now. 'I said we wanted someone who knew her *honey*. Bloody Mitchell bought boxes of it for the Gala, had some massive honey-based idea for the dessert, and held it in Scotland before they shipped it down last week.'

Anjli took this new information in, smiling.

'Well, at least you've helped with a couple of things,' she said. 'And now, Marshall Howe, I'm arresting you for the murder of Leroy Daniels. You do not have to say anything, but it may harm your defence if you do not mention when questioned something which you later rely on in court...'

Howe stared at Anjli in horror as she spoke the lines.

He wasn't croaking anymore.

22

HONEY BEES

'CAN WE HURRY THIS ALONG? I DON'T KNOW IF YOU REALISE this but we're stupidly busy today,' Helen Cage sat on her chair in her living room, literally fuming at being kept from leaving her home in Strawberry Hill less than six hours before the dinner started, knowing that the Houses of Parliament kitchens were already starting preparations.

Declan had arrived alone, and Helen had opened the door when he knocked, already pulling on her jacket as she did so.

'Oh,' she said. 'I thought you were my *Uber*.'

'I'd suggest you cancel it,' Declan waved his warrant card. 'We need to talk before you go anywhere.'

Now, in the living room, Declan sat in the same chair Anjli had the previous day. However, unlike then, this Helen Cage wasn't one that seemed to want to help with the case. Tapping on her phone, cancelling the ride, she glared sullenly at him.

'They'll give me a low-star rating for that,' she said. 'I

won't be able to get my five stars back, and all for some bull-shit harassment.'

'I understand, and I'm sorry, but give me what I need, and I can see what we can do about that,' Declan replied. 'Or, if you want, we can go into Temple Inn and we can do it there. Do you want to call for a solicitor if you're worried about harassment?'

'Do I need one?' Helen narrowed her eyes. 'I mean God, man. Tara just died. The dinner is tonight. Leroy died two days ago. Can you just hold off piling any more shit on my shoulders?'

Declan fought the urge to snap back about this, keeping his voice calm and soft.

'So you waive your right to legal counsel.'

'I did no such thing,' Helen argued. 'I asked if I needed it.'

'Probably,' Declan spoke calmly. 'But that all depends on how this goes today.'

'Christ,' Helen looked at the wall of the living room. 'Poor Harnish will be doing everything alone.'

'I get you're annoyed, and believe me, the reason I came here was to save you time,' Declan shifted in the chair as he tried to stay comfortable without slumping into it. 'We have three deaths and a serious poisoning that we're investigating. It's taken us in a lot of different directions. Mister Patel—'

'*Chef* Patel.'

'Only when he's in the kitchen,' Declan continued. '*Mister* Patel is helping us with another part of it.'

'He didn't kill Tara.'

'And how would you know that?' Declan pulled out his notepad. 'Miss Cage, I want you to know that whatever happened, we'll find out. We're good at finding out. Painfully good. We've arrested government ministers, rock bands, even quasi-satanic cults. We're the one unit you don't want hunting you if you're guilty.'

'I'm not guilty,' Helen's voice was a little more uncertain now.

'And I'm glad to hear that,' Declan continued. 'But we'll work out if you're telling the truth very soon. You see, we've found out a lot of things about the circumstances of this case so far. And currently, I'm sick of finding out. I'd like to be *told* for once. So please, how do you know that *Chef* Patel didn't kill his wife?'

Helen sighed.

'Because he was with me all afternoon,' she said. 'Right up to when he had to go find her some junk food.'

'And you were planning the dinner tonight, perhaps? Working together to guarantee the Gala went well?' Declan asked.

'We were screwing,' Helen was almost defiant in her response. 'That's what you wanted to hear, right? We were having an affair. Had been for a few months.'

'And were you anywhere we can confirm this?'

'We were in *The Counting House*,' Helen stated calmly. 'It's just down the road from *Essence*. The plan was to shack up there so that Harnish could go back when needed, but then Tara asked for a *McDonalds,* and it screwed things up a little as the closest branch was either St Pauls or Liverpool Street, and both were a bit of a trek for him.'

'I thought *The Counting House* was a pub?'

'It has rooms,' Helen's face broke into a sardonic smile. 'Probably a bit rich for you.'

'More likely I've not needed to book it for a night. Or even a couple of hours,' Declan smiled back. 'So, is this why you broke up with Johnny Mitchell?'

Helen laughed.

'Johnny broke up with me,' she said. 'He'd fallen in love with someone else.'

'Oh yes? And who was that?'

Helen leaned closer.

'Tara.'

Declan didn't write this down, his expression giving nothing away.

'You don't seem surprised.' Helen wouldn't stop bloody smiling. It was irritating Declan.

'We know she went to Edinburgh to plead with him about something,' he replied. 'We know from witnesses there that she told him she needed him while there, so although surprising to many, I'm afraid I'm not surprised.'

Helen leaned back in her chair, her face badly trying to hide an expression of delight, or even superiority. *The expression was more telling than her replies,* Declan thought to himself. There was more here than had been thought before. *Helen was happy that Declan knew of Tara being in Edinburgh. Why?*

'So Harnish hired you because you were in a relationship?' He started writing again.

'No, Leroy hired me,' Helen grinned. 'At Harnish's insistence of course, I mean, he convinced him I'd be a great spy against Johnny, help them a lot.'

She leaned back in the chair, looking up at the ceiling of the living room as she clicked her tongue.

'Tara hated me,' she said eventually. 'Partly because I was shagging Harnish better than she ever could, but also because she couldn't complain about this to anyone while doing the same to him. They both knew about the affairs, but pretended they weren't happening, carried on being husband and wife even though the bed was empty at night.'

Helen chuckled at this.

'She actually thought that I was a fling, that Harnish would get bored with me and go back to her—'

She stopped.

'Wait, why did you think I broke things off with Johnny?'

Now it was Declan's turn to shrug.

'We assumed you'd broken up with Johnny because of the Gala.'

'The Gala?' Helen looked confused. 'The one tonight?'

'Yes,' Declan confirmed. 'Your father died after the Government refused to help him, and Johnny agreed to do an event with them.'

'And you think I'd *stop* him?' Helen shook her head. 'He bought tons of our honey for it, deliberately to piss them off! Every menu had '*Manuka honey farmed by Hill's Honey*' on it to really slam a massive middle finger into their faces as they ate dessert, and when Leroy took over, he had to keep it on the menu as it was already paid for! More money spent on bloody honey than *Essence* paid me the entire year! Why the hell would I be unhappy?'

Declan considered this. *If Helen was correct, then his theory was already shot to hell.*

'Did you know that Leroy Daniels was planning on killing Johnny Mitchell?'

'Sure,' Helen shrugged. 'Never thought he'd go through with it, though. He was always talking, never walking.'

'Did you offer to help him?'

'Why would I have done that? We might have broken up, but I still loved Johnny. He was everything to me.'

Declan looked up from his notes at this line.

There was that itch again.

His phone went off; a message from Edinburgh. He read it, nodding.

'Did you have any idea Leroy was involved in the killing of Johnny Mitchell?' he asked, holding the phone in his hand.

'He wasn't,' Helen replied calmly before adding, 'wait, he wasn't, was he?'

'We have reason to believe that Leroy Daniels smuggled himself on board an *Apex* chartered jet on the morning of Johnny Mitchell's death, landing in the UK, and returning to Dubrovnik the day after.'

'That means nothing.'

'The airport the plane landed in was a two-hour drive from the restaurant, and nobody he knew would have been aware he was there,' Declan checked his notes. 'How often since Dubrovnik did Chef Daniels borrow your eight-inch knife? I understand he did this a couple of times?'

Helen nodded. 'I had a similar one to his,' she said. 'Same make, different blade. I think the Damascus ones are a bit poncy. He said the weight was close enough, and he needed to borrow it because he left his in Dubrovnik and was waiting for them to courier it over.'

'So you never saw it after he left for Dubrovnik?'

'No, but it was definitely there, because he holds it in one of the photos of the party on the first day.'

'The first day,' Declan noted this as well. 'Not after Thursday.'

'No,' Helen shook her head. 'No, you're wrong. Leroy wouldn't have done this.'

'I beg to differ,' Declan turned the phone around. On it was a photo, from De'Geer of the blade found in the tunnels.

'We have the blade he claimed was in Dubrovnik, dropped in an Edinburgh vault.'

'Bloody hell,' Helen rose, walking to the side and pouring a drink. 'Mead,' she said as she sat down. 'A stiffener that doesn't affect my performance tonight. Made from honey, you know.'

She took a long sip, as if using it as a delaying tactic. Declan didn't want to give her any chances to recover, and so pressed on.

'Did you know about the tunnels?'

'I knew there were tunnels,' she nodded. 'Everyone does. They do ghost walks.'

'Did you also know that the location that *Monet* was opened on was once a café where Johnny had worked as a teenager?' Declan asked.

Helen sipped again.

'He'd mentioned the café, but I didn't put them together.'

'Did you ever visit it?'

'I had no need for social calls by then.'

Declan changed direction.

'How do you feel about the current Government?' he asked.

'They're a bunch of money-grabbing wankers,' Helen replied. 'Why?'

'I'm curious as to your motive for helping Harnish today.'

'The Gala?' Helen laughed. 'I already said they bought a ton of honey. I've—'

'I said motive,' Declan interrupted. 'I get that they gave you money, and it's good PR for the company, but Michelle Rose, the Foreign Secretary will be there. Most of the Cabinet, in fact all the people who helped cause your father's—'

'You think *they* caused this? My dad was one croissant

away from a heart attack for years,' Helen snapped back, interrupting Declan's interruption. 'We built a cottage industry based around *honey*. You don't think he sampled it? Sure, Manuka honey is super healthy. But that's in *moderation*. Christ, dad made even diabetics nervous when he walked into the room. I'm stunned he lasted so long.'

Helen halted herself as she realised she'd spoken too much. Declan watched her, letting the moment draw out as he considered what to say next. He was pretty sure that Helen was lying, but about what, he couldn't be sure. Currently, everyone involved in all three murders had secrets they were trying to hide. If Helen was genuinely okay with the Government, that she didn't blame them for anything, then he could understand her working the Gala. But at the same time, the itch was there, pointing out that something wasn't right here.

What was he missing?

'You mentioned you'd been having the affair for a few months now, so how long exactly were you seeing Harnish?' he asked eventually. 'Was it before or after you broke up with Johnny?'

'After,' Helen admitted. 'Pretty much the day Johnny admitted he'd been screwing Tara, I went to tell Harnish. We got wasted, and by the end of the night, instead of telling him anything, I seduced him.'

'Revenge?'

'Lust,' Helen smiled. 'I don't know why I never saw it before.'

'And you stuck at it, it seems,' Declan nodded. 'And, with your exes Johnny and Leroy gone, and with his wife now dead, you don't have any obstructions in the way to carry on.'

'We never had any obstructions in the first place,' Helen rose from the chair, half in anger. 'Leroy and me were purely physical when I was young and stupid. Johnny was a fling for when I was naïve and optimistic. Harnish is reality. We know what we need to do to get on in the business.'

'So you're staying a Pastry Chef?' Declan rose to meet Helen.

'Well, I was, but then I heard an opening came up for restaurant manager,' Helen snapped, her face grimacing as she instantly regretted it.

'Sorry. That wasn't called for.'

She finished the mead, placing the glass on a side table.

'Look, either arrest me or let me go,' she said. 'I've answered all your questions. I wasn't anywhere near Tara when she was poisoned. And in fact, nobody at the restaurant was.'

'How do you mean?' Declan was confused at this. 'Because it was closed?'

'No, because she wasn't there,' Helen replied. 'Harnish told me that after your detective sergeant person, the woman who chatted to me last time went to speak to her, Tara went to Westminster, over to the Houses of Parliament to see that everything had arrived from Edinburgh on time, as it had been brought across in bits over the last few days. She went through stock, checking against the menu requirements until she left around seven-thirty.'

'And Harnish knew this because?'

'Because she texted him to tell him she was returning to the restaurant,' Helen continued. 'And as tetrodotoxin takes a couple of hours to kick in, the only place she could have been poisoned was the Houses of bloody Parliament. So get off your high horse and start checking for culprits there.'

She grabbed her jacket again, walking to the living room door, deciding that the conversation was over.

'I'm late, so you can show yourself out,' she said. 'If you want to nick me, you know where I'll be.'

And with that, Helen Cage slammed the door behind her as she stormed out of the house.

Declan sat alone in the living room now, considering his next move. If Tara had been at Parliament when she was poisoned, what did that mean? How did someone manage to get tetrodotoxin through security in the first place? And also, how did Helen know exactly how long tetrodotoxin took to kill?

'I'm sorry, but she's having a tough time,' a middle-aged woman with greying, tight-permed hair said from the doorway. 'She loved Johnny. We all did. And the death really hit her hard.'

'She's hiding it very well,' Declan rose. 'I'm—'

'Police, I know,' the woman smiled, holding out a hand to shake. 'I'm Amanda Cage, her mother.'

'My condolences on the loss of your husband,' Declan shook Amanda's hand. 'I don't know the details, but it sounds like you've had a tough time.'

'The legal kerfuffle didn't help, but the life insurance did,' Amanda made a brave face as she walked with Declan over to the front door. 'Kept us on our feet long enough to sell off the final stock.'

'Final stock?' Declan stopped at the door, looking at Amanda. 'Until the next batch?'

'No, sorry, *Hill's Honey* isn't doing Manuka anymore,' Amanda said sadly. 'We'll gain a little from the bushes we still have, and over time we might create some limited runs, but now it's mainly acacia honey and the less common honeydew.'

'The final stock,' Declan mused. 'That went to Leroy?'

'God no,' Amanda laughed. 'He's still using the stock he bought months back. A little honey goes a long way, after all. No, it was Johnny, dear Johnny that bought the remaining batch, paid us well over the odds for it too, as the Government was paying the bill. Took about a dozen large boxes of the stuff, god knows where he held it for the last five months.'

Declan nodded slowly.

'So if I get this right, Johnny bought the stock before Leroy rehired Helen?'

Amanda nodded.

'I was hoping she'd get out of the kitchen now the honey was gone, but she seems to enjoy it,' she said. 'This Gala has been all she's talked about for the last month.'

'The last month,' Declan nodded again, almost automatically, as his mind whirled. *A month ago Leroy didn't have the gig. A month ago Leroy wasn't even involved.* Even Tara, running up to Edinburgh and begging Johnny Mitchell didn't—

'When Helen broke up with Johnny, was it hard for them?' he asked as he opened the door. 'She seemed to insinuate that she was the one who'd been broken up with, while giving me the feeling she'd been the one breaking up.'

'That's what she does,' Amanda agreed, walking to the threshold as Declan walked out onto the front path. 'I think it was better for Johnny, believing that he was leaving her.'

'Did she visit him in Edinburgh?'

'Only once, when we sent the last batch of honey up,' Amanda agreed. 'But after that she never went back.'

Declan smiled one last time, thanking Amanda once more and leaving the house, walking to his Audi.

His itch was getting scratched. The staff that worked with Johnny Mitchell in Edinburgh had claimed only one woman had appeared, who told them she was Tara Wilkinson. And Helen hadn't lied, this wouldn't have been a social call.

Declan was starting to believe that 'Tara' was Helen. And if that was the case, what else was Helen Cage lying about?

'It's me,' he said as he phoned Billy. 'I'm just checking—'

'Have you seen the email from De'Geer?' Billy's voice was excited. *'About the car?'*

'No,' Declan looked at his phone, opening up the email app. 'I just have a picture of the knife through text messages. What am I—'

He stopped as he read the email labelled *HARNISH CAR NEWS* on his phone.

'Get that son of a bitch into the Unit right now,' he said.

'Already done,' Billy's voice was joyful. *'Bullman's gone personally to pick him up.'*

'I'll be there as quickly as I can.' Declan climbed into the Audi, disconnecting the call.

Things were coming together now, but Declan couldn't shake the worry that it was a little too late.

23

HOODED MEN

'IF YOU DON'T WANT TO BE HERE, LADDIE, I COMPLETELY understand,' Monroe sat back on the coffee shop chair and stared across the table at De'Geer, currently pulling at the collar of his recently purchased grey hoodie.

'Doctor Marcos would never forgive me if I let you get into trouble all on your own,' he said with a smile. 'I just don't understand why I have to wear this. It's a size too small.'

'It's all they had, and we didn't have time for next day delivery,' Derek Sutton, also wearing a grey hoodie, chuckled. 'Christ, Ali. He whines as much as you used to.'

'I could still nick you for all this,' De'Geer muttered.

'Aye, but then you'd have to arrest me too,' Monroe smiled as he straightened his own hoodie.

The idea had been simple when they first discussed it; Lennie Wright had the council in his pocket, and what he didn't gain legitimately with a large amount of donations, he stole with some equally large 'donations' to some of the more unsavoury types of Edinburgh. A return to Hendrick, now made aware of Claire Doyle's true heritage, bore little fruit, and Monroe could see the frustration on the fellow DCI's face as he explained the red tape he was currently facing.

The only way for them to actively arrest Lennie Wright for his illegal and toxic dumping was to have something solid to take when they did so. And the paid-off police in Edinburgh, of which there was likely to be one or two out there, would immediately warn Lennie of any raid.

Besides, Lennie wasn't stupid. He was old school; analogue. He preferred a more face-to-face meeting.

And that was going to be his downfall.

'And Hendrick is okay with this?' De'Geer asked, nervously.

Monroe flashed a quick smile.

'Well, let's just say we helped him big time with finding the knife and the escape route in the Mitchell case, and now owing us, he understands that sometimes you have to break the law to save the law.'

'Which is a fancy way of saying no,' Sutton laughed, shutting up at a glare from Monroe.

'All we're doing is returning Lennie's guns and having a meeting,' Monroe said, finishing his black coffee and standing up, nodding to the barista. 'The manner of how we return them is up to us.'

Walking out of the coffee shop, Monroe stared across the cobbled Edinburgh high street to the arches the other side of the road, arched entrances to a courtyard where a climate change protest was in full swing, with easily thirty or more protestors waving banners and placards outside the Edinburgh City Chambers.

Offices where, for the last thirty minutes, Lennie Wright was currently holed up, waiting for the police to disperse the rabble before he left, most likely glaring at Councillor

McCavity as the ginger haired official simply shrugged, sitting back in his chair as he explained that *recently, this happened a lot.*

Walking across the high street and entering the courtyard through the brick arches, Monroe looked at Sutton.

'If I lose my bloody job for this, I'm blaming you,' he muttered.

'Ach, quit yer whining,' Sutton smiled, his eyes shining with excitement. 'Just enjoy the bloody moment.'

'Easy for you to say,' Monroe passed through a group of protestors, reaching into his hoodie's neck and pulling out a motorcycle buff, pulling it up around his nose, the printed image of the lower half of a skull now replacing his jaw, beard and mouth. 'This is a normal weekday afternoon for you.'

De'Geer, following behind, did similar, his buff showing a red and black tie-dyed print, pulling the hood over his head as he effectively covered his entire face, except for his eyes. With Monroe and Sutton now similarly attired, they walked up to the front doors of the City Chambers, dashing through them as they entered the ornate entrance hall.

There was a solitary guard standing there. Slowly, his eyes widened as the three hooded, masked men entered, walking up to him.

'Lennie Wright,' Derek Sutton growled menacingly. 'Where is he?'

The guard squared his shoulders, as if to confront these intruders, but as he did so Monroe pulled out a gun, one of the weapons they'd confiscated from the gunmen the previous night, holding it menacingly.

'Don't be a hero, laddie,' he said. 'We're not here for you.'

At the sight of the weapon, the guard stepped back, nodding nervously.

'Next floor up, third door on the right,' he said. 'He's with Councillor McCavity.'

'Anyone else up there?'

The guard numbly shook his head.

'The protestors are blocking them out,' he said. 'There was a fire alarm, they went outside—'

Monroe nodded at this. He knew there had been a fire alarm, just as he'd known there had been a protest occurring at that very moment. In fact, it had been Monroe's idea to call the activists, contacting them through Marcy, owner of the Vegan cafe on Newhaven Harbour, explaining to them how they intended to take down Lennie once and for all. He'd also explained to Claire that he wasn't her grand-uncle after all, but hadn't yet told her the name of the real one. He felt that was a conversation that Derek and Claire needed to have separately.

Once the activists had agreed to get involved, it was easy to find a way to gain entrance for one of them, pulling the fire alarm before leaving the building through the same arched entrance while the protest began outside. Although it was likely to be a false alarm, the workers in the council building had to accept there was the smallest chance that this was real, and reluctantly went to their evacuation point, which unfortunately was the same courtyard the protest was in, causing more chaos. And Lennie Wright who, aware that the last thing he needed was press coverage of his meeting with a Councillor, especially amongst the same activists causing him trouble and now outside the door, stayed in the offices of Councillor McCavity for the next thirty minutes.

An office that was now about to receive visitors.

'I know,' Monroe replied to the guard. 'Now do me a favour, right? Call Edinburgh Police. Here's the number.'

He passed the guard a piece of paper.

'Ask for DCI Hendrick. Explain that men with guns have entered the building and are heading for councillor McCavity's office. Yeah?'

'You really want me to do that?' The guard was a little shell-shocked, and probably believed he'd heard this wrong, in that they'd said *not* to do this, even though they'd given him a number.

'We really do,' De'Geer said. 'In fact, we're counting on you.'

And, leaving the confused middle-aged guard in the hallway, Monroe lead De'Geer and Derek Sutton up the burgundy and gold carpeted stairs, following the guard's directions and stopping at the third door on the right.

With a smile, Monroe stepped aside.

'You were always better at this,' he said to Sutton. However, the large Glaswegian simply grabbed the door handle.

'What?' he asked. 'If it's not broken, don't break it.'

With a twist of the handle, Sutton opened the door to McCavity's office and, as Lennie Wright and Councillor McCavity stared in shock at the three masked, hooded, gun-toting men entering the room, McCavity rising to his feet in horror, Monroe turned to tracksuit and trainers, sitting on the sofa by the wall, training his gun on the man.

'Stay there, mate,' he said. The burly bodyguard numbly nodded.

'What the feck is this?' Lennie exclaimed. 'You think you can come in here and attack me? I'm Lennie feckin' Wright!'

'Yeah, some pussy land developer,' Sutton said in a gruff voice. 'Hiding shite in landfills.'

'I'm more than a developer, ask anyone in Glasgow,'

Lennie was angering, ignoring the gun aimed at his face. 'I'll find you and I'll feckin' kill you.'

'Chuck the prick outside, let him play with the tree huggers,' De'Geer growled, warming to the role. 'He can answer to their claims of eco-terrorism.'

'Eco-terrorism?' Lennie waved back McCavity, who went to speak. 'You don't know the meaning of the word! I'm a developer! What I use to create my foundations isn't any of their business! Or yours!'

'We want your cobalt, Wright,' Monroe snarled in the fakest cockney accent he could manage, channelling his inner Jackie Lucas. 'We hear you got a ton of lithium batteries doing nothing and we want them.'

'Make me an offer and we'll do business,' Lennie said. 'Drop your guns and masks and then we'll talk about costs.'

'Costs? We ain't paying you!' Sutton moved closer, gun in Lennie's face. 'We know you'd pay us if it meant getting rid of it!'

'Yeah,' Monroe growled, looking at McCavity. 'And we don't charge extras like that prick there.'

'Fine!' Lennie laughed. 'Take it! All that lithium you want, hundreds of EV batteries, they're currently rotting on my building site! Take as much as you want and let those hippies outside know too! It's all yours!'

'The cobalt's just lying there?' De'Geer sounded shocked. 'On your premises?'

'Lennie—' McCavity started, but Lennie Wright waved him silent again.

'Jesus, you thugs are dense,' he said. 'It's just old batteries. There's no cash value, and it's causing me a ton of hassle—'

'Lennie!' McCavity snapped, and Lennie turned back to him, raising a hand to backhand the councillor.

'Interrupt me again and I'll smack the shite out of you,' he snarled. 'Why am I paying you to hide the batteries when these buggers can take them for free? Why should I even be listening to you?'

There was the sound of running from the stairwell outside, the all-too-familiar sounds of many sets of feet coming towards the door.

'Because the big guy with the grey hoodie isn't a gangster!' McCavity pointed at De'Geer. 'I recognise his blue eyes! He was in the office this morning booking an appointment with me! He's a copper!'

'I did,' De'Geer nodded, glancing at his watch. 'For noon. Which is now.'

'But he said he was a gangster...' Lennie looked back at De'Geer now as slowly, ever so slowly, he realised that he'd been played.

'He never said he was a gangster, Lennie,' Monroe smiled as he pulled down the mask, yanking back the hood from his head, revealing his face. 'In fact, all we ever said was that we were here to take your cobalt. Which up to now you've denied owning.'

De'Geer and Sutton pulled their disguises off as well now, and Lennie stared at Sutton in horror.

'You!' he exclaimed. 'I ought to—'

The door slammed open and a dozen police officers, led by Hendrick, entered the Councillor's office.

'You threatened me at gunpoint!' Lennie screamed at Monroe.

'These?' Monroe looked at his gun, now held with the butt facing Lennie, with De'Geer and Sutton doing likewise. 'No, you've got confused, Lennie. We're just returning the guns that you left on the docks after you threatened to kill us.

Here you go.'

'I did no such thing!' Lennie was furious. 'They're mad! It's harassment!'

De'Geer, smiling now, pulled out his phone, pressing play on it. Recorded voices came out of the phone's speaker.

'You've nothing here. You're nothing. And now you've threatened me, I'm rethinking my suggestion that you leave.'

'That sounds like you, Lennie,' Monroe grinned, as his own voice came out of the speaker now.

'What, two dead London coppers on your patch aren't going to cause you issues?'

'Who said they were gonna find you? I'm gonna dump you with the batteries. You can bleed out with them and nobody's finding you until I sort things with my pet Councillor and the next building gets built here.'

'That McCavity?'

'He's one of them. And by then we're all long gone. They'll be using bloody Time Team to find you.'

Monroe looked at Hendrick.

'I reckon you'll find some interesting ballistic data when you check these guns,' he said. 'I'll guarantee they were used in Glasgow for something. His men were a little trigger-happy. Ask tracksuit guy there.'

'You were just returning his guns,' Hendricks stared at Monroe cautiously. Monroe nodded.

'We had a noon meeting with Councillor McCavity there, which is right now. We didn't realise Lennie would have ignored fire safety laws and would still be here, but when we saw him, we thought it'd be the easiest option.'

'A meeting in hoodies.'

'Activists outside,' De'Geer answered now. 'We knew

going into the building in uniform would cause us hassle. From the activists.'

'Funny that,' Hendrick looked at Lennie now. 'When we arrived, they just backed off, made a path for us. Like they knew we'd be turning up.'

'That's the joy of peaceful protest,' Monroe shrugged. 'They respect the police. Well, sometimes, anyway.'

'So you decided to give the guns back, dressed down to bypass the activists, harassed a guard—'

'He looked nervous,' Monroe smiled. 'Probably the protest outside. I gave him your mobile phone number. I thought it might make him feel safe.'

'This is bullshit!' Lennie exclaimed. 'Harassment and entrapment!'

'Are these your guns, sir?' Hendrick calmly asked, ignoring the outburst.

'Well, yes!'

'And did these men threaten you?'

'Yes!'

Monroe looked at De'Geer.

'Did you threaten him?' he asked accusingly.

De'Geer shook his head vehemently.

'No, Guv,' he replied. 'I'd have remembered if I had. Maybe Derek did?'

'Not me,' Sutton smiled. 'I'm a changed man since my release.'

'But it's his word against ours,' Monroe looked at Councillor McCavity. 'Unless you want to take a side here?'

McCavity, knowing he was up the creek, wisely kept quiet. Monroe nodded. 'If only there was a way we could—'

He stopped as his face brightened, pulling a phone out of his pocket with his free hand.

'There is!' he exclaimed delightedly. 'I accidentally recorded the whole thing!'

He glanced at Lennie.

'Like we did last night when you threatened to kill us,' he said. 'Must have turned on in my pocket. Let's see if we threatened him.'

Pressing a button on the app, Monroe scrolled back through the sound file on the screen, playing when he hit a point halfway through it.

'Good! Take it! All that lithium you want, hundreds of EV batteries, they're currently rotting on my building site! Take as much as you want and let those hippies outside know too! It's all yours!'

'The cobalt's just lying there? On your premises?'

'Lennie—'

'Jesus, you thugs are dense. It's just old batteries. There's no cash value, and it's causing me a ton of hassle—'

'Whoops,' Monroe smiled at Hendrick. 'Wrong bit.'

Hendrick looked at Lennie Wright, who looked sick.

'Sounds like these claims of cobalt poisoning might have some basis after all,' he said, now turning his attention to McCavity. 'Did you know about this, Councillor?'

'I did, yes,' McCavity now straightened up behind the desk, changing his own narrative. 'I was performing an undercover sting operation off my own initiative, with the hope I could get Mister Wright here to confess to—'

'You lying shite!' Lennie, stunned at McCavity's brazen betrayal, grabbed the gun that Monroe was holding and turned it on him, his finger trembling on the trigger.

'You think you're so feckin' clever!' he cried at Monroe. 'You got nothing! Faked recordings and me lying to save my life from a madman with a gun!'

'We have more than that,' Monroe looked at De'Geer.

'The activist Barry Mulligan died while gathering footage of your dumping, breaking his phone in the process of a fall from a bridge,' De'Geer said. 'Today, his friends out there regained access to the cloud, and the video he took.'

'How did they manage that?' Hendrick asked Monroe, who shrugged.

'It's amazing what a good hacker can do these days,' he said. 'Oh, and Lennie, did you think for one second I'd give you a gun with a bullet in it?'

As Lennie pulled the trigger, the gun providing a paltry *click* in response, Monroe swung a meaty right hand, connecting hard with Lennie's chin, sending him sprawling to the floor.

'Firing an empty gun feels like attempted murder and resisting arrest,' he said as he crouched over him. 'I said I'd end you, Lennie, and I keep my promises. This whole thing was to give you enough rope to hang yourself. Thank you for being as predictable as we needed.'

'We'll take it from here,' Hendrick said. 'I think we'll be having lots of little chats with Mister Wright and Councillor McCavity.'

Without even replying, except for a nod, Monroe turned and walked out of the office, De'Geer following, the furious screams of Lennie Wright echoing after him into the hallway.

IT WAS ANOTHER FIFTEEN MINUTES BEFORE THEY BUNDLED Lennie Wright into a police car. Monroe, now back in his suit, the hoodie discarded, stood at the side, among the watching crowd, De'Geer beside him.

'You know, you might not be my grand-uncle, but you're pretty cool,' a voice spoke from beside him, and Monroe glanced down to see Claire, smiling as she watched the car drive away.

'Your real grand-uncle will reveal himself one day,' Monroe replied. 'Just try not to get into too much trouble until then.'

'No promises,' Claire nodded to both officers and left, walking over to the cheering protestors.

'Will they get the justice they want?' De'Geer asked. Monroe shrugged at this.

'He'll likely get out, return to Glasgow and lick his wounds,' he said. 'But his relationship with the Leith and Edinburgh councils is shot. He won't be dumping toxic waste around here any time soon. And of course, there's always the chance his two female Rottweilers will take a deal to inform on him, too.'

He looked at his watch.

'Come on, laddie, let's get a car to *blues and twos* us to Waverley Station. We got a train to catch in forty minutes.'

'Back to London, Guv?'

'Aye, I need to see how much Declan's bollocksed up the case,' Monroe said it with a smile, turning from the scene in front of them as De'Geer pulled his phone out, glancing at a message on the screen.

'Can we get them to stop at *Monet*?' he enquired. 'I have to show them a photo.'

Monroe read the message, nodding.

'I can see where he's going there,' he nodded. 'We'll still make the train.'

'Do you want to say goodbye to Derek?' De'Geer looked

over at Sutton, on the other side of the crowd, talking with Hendrick. Monroe shook his head.

'Christ, no,' he replied. 'That man's a bloody nightmare. D'you know, he tried to convince me once that his own grandniece was mine?'

'The cheek of it, sir,' De'Geer smiled as they walked to a squad car and a train back home.

24

SETTING THE PLATES

HARNISH PATEL STARED ACROSS THE TABLE AT DECLAN AND Bullman with a conflicted expression that showed shock, disgust, and anger, all at the same time.

'You brought me in because of a bloody *car?*' he half shouted. 'They dragged me out of the Houses of Parliament for that?'

Declan nodded as he leaned closer.

'Yup,' he said calmly. 'You see, the problem we have is that the bloody *car,* as you so correctly describe it, was found parked near the restaurant where Chef Mitchell was brutally murdered, a couple of weeks back.'

'I was in London when he was murdered!' Harnish's face was reddening with anger.

'Yes, but the car was seen six or seven hours later,' Bullman replied. 'And as you can understand, a car in your name, seen at the murder scene of a rival, the morning after the murder makes us wonder what the killer forgot to pick up, and asked you to go fetch? His murder weapon perhaps?'

Declan slid across a photo, a print-out of the image

De'Geer had sent. Harnish stared down at Leroy Daniels' knife, shaking his head in utter shock.

'Is that—'

'We're having the blood on the blade checked, but yeah, we reckon so.'

Harnish swallowed.

'Okay, the car, sure, it's in my name, but that's because it's mainly used by—I mean it was mainly used by Tara and me, collecting supplies, that sort of thing! Anyone in the restaurant could use it! I don't even know who had the keys that week!'

'Where do you keep it?'

'In an underground car park near Bank! One of the firms gave Leroy a free spot on the condition he gave them a permanently reserved table.'

'A name? So we can check the CCTV?'

Harnish shook his head.

'I can name them, sure, but the car park doesn't have CCTV there, they have clients that prefer anonymity,' he looked around anxiously. 'Is that it? Can I go? I need to get the dinner done!'

'Your wife died last night,' Declan rested against the interview room table as he considered his words. 'Yet you seem more bothered about the dinner.'

'Yes!' Harnish snapped back. 'And if it'd been the other way round, she'd do the same! I can mourn for her tomorrow, but today is a dinner that will define the rest of my career.'

'So it's not because you don't love her?' Declan continued.

'Of course I love her!' Harnish rose from the chair. 'Why would—'

'Because you're currently sleeping with Helen Cage and,

in fact, were together last night, while your wife died,' Bullman interjected.

Harnish stopped, sitting back in the chair as he realised his secrets were out in the open.

'How—'

'We're police,' Declan shrugged. 'We find things out. So if it wasn't you, who could have been driving that car?'

'Literally anyone,' Harnish shook his head, now in his hands. 'The keys were in Tara's office. While she was gone, it was left closed.'

'I was told the Maitre d' managed you? Wouldn't she have used the office?'

'Didn't need to,' Harnish said sullenly. 'Spent most of her time in the kitchen while the staff complained about Tara. Obviously not while I was around.'

'When did the affair start?' Bullman asked.

'Why?' Harnish looked suspicious now. 'It's got nothing to do with the murder.'

'Your girlfriend is the ex of Johnny Mitchell and Leroy Daniels, both dead,' Bullman continued. 'And the rival of the victim who died last night. For someone with a lot of personal baggage, it seems to be disappearing real quick.'

'Helen's blameless,' Harnish was adamant. 'She didn't even want to come back to the restaurant.'

'She didn't?' Declan was surprised at this.

'No,' Harnish insisted. 'She feared retaliation from Tara, she knew that Leroy and Tara had a history. I had to convince Leroy it was his idea.'

'And why did you want her back?' Declan asked. 'Surely it would have been easier to have an affair with someone who wasn't in the workplace?'

'We were in love, and I worked stupid hours,' Harnish

sighed. 'Only way we could see each other was to be in the same kitchen.'

'And when did you learn about Johnny and Tara?'

'Johnny and Tara?' Harnish repeated, confused. 'They hated each other. They'd—'

There was a commotion at the door, and an elderly gentleman with a briefcase entered the briefing room.

'James Dillon, representing Chef Patel,' he said. 'I've seen the evidence you have against my client, and I feel this is nothing but a witch-hunt against him, based on the colour of his skin.'

'You what—' Bullman rose in fury, but Declan, noting Doctor Marcos in the door, nodding at him, placed an arm on her shoulder.

'Leave it, Ma'am,' he said, looking back to Dillon. 'Who sent you?'

'I work in the legal department of the Houses of Parliament,' Dillon straightened. 'I have been tasked with bringing Chef Patel back to his station, as within an hour we will be seating guests.'

Declan nodded. 'He can go, for the moment,' he said, ignoring the glare from Bullman. 'We will, however, keep the right to speak to him after the event.'

'About what?' Harnish asked. 'I heard someone say you've arrested Howe for Leroy's murder?'

'He didn't work alone,' Declan turned to watch Harnish as he spoke the next line slowly. 'He claims Tara helped him kill Leroy.'

There was a very long, awkward moment of silence as Harnish Patel took this news in.

'My wife had a lot of secrets,' he said.

'Do you think she could have done that?' Declan asked. 'Killed Leroy?'

'My client—'

'Your client can answer one more bloody question before we let him go,' Bullman snapped at Dillon. Harnish nodded, a slow, saddened motion, as if realising the truth of something horrible.

'I believe she would, yes,' he said.

'Then go to the dinner and expect us to contact you next week,' Declan said, leaning over to the interview room recorder. 'Recording ended four-twenty-five pm.'

Before Harnish could pass him, though, he raised an arm, barring the chef's way.

'You seem like a good man, if a lost one, and for what it's worth, I don't think you're involved in what's been going on, apart from accidentally. But know this. I believe there's a good chance that people will die tonight, people on your watch. I believe that Helen Cage has an agenda, and although I can't prove it, I think she intends to harm people.'

Harnish shook his head at this, as if unwilling to believe that Helen could do such a thing, but at the same time he didn't speak as Declan continued.

'You said that tonight is a dinner that will define the rest of your career,' he continued. 'And it will, but you have to decide how that definition is made and what history remembers of you. I hope you do the right thing.'

'I always have done,' Harnish replied, and Declan could see the truth behind the chef's gaze. Nodding, he stepped back.

'Then break a leg,' he said. 'Or whatever it is you say before a big meal.'

As Harnish walked out of the room with Dillon following, Bullman looked at Declan, fury in her eyes.

'You'd better have a bloody good reason for going over me and letting our prime suspect walk out like that,' she snapped. In reply, Declan glanced at the door where Doctor Marcos was walking in.

'I gave him the nod,' she said, neglecting as ever to call Bullman *Ma'am*. 'Harnish isn't guilty. We've got news.'

Following Doctor Marcos down the stairs and into the main office, Bullman saw Billy at his monitor station, turning excitedly to face them.

'You're bloody lucky to have me!' he cried triumphantly.

"Detective Constable?' Bullman said calmly.

Billy swallowed.

'I mean, you're bloody lucky to have me, Ma'am?'

Bullman smiled.

'That's better,' she said, leaning over him and looking at the monitor. 'What do we have here?'

What Billy had was a selection of CCTV footage screens, all showing petrol station forecourts at night.

'So, I started thinking once Morten, I mean PC De'Geer sent me the information about the car,' he said. 'The car's an Audi Q5, 2020 model. It's a nice one, with an all-wheel drive.'

'Okay, *Top Gear*,' Declan snapped. 'Get to the point.'

'The car has a two-litre engine, and this returns around thirty-two miles per gallon,' Billy continued, unfazed by Declan's outburst. 'This gives it an average maximum distance on one tank of petrol of about four hundred and fifty miles.'

Tapping some keys, he brought up a map of the UK, with a route heading up the M1 and the M6, from London to Edinburgh.

'This is the quickest route from the restaurant in London, to Edinburgh, for someone leaving at around midnight,' he explained. 'It's four hundred and five miles, and would take approximately six, maybe six and a half hours depending on traffic.'

'So arriving around six-fifteen in the morning,' Declan nodded. 'Harnish could have made the journey and then driven back after. It's a long drive, but he'd be home by two in the afternoon, have a couple of hours' kip and then be in the kitchen that evening.'

'Nope,' Billy grinned. 'That's why Doctor Marcos called you. There's more. The Q5 only has a four hundred and forty-mile range, give or take, and the entire journey was over eight hundred miles.'

'He would have had to have refuelled,' Declan nodded. 'But that's four hundred miles in both directions he could have done so. How do you work it out?'

'Simple,' Billy beamed. 'The driver's in a hurry, but could have refuelled early in the journey. That's a problem for us, as they could have taken one of many routes through London, paying cash. And, once filled, they could go straight up, no stops.'

'But once they leave, they have a problem,' Bullman smiled back at Billy. 'They only have about fifty, sixty miles, and that's at best.'

'And they'd be travelling on motorways and A Roads, so using service stations,' Billy tapped on the keyboard and the CCTV images sprung to life, showing time-lapsed screen captures of cars arriving and leaving. 'I put a call out, got footage from that morning between seven and ten, and checked for the Q5 with a number plate algorithm.'

On one of the screens, a black Audi Q5 pulled up, the image pausing.

'This is Abingdon Services on the A74, about forty miles from Edinburgh,' Billy explained. 'Timestamp has it as eight-fifteen am, which fits the timescale.'

He restarted the video, and Declan watched the driver of the car get out, walking to the pump and placing it into the Audi.

And just like that, the itch he'd had in the back of his head was scratched.

'Yeah, that explains everything,' he said. 'This wasn't anything to do with Johnny's murder. This was something else.'

On the screen, Helen Cage, the hood of her hoodie now off her head was seen standing by the pump.

'Why would Helen drive up there the same day?' Bullman shook her head.

'I have a suspicion, but I still don't have the proof,' Declan replied.

'We have this,' Billy pointed at the screen, but Bullman shook her head.

'And what is this exactly?' she asked. 'Helen can claim she simply took the car on a jaunt. We can't even prove she was in the restaurant.'

'We need more before we bring her in, and time's running out,' Declan looked up as Anjli entered the office, DC Davey following. 'We've got an hour before the Queen eats food that's possibly cooked by a killer, food that we can't stop without due cause.'

'I might have that due cause,' DC Davey replied. 'I know what killed Tara Wilkinson, and where.'

THE MEMBERS DINING ROOM AT THE HOUSE OF COMMONS held history within its walls, an ornate dining area adorned with stunning gold and green flock wallpaper, wooden relief sculptures and a variety of expensive paintings positioned around four ceiling-high windows on the south side. Above the entrance to the Dining Room, the ornate Royal Coat of Arms, a golden lion facing a chained unicorn with the motto *Dieu et Mon Droit*, Latin for *God And My Right* underneath was positioned proudly above the doorway, signifying the connection of the Monarchy to Parliament.

Charles Baker loved this room. He loved the paintings, the leather covered green chairs, each with the commons 'portcullis' design printed on in gold, even the view from the windows over the Thames, currently behind him as he sat on the long top table, facing the other rows of tables that ran at a ninety-degree angle from where he sat, along the entire length of the room.

Beside him on his left was the Prime Minister, currently talking to the Queen, sitting beside him and at the very centre of the table. Although it was technically the last dinner of a retiring Prime Minister, the Queen was the focal point of the meal; there were many rules relating to eating with the Queen, but the main two were to echo the Queen's behaviour, so to eat when she did, and place the cutlery down when she did, but also to only sit at the table after the Queen sat down, which she had done but moments earlier.

Charles was happy with his seating, as he'd been brought closer than he could ever have imagined. Part of this was because he'd been involved in planning this, a fact also shown by Baroness Jones, a long-time friend of the Royal

Family sitting beside the Queen, in the seat that her husband Prince Phillip would have sat in before his passing. Another was because as the 'bookies favourite' heir apparent to the soon-to-be-vacant job, Charles had therefore made several efforts to be seen in any photos as 'in the room where it happened,' to quote his favourite musical, *Hamilton*. Although he was more a fan of the political songs in the second half than the whole *American Revolution* first half, which he found jingoistic and cartoonish.

To his right was Michelle Rose, the Foreign Secretary, the other possible candidate for leader, and from her expression, Charles knew she was unhappy with her seating, and hence her place in the pecking order.

Still, could have been worse, he thought to himself. *The wives, husbands and lower Cabinet members were all stuck on a table in the corner.*

He felt bad for them, but not too bad. After all, it had been he who had helped arrange the table places to ensure this. He gave a little apologetic wave to his wife at this, and looked up as a white-clad woman walked over to him, standing quietly beside him.

'Where's Patel?' he asked irritably. The Chef was supposed to be the only member of kitchen staff that would be seen in the room.

'I'm sorry, but Chef Patel has been detained and is on his way to the Palace of Westminster right now,' the white-clad woman said, smiling sweetly as she did so. 'As you can understand, the untimely death of his wife, and the investigation into the death of Leroy Daniels is causing us a few logistical issues. But, with your permission, we can start serving the first course right now.'

Charles nodded, glancing at the Queen as he did so, in conversation with Baroness Jones.

'What was it again?' he sighed, distractedly.

'A Gleneagles pâté, comprising smoked salmon, trout and mackerel,' the woman's smile didn't waver. 'It's ready to go on your say so.'

'And it's been checked for quality?' Charles was irritated at Harnish Patel's absence, but he also knew the man had been removed from the kitchen earlier that day to answer some questions at Temple Inn. And if Declan Walsh had released him, things must now be all right.

'Oh yes,' Helen Cage nodded earnestly. 'I've checked every one of the top table plates myself. It's definitely going to be a dinner to die for.'

25

OVERCOOKED

DC DAVEY STOOD AT THE FRONT OF THE BRIEFING ROOM, AN image of the spoon found in *Essence* behind her.

'Right then,' she started, pointing at the spoon. 'We sent the spoon that was in the sink off to be checked, and as we expected, the spoon had traces of tetrodotoxin on it. We're checking the rest, confirming what the toxin was embedded in—'

'Embedded?' Billy asked.

'Yes, it was likely to have been embedded in another item,' Doctor Marcos smiled sweetly as she glared at Billy. 'People rarely take spoonfuls of poisonous toxins.'

Anjli whistled the first two bars of *A spoonful of sugar* from *Mary Poppins*, but stopped as Doctor Marcos looked over to her.

'Love that film,' Doctor Marcos muttered. 'I see so much of myself in Poppins.'

'The thing we found though, that places the moment Tara Wilkinson was poisoned, isn't what was in the contents of the spoonful, but more the spoon itself,' DC Davey nodded to

Billy to change the image and suddenly a closeup of the handle of the teaspoon was blown up on the screen, zoomed in to show a stamp on the very end.

'As you can see, this is a symbol of a portcullis,' she said.

'The Houses of Parliament,' Declan realised, straightening as he saw it. 'I saw Charles Baker using one of these when we met on the Members Terrace.'

'It's not limited to the Terrace,' Davey responded. 'But it's only for special occasions, usually.'

'Like Gala Dinners?'

'That's likely,' Davey nodded. 'However, when we asked Darryl Carr, the potwasher if he recognised it, he said that when he left, there was nothing in that sink. Furthermore, when he left, Tara Wilkinson left with him, saying she needed to check the dinner plans.'

'So she went to the Houses of Parliament,' Anjli nodded.

'Helen Cage said that she'd been told by Harnish, that Tara went to make sure everything had arrived from Edinburgh on time, checking through stock and against the menu requirements until around seven-thirty.'

'Which would have been after the time she ingested the poison,' Doctor Marcos replied. 'She ate or drank something there, using a teaspoon, and then brought it back here to be washed.'

'Why bring it back?' Billy asked. 'They have teaspoons in the restaurant, and sinks in the Commons.'

'Maybe it was a keepsake?' Declan suggested. 'A trophy from the Gala Dinner, taken, used and then effectively pilfered?'

'We need to know what was on it,' Anjli was writing in her notepad. 'Do we know when we'll get that?'

'Any time before tomorrow, but no specifics,' Davey was almost apologetic.

'And the dinner would have started by now,' Declan looked at the clock on the wall. 'We need to stop it.'

'It's a dinner with the Queen and the Prime Minister attending,' Bullman shook her head. 'I'll call Bradbury, but even a Chief Superintendent can't close it down without solid cause, and currently we still have no actual proof of anything.'

She pointed at the spoon.

'They'll say she could have taken it at any time, that she could have had it in her office for months,' she said. 'With Howe stating that Tara was his expert on toxins, our murderer is dead, seemingly having accidentally ingested her own poison. They'll tell us to shut up and stand down until after.'

'So we find the proof, or we work out another way to stop things,' Declan said. 'At least get the Prime Minister and the Queen out.'

'We don't even know if something's happening, though,' Billy argued. 'What do we really know?'

'Okay, let's look quickly,' Declan nodded, nervously pacing, wishing Monroe was here. 'Helen is with Leroy, he's a big name chef and has his college friend Tara and her husband as part of the team.'

'Leroy and Helen are sleeping together—well, more just rutting, and Helen falls for Johnny,' Anjli added. 'Around this time, or maybe before it, Helen's father also dies.'

'Yes, *Hill's Honey* is in dire financial need but doesn't get help. Dad dies,' Declan mused. 'Helen and her mum seemed to think it was more health than stress though.'

'Helen leaves Leroy, goes with Johnny, leaves Johnny,' Billy said. 'Seems a bit of a pattern.'

'Johnny at this time is in the running for the Gala Dinner, beating Leroy,' Doctor Marcos said before looking out of the briefing room's windows with a smile. 'Christ almighty, what took you?'

Everyone turned to see a flustered Monroe and De'Geer enter the office.

'Sorry we're late,' Monroe said as he entered, waving at Declan, who was about to take his usual seat. 'No you don't, laddie. You're lead on this. Don't worry, we caught ourselves up to speed on the train.'

'Okay, so we have Helen and Johnny possibly break up because of this Gala, and Johnny moves to Edinburgh, his home town. Leroy maybe sends Tara up to beg him to allow Leroy to be involved somehow—'

'Actually, she doesn't,' Monroe added from the chair he sat on. 'De'Geer?'

'Before we came back, I stopped at *Monet* and showed the staff there a photo of Helen Cage,' De'Geer explained. 'They agreed that this was the woman who turned up, had a tour around the restaurant and was heard saying that she needed Johnny, that she'd risked everything for him. But, at the same time, she told them that her name was Tara Wilkinson, manager of *Essence*.'

'Her mother stated that Helen only went up once, to check that the last batch of *Hill's Honey* went there,' Declan nodded.

'Last batch?' Anjli looked up. 'As in no more?'

'As in Johnny Mitchell bought the entire load for tonight's dinner.'

'And Helen went to check on it?'

'No,' Declan said. 'I think that's what she told her mum. I think she went to beg Johnny to help her do something. And he told her no.'

'And then a couple of months later she's back with Leroy, and Leroy kills Johnny,' Monroe nodded.

'She's with Harnish, actually,' Bullman corrected.

'Isn't he married to Tara?'

'Yeah, a lot's happened, Guv.' Billy smiled. 'Helen and Harnish were having an affair.'

'So Leroy goes to Johnny and kills him, then Harnish goes up to Edinburgh—' Monroe stopped as Bullman held up a hand. 'Christ, woman. We only found that out this morning. Don't tell me that's wrong too?'

'Helen drove the car,' Declan replied. 'We've just found proof on CCTV. But we don't yet know why.'

'Helen goes to Edinburgh. Not to kill her ex, but to help her other ex?' Monroe shook his head. 'I assumed she was picking up the dropped knife De'Geer found.'

'No, because Leroy didn't realise he dropped it,' Billy looked up from his laptop. 'Dan Lane's just admitted that Leroy gave him a rucksack to get rid of when he climbed back on the plane. Didn't know what was in it, tossed it in a skip.'

'Dan Lane's admitted *Apex* smuggled Leroy in?'

'I think he didn't have much choice when the evidence came in,' Billy grinned.

Declan nodded at this.

'Okay, so moving on, Marshall Howe gets the tetrodotoxin, is told by his source, who he claims is Tara Wilkinson that Leroy killed Johnny, and he poisons him at the pub meeting, using the dosage he's been told will cause illness. He's accidentally poisoned too, but Leroy dies.'

'And did Tara give him the tetrodotoxin too?'

'Unknown.'

'There's no way Tara could,' Declan shook his head. 'She might have known how to prepare Fugu but this was different.'

'And tetrodotoxin is only really available for biotechnology companies in the US,' Davey added.

'Say that again?' Declan looked at her. Davey shrugged.

'I said tetrodotoxin is only really available for biotechnology companies in the US.'

'*Biotechnology*. That sounds a little more academic than Tara, someone with a chef's understanding of pufferfish,' Declan glanced at Billy who, realising where Declan was going with this, was already pulling up details.

'Helen Cage did a Bachelor in Science from Bristol University, specialising in *Cellular and Molecular Medicine*,' he said. 'We never checked into the rest. But we can see here that she did her postgraduate Masters degree at Newcastle, specialising in *Biotechnology, Gene Technology, Cell Biology and Genomics* with a dissertation on *The mechanisms of tetrodotoxins and conotoxins and their applications in medicine*.'

'If you needed an expert then Helen Cage was your woman,' Doctor Marcos nodded. 'And I'd bet she knew where to source the good stuff.'

Billy was already tapping on his keyboard.

'I think I might know where, too,' he said. 'I was checking the *Hill's Honey* records, confirming the sale to Johnny Mitchell, and I found this.'

An invoice appeared on the screen, and Doctor Marcos rose.

'*Potent, selective, use-dependent Na+ channel blocker, five thousand milligrams, seven thousand and ninety dollars plus tax*,' she said as she read the line description. 'US based company too. That's tetrodotoxin, all right.'

'Bought a month after Johnny broke up with her,' Billy noted the date.

'How much is five thousand milligrams?' Declan frowned.

'About a teaspoon's worth,' Doctor Marcos thought about this. 'A drop or two was all that was needed to kill Leroy. A teaspoon? In the right manner, it could kill dozens. Hundreds even.'

DC Davey looked at her phone as it beeped.

'Oh shit,' she muttered as she looked up. 'I mean, sorry, Ma'am, Guv.'

'What?' Bullman asked.

'We got the toxicology report,' DC Davey read from the phone. 'The spoon had been washed, most likely when Tara put it in the sink, but the traces of tetrodotoxin were inter-mingled with another trace. Honey. In particular—'

'Manuka honey,' Declan finished the conversation for Davey as he looked around the briefing room. 'That's why Helen went to *Monet* that morning. She knew nobody would be there, and she had time to do what she needed.'

'Which was?' Monroe, still catching up, asked.

'She doctored some of the honey,' Declan replied. 'She did the same to it as Howe did to the sandwiches. Helen knew she couldn't walk into the Houses of Parliament with tetrodotoxin, as there was a chance security would pick it up. So, she stuck it in the pots of honey that were there for the dessert and let them bring it in for her. Tara must have tested some last night and caught one of the poisoned pots. It was completely by accident.'

'*Get them on the phone now!*' Bullman was already up,

running for her office. 'I'll call Bradbury! *Close that meal down!*'

Declan, however, was already running for the door, with Anjli and Monroe immediately behind it.

'We need to stop that meal before they get to dessert,' he said. 'It'll take too long for the calls to go through!'

'How do you intend to do it?' Monroe asked as they took the stairs down to the main entrance two at a time.

'I'm in with the next Prime Minister, remember?' Declan grinned. 'I think it's time to demand my invite.'

CHARLES BAKER'S IMPRESSIONS OF HOW THE DINNER WOULD GO was actually far more interesting than how the dinner was *actually* going.

For the last hour, he'd politely sat at the table and smiled to the other diners, allowing them to whisper between themselves about the possibilities of his leadership options, but his primary hope, that of being seen with the Queen, maybe a small joke to make her smile, to show he had her attention even, had fallen on deaf ears, with the Prime Minister hogging all the bloody limelight.

And yes, Charles knew that this was the Prime Ministers last hurrah while being shunted off to the back benches, before he inevitably stepped down ahead of his own by-election, but at the same time there was a level of Tory support he should be giving to his successor, who was currently only able to talk to his back, while the sycophant sucked up to her Majesty for a peerage.

Michelle Rose, as in the wilds as he was, glanced at him with a smile.

'Not going the way you wanted, eh?' she asked. 'Doesn't look like you'll have your moment in the spotlight after all. All that planning for nothing.'

'We'll see,' Charles smiled back, purely for the audience who watched them, unaware of what was being said. 'I've still got time to gain the narrative.'

'Better do it fast,' Michelle nodded at the waiters, already moving in. 'Old Queenie-poos has finished her fillet steak with mushroom whisky sauce.'

She looked at his own plate.

'Oh no, you've barely touched yours.'

Charles fought back the urge to loudly swear at her, remembering silently that he was a major member of an elite Westminster cabal that could end careers in a second.

He had a name for the next meeting already in his head.

More importantly, he didn't have the narrative he was so confident about, and was very aware the clock was ticking. He noticed an Indian man in chef's whites standing nervously by the door and he rose, placing his napkin on the table, tiptoeing across the hall until he was beside the nervous chef.

'Chef Patel,' he whispered. 'Your food has been spectacular. What I've managed to eat of it anyway, relying on the food habits of a nonagenarian.'

'Thank you,' Harnish visibly relaxed. 'It's not been the best of days.'

'Best of weeks either,' Charles placed a hand on Harnish's arm. 'I heard about your wife. My condolences.'

'She did it to herself,' Harnish muttered, and Charles thought he saw the slightest hint of anger in his eyes. 'She worked with Howe to kill Leroy.'

'She did?' Charles Baker was genuinely surprised at this. 'I wonder why?'

'We'll never know now,' Harnish sighed. 'We'll clear the plates and move to dessert. Crème brûlée with Sandringham oranges, generously drizzled with Manuka honey.'

'Sounds divine,' Charles smiled. 'And I'm sure her maj will love the Sandringham touch. She does so like it when it's ingredients from her estates.'

Nodding to the now far more composed Chef Patel, Charles walked back to his chair, wondering whether Declan Walsh had been behind the confession by Marshall Howe, and whether Walsh was now investigating Tara's murder. He'd heard that Pearce had been found, and regretted the way he'd treated Declan when he visited, but he knew Declan understood politics. It was nothing personal; when you're toxic, you're not wanted. It was as simple as that.

Maybe now he's clear again, I can find a way to get some PR from him, he thought to himself, nodding at Michelle Rose again as he sat back down at his place on the top table. *After all, I'm going to need something explosive to knock the smile off this bitch's face.*

IN THE WESTMINSTER KITCHEN, HARNISH SWEPT IN THROUGH the doors like a man possessed, invigorated by the comments by the soon-to-be Prime Minister.

'Come on, people!' he shouted to the staff, most of whom were Westminster cooks, assisted by his *Essence* crew, mainly there to explain what Chef Patel meant when he gave particular orders. There was no time to learn on the job tonight, after all. 'Let's sort desserts! The waiting staff are clearing plates and we need to be ready to move!'

The kitchen was enormous, built for this kind of event,

not to mention the hundreds of MPs who ate in the Dining Room every day. And across every surface Harnish could see glass crème brûlée pots, filled with desserts while chefs turned their blowtorches onto the caster sugar sprinkled onto the top, caramelising it before reaching for the pots of *Hill's Honey,* taking tablespoons and dipping the whole spoon into the liquid, pulling them out and quickly transferring generous amounts to the glass crème brûlée pots.

They moved quickly, back and forth, allowing the honey to drizzle off the end of the spoons onto the caramelised surfaces in a criss-cross pattern, one showed to them by Helen at the start of the evening. Helen herself was at her own table, spoon already drizzling honey onto the surfaces.

'Do you need help—' Harnish had started to ask; Helen had single-handedly taken responsibility for both the head table and the corner one where the Cabinet sat, grabbing one box of honey for her own usage, and was taking great care the desserts were all perfect, but as he spoke, one hand rose, stopping him.

'I'm fine,' she snapped. 'I'm just finishing up.'

'You've got a couple of minutes, they're just cleaning the tables,' Harnish finished, spying a glob of honey, fallen from the spoon and on the edge of a glass. He went to wipe it away, but Helen grabbed the hand, holding it in a vice-like grip.

'I said I'm *fine*,' she hissed, grabbing a cloth and wiping it. 'Don't touch the honey. If you want to taste it, go play with one of the finished ones on the other table.'

Harnish raised up his hands in mock surrender, turning to walk away without a word. He'd found Helen to be every-thing Tara wasn't, but the moment Tara died, Harnish had realised he'd made a terrible mistake, one he would have given anything to take back. However, that would never happen, and no matter what occurred tonight, Harnish knew that once news of his affair came out, he would always be tarnished with the label of the man who was sleeping with his mistress two hundred yards from where his wife died, and then did a paid dinner the night after.

Still, the Gala would surely gain him better press. After all, it was going so well. And, with only dessert, coffee and speeches to go, Harnish had a feeling that finally, things were going his way.

However, the words that Declan Walsh had ended with still echoed in his mind, and he couldn't help but wonder how much of what Helen had said to him over the last few months had been purely for this moment. He turned to her, now back at the dessert prep.

'You disappeared,' he noted. 'During the main course. Where did you go?'

'Security outside,' Helen didn't even look up as she spoke. 'Poor buggers, standing outside while everyone's eating, all these wonderful smells coming through, I popped outside and gave them all a snack.'

'From what?' Harnish asked. Helen laughed.

'Chocolate brownies from the MPs' stock,' she replied. 'Don't worry, I didn't use any of ours, I just tweaked them a little and sent them out.'

Harnish looked back at the hall, nervously playing back Declan's words again.

'I believe that Helen Cage has an agenda, and although I can't prove it, I think she intends to harm people.'

'You're telling me everything, right?' he asked.

'Of course not,' Helen grinned. 'You need to be on point today. I won't hassle you with the small stuff. Tomorrow, you'll be the most famous chef in the world, and we'll go over everything. *Trisha! Take these to the main door and get ready to plate them on the top table! Eight to go, eight more to come! Don't touch the food!'*

As the crème brûlée pots with Sandringham oranges, generously drizzled by Helen with Manuka honey were taken by the serving staff, Harnish wondered, not for the first time, what his legacy would truly be, and how far he would go to gain the one he wanted.

———————

26

GATECRASHERS AT THE BALL

THE TWO POLICE OFFICERS ON DUTY AT THE MAIN GATES OF THE Houses of Parliament knew it was a big night; for a start the protestors were back on Parliament Green, and on a sunny day like this, most would rather be somewhere else than standing with placards waved around in the faint hope that a Minister would see it, and have a sudden *come to Jesus* moment, changing their entire belief structure.

What the police hadn't expected were the two squad cars that screeched to a halt in front of the gates, the driver of the first, a mud-spattered grey Audi leaping out and waving a warrant card in the air.

'Detective Inspector Walsh, City Police!' he yelled. *'Call up the dinner and tell them to stop!'*

Behind him, the police officer could see another man, white bearded, emerge from a passenger door, and behind him, in the second car, two women appeared; the first was a young Indian woman, the other, an older, white-haired woman, all plain clothed. They started towards him as well as, to complete the scene, a police motorcycle pulled up, the large police officer riding it leaping off and pulling his helmet off to reveal a blond beard and furious eyes.

'Look, you can't just park there—' he started, but by this point, the first man to appear was in front of him.

'*Call your boss!*' he screamed. '*Stop the dinner!* We believe there's a terrorist attack!'

The word *terrorist* was enough for the police officer and he immediately grabbed his radio, attached to his black stab vest, speaking into it.

'Sarge, we've got police at the gate, demanding the meal be stopped.'

He listened for a moment, hearing whoever he was talking to inside his earpiece.

'Meal's already started.'

'We know!' Declan exclaimed angrily. 'We want you to stop it!'

The officer listened to his radio earpiece again.

'Did you say your name is Walsh?' he asked.

'Detective Inspector Walsh, yes,' Declan replied. 'Why?'

'You're barred,' the officer replied apologetically. 'We have a direct order from Jennifer Farnham-Ewing, aide to Charles Baker, saying not to allow you entrance, nor should we listen to any flights of fiction you claim to get in. Her own words—'

'I don't have time for this,' Declan stormed past the police officer. 'If you want to arrest me, then do it in the Members Dining Room. Otherwise speak to DCI Monroe, PC De'Geer or Detective Superintendent Bullman.'

'Sir!' The officers moved to intercept, but De'Geer moved to block their way.

'I suggest you listen to him,' he said. 'Call the guards on duty. See if anything weird is going on.'

Still following Declan as he marched across the courtyard, the police officer tried in vain to get through to anyone. The roll call of seriously superior ranks arriving with DI Walsh was unnerving, especially to a uniformed officer, and the last thing he wanted to do was make a mistake.

'It's a Royal event,' he said. 'They'll be busy.'

'Or they're already dead,' De'Geer said in an ominous tone.

There were guards at the gate; suited men who Declan knew would be ex-military, and often worked as tour guides. Beside them was an armed police officer, and Declan started to work out how to get past this, but one of the suited guards stepped forward, blocking the armed police officer's line of sight.

'Anthony Farringdon sends his regards,' he said. 'How can we help?'

Declan glanced back at Monroe, a few feet behind.

'I called him in the car,' he said. 'Thought it couldn't help.'

Declan grinned. It looked like the security for Parliament and Downing Street remembered Anthony Farringdon well, at least enough to follow a request from him when called in.

'We need to stop the Dinner,' he said. 'Before dessert.'

'That could be classed as treason,' one guard said as they walked past the confused armed guard, now facing a wealth of City Police and Parliament security officers. 'But then we work for the Commons, not the Crown, so sure, let's do it.'

Charles Baker felt his stomach rumble as he waited for dessert to arrive. The fact he had managed to eat none of the main course was all on him, too focused on being seen, and less on being seen to be eating.

The others in the Cabinet, however, seemed to be more than happy to chomp away in their troughs; even Tamara Banks, Conservative MP and member of the *Star Chamber* that Charles currently commanded, had made a point of coming over and complimenting him on a meal well made, as if he was the bloody chef or something.

Charles wasn't an idiot, he knew she was only doing this to make sure they saw her with him at the dinner, so when he took over she wasn't classed as one of the MPs that was 'against' him. And he'd smiled dutifully back, commenting that it was sad that she hadn't yet been utilised to her fullest potential, as if suggesting that she should be higher in Cabinet, *his* Cabinet perhaps.

Because he wasn't stupid either. He knew how these things worked.

A member of the white-jacketed service staff moved along the back of the top table, placing small plates of dessert before the diners. A glass container, with a crème brûlée pot resting on top of it, was positioned in front of him, and Charles breathed in the smell, his stomach growling with desire as he took in the sweet bouquet of honey. Without thinking, he picked up his spoon, about to place it into the bowl as Michelle Rose grabbed his hand, stopping him.

'What in God's name are you doing?' she hissed, nodding down the table where, two seats along, the Queen was still in conversation with Baroness Jones. 'You know you eat when she does and not before.'

'Christ,' Charles wanted to toss the spoon down in disgust, but knew it'd make a scene. Still forcing a smile, he placed the spoon back on the table, taking a sip of water instead. 'Thank you. Although, if I'd made such a *faux pas*, you'd have been a shoo in for the job.'

'You'd have just found a way to lay the blame on me,' Michelle shook her head. 'It was easier this way.'

'Well, it was appreciated. And it won't be forgotten,' Charles wondered whether his competition was realising the enormity of her challenge, and was already vying for a Cabinet spot after her inevitable loss. Saving him from royal scrutiny was a pretty good start. All he needed to do was wait a little longer to eat.

His stomach, not getting the memo, simply growled louder.

But Charles could wait. The desserts were almost all out, and eventually the Queen would start eating.

And then they all could.

DECLAN WAS RUNNING AT A SPRINT NOW; HE'D PRETTY MUCH broken the world record for the hundred metres as he ran through Westminster Great Hall, or at least it bloody felt like it, especially as he took the steps at the end two at a time like Sylvester Stallone in the training scene in *Rocky*. With the officers and guards behind him, it looked either like a ragged procession, or more likely an armed chase.

The problem was that nobody could get through to the guards on the doors; the phones and radios simply weren't being answered. And, more importantly, none of the guests in the Dinner had their phones on because the Queen was there and all phones were removed before entering. In fact, only a moment of the gravest importance would allow entrance, and a paranoid detective who might or might not be under suspension or investigation, and who was barred from entrance by a jobsworth aide, was definitely not likely to be top of that list.

The thing concerning Declan the most, as he ran through the octagonal Central Lobby with more officers behind him now, was that with nobody answering the phone, there was literally no way to know if the people in the Dining Room were even still alive.

No, don't think that. You'll get there in time.

Monroe had dropped back, wheezing halfway down the corridor, but De'Geer was matching Declan stride for stride, and an armed officer, caught up in the moment was actively in front of Declan now, effectively leading the charge, screaming for people to get out of the way. In fact, the BBC journalists in Central Lobby who always did the *live feeds to station* sections of the news, seeing the crowd run past, grabbed their cameras and joined in the scrum.

Declan reached the corridor that led to the Members Dining Room and stopped.

There were two armed men there, *Her Majesty's Body Guard of the Honourable Corps of Gentlemen at Arms,* dressed in the uniforms of 1840s Heavy Dragoon Guards officers; complete with skirted red coats with Garter blue velvet cuffs, and facings embroidered with the Tudor royal badge of the Portcullis. Helmets with white swan feather plumes, usually worn when on duty, were discarded on the ground, next to fallen ceremonial battle-axes.

The items, Declan could see, had been discarded because the two guards were now slumped against the wall, either unconscious or dead.

'Christ,' Declan stopped, checking one of the soldiers. 'Are they dead?'

'Unconscious,' one of the suited guards said, checking a pulse on the neck. 'They've been drugged.'

'By those, I guarantee it,' Declan said, looking down at the two plates of half eaten chocolate brownies on the floor between them. 'Helen's already made sure nobody's there to stop her.'

And with that, he started down the corridor, already seeing the other fallen soldiers, in Victorian Heavy Dragoon Guards uniforms ahead of him.

He only hoped this was the worst that would happen.

'CAN SOMEONE PLEASE SHUT THE BARONESS JONES UP?' Charles Baker groaned. 'The bloody woman can't read the room.'

He was correct in his complaint; the Baroness, during an anecdote to the Queen, hadn't noticed that not only had everyone been provided with a dessert, but now they all stared expectantly at both the Queen and the Baroness, waiting for Her Majesty to pick up her spoon and begin, enabling them to do so. Unfortunately, the bloody woman was so caught up in her own bullshit, she'd neglected to note that everyone was glaring at her. Eventually, glancing around while she started yet another story, Baroness Jones must have realised that nobody else in the entire room was speaking and, in the stony silence, reddened, realising why everyone was watching her.

The Queen, meanwhile, oblivious to this, egged the Baroness on, asking her to continue.

In the moment of silence before the Baroness complied, the Prime Minister leant forward.

'Perhaps, Your Majesty, you'd like to try your dessert?' he not-so-subtly suggested. 'The oranges come from your Sandringham estate.'

The Queen, looking back at the Prime Minister, smiled at this, always a fan of her own estate's food. And, with the entire room watching, salivating, she picked up her dessert spoon and broke the crust of the crème brûlée with it, taking a generous mouthful's worth onto the spoon.

'Thank Christ,' Charles said as he picked up his own dessert spoon. 'Maybe I'll be able to eat something now before something else spoils my day.'

DECLAN RAN UP TO THE DINING ROOM DOORS, NOTING THAT again, the uniformed *Gentlemen at Arms* were unconscious at their posts. Inside, and through the doors, he could see the dinner in full swing, with everyone watching the Queen, most likely to work out when to start or stop eating.

Well, this time someone else was going to control that.

With a shoulder barge, Declan slammed open the double doors to the Dining Room, stumbling into the room at speed, the chamber almost freezing in mid-motion as the diners, stunned at this stopped, many of which with their spoons halfway to their mouths.

'City Police! Don't eat the dessert!' Declan shouted.

If there was any chance this would be taken as a serious comment and responded to in kind, Declan saw it rapidly disappear as the Dining Room erupted into nervous shouts of horror, calling for the police as, behind the top table members of Special Branch rushed the Queen and the Prime Minister, pulling the former from her chair and surrounding her, prepared to remove her from the scene if the shouting man turned out to be a bigger threat.

'*Arrest that man!*' The Prime Minister, struggling against his own Special Branch officers, trying to pull him away as well was shouting, pointing at Declan.

'*Sod that, arrest her!*' Declan cried out, pointing at Helen Cage, standing beside the main door, a smug smile on her face. However, more police had arrived by this point and, following the Prime Minister's orders, moved towards Declan—

'*Stop!*' Charles stood up and shouted, his voice loud and booming. 'All of you, cease your prattle! This is Detective Inspector Declan Walsh of the City Police! A man who I owe my life to on more than one occasion, and if he believes there is foul play afoot here, I, for one, will listen to him!'

It was an impassioned plea, and it was a receptive one, with the audience immediately falling into silence. Charles smiled. He'd seen the BBC cameras appear in the back of the crowd, and he knew they'd seen the Prime Minister, held down by bodyguards, crying out for arrests. Charles, however, was the face of reason. He was a calming force. Something a potential Prime Minister should be. Even the Queen seemed interested to hear what had caused the intrusion, now that she was surrounded by her armed guards. 'Please, Declan, tell me what the meaning of this is,' he said calmly.

'The Pastry Chef has poisoned the desserts,' Declan looked around the room, finally spying the Queen, surrounded by her guards. 'My apologies, your Majesty. I would not have done this without reason. We couldn't get through to you because your own *Gentlemen at Arms* have been rendered unconscious by what looks to be chocolate brownies.'

'What sort of poison?' Charles asked nervously. 'In the desserts?'

'A rather toxic nerve agent,' Declan slowed as he saw the glass dessert bowls on the surrounding plates.

The *empty* ones.

'Oh shit,' he muttered to himself.

For he was too late, and the poisoned desserts, the ones with honey laced with tetrodotoxin, ones given out to God knows who by Helen, were already eaten.

'You missed dessert, detective inspector,' Helen crowed from the door. 'But you're in time for coffee.'

'Tell me you didn't,' Declan begged, as police started moving towards Helen. 'Tell me you did *not* poison the Queen.'

'Of course I didn't,' Helen snapped. 'I'm a monarchist. And I didn't poison anyone. I think you have the wrong suspect.'

'I don't think so,' Bullman now approached. 'Did you poison everyone, or a select few?'

'A select few,' Harnish Patel said, now stepping forward. 'She took a box of honey and only worked on a few desserts.'

Helen spun to glare at her onetime lover as Declan looked at Harnish.

'Looks like you listened to me,' he said.

Harnish shrugged.

'I did more than that,' he admitted. Nodding, as if understanding this, Declan tuned back to Helen.

'Please, tell us who,' he begged.

'I second that,' Charles said from the top table.

'You've got nothing on me,' Helen claimed. 'You know nothing.'

Declan thought for a moment, realising that everyone, even the cameramen from the BBC were focused on him.

'I know everything,' he said. 'I know the why's, the what's, the who's and the hows. And, after I explain everything, I'll tell you exactly who you poisoned.'

And, in front of Queen Elizabeth the Second, Declan began to speak.

27

DESSERT WHINE

'I KNOW, FIRST OF ALL, THAT YOU POISONED THE CRÈME brûlée,' Declan started.

'You're talking conspiracies,' Helen smiled. 'I honestly don't know what you mean.'

'Well, if we're talking conspiracies, let me go through one with you,' Declan nodded back, now pacing in the middle of the room. 'You've had a problem with the Government since you believed they effectively killed your father and ended your company, *Hill's Honey.*'

'We did no such thing!' Michelle Rose exclaimed at this, realising the connection. 'The New Zealand commission had issues with Hill's Honey that almost destroyed an entire trade deal we'd spent years on!'

'You left us in the dark to die!' Helen snapped back. 'You knew we needed those bushes! It was a small price to pay, a couple of cuttings—'

'Was all it would have taken to destroy billions of pounds of commerce!' Michelle Rose interrupted. 'We couldn't risk it.'

'And their aversion to the risk killed your father,' Declan turned back to Helen. 'Your father had a heart attack due to stress when your Manuka bushes died, and the Government wouldn't bail your company out. You almost went bust, using his insurance money to stay afloat, to try to rebuild the company. But this was when you started to plan your revenge, wasn't it?'

'I don't know what you mean,' Helen shrugged, folding her arms. 'This is fiction.'

'First, you needed to make sure Leroy Daniels would bring you back into *Essence*,' Declan continued. 'You needed the money, I get that, but what you didn't expect to do is fall in love with Johnny Mitchell, a love that caused problems between Mitchell and Daniels right up to both of their deaths.'

'If they were jealous of each other, that wasn't anything to do with me.'

'No, you can't be blamed for jealousy, I suppose,' Declan nodded. 'But what you can be blamed for is the situations that led to the murders.'

'How so?' This time it was Harnish who asked.

'Because while they were together, Helen convinced Johnny Mitchell to pitch for this dinner,' Declan replied. 'Already at that point, Helen knew what she wanted to do, to poison them somehow with the desserts.'

He looked back at Helen now.

'You'd already proven yourself to be indispensable here, Johnny's favourite pastry chef. And, because he loved you, and probably your family too, you told him of your idea, of poisoning honey with tetrodotoxin, and then using it, poisoning the very people that killed your family's company.'

'This is all circumstantial and conspiratorial.'

'True,' Declan smiled. 'But let's continue and see how conspiratorial it gets.'

He continued to pace now.

'So you're with Johnny at this point; Johnny is performing his new character, Jean-Michel Blanc, on *YouTube* and *TikTok*, making a name for himself and causing issues with Leroy with his mocking videos. Around then you'd gotten to know Marshall Howe, partly because of Johnny, but mainly through the rivalry Howe had with Daniels, and convinced him that Johnny Mitchell, or more importantly Jean-Michel Blanc was a good alternative to Leroy, somebody who Marshall could champion, annoying Leroy in the process,'

'Johnny was a charismatic man, there's nothing I can do about that. He did all that himself,' Helen admitted.

Declan nodded, conceding the point.

'Johnny and Marshall hit it off, and from the beginning Marshall saw great talent in Johnny, but all you wanted was Marshall to like Johnny so much that he would champion him for the next Gala Dinner, because at this point you'd learnt that Marshall Howe was on the committee. You realised that if you could get Johnny in there, the menu would be created by you, one that would then be eaten by the Government.'

'This is fantasy fiction!' Helen cried.

Declan waved his arms around the room.

'And yet here we are,' he said.

Helen was silent, and so Declan continued.

'But things didn't work out the way you wanted, did they?' he asked. 'When Johnny got the Gala Dinner, he realised what your plan was. Maybe you told him, maybe you explained how you wanted to play this, maybe you showed him the tetrodotoxin you'd bought under *Hill Honey's* name.'

'Tetrodotoxin's a tough thing to find,' Helen protested. 'You have to be an expert to use it. Tara Wilkinson trained in Japan to learn how to make Fugu. She could have done this.'

'What she didn't have was a Master's degree in Biotechnology, with a dissertation on how tetrodotoxin worked on the human system,' Declan smiled. 'You have one of those, don't you? If anybody would know how to kill someone with a toxin, it'd be you.'

Helen's lips inched up in the slightest of smiles.

'Okay, so *then* what, Sherlock?'

'I think at this point Johnny realised you were too far gone, you had an argument, he realised that being near you, maybe even being in the same city as Leroy, who was still trying to cause problems for him, made Johnny decide to get a fresh break, return home. The location of his first place of work came up for lease back in Edinburgh, and so he took it, moving *Monet* north of the border,' Declan suggested. 'He'd already ordered the food at this point, he'd already started the menu and the Government was giving him an open cheque book to get whatever he wanted. And as a last favour, maybe even a breakup wish, he bought the remaining Manuka honey from *Hill's Honey* at a massive markup, taking it to Edinburgh, where he started up all over again but without you.'

He stopped for a moment.

'Do you think he did all this to stop your plan?'

'Johnny did it to help my family,' Helen snapped. 'I had no plan.'

'But that's not true, as you were already working to your plan,' Declan shook his head. 'The moment Johnny walked away, you realised you still needed your revenge, and so you went for the next best thing, Leroy Daniels.'

'Leroy didn't want to hire me.'

'You didn't go to Leroy, you went to Harnish Patel, the man who secretly loved you since he met you.'

There was a gasp as the diners, watching this strange dinner theatre, broadcast their shock at this revelation. Harnish, standing to the side nodded at this.

'She came to me begging to be brought back,' he said sadly, realising this had all been a fallacy. 'She gave me the sob story about how she'd been let down by Johnny, hinted how she had feelings for me, and at the time me and Tara were having our own problems, and so Helen and I started an affair.'

'An affair that brought Helen back into *Essence* when you convinced Leroy Daniels to hire her once more.'

'I convinced Leroy that having Helen around was a good chance to have a spy against Johnny, particularly for the Gala dinner, which Leroy only just missed out on,' Harnish admitted. 'I convinced Leroy that if we could somehow sabotage Johnny's attempts, then we could gain the opportunity instead.'

'And who suggested first that you could do this?'

'Helen did,' Harnish looked at the floor as he spoke. 'She gave us a rough idea what the menus were going to be, as she'd seen them. She told us Johnny kept his briefcase of plans in the safe, but then Johnny released another video, mocking Chef Daniels and he was furious. Tara said he needed to do something about it once and for all, but she didn't mean killing Johnny Mitchell.'

'But that's what Leroy did,' Monroe now spoke from the doorway. 'In the process finding the perfect alibi, a trip to Dubrovnik where he could be seen in public in a totally different country the same time Johnny Mitchell was being murdered.'

There was a sharp intake of breath by the diners at this.

'It was well planned,' Declan slow clapped. 'Tara assisted, for whatever reason—'

'She loved Leroy, always had. She would have done anything for him,' Harnish admitted. Declan nodded at this.

'Well, on the first day of the trip, they made sure every press photographer was there taking photos, ensuring he was seen everywhere. And then, after a day or two he found a lookalike, put the glasses, the hat, all the costume on him and made him stand in the background for two days while the real Leroy caught a chartered private jet from the distribution company *Apex,* who owed him money, flying to Northumberland on the Wednesday of Johnny Mitchell's death. He then crept into *Monet*, entering through a trapdoor that led from the tunnels under the city—'

'And how would he know about that?' Helen laughed. 'A secret entrance that nobody knew. Good God.'

'*You* knew, didn't you?' Declan asked. 'Because you'd already been there when you made sure the honey had arrived. Your own mother confirmed this to me. The staff at *Monet* confirmed you visited the cellar, saw the trapdoor to the vaults. You probably copied the key for it and found a way for Leroy, or others to open it.'

'Tara Wilkinson went to *Monet*,' Helen stuck to her story. 'Mum was wrong. She has bad days. Tara went there, begging Johnny to allow Leroy to be involved.'

'Oh, we heard,' Declan said. 'And we know it was Tara Wilkinson, because she *told* everybody she was Tara Wilkinson. However, when PC De'Geer showed the *Monet* staff *your* photo, they agreed that this was the Tara Wilkinson they spoke to.'

'They're wrong.'

'Of course they are, *Mrs Wilkinson*.'

Helen stayed silent at this, so Declan continued.

'So Leroy arrives, gains entrance to the building thanks to you—sorry, Tara, hides underground until the end of the shift and once the staff are gone Leroy emerges, confronts Johnny and kills him with his own chef's knife, a personal touch he'd already promised to do, close to midnight. Then he gets in his car, drives back to the airfield and returns to Dubrovnik that night, arriving the following day.'

'Nice story.'

'More than that, I'm afraid,' Declan shook his head. 'You see, in his hurry to escape, he dropped the knife inside the tunnel. Didn't even realise it'd fallen out of his bag.'

Helen's expression was mocking.

'He has a bag now?'

'Yes,' Declan smiled. 'One Dan Lane threw away for him. It's okay, Dan's already confessed to it. You can have the police cell next to him.'

'This is insane,' Harnish said. 'I knew Leroy for years, and Tara would have never—'

'Chef Daniels burned his hand the day of the first meal,' Declan interrupted. 'A burn that was visible in photos before and after this moment, but wasn't visible on the Leroy Daniels who was seen *during* this point.'

'This is your evidence?' Helen almost laughed.

'We get an excellent shot of the hand too, as he tries to stop a photographer taking a photo in a nightclub in Dubrovnik, beside Tara. It doesn't have a burn, even though his body, days later, still did.'

'If this is true, then maybe Tara was fooled too?' Harnish offered.

'Unlikely,' Monroe replied. 'She claimed that during this time, she was sleeping with Leroy. If she was, she knew it was a double. More likely, she forgot to crumple his bedclothes, to make it look like he was sleeping there.'

'The nightclub photo proves to us that Leroy wasn't in Croatia and after learning that, it wasn't hard to work out what happened; Leroy arriving in *Monet,* killing his rival and then taking the briefcase Johnny Mitchell always used for his ideas from the open safe, so that when the Government inevitably called him, asking him to take over as a second place chef, that he already knew what Johnny's meal plan would be,' Declan explained. 'We saw it in Leroy's hand at the last Gala committee meeting in the CCTV images. Understandable really, after all, there was no way he was going to be able to change the menu too much with the menu already out there. And being forced to use pre-bought supplies, including the last amount of *Hill's Honey,* meant his hands were tied. But that wasn't everything, was it Helen?'

'I don't know what you mean.'

Declan walked towards her.

'I mean that on the night in question, you took the keys to the *Essence* car, one in Harnish Patel's name and, after your shift ended on that Wednesday night you drove all the way to Edinburgh, four hundred miles non-stop, arriving at *Monet* at six in the morning—'

'Bullshit!' Helen snapped. 'Tara did this! Not me!'

'Tara was in Dubrovnik,' Declan reminded Helen. 'You arrived at six in the morning, parking near the *Ibis Hotel.* You sneaked through the tunnels, and entered the restaurant for an hour, at which point a cleaner, the cleaner who discovered the body of Johnny Mitchell, heard you leave the office and escape through the cellar trapdoor. She believes it's ghosts, but our PC De'Geer, on checking this, realised it could only have been you making your way out of the building, after doing what you needed to do.'

'And what was that?' Charles couldn't help himself blurting out the question.

'Taking a box of *Hill's Honey* and doctoring it with tetrodotoxin, the same toxin that you gave to Marshall Howe afterwards.'

'Oh, so now I gave Marshall drugs?'

'No, you gave Marshall poisons. Toxins.'

Declan sighed.

'Come on, we know it was you,' he added. 'You're the only one who could've done it. You had the toxins, bought from America and, aside from what you saved for Marshall, you filled those pots with poison.'

He looked around the Dining Room.

'How many we don't know, but you knew that once back in their boxes they'd be brought straight here, no questions asked, especially with all the chaos following the death of Johnny Mitchell, and once here you could walk in without a problem, pick up the ones you'd fixed and get your revenge.'

'Leroy had control here, not me,' Helen replied.

'True, Leroy was now your next loose end,' Declan nodded. 'They didn't know what you'd done, but Leroy suspected you, Tara didn't want you at the dinner—and you needed to be here to kill your targets.'

'On that, should we be calling ambulances?' Charles asked. 'You seem very calm.'

'We've got time,' Declan replied, turning back to look at

Helen. 'You had to remove Leroy, and so you returned to Marshall Howe and, with your knowledge of how Leroy killed Johnny Mitchell, told Marshall everything, convincing him to wreak bloody revenge on his long-term rival. The plan was to 'hurt' him, put him out of business long enough to lose out on this meal, this lifetime opportunity and then have him arrested for the crime, but you deliberately gave him the wrong dosage, knowing he'd effectively kill Leroy by doing this, making sure you couldn't be linked to the trapdoor key or the tunnel plan. What you didn't realise was that he's screw up so badly he'd poison himself too—almost, but not dying. And guess what, he's awake now and waiting to work out a deal. How long before he names you?'

Helen laughed as the room grew silent at this.

'No, please, go on,' she said.

Declan frowned. He hadn't expected that as a response.

'So, now it's days to go before this dinner, and Harnish and Tara have been given the job to continue. Harnish who believed in you, who loved you, and who believed you felt the same, and Tara who no longer trusted you.'

Bullman, also at the door, moved forward.

'Tara, suspicious of your honey's quality, tried some yesterday while here. By pure bad luck she picked the wrong box, in the process ingesting a fatal amount of tetrodotoxin, and dying last night in the restaurant.'

'You can't prove she was poisoned in this building,' Helen spoke confidently. However, Declan simply smiled, looking back to the main door where, pushing her way through the waiting police was Doctor Marcos, following Anjli into the Dining Room.

'Actually, we can,' she said. 'The teaspoon she used was

from this very room, and was stamped with the portcullis design all Parliament cutlery has. She must have taken it as a keepsake, and that keepsake didn't just kill her, it gave us the location of her murder.'

'Or, we could look at all the CCTV footage this place has,' Monroe pointed at a camera in the corner of the room. 'Bet she's on one of those, tasing your wares.'

'Come on!' Helen laughed. 'You can't blame me for *that* murder!' she waved around the Dining Room. 'Why are you talking, anyway? I poisoned everyone, remember? And there's no antidote!'

There was a definite rumble of noise at this, and Declan held up a hand.

'You didn't have enough to poison everyone,' he said. 'And as you said, you had no issue with Her Majesty the Queen. Your attack was targeted. If I had to guess, I'd say it was pretty much only the current Conservative Cabinet, and in particular Michelle Rose, the Foreign Secretary.'

There was a confusing sound at this; in some ways it was a sigh of relief as many of the diners realised they were safe, while a more audible groan was heard from the Cabinet members there, realising they'd finished their desserts.

'You had control over the desserts that went out as Pastry Chef,' Declan waved at the tables. 'You controlled each one.'

Helen sighed.

'It's true,' she said. 'All of it. Well done. But you still arrived too late, and I still killed the Cabinet.'

'Actually, you didn't,' Harnish said, stepping forwards. 'I told them to put your bowls to the side, said they weren't right. The Cabinet had the spare desserts we always make, in case some break or aren't up to scratch.'

'You couldn't have known this!' Helen exclaimed, but Harnish simply nodded sadly at her.

'You were too forceful in stopping me going near the honey while you plated, and I remembered something DI Walsh had said to me earlier about people dying on my watch,' he replied. 'I couldn't risk it, so when we started placing desserts, they were swapped.'

'Not one dessert you plated is out here,' Declan added. 'And the guards you sedated outside will all make full recoveries.'

'Of course they will, you idiot,' Helen snapped, her voice rising. 'I didn't hate them. I just needed them not to stick their noses in here for a while. But you didn't know that when you came in. You couldn't have.'

'I knew.' Declan looked at Harnish. 'I knew because Chef Patel told me so when he said he'd done more than just listening to me. I knew he was a good man, who hadn't been involved in your madness. So yeah, we pretty much have enough to arrest you in connection to the murders of Leroy Daniels and Johnny Mitchell, manslaughter charges connected to Tara Wilkinson and conspiracy to murder the British Government, which I think is effectively treason, even though nobody ate your desserts.'

'Actually, one person did,' Helen straightened up, resigned to her cause. 'I knew when they died I'd get arrested, so once I finished sending them out, I ate the last one myself.'

She looked at Harnish.

'You killed me,' she said.

'No, Helen,' Harnish replied sadly. 'You killed yourself. But not by poisoning.'

He looked back at Declan.

'I swapped that as well,' he said, half apologetically. 'She's as safe as these people are.'

Helen stared at Harnish in shocked realisation.

'Shit,' she muttered as Declan waved for the armed police to move in, arresting Helen before she could move, the diners rising and applauding, as if this was the end of some kind of improvised theatre. Declan turned to get out as quickly as he could, but found his arm grabbed by Charles Baker, now away from the top table, and holding up the arms of Harnish and Declan like a referee in a wrestling match.

'Let's hear it for the heroes of the night!' he shouted. *'The men who saved the Government! Chef Patel and DI Walsh!'*

Declan grimaced. He'd been made election fodder again.

'Does this mean I'm allowed back on the Members Terrace again?' he asked. Charles smiled widely.

'You can go wherever you damn well want,' he said. 'I think you just made me Prime Minister with this photo.'

Declan politely pulled away, noting that Special Branch had finally moved the Queen and the Prime Minister out of the dining room, and decided that discretion was the better part of valour, starting towards the entrance, nodding at the still-applauding diners until he stopped as Anjli walked over to him, a phone in her hand and a look of horror on her face.

'What?' he whispered.

'There was a gas explosion,' she said. 'I just heard. A cottage in St Davids. One fatality, a woman.'

Declan stared back at Anjli. Francine Pearce had faked her death once before, but Declan knew this time it was real, because Declan knew Karl Schnitter would have fixed it to happen the day the US Embassy arrested him. He'd even told him as much.

'*I said I needed to make things right. I did not say that involved conversation.*'

Declan moved past Anjli, silently leaving the room, unaware of the congratulatory pats on his arms as he walked down the corridor. He needed to get to the US Embassy, to see if Karl Schnitter was still in custody, to ask him if he'd done this, and why.

But in his heart, he knew that Karl Schnitter was long gone.

———

EPILOGUE

HARNISH HAD BEEN RIGHT; HELEN DIDN'T DIE THAT NIGHT. SHE didn't even suffer any side effects from handling so much tetrodotoxin, which in a way was a testament to her skills as a Pastry Chef. Instead, she was taken by Special Branch to New Scotland Yard, where she spent the night in a cell while high-up members of the Metropolitan Police worked out what to do with her. She'd been involved in the murder of several people, which meant a court case and a trial, but she'd also committed high treason, the first for many years, and there was a strong case for dumping her in the Tower of London and leaving her to rot.

Declan liked that idea and had even suggested to Monroe that they could make her into a tourist attraction. She could even bake pastries to be sold in the shop as part of her reha-bilitation.

That said, Helen was being very talkative, trying to pin blame to a lot of this on one of the three dead people in her wake. However, Marshall Howe, also realising the truth of his own situation, had changed his story, explaining that it was actually Helen, not Tara, that had given him the tetrodotoxin in the first place. With the purchase order added to this, Helen didn't have a hope of getting out of this, especially after Doctor Marcos confirmed that not only did a batch of the honey have tetrodotoxin laced into it, but twenty desserts, dumped into a waste bin on Chef Patel's orders, had all tested positive for it.

Charles Baker, in the meantime had tried desperately to make political hay out of the event, pointing out to anyone listening that not only had Declan been a hand-picked officer of the law, mentored by Baker after Declan had saved his life (a mentorship that Declan didn't recall), but that Harnish had been hand-picked by Charles for the meal, not out of desperation, but because he knew something was *special* about him, a fact he repeated during a variety of press conferences they held together over the next few days.

Declan, unsurprisingly, wasn't invited to these, most likely because he would have called Charles Baker on his bullshit while Harnish, having lost everything and needing a silver bullet to regain his reputation, would have grasped at the first sturdy straw handed to him, knowing the media had started to decide he was an adulterer who let his own wife die, while shacking up with the woman who effectively killed her. Even Charles Baker wouldn't be able to resurrect *that* career, and after a couple of days Charles realised this, dropping Harnish as quickly as he'd picked him up. Declan felt sorry for Charles; he'd pushed so hard to be seen at the event, and the fact he *was* visible meant he was also now the public face for the whole debacle. It probably wasn't going to help his Leadership battle prospects.

That said, Charles did seem to be a bit of a cockroach where political survival was concerned.

Both Anjli and Monroe went out of their way to point out that Declan shouldn't feel spurned by Charles, as it *had* been Harnish Patel who'd saved the day, as Declan arrived after the poisons would have been injected.

It was spoken from kindness, but this weighed heavily on Declan's mind.

They were right. He had failed.

And although solving the case, he'd solved it that little bit too slowly, and people, even the Queen, could have died because of his inability to scratch an itch.

He made the *decision* two days after the event.

On the day in question, he went to the Royal Berkshire Hospital in Reading where, in a ward under the name Robert Owen, was Tom Marlowe, still recovering from his recent gunshot wounds. He was up, sitting and conscious now, hitting that point where boredom and frustration collided, so he was happy to see a familiar face.

More importantly for Declan, he'd also been speaking to Trix, and knew about the St David's gas explosion.

'So it was a crack in a pipe or something,' he explained as he leaned against a multitude of pillows, alone with Declan in a side room of the ward. 'Current belief is the house slowly filled with gas while she was away in a Haverfordwest cell, and when she returned the following day, she didn't smell anything.'

'That doesn't sound right,' Declan replied. 'Surely she'd smell the gas.'

'Yes, she would,' Tom nodded. 'Unless the story isn't giving all the facts.'

'You think it was something else?'

'All I know is a couple of hours later there was a spark and *boom*.'

'It was definitely her?' Declan asked, still uncertain. Francine Pearce had a knack of disappearing.

'She was on the cameras we planted,' Tom said. 'Trix told me she got in, checked three hiding places—'

'She obviously talked to Trisha Hawkins then.'

'Yeah. Or she was paranoid, anyway. We saw there was money and passports there, but before we could get in...'

'Yeah, I get the point,' Declan leaned back on the small chair he sat on. 'I'm sorry she went out that way. It had to be Karl.'

'Gas explosion that doesn't smell? That's definitely someone on the outside setting this up. If not him, then maybe Tricia,' Tom added. 'I'd say have a word, but it seems the US Embassy has no record of him being kept there after his arrest.'

'CIA already has him in a new life,' Declan nodded. 'Hopefully we'll never see him again.'

'I'm not sure,' Tom flexed his bandaged shoulder. 'I have questions I want to ask, after I have a word with Trica Hawkins. I'll still be looking.'

'Are you going back to active service?' Declan was surprised. 'I mean, they shot you in the leg and arm.'

'It's in the air,' Tom scowled. 'But if they desk-bench me, I'll walk.'

'And do what?'

Tom grinned.

'Maybe I'll be a cop, work for uncle Alex,' he said. 'Or take a sabbatical. I hear Langley, over in Virginia is good in the Autumn.'

Taking this as more *banter* than *active threat against the CIA*, Declan promised to return to visit soon and left the hospital, travelling back to Temple Inn.

He had another meeting to take before this day was over.

———

MONROE WAS HAVING HIS OWN MEETING, SITTING AT HIS DESK, Billy standing in front of him, a USB stick in his hand.

'And you told Declan you destroyed this?' Monroe asked.

Billy nodded.

'He didn't want to read it,' he explained. 'He knew there would be secrets within it, things he didn't want to know about you.'

Monroe nodded at this. The disk had been given to Declan by *Section D*, and therefore by his ex-wife, Emilia Wintergreen, and Monroe knew that although not deliberately offensive, it would be *warts and all.*

'Did you read it?' Monroe asked.

Billy nodded.

'And did it have what I did on it?' Monroe continued.

Again, Billy nodded, placing the USB stick on the table.

'It didn't mention Claire,' he said. 'That should have been my first alert that Sutton was playing you.'

'True, but Emilia might have missed things,' Monroe picked up the USB drive, turning it around in his fingers. 'Thank you for not telling anyone.'

'Not my place, Guv.'

Monroe nodded, looking up as Declan could be seen walking into the office.

'Get everyone into the briefing room,' he said. 'It's time to come clean.'

———

DECLAN SAT IN HIS USUAL SPOT, GLANCING OVER TO ANJLI.

'What's going on?' he asked.

Anjli shrugged.

'The whole team's in, so it's probably a fresh case.'

'We only just finished the last one.'

Anjli turned to face Declan with a piercing, withering gaze.

'Crime never sleeps,' she intoned mock-ominously.

Doctor Marcos, sitting at the back with DC Davey and PC De'Geer laughed at this.

'I can make crime sleep,' she said. 'I can make crime sleep all night with what I have in my day bag.'

Declan didn't know what was scarier; Anjli's voice or Doctor Marcos in general. Billy, sitting in his usual spot laughed at this, and Declan noted that his laptop, always by his side and connected to the plasma screens during briefings, wasn't to be seen.

This felt wrong somehow.

Bullman walked into the briefing room, her face a mask of anger and annoyance. Following her was Monroe, his face set in stone, emotionless.

'Everyone shut up,' Bullman stated and, not expecting this more serious side to her, the Unit quietened instantly.

'DCI Monroe has something to say,' she said, nodding to Monroe before walking out of the room. Monroe stared at the Unit, as if unsure of what to say.

'You're all the best in the force,' he started. 'And I know that because I brought you all in. Too good to be fired, I said. I know they'll make me proud, I said. And you proved me right.'

'What's going on, Guv?' Declan asked, feeling a sliver of ice run down his spine.

'While in Edinburgh, I went up against a man from my Glasgow past,' Monroe continued. 'Lennie Wright. His brothers killed mine, many years ago.'

There was a murmuring of surprise at this; Declan saw that Billy, Doctor Marcos and De'Geer kept silent, as if knowing this already.

'In Edinburgh, I learnt some things,' Monroe continued. 'In particular, I learnt that my brother Kenny was killed because of me. That the hit was on me instead of him, and it was an accident.'

'They had a hit on you?' Anjli asked, surprised. 'You were what, twelve?'

'Sixteen,' Monroe replied. 'I was doing small jobs for the Hutchinson Family at the time. One of them...'

He paused.

'One of them was a fire,' he said. 'They tasked me with causing a distraction while some people, people I didn't know, met. I knew there was a derelict building nearby, so I set it alight.'

'You're an arsonist?' Declan was surprised.

'I'm a murderer,' Monroe admitted. 'I learnt later that there'd been a member of the Wright Gang staking out the meeting place, using the building as a location to spy on the Hutchinsons.'

'How long have you known this?' Anjli asked. Monroe shrugged.

'I knew about the fire, and the intensity that I caused with my arson attack all my life,' he admitted. 'But I was told it was just that. A fire. It was only while in Edinburgh I learnt it was Brigid Wright, the Wright *sister* that died in the fire, unknown to me. But regardless of what I knew, the deed was done, and her brothers placed the hit on me and my brother, unsure on which of us was to blame.'

'And your brother was killed.'

'Yes. And then in retaliation the Wright brothers were also killed by the Hutchinsons, and in the end only Lennie and I lived, an entire country between us.'

Monroe took a deep breath.

'Johnny Lucas knew, and he used it to gain favours over the years. Nothing massive, but a case of turning the other way now and then. By the time I'd broken away, I had quite a little file building in Scotland Yard, a file that others knew about.'

Declan nodded at this; Monroe had been one of the faces on his father's crime board before he died.

'I've let Bullman know everything,' Monroe continued. 'She's annoyed that she has to move it up the chain, but effective immediately I'm suspended from active duty while they decide what to do with me.'

'They can't!' Billy exclaimed. 'You've made some mistakes, we all have! But you've done so much!'

'That's what I'm hoping they'll decide too,' Monroe smiled. In the meantime, DCI Farrow will take on my duties. He'll be here later today. It's been an utter pleasure working with all of you, and if I don't come back from this, remember that you're all welcome to contact me, no matter what.'

And with this, Monroe walked out of the office, as if holding back any emotion before it spilled out over his face.

'Shit,' Anjli said. 'Farrow's a good choice, though for the interim. He knows us.'

Declan nodded. DCI Farrow had also taken a personal interest in looking after his family, so he couldn't complain.

What he could complain about was that this slightly compromised his *own* plans.

BULLMAN WAS IN HER OFFICE AS DECLAN ENTERED.

'I know, I was as surprised as you,' she said. 'I'll be making sure he's well represented, and Bradbury himself has demanded that he be used as a character witness in the case. But it's going to take a while. Monroe's desire to clean his soul really couldn't have come at a better time.'

'I agree,' Declan said, straightening up. Bullman glanced at him, sighing audibly.

'Is this about Farrow?' she asked. 'I know he's sleeping with your ex-wife, but he's genuinely the best option we have right now—'

'He's sleeping with Liz?' Declan stared in shock at his superior as all the pieces fell into place. 'Of course he is. That makes so much sense now. But it isn't about Farrow.'

He reached into his inner pocket, pulling out an envelope.

'This is my resignation letter,' he explained, placing it on the table. 'I'm sorry to do this to you right now, I didn't know Monroe was going to do all that.'

Bullman watched the letter as if expecting it to attack.

'Can I ask why?' she eventually spoke. 'You just had one of your biggest wins ever.'

'I didn't though,' Declan replied. 'I failed. If Harnish Patel hadn't worked it out, I'd have arrived after the entire Cabinet was poisoned.'

Bullman nodded.

'I heard what you said in the interview room too, Declan,' she continued. 'I saw you reach out to Harnish Patel. What you said to him there made him second guess Helen. You did save them.'

'And what about the others?' Declan snapped. 'Kendis Taylor, Lydia Cornwall, Sebastian Payne, Tara Wilkinson, Rolfe Müller, even Will Harrison, Peter Suffolk, Andy Mac, Derek Salmon and Susan Devington? All of these people would be alive if I was quicker, if I was better!'

'You can't judge your successes by the people who died,' Bullman insisted.

'*I had a German car mechanic in my house, who I've known since childhood, who turned out to be a serial killer that murdered my parents!*' Declan shouted, noticing that this outburst now gained the attention of the office. 'I can't do this anymore. I can't go on wondering if my family will be safe. I can't go on knowing if others I love will be next.'

Bullman nodded at this.

'I see your pain, I do,' she said. 'I have the same. The ghost of DI White is in my dreams regularly. But he made his own bed. All of them did. And if you can't hack it right now? Then walk out of that door, Declan Walsh, because I don't want you here.'

Declan thought for a moment, and then nodded.

'Thank you, Ma'am,' he said before turning and walking out of her office door. And, as Bullman watched Declan walk to his desk, grab his jacket and leave the building, Anjli calling out after him in confusion, Bullman stared down at the envelope on her desk, the envelope that contained Declan's resignation letter.

'Shit,' she muttered. 'That was supposed to be reverse psychology.'

Picking it up, she walked out of the office, staring at the *Last Chance Saloon.*

Alexander Monroe was suspended, up for disciplinary charges that could end his career, and Declan Walsh had walked out after giving his resignation letter, unable to continue. She'd probably have to find him somewhere different to work out his notice period as well.

Bullman sighed, staring at the remnants of her Unit.

Things would never be the same again.

DI Walsh and the team of the *Last Chance Saloon* will return in their next thriller

BEHIND THE WIRE

Released 13th February 2022

Order Now at Amazon:

http://mybook.to/behindthewire

ACKNOWLEDGEMENTS

When you write a series of books, you find that there are a ton of people out there who help you, sometimes without even realising, and so I wanted to do a little acknowledgement to some of them.

There are people I need to thank, and they know who they are. People like Andy Briggs, who started me on this path over a coffee during a pandemic literally a year ago to the day as I write this, people like Barry Hutchinson, who patiently zoom-called and gave advice back in 2020, the people on various Facebook groups who encouraged me when I didn't know if I could even do this, the designers who gave advice on cover design and on book formatting all the way to my friends and family, who saw what I was doing not as mad folly, but as something good, including my brother Chris Lee, who I truly believe could make a fortune as a post-retirement copy editor, if not a solid writing career of his own.

Also, I couldn't have done this without my growing army of ARC readers who not only show me where I falter, but also raise awareness of me in the social media world, ensuring that other people learn of my books, including (but not limited to) Maureen Webb, Maryam Paulsen, Edwina Townsend, Lorraine Locke and especially Jacqueline Beard MBE, who has copyedited all nine books so far (including the prequel), line by line for me, and deserves *way more* than our agreed fee.

But mainly, I tip my hat and thank you. *The reader.* Who, five books ago took a chance on an unknown author in a pile of Kindle books, and thought you'd give them a go, and who has carried on this far with them.

I write Declan Walsh for you. He (and his team) solves crimes for you. And with luck, he'll keep on solving them for a very long time.

Jack Gatland / Tony Lee,
   London, November 2021

ABOUT THE AUTHOR

Jack Gatland is the pen name of *#1 New York Times Bestselling Author* Tony Lee, who has been writing in all media for almost thirty-five years, including comics, graphic novels, middle grade books, audio drama, TV and film for *DC Comics, Marvel, BBC, ITV, Random House, Penguin USA, Hachette* and a ton of other publishers and broadcasters.

These have included licenses such as *Doctor Who, Spider Man, X-Men, Star Trek, Battlestar Galactica, MacGyver,* BBC's *Doctors, Wallace and Gromit* and *Shrek*, as well as work created with musicians such as *Ozzy Osbourne, Joe Satriani* and *Megadeth.*

As Tony, he's toured the world talking to reluctant readers with his 'Change The Channel' school tours, and lectures on screenwriting and comic scripting for *Raindance* in London.

An introvert West Londoner by heart, he lives with his wife Tracy and dog Fosco, just outside London.

Locations In The Book

The locations that I use in my books are real, if altered slightly for dramatic intent. Here's some more information about a few of them...

Essence doesn't exist, but Cornhill, the area of London where I set it does, and is the street running between Bank Junction and Leadenhall Street. The 'Corn Hill' it takes its name from is one of the three ancient hills of London; the others are Tower Hill, site of the Tower of London (seen in *A Ritual For The Dying*), and Ludgate Hill, crowned by St Paul's Cathedral (seen in *Hunter Hunted*).

Although opposite the Bank of England on Threadneedle Street, today Cornhill is commonly associated with opticians and makers of optical apparatus such as microscopes and telescopes. A statue of the engineer James Henry Greathead was erected in 1994 in the road beside the Royal Exchange, which lies within the ward.

Also, underneath the modern pavement is the world's first underground public toilet, which opened in 1855. Users were charged a standard fee of 1d, reputedly giving rise to the saying to "spend a penny".

The Edinburgh Tunnels are also real, and although I use a fictional tunnel under Lawnmarket, there are dozens of tunnels, still uncovered under the city from when it was paved over, and it's believed they travel under the area of the street I used, so perhaps not as fictional as I state?

The *Ibis Hotel* is also real, but doesn't have a metal door leading into any tunnels in the basement. However the *Tron Tavern* across the road does have a trapdoor leading to the tunnels, rediscovered by former Scotland rugby star Norrie Rowan in the 1980s, the man credited with finding and bringing back to life the Edinburgh Tunnels and Vaults.

After finding the first tunnel, he excavated the rubble by hand, and later on used this same trapdoor to enable former Romanian internationalist Cristian Raducanu to evade capture by the Romanian secret police, and seek political asylum weeks before the Romanian uprising of 1989.

Dubrovnik in Croatia of course exists, but the hotel that Leroy and Tara visited doesn't. That said, it's modelled on the *Hotel Bellevue,* a five-star hotel I stayed in earlier this year while researching this book (and another project), the Michelin-Star *Vapor* restaurant the hotel's main attraction, with a view looking out over the hotel's private beach.

Lapad Beach also exists, and is a touristy area where bars, nightclubs and a multi-screen cinema all reside.

Strawberry Hill exists, and shouldn't be confused with the *Strawberry Fields Salvation Army* garden that John Lennon used as the inspiration for his *Beatles* song.

In fact, Strawberry Hill is an affluent area of the London Borough of Richmond upon Thames in Twickenham, situated ten miles south-west of Charing Cross station. It's also the inspiration for 'Strawberry Hill House', the fanciful Gothic Revival villa designed by author Horace

Walpole between 1749 and 1776. It began as a small 17th century house "little more than a cottage", with only five acres of land and ended up as a "little Gothic castle" with forty-six acres.

The original owner had named the house "Chopped Straw Hall", but Walpole wanted it to be called something more distinctive and after finding an old lease that described his land as "Strawberry Hill Shot", he adopted this name.

After a £9 million, two year restoration, Strawberry Hill House re-opened to the public in October 2010.

Finally, The Members Dining Room of the *Houses of Parliament* exists, and has been the location of the *Sherlock Holmes Society of London's* January Dinner for many years now, a dinner I've been honoured to attend on several occasions.

The desserts are usually excellent.

If you're interested in seeing what the *real* locations look like, I post 'behind the scenes' location images on my Instagram feed. This will continue through all the books, and I suggest you follow it.

In fact, feel free to follow me on all my social media by clicking on the links below. Over time these can be places where we can engage, discuss Declan and put the world to rights.

www.jackgatland.com

Subscribe to my Readers List: **www. subscribepage.com/jackgatland**

www.facebook.com/jackgatlandbooks
www.twitter.com/jackgatlandbook
ww.instagram.com/jackgatland

HUNT THE GREATEST TREASURES
PAY THE GREATEST PRICE

JACK GATLAND

THE
LIONHEART
CURSE

BOOK 1 IN A NEW SERIES OF ADVENTURES
IN THE STYLE OF 'THE DA VINCI CODE'
FROM THE CREATOR OF DECLAN WALSH

**AVAILABLE ON AMAZON / KINDLEUNLIMITED
FROM SUNDAY 9TH JANUARY 2022**

Made in the USA
Coppell, TX
06 February 2022